BERKELEY BRED

GREYHUFFINGTON

LET'S GET SOCIAL

Instagram:

Grey Huffington
(Cover reveals, releases, etc)
Instagram.com/greyhuffington

HuffingtonHQ
(News, updates, etc —headed by Team Huffington)
Instagram.com/huffingtonhq

TikTok:

Grey Huffington
(Vlogs, updates, promotional images/videos, etc — headed by Team Huffington)
TikTok.com/@greyhuffington.com

Pinterest:

Grey Huffington
(*Inspiration, quotes, snippets, visuals, boards, lifestyle, etc —
headed by Team Huffington*)
https://pin.it/695pEOV9m

TRIGGER WARNING

PLEASE READ THIS SECTION!

Seeing this note means the book you are about to read could contain triggering situations or actions. This book is subject to one or more of the triggers listed below.

Please note that this a universal trigger warning page that is included in Grey Huffington books and is not specified for any particular set of characters, book, couple, etc.
This book does not contain all the warnings listed. It is simply a way to warn you that this particular book contains things/a thing that may be triggering for some.

This is my way of recognizing the reality and life experiences of my Romance friends and making sure I properly prepare you for what is to unfold within the pages of this book.

violence
sexual assault
drug addiction
suicide
homicide
miscarriage/child loss
child abuse
emotional abuse
mental illness
infidelity
infertility
cancer
criminal activity

As I penned this book, I couldn't help but come to terms with the reason I've made a mess of these boys' hearts with the deaths of their mother and father (and Anna).
The truth is, I'm still healing myself. I lost two people very dear to me and their deaths are just something that I can't let go of. Not yet. My heart and my head, they aren't ready. So, until then, I'll write the pain away.

This book is dedicated to anyone that's lost someone who made their days better. It never stop hurting. The hurt just hurts a little less.

I hope you're resting well, Tierra. I miss you bad, babes.

Grandad, I can't, won't believe that you're not here. Maybe we'll talk about it later.

g.

P.S. This book is fluffy, fun, stressful, and overall a breath of freshness.

CONTENTS

GREY**HUFFINGTON**

PROLOGUE

MY INTERNAL ALARM abruptly woke me from my sleep. The low light of the sun's pending horizon was softer and gentler on my eyes at this hour, which was appreciated. Scorching eyes wouldn't pair well with the piercing headache that instantly forced a groan from my chapped lips.

"Urgh."

With my middle finger and thumb, I massaged my temple to distribute and possibly diminish the pain. I felt like shit. The dryness of my mouth proved to be discomforting. Hydration was necessary. A sip of water, a Gatorade, or anything revitalizing would suffice.

The simple task of retrieving a thirst quencher grew complicated as the numbness of my arm became more apparent. Long, dark hair covered the upper half while sandy skin rested against my forearm. My eyes scanned the naked frame as blurred memories of an eventful night came rushing in, explaining the unclothed woman, splintering headache, and chalkiness at the back of my throat.

Sure not to wake my guest, I slowly slid my arm from underneath her and replaced it with a pillow. She stirred slightly but remained semi-unconscious. I stood off to the side of the bed, clothed in only a pair of black briefs, trying to determine the exact order of events that led to this moment and if the night had been satisfying enough to continue into the morning or politely wake my guest to make her exit.

My phone's screen glowed in the distance, summoning my attention. I grabbed it from the nightstand and quickly scanned the notification that appeared. Somehow, I managed to conjure enough saliva to hydrate the desert of a mouth I was suffering from, putting a few more seconds on the clock before dehydration choked me to death.

Dear Milo Domino,

Your order has been processed and is preparing for delivery.

Delivery window: 9:00 a.m.-12:00 p.m.

Thanks for choosing, Treat Someone.

My heart's BPM increased substantially as I concluded the reading of what was viewable on the screen notification. Rolling the flesh of my inner, lower lip between both rows of teeth, I unlocked the phone to find the lone contact on my *Favorite* list, though it was the most under-utilized among all others.

The flowers that replaced her government name were a reminder of how much she'd bloomed over the years, and though I'd watched from a distance, it had been enjoyable, nonetheless. Words, a plethora of them, crowded me, making it hard to eliminate those that were unnecessary and keep those that would mirror my sentiments. Sighing, I chose a few that were fitting and best described my feelings on this special day.

Nature... Thirty-six candles, today, love. We're getting on up there, huh? I'm wishing the happiest of birthdays, continued wealth, prosperity, peace, and ultimate success for my favorite girl in the entire world. May this day be as magical as you imagined. I love you. Milo.

I read the text a number of times before pushing the arrow to send the message. With the most important task of the day out of the way, I began trekking through the house, en route to the kitchen.

The distance from the bedroom to the kitchen in the condo was substantially different from my home. It was crucial to my survival this morning, so I appreciated it more than I'd imagined I would once the cold water hit the back of my throat. I didn't stop chugging until the container was empty and the bottle began to crackle.

"Urgh. Shit."

Alleviated from the dehydration manacles, my brain function improved tremendously. My thoughts were clearer. My vision improved. And my body was in overall better health. I grabbed another bottle from the fridge and headed back to the bedroom.

The relevance of the body in my bed no longer registered with me. Ready to clear the space, prepare for my departure, and get my day at the office started, I nudged the dark-haired woman who was still unconscious.

"Ummm?" She groaned.

The scrunching of her features revealed the painful movement of her frame and the opening of her eyes.

"Ummm."

"Checkout time, baby girl," I announced, pecking the screen of my phone to secure her transportation.

"Hmm?"

"Your ride will be here in – *six minutes*."

"My ride?"

"Yes. It's time to head out. Would you like a bottle of water?"

"Um hmm."

She nodded, finally opening her eyes and sitting up in bed, pulling the cover up with her. From the looks of things, it had been a hell of a night for us both. She uncapped the bottle and turned it up until she was satisfied. By the time she lowered it, she'd finished a third of the water.

"I didn't get your name," she exclaimed, much louder than anticipated.

"I didn't give it to you. Four minutes. Your ride will be here in four minutes."

"Well, I'm N–"

"It doesn't even matter, baby girl. You need a shirt or some shit to throw on?"

"That would be great. Are you always this rude? I don't remember you being this way last night."

"Probably because you don't remember much of anything from last night. I'm not rude. I'm blunt. Honest. Upfront. I can bet my last dollar I was last night as well. It takes too much energy to be anything other than myself. Briefs?" I yelled over my shoulder as I began searching through the closet for a few pieces I didn't care too much about.

The selection was much smaller than the one at my

primary residence, so the options were very limited. I settled on a previously worn and washed white T-shirt.

"Yes. Please."

I opened a fresh pack of briefs to pair with the shirt and headed back into the bedroom where my guest was finally up and stretching her naked frame. It became very clear to me why I'd chosen to bring her home with me.

Shit, she holding.

The possibility of seeing her again quickly increased. Suddenly, her name wasn't a bad topic of conversation.

"On second thought, what's your name, baby girl?"

I tossed the clothes in her direction. She caught them mid-air. As she leaned over to place the shirt on the bed, I observed. I could even see that ass from the front. But when she slid my briefs up her thighs and over her cheeks, I was intrigued. She was ridiculously thick. Conflicting thoughts led me to my screen, again, wondering if I should cancel the ride back to her car and order her another one in thirty-five minutes or let her walk out of the door in the next two.

"Yours first," she responded, sucking the skin of her teeth.

"Milo."

"Neisha."

"What's your contact information, Neisha? Maybe we can do this again sometime."

"555-902-9665."

I jotted her number just before saving the contact. Knowing that I had a full day of scheduled events ahead of me, I decided to let her go about her day. There was a four-mile run waiting on me in The Peaks. I needed to get out of

Berks and back home as soon as possible before heading to the office.

"Your ride will be here in about a minute."

"Don't be a stranger."

"I won't be. Not at all," I assured her, watching as she pushed past the loveseat and out of the bedroom.

When my eyes lost sight, I moved through the room, down the hallway, and into the living room where she pulled the door open to exit.

"I guess this means I'll see you another time."

She turned slightly, just as her feet hit the threshold.

"Without a doubt, baby girl." I nodded, unable to detach my eyes from her backside.

"I look forward to it."

"A black Lincoln."

"Hmm?"

"The truck waiting for you out front is a Lincoln truck."

She smiled, lowering her head to watch the steps she was taking in the heels she'd slid into. Evidence of the night she'd had was all over her body. The itty bitty piece of fabric she'd worn dangled over her shoulder.

With a shake of my head, I tittered, realizing she was about to commence the morning-after walk of shame. I prayed anyone she encountered was generous enough to mind their fucking business and stay out of hers. It was possibly asking too much in a neighborhood full of mother-fuckers who had a plethora of time on their hands and gossip groups dedicated to wealthy housewives.

The door slammed behind her, jolting me back to reality. For a second, my mind roamed, but thoughts of the tasks of my day got me back to where I needed to be. I just hoped by the end of the day, I could piece together my night to the fullest. Fucking around with Lawe, it was almost impossible.

After getting dressed, I settled for another bottle of water and a protein shake from the fridge. I cleared the pad of any traces of human activity and headed out the door without delay. The trip to my car was quick and uneventful, making it rather pleasurable, to say the least.

Sunrise was in full bloom as my altitude climbed, setting a beautiful scene right in front of me. My ears were like small explosives waiting to erupt as elevation continued. As magnetic as the ascent was, it was sometimes jarring. The Peaks sat atop the hills of Berkeley, serving as a partition for the mountains behind us.

Black gates parted, prompting me to pull forward and into my driveway after punching in the code to gain access. The engine of my i8 purred quietly as I tapped the gas slightly, carefully creeping beside the Ashton inside of my four-car garage. With each bay full, an extension of the design was climbing its way up my priority list.

My long limbs stretched until my bones popped, submerging me in relief. With haste, I exited the garage and the gate that had cost six figures to install. After receiving the quote, I was convinced I was in the wrong profession and that a career as a neuropsychologist wasn't as nearly as lucrative as one spent building fences. I imagined the owner of *Founder Fencing* lived just up the road in a house just as stunning as all the homes on my block with a fence that made neighbors envious.

My index and thumb pressured the buttons on the side of my sports watch, starting the timer that began ticking immediately. I picked up the pace, going from a brisk walk to a full jog, and stayed there until the first two beeps sounded. They signified the ten-minute mark, kicking me into high gear. Once I began running, my legs didn't rest until I was inside the ridiculously expensive fence, leaning forward with my hands on my knees in an attempt to catch my breath.

"FUCK! That was rough," I admitted out loud, thinking of the three times I regretted the decisions I'd made last night.

Mornings after were always the toughest runs, forcing me to reconsider my way of life and some changes that needed to occur. A creature of habit, I always found myself back in the same predicament at least twice a week. It was hard to decipher if I was simply in search of a good time or escaping the things that hid in the tiny folds of my mind. They were small but they were mighty, with the power to humble even the strongest soldier.

No pity for me, I reminded myself of the words often spoken in my childhood dwelling.

Cool air escaped as I opened the door. The scent of fresh linen, sage, and cedarwood welcomed me home. I loosened the straps of my watch, tossing it onto the console in the entryway. My phone was next, but not before checking for new notifications. There were none.

Sucking the skin of my teeth, I tilted my head as I stared at the message thread that was full of short phrases and dry replies. I was still praying daily that the reality of it all shifted in my favor. Until it did, I'd continue putting in my bid, recognizing special days, and reminding her that I was still here... *still waiting and still ready.*

I climbed the steps two at a time, desperate to spend time underneath the massaging showerhead before the clock struck eight. Warm towels waited next to the shower in the linen dispenser. I added a new white T-shirt, fresh out of the pack.

My morning showers ended on a cooler note, making sure I was alert and prepared for the duration of the day. Otherwise, I'd find myself climbing into bed to get a few minutes of sleep, which resulted in hours of uninterrupted, forbidden rest that threw my entire day off.

I stepped behind the glass door after stripping completely. The motion sensors detected my presence, starting the shower automatically. The science behind the perfected temperature within the first second of dispensing would always be a mystery to me but I appreciated the fellow wiz who mastered it. A sucker for all things scientific, I was intrigued.

Nature... Thirty-six candles, today, love. We're getting on up there, huh? I'm wishing the happiest of birthdays, continued wealth, prosperity, peace, and ultimate success for my favorite girl in the entire world. May this day be as magical as you imagined. I love you. Milo.

I reviewed the message in my head a fourth time, wondering if I'd said the right words and if they were enough to garner a response. Quite honestly, I was counting on one. I could use the improvement of my day. Though it wasn't shaping up to be a bad one, it could always be better. Nature held the power to make that happen.

With a soaped towel, I scrubbed the remnants of my night and the evidence of my four-mile run from my skin. A second and third time summoned contentment, clearing my conscious as I stepped out and into the coolness feeling squeaky clean. The warm towel soaked up the cold water from the last leg of my shower that trickled down my body.

"Shit!" I shivered, feeling like I'd been drenched in ice.

Once clean, it was unlawful to touch the floor's surface without a layer of protection. Pure white bath slippers lined the bottom of the cabinet, waiting for my size twelve feet to fill them. Burying my feet in the terry cloth fabric, my temperature rose even more. Feeling somewhat toasty, I strolled to my closet where I chose the day's attire.

A simple pair of denim and a white button-down managed to get the job done. Before slipping into either, I hydrated and moisturized my skin. Ashy ass skin was a pet peeve I'd developed as a kid and it stuck with me throughout adulthood.

I never stepped out the door without drenching myself in the best moisturizer on the market. I was too Black to even consider it. My ashy was a different kind of ashy, and after one too many experiences, I never wanted to be on the receiving end of bulging eyes and critical colorism jokes that almost ended with motherfuckers' teeth on the pavement.

Fully dressed and standing in the mirror, I added the final details. Rolex watch. Cuban link chain and bracelet duo. Cologne. And last, the plate of gold open faces that partially covered six of my bottom teeth. It was subtle, but it was the perfect touch for a Black doctor who defied every stereotype attached to Black men by society.

"Alrighty."

Anxiously, I grabbed my phone as I headed out of the door. My day had officially started. Down the stairs and through the first level, I floated. I unlocked my phone just as

I stepped outside. The blank screen forced hard, sharp air from my nose as I sighed in despair.

Still nothing, I thought as I lowered my body into the car and started the engine. I imagined it was Nature's intention to push me as close to the edge as possible, the few times of year I texted her, by dragging with her response. There was almost always a wait.

Without a doubt, I knew she'd already opened and read my message back and forth. She hated unopened notifications on her phone and always had. A well-calculated and prideful woman, more than likely, Nature was perfecting her response before sending it, no matter how simple it might be.

Lil Baby's track filled the car. The chorus began as I pulled out of the gate. By the time I pushed the gas and shot down the street, the first verse came through.

"How we get so deep so fast? Bae stop playing I'll beat yo' ass. You be on some toxic shit but I cannot get off this bitch. I haven't seen you in three m—"

The music halted as a text came through. I felt around the middle console to locate my phone while keeping my eyes on the road.

"Every time I see one of yo' pictures, that shit drives me cra—"

Flowers. They crossed the screen, reminding me that I still needed to update Nature's contact. As symbolic as they were, and as much as I loved them, I was ready for the change. She was a year older, a year wiser, more beautiful, yet still prickly to the touch. A rose, a single rose, suited her best now. I'd come to the conclusion while in the shower.

Because she altered the functionality of my cerebrum,

my safety was in question. Before my journey to the office had completely begun, it was put on pause. Pulling into my neighbor's yard, I stopped just where their gate began. I shifted the gear until it was in park. I had no intention of entering their property.

My heart drummed against my chest. The bit of saliva that was keeping me from choking off complete dryness, I used to push the lump down my throat. I gripped the skin of my lip between my teeth, drawing blood instantly.

It didn't matter how much time passed between us, there was a special place in my heart for Nature. She was the one that had gotten away, and all these years later, I was still kicking my ass for letting her. I could've easily blamed it on immaturity, but it wasn't the case for me.

Fear. Fear of failure, fear of failing her, was what kept me from chasing her down and forcing her to see our potential. To this day, I regretted that decision. Every time I saw her contact cross my screen, I was reminded that I'd never stop regretting it.

Thank you, Milo. Love you back.

Her response gave me little to go on. The simple thanks should've taken a few seconds to send, but it had taken her hours. It was shit like that, when it came to her, that led me to believe the feelings were mutual and I, too, still held a special place in her heart.

"Love you back?"

I hated that shit. It was the most casual, unflattering response to my yearly confession she'd ever given and it made me sick to my stomach.

She doesn't even use incomplete sentences, I thought, reviving control of my cerebrum and the ability to think clearly. As I reversed out of the driveway, I repeated the six-word text in my head over and over.

A smile pulled my features upward until it reached my eyes. Nodding, I realized that her response had been studied and erased, and retyped several times before being sent. It was very intentional. Yet, after it all, the fact still remained that I'd received a response at all.

To some capacity, she still cared enough to send one. Hadn't she, I'd be left in the pile of notifications she didn't have the energy to reply to. Taking my small win for what it truly was, I continued down the road at full speed ahead.

MY MORNING WAS off to a great start. A visit to the florist that was only a few blocks away from the office led me to the pressed sandwich shop next door. I grabbed a turkey bacon, egg, and cheese flat with pressed orange and ginger juice as my beverage.

I'd parked my car in the garage attached to my office and struck out on foot. My goal of two-thousand steps per day was easily consumed by the commute. The morning runs weren't calculated in the equation or else I would've hit that goal before I even stepped into the shower this morning.

The doors of the Richmond Medical Lofts opened automatically, keeping my hands free for me to continue scarfing down the sandwich between my thumb and four fingers. In the main lobby were a host of other business owners who were coming and going just as I was. Once I made it to the elevator, I pushed the button that led directly to my office. It was the only office on the floor, unlike most of the levels.

The transparent doors of the elevator confined me, trapping me inside alone. Imprisoned with my thoughts, I crumbled the parchment paper and napkin that my sandwich had been wrapped inside. The ginger from my juice tackled my tastebuds as brown strands of perfectly curled hair, quarter-sized eyes, and bushy brows pushed aside every memory from my frontal lobe.

Her smile. Her scent. Her touch. Her laugh. Her company. Her heart. Every aspect of her, I craved, deeply. Her body, I thirsted for it, nightly. And after over a decade, one would believe that my yearning would subside, but with each passing year, it only intensified. Settling down and having someone to call home were slowly inching their way up my priority list, which complicated my plight.

Valentine's Day surprises. Wedding bells. Honeymoon. Babymoon. Children. Family. Vacations. Drop offs. Pickups. Lunch dates. Recitals. Afterschool activities. I wanted that shit like I wanted the next breath to pass through my lungs.

The girl I'd befriended in my early days of college and later fell in love with was the only person in the world I was interested in creating that life with. And until she returned home, I'd continue to roam the streets. She was my destination. There was no alternative. There was no settlement.

Forgetting Nature hadn't happened in the last ten years, and it wouldn't happen tomorrow, either. We were in our teens when we met, the youngest on the college campus. After almost five years of friendship, three years of a flawless relationship, it took one night, one mistake to break her heart a hundred different ways. I'd been trying to find my way back ever since. But true to her word, Nature hadn't let me back in.

The woman she'd trusted with her secrets and used as a shoulder to lean on was the woman who took advantage of her vulnerability and turned her into someone I hardly recognized for far too many years to keep count. And in some sick, fucked-up way, although I was the one who had put her in the predicament, I felt as though I needed to be the one to rescue her, too.

That was why letting go completely wasn't an option. I still *needed* to right my wrongs. I still *needed* to fix the person I'd broken. I still *needed* to mend her, mend us.

"Good morning, Mr. Domino," Christina cooed softly, stepping backward as I stepped off the elevator.

She was only three weeks into her probationary period, and I was heavily considering terminating her employment to give her the dick she desperately wanted. Like a dog in heat, she followed me through the office with her mouth agape and invisible hearts flying around her head in perfect circles. Remembering to push my one o'clock meeting back to one-fifteen, I stopped in my tracks, turned and collided with Christina, immediately.

"Oh, God. I'm sorry, Mr. Domino. I'm sorry," she apologized, grabbing the remainder of the orange and ginger juice from my hand.

My fingers were covered in the concoction, but the fact that not even a drop had gotten on my white shirt kept me level-headed and at ease.

"You riding my bumper too tough, Christina. I don't need a puppy. I need a receptionist. There's no need for you to meet me at the elevator every morning. Rest your bones.

Stay in your seat. If I need you to get up, I'll make the request. Otherwise, stay out of my personal space."

The first two warnings had been much more professional and considerate. I hardly had any patience at this point. It was unfortunate for her, but it was necessary that I gave it to her straight.

"Yes. Okay. I understand," she rushed out, leaning over her desk to grab wet wipes. "I'm so sorry. Here. This should help."

"Thanks."

"Was there something you were about to say to me?"

"Yeah."

I'd nearly forgotten.

"Push the one o'clock back fifteen minutes. I have a very important call to make before I head in."

"Sure. Should I add this call to your calendar? It's not on the schedule."

"It doesn't have to be. Just know it'll be made during that timeframe."

"Got it. I'll keep your availability shut off during that time."

"Please," I agreed, wiping the last of the juice from my fingers and handing the wet wipe over.

Because I felt sticky, I'd still visit the bathroom in my office, but for now, the clean-up job I'd managed would do. When I finally walked off, I didn't make it very far before Christina was on my heels again.

"Just one more thing, Mr. Domino," she huffed.

"Yes, Christina?" I asked, never breaking my stride.

"Would you like lunch from Bertos?"

"Christin—"

"My treat," she added.

"No. But if you'd like Bertos for lunch, be my guest. Charge it to the company's card this once."

"No. It's fine. I just... I know you love Bertos and figur—"

"Enjoy the rest of your morning. I'll see you once meetings have concluded and it's time for me to head over to the hospital. If you need me, buzz my office. Please... please don't need me."

"Yes, sir!" She nodded, watching from afar as I widened the gap between us. "Wait, but what if I actually need you?" she yelled after me.

Deciding against answering the question, I entered my office just as my cell chimed. I nearly tumbled over my desk as my cerebellum completely crashed, throwing off my coordination. The red rose I'd replaced the bouquet of flowers with popped up at the bottom of my screen, throwing me all out of whack and fuzzing my brain. The notification was unexpected, but simultaneously treasured.

I settled in the cushioned seat before unlocking my screen to read the message that had been sent. Nature's pretty face appeared in the small circle at the top of the message box and right beside the last message she'd sent. My eyes were glued to the five lines, unable to read a single word as I attempted to lower the amount of beats produced by my heart per minute with long, slow breaths.

Milo, your kindness hasn't gone unnoticed — this year or any before. As always, you've made this day a bit more special. Thanks for the flowers and the chocolates. They're still my favorite.

Nay.

A stroke of pain ran through me, making my entire face twitch. The melancholy message that stared back at me left me stuck, unable to decipher between returning the text or making a call. Nature hadn't given direct signs of her despair, but I could feel it in each word she sent. Evidence was all throughout the message, making my decision easier after reading it a third time.

"Milo," she murmured on the other end, answering her phone on the second ring.

I clammed, pausing for a few seconds to savor the moment. Her voice was like the sweetest melody, settling my heart and my head at the same fucking time. Whatever magic she possessed left me feeling pathetic every time we encountered one another. After so long, I should have washed my hands and put her in my rearview but I still wanted her riding passenger seat. I couldn't see it any other way.

"What's the matter, Nay?"

The nickname I'd given her rolled off my tongue effortlessly. She'd set so many boundaries when shutting me out that she'd forbid the name slip from my slips, but somehow, it made it into our message thread this morning, giving me the green light to reinstate it in my vocabulary and our rare conversations.

"Nay, huh?"

"Yes."

"When did I become N—"

"You want to beat around the bush or you want to tell me why the prettiest girl in the world is sounding a bit flustered on her special day?"

"I'm fine, Milo," she lied.

"Special plans?" I deflected, understanding she wouldn't be letting me in. Probing wasn't an option, but there were other, more satisfying options.

"I don't know. I was thinking of taking the day to rest and relax. I've made no plans and I'm okay with that this year."

"Hannah?"

"Long story." She chuckled, nervously. "But thanks, Milo, for the flowers and strawber—"

"Eight," I blurted, refusing to let the opportunity pass me by.

"Huh?"

"Eight o'clock. Be ready and at your mom's at eight."

"Milo. I don't think that—"

"Would you rather I pull at to your house and knock on the front door? Because I will. I don't give a fuck, Nature. You don't have plans, but I do, and they happen to include the birthday girl."

"Still demanding, I see," she sighed.

My silence forced a response. I had little to say. I simply needed Nature to understand that her night just got a bit more interesting and it wouldn't end until she felt better about herself, better about her day.

"Alright."

"Still knee deep," I corrected her. "I'll see you at eight, Nay, and not a minute later."

I moved to disconnect the call but was halted by her voice.

"Milo?"

"Yeah?"

"What should I wear?"

Nothing. I drew blood from my bottom lip as I closed my eyes to shove my true thoughts back and allowed the more pleasant ones room to surface.

"A piece that makes you feel insanely beautiful. It's your day, baby girl. If you don't have that piece in your closet, I have no problem sending that, too."

"No. You've done enough already. I can figure out the rest."

"Just let me know. If you come up em—"

"I can handle it, Milo. I promise."

"Alright. Eight."

"Eight," she confirmed.

Synchronously, we ended the call. And for ten minutes in total, I was unmoving. Temporary paralysis left me with stiffened limbs and dry eyes. It wasn't until a knock at my door startled me that I managed to snap out of the state I was in.

"Mr. Domino," Christina exclaimed. "Just one more thing."

Squeezing my eyelids together, I inhaled deeply before exhaling.

"Yes?"

"The expense report. You requested it yesterday. I have it for you right here."

"You printed it out?"

"Yes. Is that a problem?"

"The fact that it could've been emailed poses the problem, Christina. There was no need to waste paper, ink, or steps making your way to my office."

"Oh. Okay. I didn't know. I just thought maybe you wanted a physical copy."

"Please email the report."

"I will. Your first meeting is in less than twenty minutes. Is there anything I can ge—"

"Out. You can get out, Christina."

"Yup. Doing that now."

She scurried out of the door, leaving me alone, again. I tried keeping a level head with Christina, but she was a lot to handle. Every chance she got, she was in my space. As a man who loved the smell, feel, and view of pussy, I had no problem taking her thin ass down, but I wasn't on that type of time.

Remaining professional was the goal and I was determined to keep it. I'd blurred the lines of business and pleasure too many times and had learned my lesson. This time, things had to be different. I'd ran through too many assistants in the last four years to chance it again.

Looking past my watch to check the time on my phone, I realized I had less than fifteen minutes, actually, before my first meeting started. The task at hand would only take five, ten at the most. I stood and pushed my door closed.

Seconds later, I was tapping icons on the screen that led me to FaceTime. The call I initiated included everyone from the group message dedicated to the five boys my mother had spat out without complications or medication.

"Yeah?" Malachi was the first on the line.

Judging by his background, he was stuck in the nursery. And from the motion, I quickly determined he was rocking my nephew in his arms.

"Maaaaaaaz, what's up, my nigga."

"Milo, it's not even ten. Why are you this loud?"

"Why are you so fucking quiet?"

"Probably because I'm trying to get him back to sleep after being up all night, wearing me and my wife out. Please keep it down."

I softened, hearing the exhaustion and frustration in his voice. A yawn nearly split his face in two. His eyes watered from the intensity of it all. I chewed on the pink flesh of my inner lip, imagining myself in his position.

The wife. The son. The tired eyes. The lazy words. The lack of energy. My palms began itching at the thought of soiled diapers and shirts that reeked of puke. My chest tightened with fear. The possibility that something I needed just as much as I needed to succeed in life slipping from my grasp as time ticked away made me clam momentarily.

"Milo," Malachi spoke, reeling me back in.

"Bet. Maaaaaz, Unc gon' catch you later, youngin," I whispered, refusing to contribute to my brother's misery.

A smile crossed Malachi's face, making me smile in return.

"Fuck you smiling about?"

"You, jolly and shit. Talk to me, bro."

"What's up?" Makai joined the call.

"This nigga answering the phone all smooth and shit like we some pussy on the line," I scoffed.

"Pussy won't be on my line. It'll be in my bed, on my face, on my di–"

"Aight. Aight," Mercer interrupted, answering at the perfect time.

"I don't know why you added your boy to the call. That nigga probably done went through twelve phones since this group started," Makai tittered, referring to the oldest of my mother's children.

We didn't share the same father. When our mother committed suicide during a psychotic episode, he didn't come to Pop's house with us. We didn't have the same grandfather, either. The moment our mother's mental health began to decline, his father gained sole custody of him. My parents knew it was best for everyone. Willingly, our mother signed over her rights.

"Nah. He st—" I started, but was quickly cut off by the man in question.

Nightfall surrounded him as the stars in the sky shined brightly. We lived in opposing time zones.

"Mercer. Malachi. Makai. Milo."

Chem paused and nodded between each of our names.

"In order, though?" Makai huffed, shaking his head.

"You got a problem with that?" Chem cleared his throat and spoke up. After asking, he pulled from the blunt that appeared in the camera.

"Jumping on a plane to beat your ass has crossed my mind a few times. Don't push it."

"Good luck finding me."

He'd willingly given up his citizenship to roam the streets of his country freely and without the threat of the FBI, DEA, and the rest of the federal agencies that had him on their radar.

"Fuck all that," I intervened.

"Why is he so excited?" Mercer asked anyone who'd listen.

"Shut up long enough and we'll figure it out," Malachi suggested.

"Aye!" I warned. "Chill. Everybody. This is very important."

Long and exaggerated sighs followed one after the other. I didn't give a damn how tired of me they were, everybody was about to listen to what I had to say.

"I'm getting my bit—Nature back!"

"Rain Forest?" Makai grunted.

Chem sucked the skin of his teeth and shook his head.

"This nigga," Mercer hissed, ending the call.

I quickly added him to the call again through the settings.

"Don't ever fix them fat ass knuckles to hang up in my face."

"I got shit to do, Milo. Nature?"

"Yes, dog. Desert!" Makai bellowed.

"Makai!" I grimaced.

"Please, Makai," Malachi added.

"Nigga has absolutely no respect for this man's woman." Chem pulled on his blunt again.

"Not his woman," Makai corrected. "And you sound like you got some shit to get off your chest. What's up?"

"Remember I used to kick your ass as a kid, Makai?"

"So, what, nigga?"

"Ain't shit changed, but I don't have the energy. I don't throw hands, kid. I erase any traces of niggas' existence."

"So, you niggas don't hear me?"

"I'm listening, Milo."

"Today is her birthday."

"I hope you doing some tricking." Though over my shit when it came to Nature, Mercer always had an input.

"Plenty," I admitted.

"Type of shit I like to hear." Chem approved with a few nods.

"What makes you say you've gotten her back?" Malachi was asking the real questions.

"I did the usual, ya know, sending birthday gifts to her mom's crib. She texted me to tell me thanks, but this year was different. She sends a word or two. Some nonchalant shit. But this time, she loaded my text down. I could sense the sadness in her words, like something was bothering her so I called her ass instead of texting back."

"Good shit," Makai commended me.

"Hit her up and she's sounding as sad as I imagined. You know I can't have Baby sad on her birthday, so I tell her to be ready at eight. I'm coming to get her. I don't give a damn what's going on; at eight, I need her to be ready."

"What about the carpet muncher she been playing house with all these years?"

"Do it look like I give a fuck where she at or how the fuck she feels? Nature done agreed to dinner, so she as good as gone. When I get through knocking her walls down and reminding her of all the dick she been missing, she won't give a fuck about her, either."

"Not you 'bout to double cross the—"

"Makai," Chem sighed.

"This dick can do shit that strap-on simply can't. Nature gone remember that when she limping up on the porch after I've rearranged her shit."

"You be talking so tough until she in your mix. Then you're quiet like a bitch."

"When she leave, I be talking again," I explained to Makai, garnering a laugh from everyone on the phone.

"Knock, knock!"

Knuckles pounded on the door of my office as Christina's voice rose above all others. I tuned out the sounds of cheer in my brothers' voices and waited for her to enter.

"It's unlocked."

"Your conference call has started. They're waiting for you to join the meeting."

"Thank you."

"Of course. If there's anything you need, just give me a buzz."

I nodded while pointing two fingers toward the door she'd just come into. Before logging into my first meeting of the day, I needed to end the call I was on.

"I have a meeting that's supposed to be happening right now, so I have to go."

"Dr. Domino," Chem praised, pulling from his blunt.

"Dr. Childers," I reminded him of his credentials.

A scholar at heart, he'd obtained his doctorate eight years ago, in chemistry, nonetheless. Our shared interest in science led to the career decisions we'd both made. Though his interest derived from his fascination with the anatomy of pharmaceuticals, it pushed him into pursuing a life that didn't appeal to officials. He was a threat to their government and a god on the streets.

"I wanted to update everyone on the status of Nature and I. Don't hesitate to reinstate your gym membership if you need one. You'll be getting fitted for suits soon."

"Gym membership?" Makai questioned.

"I'm insulted," Malachi scoffed.

"And to think, the gym is the smallest room in my quarters."

"Ah. The flexing begins," Mercer groaned.

"I don't f—" Chem started.

"Nah. No flexing," I told Mercer. "That's my bad. I forgot who I had on the line. If she gives me the opportunity, I might walk out of the Stacks an engaged man, so power up your treadmills and whatever other unused equipment is in those home gyms y'all speak of. I love each and every one of you. Eyes open. Head to the sky."

"One love."

"One love."

"One love."

One after the other, their remarks piled in. When the call ended, I powered up the large display screen behind me and logged into my account to begin the meeting I was scheduled for.

"Dr. Domino," Shelene greeted me.

"My apologies for my tardiness."

"We still have one minute before we're set to start the meeting," she explained.

I took a peek at the clock. Satisfied with my timing, I rested my bones. Promptness was part of my genetic makeup, it seemed. If there was nothing else we hated more as a family, it was showing up tardy. It was a form of disrespect in our eyes. Time was precious and to be valued as such. It was the only thing in life that you couldn't redeem.

"Good. Let's begin."

Milo Nature

JOHN B'S voice was eliminated from the equation and replaced with the loud, increasingly annoying sounds of my phone ringing. It was the second call to come through since starting my engine. The large screen in front of me forced me to withhold the thick, steamy air that was prepared to push forward and through my nostrils. Inclination replaced the budding frustration as I connected the call.

"Pops!"

"Mi. Mi. Mi."

Three times, he repeated the nickname he'd given me as a very small child.

"Talk to me, old man."

Hearing his voice was a pleasure of mine. With his increase in age, it wasn't an unrecognized blessing that he was still around. Since teens and preteens, he'd raised four boys to be productive members of society, for the most part, and had done so gracefully. The creases in his eyes when he smiled, showed no evidence of the hardships we faced or the pain of losing his son to his daughter-in-law's mental illness caused.

He paused briefly before replying, "I, uh, wanted to catch you before the day ends and remind you that it's no ordinary day. It's sort of a special one that I won't let you forget as long as I'm breathing."

"I know, Pop."

"Well, I imagine you've already called to wish her a happy birthday?"

"I have. I texted, but yes."

"Good. Did you get her something?"

"Of course. They were delivered this morning."

"What did you come up with?"

"Flowers, the usual. I sent white chocolate-covered strawberries as well."

"Good. Good. That's about all I wanted."

From the moment he laid eyes on Nature all those years ago, he claimed her as mine forever. Pops didn't let a year go by, even after our split, without wishing her a happy birthday and making sure I did the same. He knew her number better than he did any of us boys, although, he hardly used it.

She was somewhat like a daughter to him. He'd lost his daughter-in-law so long ago. The death of my aunt triggered those emotions he felt when my mother and father died of murder-suicide. Those were scary times for him, but he mustered the strength and kept pushing. He never imagined a world without his children.

Pops always knew that he'd leave the earth before they did, but he was wrong. His wife, son, and daughter were gone. Anna, Malachi's wife, had even left him. All he had was his six grandsons, great-granddaughter, and great-grandson. He cherished each and every one of us because he knew tomorrow wasn't promised to anyone.

"Every year, Pops?" I chuckled.

"Until you stop making a mockery of the love you two birthed and won't ever find again, yes, son. Every year. She might not act like it, but she'd be crushed if either of us forgot her day. Those gifts you send to her parents' home each year, she secretly looks forward to them. Waits for them. Expects them.

"It's the only reason she visits on that day in particular. Don't stop. They maintain your relevance in her world and keep hope for you two alive. If she didn't believe there was any, she would've asked you to stop sending them long, long ago."

Taking in his words, I inhaled until my lungs filled to capacity.

"You think there's a chance for us?"

My delusion was apparent. Everyone knew that when it came to Nature, I believed the unbelievable. But confirmation from my grandfather on this very day would assure me that I wasn't a complete fool and there was a bit of truth to my delusion.

It didn't matter how many years passed, how many women I'd gone through, how many years she's spent sporting a title that she was untrue to, or how much she pretended not to harbor feelings for me; I, wholeheartedly, believed that Nature was the end for me. Everything stopped with her, for her. The second she professed her undying love for me or aspirations of being in my world and letting me back into hers, it would all end.

"When you truly, truly love someone, Milo, it doesn't just die. Life happens and that love creeps into a dark hole, hoping to never be discovered again. Even if they've wronged you, you learn to love them less, but it's almost impossible not to love them anymore if you ever really did. Nature's love for you has been shelved, but it exists.

"Each year on the morning of her birthday when she opens her eyes, she's reminded of that package she sat on the shelf. When she hurries to her childhood home to see what's waiting for her there, she's climbing that shelf. And just as she opens the pleasant surprises you have for her, she opens that box she sealed your history and her love for you inside.

"It's not until the day ends and another begins that she sits it back up there, right where she put it so that she'll know where to find it the next year. I'm not telling you to wait around until she's ready to keep that box open forever, but I am telling you that it'll happen one day."

"Maybe it's today."

"How do you figure?"

"She agreed to go on a date with me."

"Shut yo' mouth, boy," he exclaimed.

I could hear the inclination of his mood. His heart was happy hearing the news.

"Nah, Pops. I'm serious. I just left the hospital, making my rounds. I feel like a damn boy about to get his first piece of pussy back in the day. It's only a date. We've had plenty, but it feels like a first."

"First of many," he interrupted. "That's good. That's good. It should feel this way. It's been a while for the two of you, but I'm wishing nothing but the best for both of you, whether together or apart. I just hope like hell it's together."

"I'm taking her to Stacks."

"The steakhouse?"

"Yes."

"Yeah. She might not shelve that box so soon after tonight. A Stack's steak is worth just about as much as what's in that bo—"

"Woah! I disagree."

"Yeah. I hear ya."

"I'm pulling up to the house, old man. I'll catch you later, aight?"

"Yeah. Sure thing, son. I love ya."

"One love, Pops."

I ended the call just as a message came through. My entire hand shook from the force of the vibrations. Instantly,

I pushed the small button on the side forward to remove the silencer.

The red rose appeared. Serving as a defibrillator, it produced a current *so intense* that it resulted in a deafening heartbeat that drowned out every sound around me. It was as if I was underwater, unable to hear anything because the chlorine-filled liquid was far above my ears.

Apprehension swallowed me whole as I unlocked my screen. Ignoring every word in the text message that was four lines long, I began my reply. Whatever Nature was saying to me didn't matter. All that mattered was my response.

You don't get to stand me up, Nay. I don't give a damn what that message says. We're doing this. Get dressed and stay off your phone and out of your head. I prefer remaining respectful, but I don't have an issue pulling up to your address instead of the one that belongs to your parents. See you at eight.

The message was long and much more winded than I would've liked, but Nature needed to understand what was being requested of her. I didn't have to read the message she'd sent to know it contained doubts and apologies for agreeing to a date that she no longer thought was a good idea to attend.

She was coming along with me for the night, even if I had to go get her ass from the crib she shared with her partner. I wasn't opposed to the idea if she brought me to that point. The sadness in her voice wouldn't allow me to go on about my day as if it didn't exist. It was her birthday, and more than anything, I wanted to make sure she enjoyed at least the last few hours of it.

Gray bubbles appeared, hiking my adrenaline and toying with my patience. She was superjacent on my nerves but I couldn't say I'd rather have it any other way. When we sat down for dinner in less than two hours, it would all be worth it.

OK.

Her response was simple but the complexity of the thought process that went behind it wasn't as quickly forgotten as the single-word reply. She understood my yearning for her presence and knew that her night would be so much better with me. Nature was well aware that whatever was bothering her, I'd see to it that it was fixed before we got up from dinner. I was a source of relief for Nay.

It was always that way. Whatever problems arose for her, if I had the power, I'd make them disappear. So many years had passed since I'd contributed to her worrying less and thriving more. I missed that shit. I missed her. She knew it, too.

Satisfied with the trajectory of our night, I marched into my home calmly, heading straight for the kitchen. A bottle of water and a few pieces of cantaloupe would suffice for now, holding me over until I saw that beautiful face of Nature's. Long, jet-black lashes, well-defined cheekbones, pouty lips, and perfect white teeth would keep me full to capacity until we sat down to dine.

Cold and fresh fruit filled my fridge, replacing the harsh, processed foods that slowly decomposed the body over time. Though I had no issue eating that shit when I was out on the town, it had no place in my home. Four pieces of cantaloupe and two pieces of honeydew melon sat at the bottom of my bowl, waiting to be devoured along with the bottle of water in my hand.

One by one, I popped them into my mouth as I floated up the rounding staircase while mentally noting to remove the bowl and empty bottle from my room before leaving for the night. The smell of teakwood swarmed me upon entrance. Signs of human activity were absent, a preference of mine. A spotless home was the epitome of peace for me. Without it, I was restless, unfocused, and completely annoyed.

Wasting little time, the closet was my first destination. I settled on a pair of dark denim that was only a few shades lighter than the black ones right next to them. The acid-wash effect made them appear slightly gray. Still, I paired them with a black Amiri shirt. Black and red Jordan Ones were the shoe of choice, being that the letters on my shirt were the color of fresh blood.

With my free hand, I laid everything on the island in the middle of my closet, making sure it all coordinated well. Satisfaction was easily obtained, shaving off a few minutes of my preparation time. The empty bowl hit the glass on the top of the jewelry case that was next to me. I stripped out of the clothes I'd walked the hospital halls and visited patients in, shoving them down the laundry shoot before heading out of the closet and into the shower room, which was just through the second door in the large space.

I stepped inside the shower to get the water started, but immediately stepped back out because I wasn't quite ready to get in. The screen of my phone unlocked as I placed it in front of me. I disabled the Bluetooth connection to the speaker in my bedroom and connected it to the bathroom's system. Drake's harmonizing ass rushed through the speaker above the shower, filling the room with his voice.

As if anyone besides me and the housekeeper had been inside my home, I checked the towel warmer beside the shower to make sure there were towels inside. It was a habit stemming from a childhood that included living among four other males who would clown you for not checking the cabinet for towels before stepping into the shower. Many days, I'd skipped the step and ended up running through the house in search of clean, dry towels on laundry day.

This time, when I stepped behind the glass door, I didn't emerge until my body was covered in small beads of water that had been working the sweat and gunk of the day from my skin. The warm towel scrubbed away evidence of the H_2O upon reaching my bedroom. Moisturizer was quickly added for easy and thorough absorption.

Taking a look at the clock, I noticed I had less than thirty minutes to get out of the door and make my way toward Berks, where Nature's parents rested their heads each night. The mutual meeting spot was ideal because it was not too far from Stacks. Though I'd pass it on my way through The Peaks, it wasn't too far of a drive and wouldn't feel like the quick turnaround it really was.

Within twenty of those thirty minutes, I was dressed and inside the Aston Martin. Speeding down the street, I spritzed my neck a few more times with the cologne choice of the night. My windows were rolled down, airing out the heaviness of the aroma. I tossed the travel-sized bottle in the door pocket next to me and tightened my grip on the steering wheel.

My gratification peaked as a smile curved my lips up

and into a smile. If Nature didn't feel like home for me, my nerves wouldn't have survived the drive, but the comfort her presence granted me wouldn't allow it. For the first time in a long time, I truly felt like I was on my way home. *On my way back to her.*

I wasn't sure what this dinner would mean for either of us, but I couldn't deny the tingling in my gut that told me it wouldn't be our last one. Before I left her for the night, I'd make sure of it. Too much time had passed since I'd been graced with her smile and pretty brown hair and witty responses.

I missed that shit. I missed her. And after years of fucking around and lending my attention to undeserving participants, I was ready to fight until my death to make sure that I secured a new position in her world. It was my fault that we were in the spaces we were in. Tonight was the opportunity to make amends.

The sight of the snow-white Porsche Cayenne parked directly in front of the newly remodeled family dwelling as I pulled into the driveway loaded my abdomen with swarming butterflies. A quick chuckle forced me to sit a bit longer than anticipated as I got my shit together.

"Really, nigga?" I asked, massaging my temple with my index finger and thumb.

Nervous? I couldn't believe it. Nature was a source of comfort, which made it quite difficult to process. Nevertheless, with a shake of the head, I climbed out of the car and made my way up to the door.

Picture-perfect landscaping make me question my yard guy and what the fuck he was doing in my yard once a month because mine looked nothing like theirs. I refrained from snapping images, but made a promise to find out who they were working with so I could hire the same company. An assortment of plants led me to the steps that led to the front door. I stretched my right arm, preparing to ring the doorbell, when the door opened.

Sandy hair, lean limbs, chiseled cheeks, angelic eyes, mascara-encrusted eyelashes, and perfectly waxed brows rendered me speechless. So beautifully, Nature had aged. I swallowed to get rid of the chalkiness of my throat, still wondering if words were even possible.

Emotions choked me, assuring me that it wasn't yet time to speak. The pricking of my eyes forced a chuckle out. It was a habit of mine, one that collected my feelings and helped me gather myself when they were too big to voice or too much to handle. I cleared my throat again, unsure of what was going on inside my chest. The achiness forced me to rub it, twice right and twice left, before dropping my hand completely.

Subtle makeup covered her features, enhancing each and every one of them, making her even more beautiful than I'd imagined. I forced myself to look away. She was breathtaking and had surely summoned every ounce of air from not only my lungs but my bloodstream as well. I wasn't sure if I'd faint from the lack of oxygen or if I should place my lips on hers and inhale until my body was refilled with a decent supply of oxygen.

Soundlessly, we both gazed, neither in a hurry to say much. Silence was enough for once. I had no words. I'd waited patiently for this moment for far too many years to count and I wanted to savor it. I needed to savor it. For the rest of my life, I wanted to remember the enormous feelings it produced and the gratification it pumped me with.

After what felt like twenty-hundred hours, she finally said to me, "Hi."

Her voice along with its sensual, sultry delivery left me tongue-tied. With a shake of my head, I let out another chuckle.

Get ya shit together, Milo, I warned. Losing it wasn't part of the plan and neither was it becoming. I almost hated her for stripping me so soon, leaving me bare, in the nude on her parents' front porch.

"Hi." I cleared my throat, stepping back so she was able to join me outside.

I mustered as much strength as I possibly could to restrain my hands. Desperately, I wanted to pull her in, kiss her lips, and tell her how sorry I was for the hurt I caused her until I no longer had a voice to speak and she believed me.

But I didn't. Unfortunately, I didn't deserve that privilege as much as I wanted to believe differently. At that moment, I accepted my position and waited for initiated contact. As if the universe was working in my favor, she inched forward, nervously placing one arm over my shoulder, sure not to rest her head on my chest in the process.

And then, there was a pat.

A second one.

A third one.

The church hug. I tittered, sucking the skin of my teeth. The ability to control my impulses failed as I expanded, opening wide enough to accept all of her. In my arms, I wrapped Nature, clinging to her skin as if it was my soul's supply of nourishment and the central center for all good things in my life. In a way, both could be true.

She smelled of peaches, flowers, and baby powder. The combination was oddly satisfying, leaving me with no choice but to bury my nose in her neck. She trembled underneath my grasp, confirming her hesitancy and stomping all over my chest in the same breath. I pulled back, giving her the space her nervous system protested for.

"It's... uh... It's been a long time." She sighed with a smile that was so quick and so small that I almost missed it.

"Too long," I confirmed. "Your people here?"

Refusing to leave without at least saying hello to her parents, I inquired about their location.

"Well, of course, my mother is inside. She just went down for the night. My father..."

Those big, pretty eyes saddened at once as she looked up at me, rolled them, and then focused on me again. Her father was always a sore subject. After all this time, I noticed nothing had changed. His behavior throughout her childhood was a driving force in her decision to end things with me and it seemed it had continued.

Nodding, I completed her sentence. "Is out. It's good. I'll catch him another time."

Every few weeks, when he made his way through the halls of Benedict Berkeley, where I was Chief of Medicine in the Neuropsychiatrist department, we shared a few words. Though small, it was a driving force in the third largest hospital in the world. We were making strides to improve the brain's function and its relationship with the nervous system.

Even at his age, he was still on the go, unable to sit down

for even a few hours. He was a leader. A helper, by nature. However, the person he neglected to help was the person who needed it most, needed him most.

"Shall we?" she insisted, brushing off the temporary moment of disappointment.

"After you."

Nodding toward the short set of stairs, I urged her to move forward because I'd be right behind her. She slid past me, forcing me to plant my feet where they were. Unmoving, I acknowledged the small weight gain that age accompanied. Slowed metabolism and increased consumption of wine or other alcoholic beverages could all be factored into the pounds that expanded those already wide hips and ass. Neither were ridiculously large, but they were heavy on that thin frame of hers. She was gifted with subtle, yet notable curves that demanded the attention of any man in her presence.

The ratio hardly made any sense, but previous run-ins, family dinners, and store runs with her mother proved what was genetically possible. They were built like that. Her and almost every woman in their family. Thin, lean frames with asses that made you do a double take or immobilized you momentarily.

"Are you coming, Milo, or will you stay on the porch all night long and force me to eat dinner alone?"

She waited on the passenger side of the car, staring back up at me still on the porch as I waited for my body to regain consciousness. With daring eyes, I glared in her direction, heading straight toward her. My legs didn't stop moving until I was right in front of Nature. For a second, my heart stopped too.

Hadn't she been almost a full foot shorter than me at 5'7, we would've been chest to chest, face to face, nose to nose. That was how magnetic her presence was for me. I had no intention of invading whatever personal space she'd claimed before I came into her life but some way, somehow, it never existed for me, *to me*.

"Milo." Breathlessly, she all but pleaded, reaching forward.

In an instant, her palm slid against my fingers as I redirected her hand from the door she was attempting to open and flee from me.

"If you touch that door, Nature, I'm going to be very fucking offended."

"I-I..." she stuttered, tripping over her words. "I wasn't."

It was refreshing knowing that she hadn't forgotten. Instead of admitting as much, I peered down at her, waiting for her to look up at me. And when she did, she cracked my chest right open and gutted me of my heart. It was hers.

She owned it. Always had. Always would. Ownership had never been questioned, and as my orbs focused on the golden-colored beauty inches beneath me, I knew it never would be a question of mine.

Finally, she gave me those honey-drizzled rounds. Gnawing on her bottom lip, revealing her array of emotions and feelings as well as their displacement, she looked up at me. She didn't bat a single lash while waiting for me to say something, anything. She clung to the breath she'd taken, not letting go until words surfaced.

"Fix your face."

"Milo," she huffed.

"Fix it before you get in this car, Nay. I don't give a fuck what happened before I showed up. From this moment forward, you are only to feel good things. Shit that makes your lips stretch for your eyes and that heart of yours beat so hard against your chest that you think you need to see a cardiologist. I'm not accepting anything less and neither should you. So, fix your face. I'm here. Whatever it is, I'm going to make it better now."

Slowly, she released a long stream of air, ridding herself of everything that was hindering her happiness on such a special day. It wasn't until I saw her ears lift and cheeks rise slightly that I opened the door and allowed her to slide into the passenger seat where she belonged.

Enclosed in the small space with her, the scent of her perfume ignited my senses. Closing my eyes, momentarily, I tried hard to define the moment and the value it carried but failed. Nature Dupree, a college graduate at the age of eighteen and the youngest OB/GYN Berkeley had ever known, was once again, my passenger.

"You really don't have to," politely, she responded to my outstretched hand with the box in the center.

"But I did."

She accepted the Rolex-branded box with the softest of smiles spreading her lips across her entire face.

"How'd you know?"

"Homework. You're a subject I'll study until the death of me. It's detrimental to stay up to date on all things Nature as much as I pray for our reunion."

"Pray?" She chuckled, pulling the top of the box backward.

"Yes. I saw a few weeks ago that you'd misplaced your favorite watch."

"My Datejust."

"Your Datejust. I ordered an upgrade, immediately, and included a few customizations. Within a week, it was at my doorstep. I wasn't sure when I'd have the chance, but there was just something warning me against sending it here to your parents' home. I'm happy I didn't fight that feeling and followed it, instead."

"Why?" She chuckled. "My arm wouldn't have been so bare for so long."

"Because I wouldn't have gotten to see this look on your face."

"Milo." She was amused, covering her face, but not before I got a peek at the redness of her cheeks and all those pearly white teeth. "I have no idea what you're talking about."

She wasn't a good liar. That hadn't changed, either. But instead of calling her on her shit, I pulled out of the driveway as "Misunderstood" by Lucky Daye began on the stereo.

Thank you, she mouthed while we exited the driveway.

Twice, I tapped the middle of my chest with my palm with a nod. As the soundtrack of our night poured through the speakers, I pressed the pedal. Nature occupying my passenger seat was paramount to my week. I couldn't imagine a better way to end it.

As college kids, we hardly had much of anything to our names. Long walks to classes and labs felt much different from the buttery seats of the Aston, but just as good. Watching her hair fight the wind and get stuck in the lip gloss she'd painted her lips with was as comical as it was heartwarming, reminding me of the windy days we struggled to keep our bodies from flying in the opposite direction as we trekked the campus to our next destination.

The diamonds that circled her watch glistened under the light that bounced off her brown skin every other second. *Flawless. Perfectly made.* Nature was such a beautiful creature, unlike anything I'd ever seen. Her cinnamon-colored hair, honey-drizzled eyes, and sandy skin tone were only a few of my favorite things about her. The list was almost never-ending.

Bobbing her head, she matched the beat of the stereo. Somehow, someway, Kehlani's voice had made it into the mix. Because Nature was so enthralled in the record playing, I decided against changing it and listened to the words she seemed to know quite well.

Her sentiments included taking turns being grown, being accountable, feeling crazy for missing someone, being problematic, feeling addicted to someone, putting the pussy up and waiting for someone, and an array of other things. But the ones that stood out most were the lines she felt it necessary to harmonize.

"You a damn drug. You're... *toxic*," she sang, lowly.

"I was this way for you. Put the pussy away for you. Thinking I would wait for you."

"Problematic. You know that dick always been problematic."

I continued listening until the song ended and she busied herself with her phone. A peek in her direction confirmed my suspicions. She was checking her emails. It was a habit of mine, too. As if the universe was working in my favor, the next song was a repeat of one that had played not long ago. I didn't understand how it reappeared in the rotation, but was thankful when I heard Lucky Daye's voice. I mashed the button on the steering wheel, pumping the volume and drawing Nature's attention. This time, it was my turn to talk my shit.

"We ain't gotta be all put together girl. Maybe we're better misunderstood. I been tryna be clear in my feelings girl."

The opening lines were enough to solidify her piqued interest. I allowed Lucky to continue doing his thing, only tagging along when it was absolutely necessary.

"I try to do it. I push 'em back any time you come and see me. Is it mine all mine all mine? All I know is it just feels right. Don't it feel right?"

My hand with a mind of its own, escaped my side of the vehicle and migrated over toward Nature's side. It landed on her thigh. The dress she wore had risen as she'd sat in the car, giving me the privilege of skin-to-skin contact. Gently, I squeezed, taking a second to look in her direction.

"My thoughts be doing what they wanna. Got me thinking that I can't have ya like I want ya."

Every few lines that appealed to me and our situation, I matched, word for word. Nature's eyes never left me, and if I wasn't driving, my eyes wouldn't have left her. As if our batteries just needed to be recharged, our connection was beginning to spark fire again.

Another song and then another song played before she tore her orbs away from me. I released her body as I turned the corner that Stacks sat on. Pulling up to the valet attendant was almost torture. Pulling the plug on our parallel energy at the moment would require another boost of our batteries by the time we were seated inside.

"Good evening. Welcome to Stacks, Mr. Domino."

Closing my eyes briefly, I pushed away the saltiness and embraced what was to come.

"A regular, huh?" Nature chuckled, gathering her belongings in preparation to exit.

"For the amount required to reserve, they better know my name every time I pull up."

I stepped out of the car and watched the attendant run around toward the passenger side.

"Broken fingers are no fun. As a physician, please trust me on this. Touch her door, my nigga, and you'll be forced to figure out how to straighten each one on your right hand as you wait for paramedics arrival."

Tossing both hands in the air, the young, dread headed brother stepped back with a smile on his face. His head lifted and fell continuously as I approached the passenger side and opened the door.

"I get it," he exclaimed. "I get it."

Admiring Nature's frame as she stood to her full potential. The sexy, strapless number she wore was a fucking sight. Black in color, it matched my attire. Though unplanned, we looked like a well-coordinated unit.

"Physician?" he asked.

"Yeah."

"Undergrad, majoring in Biochemistry."

"What's the end goal?"

"Surgeon."

"You're going to need those fucking fingers." I chuckled.

"I am," he agreed. "Any advice?"

"Yeah. But not at this moment. I'm occupied, and so are my thoughts."

We both eyed a smiling Nature. The innocence in her eyes spread down her face and infected her smile.

"Monday morning, come by my office."

I dipped into my car to grab a card and hand it to the young man.

"Ah. Shit. A brain guy."

His eyes bulged from his skull as he read the card.

"Damn, Chief?"

"Anything is possible, Black man," I assured him, closing the distance between my date and I.

With my hand on the small of Nature's back, we pushed forward. Before we got too far away, she turned back, hesitating as she gathered her thoughts.

"It will get hard. So hard you'll want to give up. It'll get lonely. So lonely you'll question what you're really doing it for or who you're really doing it for. But whatever you do, don't give up. I studied medicine, too, and as a woman who delivers multiple babies a week, saving so many Black women's lives, the hardships I faced in school seems so... small. I'd do it again a hundred times."

"You, too? A doctor?"

"I'm whatever my patients need me to be. A therapist. A friend. A physician. A shoulder to cry on. A surgeon. Anything," she admitted.

"Mom's not going to believe my luck today. Just the motivation I needed. I'm just... wow."

"Have a good night..."

Nature paused, remembering she hadn't gotten his name.

"Jeremiah."

"Goodnight, Jeremiah."

"Goodnight, ma'am... sir."

Milo Nature

DIMNESS SHEETED THE RESTAURANT, offering the moody, mellow vibe that I preferred over the live, brightly lit atmosphere of many establishments. Across the table, in the seclusion of our private dining suit, sat Nature with her eyes nervously bouncing around the room. The Van Cleef bracelets slid up and down her arm as she pushed and pulled on them over and over.

Red wine was in front of her. Brown liquor covered the bottom of the glass that I swirled around before taking a second sip, clearing it completely. As the glass cleared my line of vision, Nature's eyes had found me and remained fixated on me as she lifted her glass to sip from.

"How are you, Nature?"

Resting my back against the seat with expanded limbs that acquired space beyond the necessary, I cracked my knuckles with my thumb, starting with my index finger. Patience failed me as I waited for her voice to serenade the moment. It wasn't until she was ready that her lips parted. And when they did, I was all ears.

"I'd say that I'm perfectly fine." Slowly, she sighed. "But that would be a lie. I've been better, but it's not all bad."

"How can I fix it?"

"Fix it?"

"Your issue."

"You don't even know what it is, Milo."

"It doesn't matter. How can I fix it?"

"You can't," she scoffed. "Unless you have some sperm to donate in the next forty-eight hours."

To lighten the load of the words she'd just spoken, she laughed. Her right hand went up toward her chest as she began to rub. Nature was a creature of habit. I remembered the gesture. It was a sign of discomfort and shattering nerves.

With hiked brows, I responded, "Your master plan?"

"My master plan."

"What does Chasity have to say about you—"

"Chasity was never a part of my master plan and I doubt you care what she thinks."

"I really don't give a fuck. For once, I didn't have a response, so I followed up with something that's especially irrelevant to me."

"Figured."

"Continue."

"Had I realized plugging her into my plan wouldn't work when it was all said and done, I could've saved us both some headache and hard times."

"Is that where this sadness is coming from?"

"Sadness?"

"I can feel it, Nay. It's all over you. From the look in your eyes to the movements of your body to the sound of your voice."

"Chasity in particular, no. But where my life is right now? Yes. Yes, that's where it's coming from. I ended things with Chasity, officially, just two days ago. We'd already separated six months ago. I guess we were both just sticking around for our heart's sake. Because she was once my best friend, I've never spent much time without her around. In some way, I dreaded the day I'd have to end it all, but I knew that I wouldn't step into year thirty-six, holding onto anything or anyone that didn't align with that plan. As delusional as it might seem, it's true."

"Six months?"

"Is that all you retained from everything I said, Milo?" She took another sip from her glass.

"No. It's one of the three most important things, though."

"What else did you manage to pull?"

"The fact that you feel as if you fell off track somewhere and your thirty-sixth birthday is your marker. Your new starting point. Your relationship with Chasity ended long before the six-month separation but you held on three months after that because you're not accustomed to living life without her. She was once your best and often times your only friend."

"You were listening."

"It's disheartening learning that you thought otherwise."

"The clock is ticking for me, Milo, and it's filling me with so much unwarranted anxiety. I can feel it swell in my throat every time I open my mouth to speak. By thirty-six, I always saw myself with children and a husband living in a house that made my younger self extremely proud. It's like I've been busting my ass since I was a kid for that life, only to feel empty every day that I walk inside of my home and no one is running up to me, screaming their little heads off.

"I've come to terms with the fact that I won't marry. I'm okay with that, but I'm not okay with continuing life childless. It's daunting. The thought. And the fact that I deliver babies every day just makes it even worse. It's like salt is being poured on fresh wounds each time I hear another one cry. Instead of continuing to wait or putting myself through the torture any longer, I have an appointment with Jessie this Sunday. She's not open on Sundays, but she's taking me, anyway. Privacy is a concern for us both and—"

"Jessie?"

I remembered only one Jessie, an old college buddy of hers who was into reproductive health.

"Yes."

"For what?"

"IUI," she clarified.

"IU..." I trailed off, mired with disbelief.

"I'm not getting any younger, Milo. So many risk factors increase in women over thirty-five. Yes, I see hundreds of women each year who have perfectly healthy babies after thirty-five, but it's the twenty to thirty women who aren't as lucky that haunt me when I fall asleep at night.

"Gosh, I'm making this all about me. I'm sor... I'm sorry. I'm piling my problems on you and that is not how I intended to spend the night. We haven't seen each other in forever. I shouldn't be so wasteful of our time together. Please forgive me."

"Nature."

"Sorry. I promise. I won't talk abo—"

She was always apologizing for nothing, as if everything was her fault when it wasn't. This... this was, in fact, my fault. The fact that her master plan had derailed, I was to blame. That family and home she spoke of included me. It stung, knowing how one bad decision had changed the entire life story for someone I wanted nothing but the best for.

"How can I help?"

"You can't, Milo."

Her words paralyzed me. Immediately after the pain, I numbed as she continued.

"Not this time. This is something that I have to fix on my own. I waited so long and I can't tell you why. I don't even know. But I do know that I'm done waiting. I'm ready to hold my daughter or my son in my arms for the first time and I don't want to be thirty-seven when it happens. So, let's talk about something else. Please. I got so carried away. I'm sorry."

"Stop apologizing for expressing yourself. I asked and you unloaded. I'm appreciative of your ability to flow so effortlessly as I listen."

"It's always been so easy."

"What?" I questioned.

"Talking to you."

She looked up at me, sipping again. Those eyes of hers had always gotten her in big trouble, and tonight, I didn't think things would be any different.

"Yeah? Because I remember a time you wouldn't."

"Whose fault had it been?" She tilted her head, waiting for a response.

With a nod, I leaned forward and let her have that one. We both shared gazes as silence toyed between us. After a few seconds, she ripped her eyes away from me. I watched her chest rise and fall, dramatically. She was a mess inside.

"I've missed you," I confessed, slamming my back against the chair again as I rubbed a hand down my face.

"Milo, please," she begged.

"Would you prefer I lied?"

"I'd prefer you didn't make this night harder than it is already, is all."

"Watching you from afar isn't as nearly as glorious as the front-row seat. You've grown into an even more stunning being than I had imagined."

Blushing, she sucked the skin of her teeth before responding, "Admittedly, I knew you'd become every bit of the man you are today."

"Remind me to write you a check for your contributions to this man."

"Ahhh. Stop it. I didn't do much. That was all you, Milo. You're brilliant. Til this day, I've never encountered anyone as sharp as you."

"Nature, have you forgotten you started college at sixteen?"

"You were fifteen," she reminded me. "I wasn't quick enough."

We both joined in laughter as memories of our college days soared through our heads. It was much different from those around us, being that we were the youngest students on campus. It was part of the reason we bonded. And after years of friendship, we sought out more of each other. Our relationship was blissful until it wasn't.

The food arrived before I was able to conjure a reply. The smell of sizzling steak made my stomach rumble. I could hear the evidence of its medium-well nature on the skillet it was still being cooked on. Before it was set in front of me, the waitress set the seafood pasta on the other side of the table. Nature pulled it closer, lowering her head to take a whiff.

"If there's anything else I can get for you all, just flag me down or request it from the tablet," our waitress said, pointing to the tablet we'd placed our order on. "Another round of drinks is on the way."

"Thank you."

"Thanks," Nature added.

We fell into comfortable conversation as forks began clinking against the glasses our food was in. Those sad eyes began to sparkle again, glistening as she spoke and listened to me do the same. Her cheeks lifted and fell more times than I could count.

Two hours and too many glasses of liquor later, the check had been settled and I watched Nature wobble out of the door as I held it open. My heart pumped with joy and sadness, simultaneously. I wasn't prepared for the night to end, and neither was I willing to push past boundaries that Nature had put into place.

Though this night hadn't led to much more than a pleasant time, I didn't regret a minute of it. I'd turned her frown upside down and it was the least I could do after all she'd gone through on my account. Her shell had softened. That was a start for me. For us. When the opportunity to be more than a listening ear presented itself, I'd gladly take it.

Jeremiah, the valet attendant, stood beside Nature's door, allowing me to open it in order for her to get inside. Once she was settled, without haste, I circled the car and slid into the driver's seat. The door was ajar, making the transition smooth.

"See you, Monday," he shouted as I closed the door.

With the wind, we were gone, cruising the Berkeley streets with full bellies and jaws that ached from laughter. Every few seconds, I could feel Nature's eyes on me.

"Clear your mind, Nay," I advised, lowering the volume on the music right after.

"Nothing is there, really. Just thinking about how we've both grown into the people we once dreamed we could be."

"And making this shit look easy when—"

"It isn't."

"Not at all."

"How is everyone?" She changed the subject.

"Pops, I don't have to tell you how that nigga is doing. You probably hear from him more than I do."

"Stop it."

"He still on my ass about fucking up with you," I shared.

"Tell him it's fine. Life goes on."

Her words were like little daggers, piercing my heart. Finding it hard to recover quickly, I cracked my neck to release some of the tension that was building.

"How's Malachi?" She continued in a somber tone that expressed her genuine concern for my brother's well-being. Though distant, she wasn't a stranger to his circumstances. It was her phone that I found myself texting when I needed a few words of reasoning as it related to the strain on the relationship my brother and I had.

"Malachi is better. Much better. Remarried. Just had a son. Back in the city."

"Good. And Mercer was released. That reunion must've been precious."

"Yeah. He's home. Adjusting for him hasn't been the easiest, but he's home, nevertheless."

"Makai?"

"Still foolish."

Chuckling, she tossed her head back and exposed those perfect white teeth between her lips.

"He's truly a wild card."

"You never know what to expect with that nigga. Every time you think you know him, he shows you that nobody truly knows him. Not even him."

"He wakes up and unboxes a new version of himself each day."

"Every fucking day." I laughed, realizing how true that was.

Our time together crept to an end as I pulled into her parents' driveway. Before the wheels came to a halt, she was already saying her goodbyes.

"It's been great, Milo. I promise not to let so much time pass before we do this again."

"Happy birthday, Nature."

"Thank you for dinner and thank you for the watch."

She lifted her arm, flexing the piece of gold back and forward.

"You like it?"

"I love it." Nature yawned. "Whew. I need to get home."

It was getting late. Acknowledging she was an early bird and her bedtime had passed long ago, I exited the vehicle and ran around to her door. When I opened it, she stepped out and right into my outstretched arms. I wrapped them around her, inhaling the unique fragrance on her skin. Her warmth was encompassing. I wanted to live and die within it.

"You're up next," she reminded me, pulling back.

"It's September, Nay. I have a while."

"I'll reserve a table somewhere just in case. If you don't have any other plans."

"I'll cancel them." Shrugging, I leaned against the car and pulled her close to me.

"There's no need. Maybe another time."

"Maybe not another year. This year. Why are we waiting?"

"Because, Milo, it's important that I take you in doses."

"For once, overdosing doesn't sound too bad."

"The medical board would have your head for saying something like that."

"Let 'em."

"What was your end game here?" She chuckled, standing in front of me, looking like a much better meal than the one I'd just eaten. I wanted to devour her next. "What are you trying to do, Milo? I'm no fool. I know you really well. What's your aim?"

"To be your nigga."

Nodding, she slowly backed up a bit.

"Haven't we gone over this before?"

"Shit done changed."

"It didn't change soon enough," she told me.

"I don't like the idea of a stranger fathering your child," I admitted. "It's been on my mind all fucking night."

"I didn't like the idea, either, but it's now or never for me. I've grown to appreciate the structure that will accompany having a child of my own without anyone to share them with. Unlimited hugs and kisses," she joked.

"Is that really enough?"

"It has to be."

"Give me three months, Nay. And everything on that master plan of yours, I can make happen for you. For us. I know we're getting older and I, too, am ready for all that shit you are. I don't see the issue with giving our situation another shot."

"I can't, Milo."

"Why not?"

"All those years ago," she said before pausing. "When you hurt me, Milo, I made myself a promise that I'm going to keep."

"What's that, Nay?"

She dropped her head before looking back up at me with pain in her smile. Sighing, she turned her head as the words fell from her lips.

"I'd never give you the chance to hurt me twice."

Silenced by the impact of my heart slamming against my chest, I closed my eyes and let the words soak. Everything hurt. Before I managed to recover, she was gone.

"Goodnight, Milo," she called out over her shoulder as she slid into her truck and took off into the dark of the night.

I wasn't sure how long I remained on the passenger side, trying to recuperate until I made it back to my side and inside of my whip. My heart led the way as my foot mashed the metal, assisting it to its destination. And it wasn't until I was parked alongside the white fence that was lined with greenery that I stopped. Out and on foot, I pushed through the barrier and made my way up onto the porch where beautiful plants lined the stairs up.

"Milo?" Nature gasped.

Flustered cheeks and furrowed brows were evidence of her state of confusion. She had barely gotten her key into the front door by the time I invaded that personal space that didn't exist in my head or my heart. Filled to the brim with regret and grief for the loss of us, I folded my hands in front of me to keep from wrapping them around her body, lifting her into the air, ripping her out of that dress and fucking her on this porch until she forgot all the pain I caused her all those years ago.

"I'll do it."

"I'm sorry," she apologized for nothing. "But what is it, Milo? What are you referring to?"

"The sperm. I'll do it."

"Milo, I wasn't ser—"

"I'll do it. I want to do it. Let it be mine."

"Milo, you don't have... I have a donor."

"It should be me, Nature. It would be an honor and it would be a small token of appreciation for your contributions to the person I am today. It's the least I can do, Nay. Gift you with the one thing that will unbreak the heart I broke back then and screwed up your whole life plan. Let me get you back on track. Let me contribute to the woman, the mother, you're trying to become."

"Milo, are you sure?" she asked, tears making her eyeballs glisten in the dark of the night.

"I'm so fucking for real. Let me do that for you. Genes, family history, physical disabilities and attributions, all of that is right in front of you. It's not something you have to question or worry about down the line. You know me. You know my history. You've seen the niggas in my family too many times to count."

"This is... I didn't expect... I'm sorry. I'm just trying to process everything. This is... this is. Why are you doing this, Milo?"

"Because I don't want to see you do this alone. I have no doubt that you can, but I want in, Nay. I'm not getting younger, either."

"Co-parent?" She groaned through her tears. "What else is in this for you? I know you've thought about this on that short ride over. Lay it all on the line, Milo. Don't lie and don't hold anything back. Tell me everything."

"Natural conception."

"Ha!" Sarcastically, she chuckled. "Of course you would wan—"

"Co-parenting."

Shaking her head, she continued listening as she cleared her face of tears.

"A second chance."

"Milo, I—"

"Hear me out, Nature. I'm not asking for that today or next month or the month after. I am simply saying that, whenever you decide to date, I want first in line. It'll only make sense for us to at least try and maybe co-parenting won't be the dynamic forever, ya know? Maybe our child could eventually experience a two-parent household. Maybe we could walk down the aisle and jump that broom.

"Your plan is still viable. It can survive if you'd just give it a chance to. I won't beg you. I won't bother you. I won't try to force you into anything. Time will do for us all that needs to be done. Just give me the chance to truly father our child before the next nigga. That's all I'm asking."

"It's asking a lot, Milo."

"I understand that, but I'm worth it, Nay. I know it and so do you."

Pausing momentarily, she nodded after some thought.

"That's three requests to make one of my dreams come true."

"Four."

Her eyes shifted as she nodded again.

"Natural conception. Co-parenting. A chance to father our child if ever you decide to date again. First in line."

"That's three."

"M. Their name has to start with an M."

"Self-centered, much?" she tittered.

"Please."

"Okay." With a sigh, she continued. "But I have some rules and regulations of my own."

"Spill."

"Monthly check-ins during the pregnancy. I don't need you holding my hand the entire pregnancy. I can manage alone and prepared to. I don't want that to change. I don't need company at appointments or anything like that. We can meet monthly for check-ins. A common place. Maybe a restaurant or coffee shop or something of the sorts. We split ultrasound images."

"Okay. Baby shower, delivery room, ride home from the hospital, you can't say no to those."

"Why can't I?"

"Because you can't."

"Fine."

"What else?"

"I didn't want a baby shower, honestly."

"Alright. What else?"

"We don't share supplies or bags or car seats."

"From the delivery room and beyond, I'm there for every appointment. I'll give you the pregnancy appointments. I don't want to, but cool."

"Milo, are you sure? I had this all figure out. I don't want to drag you in—"

"You're not dragging me into shit that I don't want to be a part of. I'm no young nigga and I don't want anyone birthing my child if their name isn't Nature Dupree."

"Thank you."

"Nah. Thank you. I thought you'd tell a nigga no and send me on about my way."

"Being that I didn't, can you be honest with me?"

"I've never been anything but honest with you."

"I know."

She lowered her head. When she lifted it again, she released heavy, warm air from her nostrils.

"What is it?"

"Will you have time? Will you be there? I mean, really be there? Mentally, physically, emotionally, and not just financially? I can provide for a child alone. I don't need you for that. Will you have time?"

Her father had ripped her heart out so many times that he was still trying to situate it in her chest. His obsession with work and the betterment of his patients left her and her mom scrambling for his time, attention, and emotional support. Financially, they wanted for nothing, but it was never enough for Nature. She'd trade the finances for his undivided attention almost any day.

"I'll make time. It won't be an issue. It won't ever be a problem. Alright?"

"Sorry. I just... My father never..." She stammered over her words.

"I'll make time."

Peering down, I looked into those glossy eyes to help her understand I had every intention of showing up every time our child needed me.

"I need some time to process all of this."

Nature stepped back and closer to her door. The last few minutes had overwhelmed her, forcing her hand on her chest as she rubbed it over and over.

"Understood."

"I'll call you tomorrow, okay? Maybe around noon if you're not busy."

"Call me at any time of the day, Nature, and I'll get unbusy. Just hit my line."

"Okay."

I rested my lips on her forehead, pecking it quickly before stepping off. I made it near the gate before something prompted me to request more details surrounding her body's cycle.

"When does your ovulation window open?"

"Tomorrow!" she yelled down the stairs.

Turning on the heels of my feet, I watched as she unlocked her door.

"You're most likely to conceive before or after that twenty-four-hour window."

"I'm aware, Milo. I'm an OB/G—"

Before she managed to finish her sassy ass response, my long legs had tackled the steps and her body was being shoved forward, into the house. My hands, with minds of their own, caressed every centimeter of skin accessible. And at the realization that her fabric was restricting the rest, I tore through it all, not loosening my grip until she stood in front of me bare.

I slammed the front door shut with my foot. The force rattled the frame, taking Nature by surprise. Her gapped lips drew me closer. Like little whispers, they summoned me. And when I gave into their demands, I almost exploded.

Pre-ejaculation hadn't seeped from my dick since I was a boy, waiting to get my dick wet for the first time. It was the summer that I graduated from high school and would be heading to college in a few short weeks. At fifteen, I'd kept my head in the book, not involved with or intrigued by any of the young girls around the way. It wasn't until Makai dragged me on a double date with Arnisha and her sister that I became genuinely interested in losing my virginity. Two weeks of phone conversations and walks to the court in our neighborhood led Jayla to my bed.

"Milo," she whispered in my mouth.

"Shhhh."

I quieted her by muffling her cries with deeper, sloppier movements of my tongue and lips. She tasted like sweet, fresh nectar. Remnants of her gloss added a strawberry flavor that I wasn't exactly opposed to. My forcefulness pushed her backward, in the opposite direction. When I felt her slipping away, I began longing for her instantly. My long, anguished hand wrapped around her slender neck, desperate to have her nearer. It was her skin I craved being a part of because even when she was close, again, she wasn't close enough. I pulled away from her mouth to whisper in her ear.

"Where the fuck you going, Nay?"

"My God," she called out, melting in my grasp.

"May He be with you tonight."

I bit her ear, then slowly trailed my tongue across her face and bit her cheek.

"Milooo."

Then down her face, biting her lower jaw.

"Milo."

Over and over until her chin was between my teeth. She was obsessed with pleasurable pain. It made her center secrete.

"Miloooo."

"I've waited a long fucking time," I admitted, "to give you this dick."

"Ummm. Milo."

"I just need to know if you really want it or if you're ju—"

She covered my lips with her hand before looking up at me with those curious, cautious eyes. I loved her. I loved this woman with every fucking fiber in my being. And until I did, I'd never stop trying to get back to her.

"I've been grinding on a manmade erection for a decade," she breathed out. "Regardless of the circumstances and it being just this one time, I could use the reminder."

She didn't wait for a response before she was on her knees, tugging at my waistline feverishly. I helped her loosen my belt and slide everything that was between her and my dick down my legs. Swiftly, I relieved myself of my shoes, pants, and briefs at the same time.

Nature, on her knees, waited. My hardness addressed her desperation. She clung to both of my legs, staring at the erection with blossoming eyes and a wet mouth. I watched her chest rise and fall, unsure of her next step.

"You gon' stare at it or you gon' put this motherfucker in your mouuuuu—"

"Spuuuh!" As the words left my mouth, spit came flying from Nature's.

I shivered, quickly reminded that she had a good head on her shoulders and I wasn't only referring to her genius-level of knowledge. It was that sloppy ass top that I remembered at that moment.

Her lips surrounded my shit. Warm, gushiness followed immediately after. She tried her hardest to accommodate every inch of me but she was out of practice. Though capable, she needed time to readjust.

"Slow down," I instructed. "This dick not going nowhere."

Nature lubricated my rod and began using both hands to twist upward and then downward while she focused on the head. It was a much easier task for her, one she could perform with ease.

"Shit."

She dropped one hand leaving the other and working her way down my pole until her lips touched her thumb and index finger. My toes curled until they popped.

"Damn, girl."

Excitement drove her to the brinks of insanity. The back of her throat touched the tip of my dick, causing her to heave each time. Her eyes watered and her stomach caved, but she was determined. Finally, she was able to stuff me between her jaws comfortably, but it didn't come without a price to pay.

"Ahhhh," she grunted, removing me from her mouth completely.

Hot tears stained her pretty face as a trail of saliva maintained our connection. If my sperm wasn't the guest of honor for the night and needed somewhere special, right there was exactly where I would've put it. On those lips. On those cheeks. Across her forehead. Anywhere on that beautiful face.

"Ummmm."

Her moans were gratifying. When she took me into her mouth again, I knew I wouldn't last long this time. My climax was vastly approaching. Nature's jaws suctioned my dick as my fingertips dug through her hair until I felt scalp. I pushed her head forward, fucking her mouth as she took it like a fucking champ.

"Get up," I murmured, nearing my peak. "Get up. I-I'm 'bout to nut."

"Umm. Um."

"Nature."

"Right here."

She removed my dick from her mouth and rubbed it across her face, showing me exactly where she wanted it. As if she'd manifested it, semen shot from my dick and onto her face. I stiffened, unable to move a muscle for a full minute as labored breathing burdened us both.

"We could've used that," I grunted, marveling at my thick cum against her skin.

Slowly, she replied, "We still can."

I drew blood from my bottom lip, watching as Nature swept mounds of semen from her face, muddling her index and middle fingers before inserting them into her vagina. From atop, I monitored as she stroked her pussy with both fingers, using her thumb to press against her pearl. She'd ruined my chances of eating her pussy before I stuck my dick in her, but I wasn't complaining. The view was too fucking good to sweat the small shit.

Besides, I had no intention of leaving her until her ovulation window closed and we were damn near certain she had been impregnated. One time was fine. I just wanted to make sure it lasted a while.

The sound of her cream oozing from her pussy and mixing with my sperm made my dick even harder. But with patience, I waited and watched her lean backward to give me an even better view of her playtime. The way she worked her pussy made me jealous, almost.

Twirl.

Swirl.

In.

Out.

Side.

Side.

Stroke.

Twirl.

Mouth?

She'd breached my boundaries, taking shit too far. One by one, she licked her fingers from the bottom to the top. By the time she made it to her thumb, her body was in my hands and her back was against the wall. I slid her down onto my erection and replaced her fingers with my tongue. I tried prying hers out of her mouth so that I could take it as a souvenir but I couldn't unroot it for the life of me.

"Geeeeentle, please," she begged as I tapped at her entry.

When she finally let me in, her snugness silenced me. It was unhinged. Gushy, lubricated walls made silent promises to undo me. Unman me. Unravel me. Unearth me. Dismantle me. And I looked forward to every second of my deconstruction.

"Fuck."

I sank my teeth into her shoulder, desperately trying to relieve the mounting pleasure. Her shit was ridiculous. Top fucking tier. There was no such thing as better. It didn't exist. I'd gone through enough to know.

"Damn. I've missed you."

I kissed her lips, again, finally able to move and put the initial shock behind me. We were here and this was our moment. I never wanted it to end. Reality was nothing in comparison to the state of delusion I was in. there, I wanted to remain forever.

Time stood still. Everything around us was obliterated. It was only us, the way that I'd dreamed too many times to count. Her arms laced around me, deepening the imprints in my back. Heavy breaths from her lips heated my skin. Her low, pleasure-filled voice made the hairs on the back of my neck stand as she called my name over and over again.

"Miloooo."

Up and down, her back scrubbed against the wall.

"Milo!"

It was all so surreal. Tonight, we were creating a child,

our child. It wasn't how either of us had planned it, but it was as magical as I'd ever imagined it.

"Millllllooo."

I stroked her gently, as she'd requested, filling her with as much of me as possible. Her wetness helped me glide without friction. She was almost too fucking wet to remain lodged inside of her but her lack of expansion kept me buried.

"Yesssssss. Yesssss. Oh my G— I'm cu— Ummm!"

I gathered her hair and pulled her head backward. I was immediately given unrestricted access to her neck. When I clamped down, her body began to quiver.

Pulling away, I rested my lips against her ear and whispered, "That's it, Nay. Cum all over this dick."

I sank my teeth into her lobe, forcing her to cry out in pleasurable agony before going limp. Her orgasm had drained her of her energy and ability to remain upright. I carried the weight for us both as I made my way upstairs. I had no idea where the fuck I was going, but I pushed open every door until I found the one I was certain belonged to her.

I laid her down on the bed, never releasing myself. We were still connected as she gathered strength from some unknown source. I stood at the edge of the tall bed that was covered in cream linen, spreading her legs even wider.

Even in the dark, I could see her. Feel her. Her naked body was my playground. I remembered where everything was. Finding her most sensitive button was no obstacle.

"Ummmm. Mi—"

I stroked her pussy, listening to the sound of her creaminess being slathered against her walls and all over my dick.

My thumb pressured her bulb, exploring her sensitivity. As if that wasn't enough to mount her again, I leaned forward and took her right nipple into my mouth.

"Oh God! I'm going—Ima cum." She cried.

Nature was the closest thing to heaven. Her pussy pulled me in, suffocating my dick, ready to choke the semen straight out of that motherfucker. My end was near. I could feel my nut rising to the head of my shaft. It wasn't until it began to escape that I let her breast fall from my mouth and tucked my head between her shoulder and chin. I continued drilling her from below, preparing for our first round to come to a screeching halt.

This was my safe space. My heart was content here. Though she probably didn't believe it anymore, she was home for me. There was no one in the world I'd rather spend my best and worst days with. There was no other person in the world that I'd rather spend my long nights with.

We were one and the same. Both of us wanted the same things. I wasn't sure how we'd get to the end of the road hand in hand but I had faith it would happen. But first, there was something I needed from her. Something specific. Something irreplaceable. Something solid.

"Give me a son," I pled, continuing to unload in her womb.

It was open season for once in my lifetime. If this was my only chance, I wanted a boy.

"Okay," she agreed, body convulsing underneath me.

NOTE.

Between the covers of this book is **my** art piece —
beautifully paired words structured for **my** creative
satisfaction and later consumed by others for enjoyment.

It's **leisure for you**, it's **life for me**.
This is just a book to most. **It's art for me**.
My art. I've had *my* time. Have **yours**.

happy reading

GREY**HUFFINGTON**

ONE

Nature

"I DON'T UNDERSTAND IT, SHAYLA," I groaned, leaning back in my seat.

My right hand caressed my growing belly, rubbing in circles as I tried to decipher the message I'd received twenty-six hours ago from Milo. Though simple, there was an underlying level of complexity that accompanied it.

"What's there to understand?" Shayla asked, shrugging her shoulders.

"I miss y'all?" I scoffed. "What does that even mean?"

"It means what it says," she chuckled, "He misses his ex and the child you two conceived. You're a smart girl,

Nature, but it doesn't take a woman with a brain like yours to figure out what that message is saying. He didn't sugar-coat it or beat around the bush like he has the last couple of months. He just came right out and said it."

"Which leaves me puzzled. I've read it twenty times today and I'm still as lost as I was when I got it. We're almost at the finish line. He hasn't said anything like this the entire pregnancy. Why now? I guess that's what I mean. You know?"

"Why did he take so long? Why hasn't he said it sooner? Is he for real? Does he mean in the way you're hoping he does? Do you respond telling him the truth or keep lying to him and keep lying to yourself? Is that what you're asking yourself, because continuing to ask what he means by that message is irrelevant. It's me you're talking to, Nature. Come on, now."

Sighing, I lifted my right hand to my chest, rubbing back and forth hoping the aching subsided. Maybe I wasn't asking the correct question. Hearing Shayla express my truest feelings so effortlessly was almost triggering.

"Listen, Nature, I've heard you from the very beginning of this journey. I've lent you an ear any time you've needed one. Only when you've asked for my opinion, did I give one, but today, babe, I have to just lay it all on the table. I hate giving unsolicited advice, but I'd be damned if I don't. Watching you burn with desire for a man that clearly wants you as much as you want him is torture, and that's putting it lightly."

"I'm not burning with—"

"Girl, please. Those monthly meetings you have with Milo are the highlight of your existence."

"Actually, my child is."

"And the man that helped you create your child. You can fool a lot of people, but I'm not one of them, Nature. So, either, we're going to be real about your feelings or you can consider this the final conversation we'll have about your co-parent."

Inhaling deeply, I stared off into the distance. I could feel the dryness of my throat increase and began choking me. Blood filled my mouth from the piece of flesh I'd bitten through. My heart hammered against my chest, begging to be relieved of its barriers to beat freely for the one person in the world it ever held space for.

"OK. Alright."

The words rushed from my mouth as I tossed my hands in the air.

"Maybe you're right, Shayla."

"Maybe?"

She sipped from her drink, sniggering in the process.

"What's so funny?"

I smiled through the pain. It was so familiar that I'd learn to live with it. Since the day that Milo delivered the mind-boggling news that broke me down to the core, it lived with me, owning residency that wasn't up for sale.

"Awww. Poor baby. I'm sorry. I'm not laughing at your p —I just think it's the cutest thing. Seeing you this way. I haven't seen you this flustered in years. I, once, had my doubts about Milo from the things I've heard through the grapevine, but this situation has brought so much light to his character. I have to admit that I'm rooting for him."

"You're supposed to be on my side, Shayla."

"I am, which is why it's time to tell you what's really been on my mind."

"Spill it," I mumbled, placing a hand on my belly.

Shayla was my friend of six years. She'd quickly become my confidant, my listening ear, and my therapist in many instances. I wasn't a patient of hers officially, but it sure felt like it most days.

"Chasity was never your partner. Chastity was a means of suppression. You didn't love her beyond the friendship that you once had. You weren't invested in your relationship. You were comfortable. She brought you comfort. She was a safe space and had been since you were kids.

"In my opinion, I think it was selfish and heartless of her to capitalize on your vulnerability and force you into a situation that stemmed from an unhealthy obsession she had with you from day one. She practically tried to turn you out but judging by your round belly and growing feelings for the man that helped you create the child inside of it, dick prevailed. Once again. But she's another subject for another day. Moving forward.

"Your relationship with Chasity helped curb your true appetite. Now that it's over, those feelings you stuffed way down in some black hole, they've surfaced. For so long you convinced yourself they didn't exist, but they do, Nature. That text isn't the first and neither will it be the last of Milo's advances but you didn't need me to tell you that much.

"You knew it already. You knew it from the moment you agreed to co-parent a child with him. You knew it from the moment he stuck his dick in you. You knew it from the moment that pregnancy test came out positive. You've known for the last eight months. You're just a little disappointed that it took eight whole months. You thought it would be sooner. Now, you're a bit salty about the timing and wondering if you should embark on those feelings you two share or leave it alone. Because I can bet my entire practice that you miss that man, too."

"Are you licensed in reading someone, too?"

"I'm serious, Nature. You can try your damnedest to ignore your true feelings but they'll only continue to grow and frustrate you every time you think about how much you truly want him and everything that a life together has in store for you. He hurt you. I get it. And I commend you for breaking it off instead of staying. But you two were kids. This is a grown ass, fine ass Milo we're referring to now. He's not that boy you knew all those years ago. He's someone new. Why not give him another chance? It's going to eat you up inside out if you don't."

Sliding my bracelets up and down my wrist, I digested everything that was being poured onto my plate. After considering my feels and the words she'd just shared, relief still hadn't found me.

"Just be honest with yourself."

"I'm miserable without him." The confession slowly escaped my lips.

As if an anchor was lifted from my chest, I could finally breathe clearly. I'd never admitted that tiny truth to anyone. Too afraid to say it out loud because it would make it true, I held it in for so many years I'd lost count. His presence intensified my misery, which is why I communicated with him as less as possible and kept it very short with Milo prior to my pregnancy. Now, it wasn't as easy and the facts were glaring at me every morning I opened my eyes.

"Awwwww."

Gathering the napkins in front of her, Shayla prepared for the influx of pregnancy emotions that I suffered through daily. I grabbed the bunch from her hand and patted underneath my eyes before the tears managed to fall.

"God!" I coughed. "That feels so much better in the atmosphere."

"I'm sure, babe. I'm just happy you've had this breakthrough. To admit something so powerful is a great start to finding a resolution."

"The resolution is so clear, Shayla. It's always been clear but I can't put my heart in harm's way. That man has the power to destroy me. He did once. I can't risk it happening again. It's like, I'm damned if I do and damned if I don't. In a way, this child, our son, was my piece of Milo that I thought I'd be content with. Ya know? Having some of him. A little. But it's strengthened my craving. I wish he was there every time I lay down at night. I wish he was there every time I wake up in the morning. When my back hurts, I wish he was there to rub it. When my feet hurt, I wish he was there to massage them. The list is never-ending."

"Then tell him. Why drown in misery when it's not necessary? It's not the only option."

"The pain, Shayla. You don't understand. It's a different kind of beast. It's no—"

"Today, if you found another man and fell in love, the risk would still be significant. By not following your heart and seeking solace in Milo, you're saying that you will never, ever attempt to fall in love again. Because, when it's all said and done, risk is involved. It doesn't matter who the relationship is with."

It was agonizing how true her revelation was.

"I don't know," I admitted.

"You do know, babe. Fear is fighting to keep you stagnant, stubborn, and prideful. But what's pride when it comes to falling and being in love?"

"It has no place."

"No place at all. So stop fooling yourself into believing it does. The only questions you need to be asking yourself is if you truly love this man enough to take that risk. Is he worth it? Will it hurt worse to love him out loud or keep suppressing your love for him?"

"I do."

"You do?"

"I love him enough."

"Then what are you waiting for, Nature?"

"I don't know. Him, I guess."

"You won't even say more than ten words to the man. Are you expecting him to be a fucking mind reader?"

"He used to be."

"Well, he isn't anymore. And he promised not to push any boundaries."

"He's never cared about boundaries before. Why now?"

"Maybe because you're carrying his child and stress levels matter. Maybe because he's waiting for the green light."

"Or maybe because this isn't what he wants."

"Have you convinced yourself of that, too?"

"No. The thought just came to mind."

"I think he's simply playing the part until time is on his side. A man of patience. One has to appreciate that."

Sighing, I shook my head from one side to the other, "I have so many mixed emotions about all of this."

"If I were in your shoes, I wouldn't let another night past with me sleeping alone in my bed. I'd be jumping that nigga's bones by nine. You two have a few more weeks before the baby comes. They pretty much ruin all the fun. Not to mention you're advised to wait six weeks after they get here to fuck again. Just a whole pain in the ass. The last few weeks of your pregnancy don't have to be spent alone, babe. Go get your man."

There was no rebuttal. Sitting with a heavy heart and loaded thoughts, I meditated in the silence. As the sinking feeling submerged me in concern, doubt, and conflicted me, the pros and cons of starting anew with Milo began weighing themselves in my head, involuntarily.

"Are you ready to get going?" Shayla broke my train of thought.

Still staring into the blankness, I twirled the necklace that fell right below my collarbone.

"Yes, but first I need to cover the tab."

"Already handled."

Dislodged from the trance by her words, I snapped my head in her direction. Remorse plagued me as I was unsure how long I'd drifted.

"Sorry," I apologized.

"It's okay, babe. I'm aware that you have a lot on your mind right now. I just hope this conversation shed a little light on how to move forward."

Tilting my head and pulling in air, I asked, "What would you do?"

"I'd risk it all. Everything I have. If my heart still refused to make room for anyone else after all this time, it would be all the proof needed to know I made the right decision."

Gracefully, she stood tall and grabbed her purse from the hook to the far left of the marble tabletop. It wasn't until she grabbed mine and placed it on her other shoulder that I realized I hadn't budged. Delayed cognition and mobility was solely based upon my inability to push aside thoughts that related to the father of my child.

Eventually, however, I managed. When I began my waddle, I didn't stop until I reached my vehicle and started the engine.

"Call me once you've sorted things out. You'll be fine. I promise!" Shayla yelled from a short distance.

With a head nod, I dismissed us both. Inside of my car, the cool air brushed against my skin. The white, loosely fitting shirt I wore clung to me as the pressure from the AC assaulted it. Summer hadn't reached Berkeley yet. We still had weeks before the true temperatures crippled us all. Nonetheless, May had just started and it came in swinging.

Ironically, Summer Walker mumbled words over a beat that I could hardly hear because my stereo's volume had been lowered before I exited to go inside of John Pione, the restaurant where Shayla and I dined bi-weekly. I pumped the volume as I pulled out of the parking spot and into traffic. At the realization of what was playing, I started the song, again, this time signing right along with her.

"Threw away your love letters. I– thought it'd make me

feel better. I– finally got you out my bed but I still can't get you out my head. Oooh."

Together, we concluded the song a minute later. Wishing she'd made a full-length single of the track, I hit the back button to restart it again. Visions of Milo's long arms surrounding me as he read the first letter he'd ever written in response to the letter I'd given him a day earlier bombarded me. It felt like a lifetime ago.

We'd both graduated our undergrad programs a year and a half prior, but still lived on campus as part of a program that provided us with campus housing until we completed our medical degrees. The program was dedicated to young scholars much like Milo and me who weren't ready for the ways of the world to interrupt our thought process, the way we acquired knowledge, or our chances of finishing our degrees flawlessly.

A mere four months prior, we'd made things official. Years of uninterrupted studies, summer hours, and loaded schedules each semester had kept us apart for years, but neither were enough to completely smolder the burning desire we both suffered through for one another while making our education our top priority. And finally, when we couldn't withstand the idea of being apart, we merged as one.

Every song that played after left me a bit deeper in my feelings than I was before starting the journey home. Finally, in my driveway, I made my way into the house at a snail's pace. The additional weight was still taking some adjusting.

The smell of vanilla and caramel welcomed me, squeezing me like the hug I desperately needed. Exhaustion burdened me with tired eyes and legs. In the shower and then to bed was where I was headed, but the sound of my doorbell put a dent in my plans.

Ding Dong.

I'd only managed to make it up the first few steps when I turned and headed back down. Chalking the visit up as one of the twelve things I ordered from online on a daily basis in preparation for my son, I opened the door, expecting to be greeted by boxes. Instead, there was a delivery guy, dressed in red, waiting to greet me. Both hands were full, one with a bouquet of fresh roses that matched his shirt and the other with a fruit bouquet. My stomach growled at the sight of them, though I'd just eaten.

"For Nature Dupree."

"Yes."

"I was instructed by Mr. Domino to bring them inside if you don't mind."

Of course. Reading the card to find out where the gifts had come from was almost pointless, and so was the name-dropping he'd just done. When I swung the door open to find him behind it, I knew who'd sent him.

"Sure."

He didn't go far when I stepped aside to let him in. I was almost certain he'd gotten clear instructions on where to rest the gifts and how quickly he should depart because he was out of the door faster than he'd come in. I locked up behind him and wobbled my way over to the console where he'd left my things. After busting open the fruit bag, I removed the note card from the center of the roses.

To my surprise, it wasn't a computer generated message or one that the flower shop owner had written herself like she usually did. Milo's handwriting was scribbled across the card, halting all movement as I peered at the words he'd used to describe me and the feelings that he'd been having since the start of our pregnancy.

Nay,

I was on my way out of the office this evening when I thought of you. This isn't a new occurrence. It happens throughout the day, all day, every day. But today was different. I thought about how you've mustered the strength to carry our son through a healthy, flawless pregnancy while making it look so easy though I know it's not.

Somehow, saying thank you just doesn't seem like enough. I wish I could bear some of the load but God ain't have men in mind when tasking women with the beautiful burden of birthing life. We're in the final stretch. I can't wait to hold Mason in my arms. I'm looking forward to our check-in next week. Bring me good news, love.

Milo.

Holding the card up to my chest, I groaned as my lips curved upward and my heart began to ache. Deep down, right at his core, he was everything. Gentle. Kind. Caring. Attentive. Affectionate. Wise. Remarkable, in every sense of the word. But he'd buried those traits the day that he gained the title that made it easy to cover the hole he'd dug for me to put them in.

Cheater.

Sighing, I pushed past the disappointment that pooled at the bottom of my belly, turning my stomach and nearly forcing vomit from my mouth. Once the feeling subsided, I embraced the emotions that accompanied the handwritten note still resting against my chest.

I pushed a piece of cantaloupe in my mouth as I read it a second time. By the third time I finished, some of my fruit were in the fridge and the rest were in the bowl I was headed upstairs with. The fruit never made it to my bedroom as intended. I left the note and the bowl they were in on my dresser while preparing to shower, hoping that sleep found me easily.

Cushioned slippers protected my feet from the cold beneath them. I reached behind the glass door and turned the knob of the shower until it reached the red gem I'd installed years ago. It marked the spot for the perfect pressure and temperature so I never had to guess.

Soon. I dreamed about upgrades in my next home that included automatic showers and toilets that flushed when I was finished handling my business. To build the perfect private practice over the last five years, I'd put those aspirations aside. Now that my child was about to make his grand entrance, those aspirations were becoming my reality.

When the water was nice and warm, I peeled my clothes off my body and placed them in the laundry bin next to the shower. I stepped inside and let the steam rise above me. The silk scarf and shower cap I'd put on just before getting in saved my silk press from destruction. For them both, I was grateful.

I closed my eyes as Milo's words resurrected my rapidly beating heart. His kindness was exactly what had drawn me to him all those years ago. His leadership kept me by his side for as long as I was. No one could've ever told me that we'd never amount to anything together but would come the best versions of the people we were striving to be... apart.

The day that I discovered Milo cheated on me was the

day I thought my life was over. I hadn't experienced a heart attack, but medical schooling and the symptoms I felt for weeks after the breakup led me to believe that I was suffering from one. My suspicions landed me in the hospital, hyperventilating and confused as they ran every test known to man on my tiny frame, trying to discover the root of my heart's behavior. In the end, I was sent home with anxiety medication and a diagnosis that wasn't often given to patients. The emergency room physician informed me that I was suffering from a broken heart and the only cure was time, patience, and rest.

Inhaling, I recalled the moment my heart shattered. Nearly three days of unanswered calls, avoidance, and twelve voicemails, I was led to Milo's dorm where I found him sitting in the dark with the weight of the world on his shoulders.

"MILO, WHAT'S THE MATTER?" *I asked, but he remained silent.*

"Milo. What's wrong? Is everyone okay? In your family?" The fear that he'd lost someone else close to him left me wondering if he'd heard bad news.

"Yeah," he mumbled, head still low.

"Then, what's the matter? Talk to me."

"I– jus– Not right now, Nay."

"You've been ignoring my calls for the last two days and avoiding me on campus altogether. What do you mean, not right now? What is going on? Talk to me."

"Shit just crazy right now."

"Tell me what the hell is going on, Milo!" I demanded, finally at my breaking point.

As the words left my mouth, there was a knock at his door.

"Knock, knock," a familiar, soft tone sang out loud.

My head whipped in the opposite direction. Big, unconcealable knots began to form in my stomach as I became physically ill. When I turned back around to face Milo, it was as if his deep, dark skin had darkened a few more shades. I wasn't sure if that was scientifically possible, but it had to be because I was staring right at the blackest version of Milo I'd ever seen.

Because the door wasn't locked, LaKia, his mentee, was granted access immediately. Her presence was a surprise, one that I wished I could claim was pleasant, but it wasn't. She had no business in Milo's dorm room. Their meetings were in Founder's Hall every Wednesday and Friday at six in the evening. It was nine on a Sunday night.

"Miiiiiil—"

My presence was a surprise to her as well. She stopped mid-stride upon recognizing me standing in front of a shrunken version of the person she'd come to see. My eyes never left her as she began retracting, backing toward the door she'd come in.

"Can I help you, LaKia?" I was led to ask.

"Uh. I have an exam tomorrow and was... I just wanted to see if Milo could help me prepare."

"Today isn't Wednesday and neither is it Friday."

"Right. Uh. I'll just g—"

"Please."

She closed the door behind her, leaving us alone again.

The sound of Milo cracking his knuckles one by one rattled every nerve in my body. Downward brows and lowered eyes proved I was losing the war that had been waged on my heart in my absence.

"Milo," I murmured.

A million tiny needles pricked my orbs. The hairs on the nape of my neck stood in solidarity. As if I'd been drenched in cement, the ability of movement quickly diminished. My heart was heavy but my body was heavier. Slowly, I turned in his direction.

In the corner, at the edge of his bed, Milo continued to crumble under pressure that hadn't derived from me, personally. From the moment I walked through his door, I recognized it and knew it had been crushing him long before he saw my face. Defeat covered his entirety. Like glue, it was stuck on him. It was in his posture. The tone of his voice. In his movements. And in those dark eyes of his.

"Nature. Please. Just, let's not– I– baby," he stuttered.

A whiz, his vocabulary was expansive. Whether he chose to use it or not was completely up to him. He had total control and was a professional when it came to code shifting. But not now. The very brain he studied day and night, tirelessly, until his hurt, managed to malfunction for the first time since I'd known him.

He glitched.

Right before my very eyes.

"What did you do?" I mustered the strength to ask.

Shaking his head, he palmed his handsome, flustered face.

"I fucked up, Nay."

He refused to look at me as the words came rushing through his lips. Lips that I couldn't see because he'd hidden from me. Hidden his eyes that the truth lie within. Hidden his mouth that spoke truths that I refused to believe. Hidden. He'd retreated in the palms of his hands which weren't big enough to conceal him entirely.

He'd sought refuge within those two small, insignificant parts of him and not within me. He safe space. His safe haven. His home.

"I fucked up," he choked out. "I fucked up."

He repeated the words over and over, pounding them into my chest time and time again, making it hard for me to see. Making it hard for me to breathe.

"I fucked up."

Hard for me to stand. Hard for me to hear. But even with limited sound, I heard my heart as it still beat for him.

Boom. boom.

Boom boom.

Boom. boom.

Dummy! I screamed inside.

Him, yes. But me too. Because, how could my heart be such a fucking fool?

My feet began moving in the opposite direction of him, my lover, homie and friend. As if fire had been set to the carpet beneath me, I scurried toward the door, desperate to free myself from the suffocation he was administering. Just as my hand grazed the handle, I felt his arms around me and his hot tears on my shoulder as he held me.

Rocking me from side to side, he pleaded, "Don't leave. Just don't leave. I can explain, Nay."

"*Get off me.*"

"*Please.*"

"*Get off!*"

I struggled against his frame. Warmth covered my face as my tears fell freely.

"*Nay.*"

"*Milo. get off,*" *I begged.*

"*It was a fucking mistake.*" *He cried into my shoulders, tears wetting my shirt.*

"*Let me go.*"

"*I can fix this. I have to fix this. Let me make it right. Tell me how I can fix this.*"

With all the strength I had left in my body, I freed myself from his grasp and pulled open his door. A mere foot outside of his door was how far I managed before my world caved. My limbs weakened as blurriness covered the fixtures and features of the dormitory halls.

"*Nay?*" *His voice rang out just before my entire world blackened.*

I CLENCHED the bar in the shower to steady my weight as the memories threatened my stability. Blinking back the tears, I chose to focus on the present and rid myself of moments that weren't reflective of where Milo and I were now.

Where are we, even? I asked, grabbing the towel to soap up.

I scrubbed my body from head to toe as best as I could with a protruding belly and an eight-pound boy residing inside of it while the question continued to play in the background. Upon exiting, I came to the conclusion that we weren't any closer to where we needed to be and until I was honest with myself and honest with Milo, we wouldn't be.

"We belong together," I whispered, the revelation releasing the budding tension in my frame. Hearing the words was much more freeing than burying them inside.

It just makes sense. It makes sense!

As I patted my body dry, I raced to my closet, still feeling like a snail that just wasn't moving nearly as fast as I imagined in my head. Nevertheless, I reached the closet where I tossed my overnight bag onto the floor and began my search for my most comfortable clothes. One by one, I stuffed pieces inside, packing enough for a few days because I didn't have intentions of returning home for a while.

Don't forget the fruit, I thought, zipping the bag and pulling it up on my bare shoulder.

I carried it into the bedroom where I slid into the pajama top and bottom that laid on the bed. A subtle, floral perfume with a name I hated pronouncing was spritzed all over my body. I stood in the mirror and unwrapped my hair, allowing it to fall into place.

My fingers massaged the rebellious strands into their final resting spots. The gloss on my vanity was perfect for the journey I was preparing to embark on. It was light and it was balmy. With my overnight bag in hand I flipped off the light, exited my bedroom, and headed down the stairs.

On my descend, I pulled up Milo's contact and copied the address to his home in the GPS. Twice, since discovering the pregnancy, I'd been to his place. Once for a grand tour of where our son would spend some of his time and another to help Milo decide on the nursery color and furniture.

Third time's the charm. I shrugged as my feet graced the first level of my home.

TWO

WITH A MIRED CONSCIOUS, I contemplated turning around and heading in the opposite direction eleven times before I made it to the first red light on my side of town.

Just abort the mission. I tried convincing myself as I sat underneath the bright red glow of the streetlight. But as it turned green, naturally, my foot switched pedals and continued on the path the GPS was suggesting.

God, Nature. What are you doing? Nervously, I grimaced, so unsure of myself.

As an incredibly cautious and calculated woman, spontaneity was never in the deck that my cards were dealt from.

Nothingness swelled in my chest and throat. My oxygen levels decreased as my blood began rushing through me at an alarming rate.

Boom. Boom.

Boom. Boom.

Boom. Boom.

My heart beat loud in the silence.

Boom. Boom.

Boom. Boom.

Boom. Boom.

Quiet, I begged.

Trembling fingers steered the wheel, making each turn as instructed until I reached the gates of the dreamy, lake-front property that Milo called home. I was envious of the piece of art. It was almost impossible believing the same man I clutched my pearls in the presence of had the brains to build such a masterpiece.

Lawe Domino was a special case and anyone he'd ever encountered would agree. However, just like the other members of the Domino family, he was gifted. The folds of his brain held genius-level knowledge of a certain subject, one that he excelled in, making a fool of anyone else in the same realm.

Using the pad at the end of the property, I punched in the code that had been given to me months ago. Somehow, I remembered it without referencing the text. I held my breath as I punched in the final number.

Zero nine. Zero three. *Zero four. Twenty-two.*

"Zero nine. Zero three. Zero four. *Twenty-two.*"

I repeated the numbers aloud, startled by the discovery. *Our birthdays.*

Flared nostrils and reeling thoughts led to a reassuring smile.

Oh, Milo.

The tires of my truck pressured the concrete beneath it as I drove through the property, up the never-ending driveway. Finally making it to the roundabout, I parked alongside his i8. Contentment lulled my heart as I exited the driver's side.

Patience befriended me as I opened the back door and grabbed the bag I'd packed for the duration of my stay. When I finally took the steps, one by one, my confidence level had risen tremendously. The boldness of my actions no longer terrified me, but empowered me.

For once, I was throwing all caution to the wind and taking a chance on something I'd tried forgetting and dismantling over the years. As I stood at the door, ringing the bell, I settled on the fact that it wasn't easily forgotten and impossible to dismantle.

Ding Dong.

The bell sounded throughout the house and on the porch where I stood, preparing to wait. Factoring in the size of his home, an immediate answer was impossible unless he was near. With it being highly unlikely, I switched the bag from my right shoulder to the left as I balanced the weight of my body so that it was distributed evenly.

I rubbed my hands down the sides of the pajama pants I wore, peeping around me as the sounds of the creatures in the night became more apparent. Long, uneven breaths kept my anxiety at bay. With my right foot, I patted the concrete.

I should just... Maybe I should go.

Again, I'd entered the ring of fiery and was fighting my

fears. The silence was deafening. It made so much room for doubt and discouragement.

You can't, I commanded.

Bowing my head, I remained planted in place, refusing to take a step in the direction that felt most comforting for me at the moment. I shifted my line of vision toward my truck, wondering how long it would take me to return if necessary. Before the entertainment of the thought began, the locks began turning and the smile that I'd shed peeled my lips backward.

The door opened, exposing a shirtless Milo with dampened skin. Evidence of his fitness addiction left me breathless as I pushed through the door, past his dark figure, and into his home. The carefully chosen, ever-provoking scents of his home pushed any words that I managed to come up with down my throat and into the pit of my belly. And when he turned to face me, exposing the thick, mouthwatering print against his legs, I contemplated running out of the door I'd just come inside of.

"Nature," he rushed out, inhaling deeply before releasing more words. "I wasn—"

"No," I interjected, stopping him before he could continue.

If it wasn't now, for me, then it would be never. The words I'd practiced in my head as I dried my body and prepared for this moment right after my shower showed grace and appeared on a prompter in my head. Sighing, I allowed the bag on my shoulder to fall to the floor.

"Listen, I-I have so much to get off my chest. And for once, I don't want to keep it to myself. I don't want to hide it. I want to put it all out there. Lay all of my cards on the table. I'm tired, Milo, of pretending. I can't do it anymore."

"Nature, now is—"

"I'm still in love with you!" I blurted, shaking my head as I chastised myself for waiting so long to tell him.

"I've never stopped loving you. Like, not even a little. This child, this child was my security blanket. A way to keep pieces of you in my world, safe pieces. Pieces that weren't threatening. Pieces that I loved most about you. Pieces that I still remember and won't ever forget. But since our son has been growing inside of me and we've gotten a bit closer over the months, I'm able to be honest with myself now.

"We're just not close enough. I want to try to start anew. I want the late nights and early mornings with Mason... but I want them with you, too. I see it all the time. You. Me. Him. All of us. A family. I don't want to do this alone. And I don't want to co-parent, either. I want a solid, unbreakable bond. The one I thought we had all those years ago. I want that now. Maybe I'm selfish, but I can't help but feel like you owe me that. You owe me a happily ever after. And you have to give it to me because there's no one else in this world that has the power to.

"I know I've been a bitch to you over the last month. Holding onto this information and ignoring my truest feelings, but you scare me. You scare the shit out of me, Milo," I scoffed. "But fuck fear. The risk can't be heavier than the burden of not being able to love you loudly is. No one can convince me of that. In some crazy, perfect world, I can't help but imagine we belong toge—"

Milo's eyes cut toward the large, state-of-the-art staircase as the sound of human activity startled me. I followed his orbs. Simultaneously, our eyes landed on the thin, beautiful woman descending the stairs behind us.

At a loss of words, I turned around to find Milo staring at me again. This time, he moved closer, placing both hands on my arms. I caved, internally, but willed myself to remain composed as I gazed into his remorseful, regretful dark eyes. I felt my heart break all over again, watching as his lips tried forming words beyond my comprehension at the moment. Shattered, on the floor between us, my focus was leaning toward trying to capture as many pieces as possible of it before my life ended in tragedy and unexpectedly from the blunt force trauma to the chest.

"Nay. Look at me. Listen to me," he begged. "Focus on me."

My head turned, slowly peering over my shoulder as the young lady continued down the stairs. Milo's hand touched my cheek, ever so gently, forcing me to face him. His handsome face displayed thick, bushy brows that folded as fear drove him to desperate measures.

"Please. Just focus on me. Listen—"

He didn't have the words he wished did.

"I-I'm sorry. I shouldn't ha—"

"Any time. Any time. Nay. Don't do that. Don't say that. FUCK!"

"I'm sorry."

I pulled in the opposite direction.

"You don't have to leave. Stay. Please. Ayo, it's time to go!" he yelled at his company. "It's time to roll."

"No. sweetie. It's fine. You can stay," I belted over my shoulder.

"Nature. Don't do this shit," he gritted, tilting his head in agony.

"I'm sorry for popping up."

Shaking my head, I leaned down and picked up the bag that I'd brought with me. Milo reached for it, but wasn't quick enough. I managed to dodge his attempt at retrieving the bag, then stepped around him.

"Nay. Just let me fucking explain. Please."

"You're not mine, Milo. There's nothing to explain. I'm sorry. I shouldn't have come."

With every ounce of strength I could muster, I fled through the door I'd just come through. Out of the house and onto the porch, the third vehicle suddenly came into view. I'd completely missed it on my quest to regurgitate my feelings and have them heard by the one person who could reciprocate them.

The actualization that his car wasn't the only one in the driveway, vomit rose and tickled the back of my throat. I leaned over the flower bush, ready to release if necessary. When the nausea subsided, I continued toward my truck, moving much faster than I had in the last three months since my belly had grown so large.

My swollen belly brushed against the steering wheel as I settled in my seat. My engine started at the push of a button. The speed my body couldn't produce, the wheels of my truck could. I burned rubber down the path to the fence, only stopping momentarily to allow it to part. Once it set me free, I nearly bald my tires getting off the property.

Two miles down the road, in the comfort of my peanut butter seats and tinted windows, I came to a complete stop, and buried my face in the palms of my hands. Tears stung my eyes as they fell, collapsing and combining in my hand.

On the side of the road, where my dreams of a life with Milo died, I wept like a newborn with colic whom was inconsolable. Not until my tear ducts failed to produce more tears did I gather my bearings and give myself grace. I rubbed my wet, sweaty palms against the softness of my pants as large, notable movements caused my stomach to cave in on the left side and protrude on the right.

My son reminded me that he was with me. A smile etched away at the sadness that held me hostage. I laid both hands on my belly, lowering my head so that he could hear me a bit better.

"I'm sorry, little guy," I apologized for my emotional melt down. "Mommy is so sorry."

I sucked in the oxygen around me, determined to rid myself of the incredible gloom that had been cast over my world at once. The silent chastisement didn't go unnoticed as disappointment crept in where the sadness was exiting.

It's all my fault, I admitted, cleaning my face with a dry napkin from the armrest.

I flipped the mirror above the steering wheel as I patted away the wetness. Taking the blame was so much easier than blaming Milo for the mixed signals he was sending. It was much easier than focusing on the fact that he'd given me free range and unrestricted access to his home at any point since discovering my pregnancy, though he was aware that he was bringing other women to his residence.

He'd assured me in the very beginning that he entertained women elsewhere and they'd never cross paths with me or my son. Like a fool, I believed him. Now, it all felt like a lie. And with all honesty, I think that hurt worse than anything. Milo was many things, but a liar wasn't one of them. To know that he'd stooped to such barbaric levels left me puzzled and extremely intolerant.

"Unbelievable."

Once I was on the road again, my wheels didn't stop rolling until I reached *The Hammond at River Town*, the waterfront hotel with views that made you sick to the stomach with jealousy. At the edge of town, where the water was still and beautiful, it was easily my favorite place to get away. Often, my staycations commenced and ended at this very hotel. Though I hadn't planned one, that's exactly where my mind was when the attendant opened my door and welcomed me to the property.

"Welcome to The Hammond at River Town. Turning in for the night?"

"Yes. The keys are inside."

I wasted little time exiting.

"Room number?"

"I'm not sure, but I will know in a few minutes."

"Would you like us to bring your bag inside?"

"Yes, please."

"Eddie will be right behind you."

"Thank you."

Through the lobby of the hotel, I floated, ready to secure a room and rest my worries. The hole in my chest made it rather complicated to even think logically, but it wouldn't be long before I could unravel in the privacy of my hotel room. That fact kept my head high and my chest out.

"Welcome to The Hammond at River Town. I'm Rebecca. How can I be of assistance?"

"Rebecca, I need a room with a fabulous view for the next two, three nights. The closer to the water, the better. I know this is last minute, so give me what you have."

"Sure thing. Let me see what I can do. We had a few cancelations tonight, so you're in luck."

"Sounds good."

Sighing, I shifted my weight from one foot to the other. The massive lobby was full of Berkeley's finest, in addition to the prestigious out-of-towners who preferred lodging in class. The corner bar that I once loved so much caught my eye.

Pregnancy kept my system clear of alcohol, but a virgin beverage didn't sound so bad. With the night I'd had, I deserved the closest thing to a drink that I could get my hands on. Settling on the idea of visiting the small bar later, I waited for Rebecca to give me some good news.

Milo · Nature

I ADMIRED my reflection in the elevator mirror. My stomach had grown tremendously over the last few weeks, but it seemed to be the only thing on my body growing. I was all baby. The twelve pounds I'd gained during pregnancy was hardly anything to complain about. Eight of them belonged to my baby boy.

The first trimester was hell. I lost eleven pounds and was wondering if I'd ever get them back. I managed to add an additional twelve to the mix for a total of twenty-three pounds. They were all in my midsection and chest. My breast felt like bags of sand. Removing my bra for any amount of time was like shedding anchors.

Ping.

My phone vibrated in my hand as the doors of the elevator opened. Without checking the screen to determine the caller, I silenced the buzzing with my index finger and continued through the lobby. The pain that rested in my swollen eyes reminded me of where I was less than an hour ago and how I felt.

The visit to his home was supposed to be the paracme of my night, but quickly proved to be the decline of it, catapulting me into the pits of darkness. A simple dress, beautiful view, and corner bar at The Hammond were promising in efforts to relocate my light, the one the darkness concealed within me.

The silk pajamas were replaced with a strappy satin dress that clung to my belly and stopped right above the Hermès flats on my feet. In addition to the two-piece athleisure set I'd packed, the dress was the only piece of real clothing to claim in the overnight bag I'd packed for Milo's house. My intentions were to be underdressed and overstimulated my entire weekend, but life had other plans for me.

Dimly lit with jazz serenading the guest upon entry, the little bar stole a piece of my heart immediately. I was instantly reminded of my last visit, when alcohol was part of my ritual and included in every recipe for a damn good evening. Tucking the dress under my bottom, I slid onto the bar stool with ease.

"What can I get started for you?" the bartender asked, drying the glass in his hand with a white cloth.

"Let's see. Obviously, the part of the drink that makes it

fabulous can't be in the equation." I chuckled, rubbing my belly.

"Figured when you walked in. Mocktail?"

"Is that what they're calling it these days?"

"Yes."

"Well, yes. One of those."

"Anything in particular?"

"Surprise me. Tonight has been full of surprises. Another one won't hurt, right?"

"I don't see why not."

"Thanks."

"Another one, coming right up."

Smiling, I saved myself from more embarrassment by silencing another call. Milo's persistence would not prevail in this instance. Over a decade of avoidance should've taught him something by now, but it seemed it hadn't. After the call was silenced, he followed up with a text. On the screen, a long rectangle with **Mason's Father** bolded appeared.

Where are you?

"Here's a lemon berry drop, hold the fun stuff."

Accepting the light purple drink, I thanked the bartender with a nod and a smile. The chair beside me seemed to magically rearrange itself until I noticed, out of the corner of my eye, the culprit was seating himself in the chair right next to it. Another message appeared on the screen, disrupting my train of thought and demanding my undivided attention.

We need to talk, Nay. Where you at?

"Old fashion, please."

My God. I clenched down below, swallowing the

saliva that pooled in my mouth, trying to recall ever hearing a voice as delicate, yet raspy as the one I'd just heard.

Another call came through. I silenced it as well. After, another text vibrated the phone. Growing frustrated, I opened the messages to read the last one. Milo made an eirenicon in an effort to defuse the situation at hand.

I apologize for you having to see that, see her. There's nothing to that. It's just something that happened, unplanned. You don't have to pick up the phone. Just tell me where you are. I'll come to you. Hear me out.

Though I wanted to end my night with Milo hours ago, it wasn't on these terms. Instead of declining the offer, I closed the chat and flipped my phone over on the counter. Exhaustion from the night's activities forced a long, exaggerated breath from me.

"Long day?" the insanely sexy voice questioned.

As if he was a debt collector that I owed a lump sum, I felt obligated to respond. Words flowed without preparation.

"Long night."

"It's only nine-forty, baby. The night is hardly over."

I waited to feel my flesh crawl at the sound of a stranger calling me baby. The wait was in vain.

"For me, it's over in the next ten or fifteen minutes. I'm already awake way past my bedtime."

"That means I can't ask the man to grab you something to eat so you can chill with me, right here, for a little while longer?"

"Unfortunately, I don't have an appetite."

"I think that's the first time I've ever heard a pregnant woman say she doesn't have an appetite."

"Oh, so, this is normal for you? Offering pregnant women at the bar food?" I chuckled, prying.

"No. I've never seen a pregnant woman at the bar," he tittered, stifling a very mature, deep grunt that I wished he'd set free.

"Luckily, it's a mocktail."

"Mocktail?"

"That's what he calls it." I shrugged, nodding toward the bartender. "A girl can pretend, right?"

"I fully support."

"Good."

"Married? Engaged? Widowed? Situationship?"

He sipped from his glass as he stared in my direction, waiting for a response.

"Single."

He kissed the skin of his teeth and tilted his head in the opposite direction.

"I wasn't expecting that shit," he admitted. "Some motherfucker fumbled, for real."

"How you know they didn't dodge a bullet?"

"Hit me right here wit' it." He chuckled, tapping the area where his heart rested.

Finding his gesture comical, I tossed my head back as giggles escaped my mouth, loudly and obnoxiously.

"I'm Zane."

He leaned over, stretching an arm until our hands met. Zane's smile was as alluring as his voice. His pecan brown skin was flawless. His eyes were large and curious and his lips were stained with evidence of his recreational hobbies.

"Nature."

"Nature?"

His brows raised as his lips turned downward.

"Yes."

"A really pretty name. How'd that come about? What's the story behind it?"

"My mother. Long story short, my mother and father went on a small hiking adventure the month before my scheduled induction. My father had a little free time, which was very rare. Mid-hike, my mother went into full, active labor. Before they reached the bottom of the mountain, I breathed in fresh air. I was born in nature, prematurely but perfectly healthy."

"Ya people didn't shit themselves, having a baby in the wilderness?"

"My father is a physician. My mother was a nurse until she retired early. My birth was the moment of her self-discovery. An awakening of some sort."

"Damn. That's dope. Do you live up to your name?"

"Meaning?"

"Are you some wildlife rescuer or some shit?"

"I'm not. I'm a physician."

"Family full of doctors."

"I imagine so."

"What kind?"

"I deliver babies."

"Bullshit!" he exclaimed.

"No. Seriously. I'm an OB/GYN."

"Wow. Yeah. Very fucking different. I thought you were going to say you were a banker or a data specialist or something glass office, team of coworkers all racing for job security related."

"I employ, Zane. I'm not an employee."

"Forgive me," he apologized, tossing his hands up. "Talk your shit."

"That was in no way a moment of haughtiness. I'm simply a woman who has worked very hard to get to where I am. I just don't want anyone to ever confuse it."

"Noted."

I finished off my drink, still staring at his pretty brown skin.

"My time has come, Zane. It was a pleasure talking to you. I really needed that entertainment, as brief as it was."

"Maybe tomorrow won't be as brief."

"Tomorrow?"

"At dinner, at Ragland." He mentioned the restaurant that was on the other opposite side of the lobby.

"Thanks, but tomorrow is no good for me."

"Understood. How about you take my number and tell me when a good time for you arrives?"

"I see what you did there."

"Do you approve?" He smiled as I stood.

"Yes, but I'll be honest. If I take your number, you'll never hear from me again. If you're willing to wait, a good time for me will be in about..." I paused to look down at my belly, quickly doing the math. "Five to six months."

"Understood and willing. Patience has never scared me."

"Good. 555-211-1990."

"Once more."

"211-1990. Goodnight, Zane."

Before waiting to find out if he'd copied it correctly or heard me clearly, I made my way out of the bar and toward my room, not bothering to pay. If he was interested in using that number of mine, he'd better handle the small bill himself.

The silence of the elevator was like cold water to the face. Reality hit me and it didn't hesitate, either, thrusting me into the storm without warning or regard for the exhaustion of my heart. My cell buzzed for the tenth time since I'd left Milo's home. Taking a look at the screen, I silenced the vibrating with my thumb.

Milo, please, I begged internally.

I was freed from the elevator and let off on the eighteenth floor where the views were immaculate. Upon entering my hotel room, I rushed to remove the dress. Anxiety perched on my chest, making me feel as if I was suffocating with restricted airways and limited oxygen.

Nearly bare, in only my panties and Hermès slides, I sat on the edge of the bed, pulling in deeply and releasing slow breaths. Over and over, I repeated the exercise until the pricking of my skin subsided and the weight of my chest lightened. Just as I managed to gain control of my conscious, my phone vibrated again. Another text appeared on my screen.

Alright. You don't want to talk. Just let me know you're good. Let me know you're okay. Let me know my son is alright.

"I'm not!" I declared, fighting back the tears that blurred my vision.

I failed. Miserably. Pregnancy emotions coupled with pent-up frustration spilled onto the screen of my phone.

Damn you, Milo. I grimaced, spelling out a simple response.

He's fine, I replied.

I didn't have it in me to pretend that I was well. I wasn't. I'd put my pride aside, risking it all to proclaim my love and deepest desires for him, only to find that he was preoccupied and the hard dick that I assumed was because of me was the result of an eventful evening with someone else. I was the furthest from okay.

Before the message he attempted to send replaced the gray bubble, I tossed my phone across the room, into my suitcase where it landed softly. I crawled up the bed, peeling the sheets back, and stretching my legs underneath them. As I pulled the comforter up, my tears soaked the very top, blending with the white and disappearing completely.

THREE

"ARE YOU THERE?" Jack asked, garnering my attention.

"Uh, yeah. Is that all?"

"We didn't get a solid vote from you," he reminded me.

"Sorry. My vote still stands. No."

"Do you mind elabor—"

"I've done so over the last hour in this meeting. My concern is the patient, not the earning potential for the trial."

"Our concern is the patient as well. That's the top priority here. We're all—"

"Jack, I haven't heard the patient mentioned but maybe

three times here. I've seen numbers and estimations for the trial the entire time we've been here. I haven't seen the patient's medical history, family history, allergies, weight, height, current medications, nothing."

"We haven't gotten a chance to share that information."

"Then I can't give an informed decision. So, as of now, I'm voting no. When you can give me some concrete evidence that this is the best course of action, it might change. But as of now, as this hour-long meeting with hardly any mention of the patient ends, I'm standing on that no. If you need me, feel free to reach out and schedule another meeting with my receptionist. Until then, I have business to tend to. Have a good day, everyone."

I signed out of the meeting by shutting down my computer completely. My focus was far from intact. Seven days had passed and there was still no word from Nature. I picked up my cell, checking for notifications attached to the lone rose that replaced her name in my contact list. There were none, as expected.

"Cut me some fucking slack, Nay. Shit," I hissed, tapping the screen until her phone began to ring. I was sent to voicemail almost instantly.

I checked the day's schedule from my iPad, realizing it was much tighter than I'd imagined and a break in between meetings to pull up on her was impossible. Too many days had passed since I'd heard Nature's voice. Too many days had passed without making amends.

Desperate times cause for desperate measures. I remixed the phrase as I dialed the number from the listing I'd just pulled up. The phone rang three times before there was an answer.

"*Womb Health*, this is Jasmine speaking. How can I help you?"

"Yes. Dr. Dupree, please."

"One second. Please hold."

My thumb pressure my other fingers one at a time until they cracked. By the time I popped my neck on both sides, the music halted and her silky voice was on the other end of the line.

"Dr. Dupree. How can I help you?"

I paused, allowing the softness of her voice to calm my raging heart.

"Hello? Dr. Dupr—"

"I miss you," I confessed, sitting back in my seat while massaging my temple.

"Seriously, Milo?" she whispered.

"You left me no choice."

She didn't utter a word in response.

"Nature?"

"I'm here."

"I miss you."

"I heard you the first time, Milo."

"I'm coming to get you this evening, when you're done at the office."

"Not tonight, Milo."

"Why not?"

Flustered, I questioned the reasoning behind her decline.

"Because I have three mothers in labor right now and they'll all be pushing tonight."

"Tomorrow night, then," I settled.

"Not then, either."

"Why?"

"Because I don't want to go anywhere with you, Milo. Not tonight. Tomorrow. The next day. No day. So, please, spare us both and don't call the office anymore."

"I won't. I'll just come through."

That was factual. Nature knew that it was better not to back me into a corner but that was exactly what she was doing at the moment.

"Milo," she sighed. "Listen, I'm sor—"

"You had every right to be there, Nature."

Before she could begin apologizing, I cut it short. There was no need. Some things had gotten out of hand before her arrival. On any other day, she could've popped up without incident. But it was that particular night I wished she hadn't.

"No, I didn't and we both see where popping up gets you."

The thought of walking into what she had made my blood boil. Biting into the flesh of my lip, I chose my words carefully, holding back the ones I really wanted to say.

"If a nigga wants his legs or his life, he ain't gon' be coming down ya fucking steps."

"Goodbye, Milo."

"Nature."

"What?" she sassed, but refused to end the call.

"I'm done pretending, too."

"Forget everything I said, Milo. Those were only my pregnancy emotions talking. I meant none of it. I just... It was an emotional night and I needed support. I'm past that now. Those words meant nothing. Let it go. I have to get out of here. I'm being paged to come to the hospital."

She ended the call immediately after dropping her bomb on me. Calling back wasn't an option. She was on her way into labor and delivery at eight months pregnant. I admired her strength and resilience, but it worried me at times.

Though I encouraged her to begin her leave of absence, she refused to stay home until the baby was threatening to burst from the seams of her vagina. Boredom was not on her list of things to fall victim to while there were patients she loved and whom trusted her through their entire pregnancy that she wanted to see until the finish line.

"Good afternoon," Christina cheered, stepping into my office and closing the door behind her.

I watched as she twisted the knob until it locked before turning around to face me. Falling back into my chair, I waited for whatever was next. Since the incident that happened at my home, she couldn't resist visiting my office daily to see how much work she could distract me from.

As much as I hated to admit it, she wasn't as easy as I wished she was to deny access. The back of her throat made me feel a little better about the bullshit her impromptu visit to my crib to drop off papers for the conference I was set to attend the next morning had caused. I wasn't sure who had equipped her with the skills she possessed, but I wanted to buy the nigga a bottle of the finest on the shelf.

"Not today, Christina," I groaned, still salty from the way Nature had ended our call.

Refusing to take heed to my warning, she fell to her knees in front of me. Her slim fingers worked their way up my thighs. When she reached the tip of my dick, her eyes lit up.

"Somebody seems to think otherwise," she purred, rubbing my hard dick through my pants.

"That's for my son's mother, not you," I informed her, sliding her hand off my thigh.

"Hmph." She pouted, folding her arms in front of her.

"Get up. I've got shit to do. Let's make this the last time you find your way into my office during work hours. What happened the other night was a big fucking mistake. It won't happen again."

"And yesterday, too? What about the day before that?"

"Get up, Christina."

"Whatever you say, *Boss*."

Chuckling, she rose to her feet and headed for the door.

"If ever you change your mind or want to feel a little better, I'm on—"

With a shake of the head, I dismissed her, pointing toward the door that I wanted her out of. Slowly, she sauntered, seemingly waiting for me to change my mind. Closing my eyes, I forced the words down my throat, refusing to indulge, though I wanted to bend her over in that tight ass skirt and make her pay for the turmoil she'd caused.

In the privacy of my home, the evening she delivered the papers to me, her advances were met with compliance. I gave Christina exactly what she'd been begging for since the day she was hired. Sitting behind my desk, realizing how it might've ruined my chances of rekindling things with Nature, regret taunted me. The second I allowed her to lower my shorts and attempt to suck the melanin out of my soldier, I fucked up, royally.

"Fuck!"

Slamming my hand against my desk, I released my frustrations. Simultaneously, a notification from my phone sounded. Taking a peek at the screen, I noticed the calendar notification included Nature's name as well as a location and date.

Long fingers and a collapsed palm covered my mouth as I nodded up and down. Sheer joy replaced the frustration and uncertainty Nature's absence was causing. I scribbled the time on the notepad that was in front of me out of habit and because if I didn't write the words with my own hands, then I'd forget.

I'd always been that way. It didn't matter how many times the calendar reminded me of appointments and meetings, personally written reminders was the only way to embed them in my brain without the possibility of forgetting. Our monthly check-in was upon us and the timing couldn't have been more perfect. Nature assumed she wouldn't be spending the evening with me tomorrow, but our synced calendar proved otherwise. As excitement crept through my veins, I began preparing for my next meeting. Before burying my brain in the notes from the previous meeting I'd had with Gamber and Sons, I picked up the line and pressed zero.

"Yes, Dr.?" Christina asked lowly, mind completely muddled.

"Clear my schedule tomorrow. Anything after 10:00 a.m. is a no for me."

"I, um. I can't. You have to—"

"Clear it."

I ended the call, ready to focus.

Milo Nature

THE COMBATIVE NATURE of medical dwellings as it related to bacteria growth and cleanliness left 90 percent of its patience shivering in waiting rooms for hours. Hadn't the white coat that draped my body been present, I would've fallen victim to the field's standards as well. Fortunately, I'd grown tolerant of the discomfort after spending more of my life in labs and facilities than I had in my childhood home.

Like a moth to a fiery flame, I was drawn to the sandy-haired, bronzed beauty sitting in the corner with her eyes planted in a book. I pulled the fitted lower on my head as I made strides in her direction. Her lack of awareness reminded me of her honorable and admirable traits. Wholesome, she was, and assumed everyone around her was the same until they proved differently. *Honest. Centered. Calm. Patient. Simple.*

She was so fucking simple, much like I wanted this thing between her and I to be but it wasn't. It was as complex as the relationship between the neurological and psychological systems of the body. Though I'd mastered both of those, I was demoted and classified as a freshman on the campus of Dupree U. It was my very first day and I was determined to graduate with a master's in all things Nature.

Standing over her, I peered at her perfectly straightened hair with slight bends that kept it out of her face. It framed it perfectly. The epitome of beauty, I could stare all fucking day without tiring. Our son had hardly altered her structure, but if he had, I could only imagine how much more her features would have bloomed, giving me a little more of her to love down.

Noticing my harboring presence, she looked upward, eyes shifting until they rested where my line of vision ended. The air drained from her lungs. I watched her body slump as her nostrils flared and eyes glossed over. Aiming to keep those big, heart-shattering tears at bay, she failed. Before the first one hit the white coat she wore, I caught it with the tip of my thumb. And then, the second one, I swiped away, too.

Leaning forward, I whispered in her ear, "No more tears, Nay."

On my ascend, I paused, mere inches away from her face. Full, succulent lips provoked me, leaving me no choice but to rest mine against them before taking the seat beside her. Stunned into silence, Nature traced the edges of her sugared lips with the tip of her index finger, staring straight ahead in utter shock.

I folded the page of the book she was reading and then removed it from her free hand. I tucked it under my arm and replaced it with my hand. Her fingers stretched, reflecting her hesitancy and opposition. Slowly, gently, I pushed them down and between my fingers one after the other. When we were finally entangled, I brought her hand up to my lips and planted a kiss on the very back.

Nature remained silent, taking in more oxygen than necessary before letting it out. Appointments prior to the birth of our son were not in our agreement. They were specifically for Nature's involvement only. However, circumstances were different. Things were shifting, or at least they'd start very soon. Her appointments were bi-weekly this month. Next, they'd be every single week. If I could, I wanted to be present for each and every one of them.

"I heard you," I said to her.

Gradually, her head turned in my direction. Silence haunted us. No words exited her lips initially and until they did, I held my breath.

"Please," she begged, sending arrows straight through my heart, "Forget that night. I have."

She was asking the impossible. Her words had stuck with me, looping in my head like a broken record. Denying me access to her heart after claiming I could have it, wholly, was inconsiderate. However, she'd said the shit and there was no way she could make me forget them. Maybe she'd changed her mind but I hadn't changed mine.

"Unfair."

"Milo, no–"

"You can't do that to me, Nay."

"Not here."

"Agreed."

I settled, feeling her slip from my grasp, literally and figuratively. The sinking of my stomach assured me that my fears were coming to fruition. She was retreating, returning to that hard shell she'd shed for me, for us. And there wasn't shit I could do about it but cling to pieces and parts of her that remained accessible, using them as entry points to her head and her heart, hoping she'd soften again.

She freed her hand dismantling our connection. The analogy was disheartening. However, I'd learned a very long time ago that Nature didn't respond well to discomfort and forcing her to open for me, again, would push her further away. The only solution when it came to her was patience. But waiting for a moment like the one she'd had seven nights ago felt too much like torture. I'd waited long enough.

"Nature Dupree."

Simultaneously, we were on our feet. I followed her lead. Though Marcie was a mutual friend of ours and we'd chosen her practice together for Nature's prenatal care, I'd never visited and was clueless as to where we were headed. Nature, however, was familiar, strutting through the halls as if they were her runway. I withheld my chuckle, watching her wobble from one side to the other as she tried to manage the bulging belly in front of her that was growing rapidly.

White walls and beige accents made the room seem far more spacious and airy than it was. The minimalistic set up was admirable and reminded me a lot of my office without the hints of black in places where I wanted contrast. Because I was well aware of color psychology and the way it affected the mental state, black paint in the office was limited.

Nature's round belly made it impossible to close the gown at the center, where it was split for easy access. Exasperated from the walk and getting undressed, she lie on the bed, suffering from labored breathing and tired limbs. Wishing I could bear the weight of her pregnancy, I found myself beside the bed, pushing the cloth aside.

A dark line centered her belly, stopping right at her enlarged navel and then continuing underneath it. I'd seen her belly a number of times, but a modest woman, she refused to expose it in the middle of restaurants during our check-ins. That limited my views to private settings, which Nature tried her hardest to avoid with me. My home and hers were the only locations I'd gotten to caress her skin and admire the canvas that was creating such beautiful art.

I placed my right hand on the center of her stomach. Leaning forward, I placed my ear against it as if I'd hear what was going on inside. Though it was highly unlikely, I still strived for the unimaginable.

"Seriously?" She sniggered, thinking I was incredibly insane. Maybe I was.

"Trying to see what's going on with this little dude," I admitted.

The sound of my voice caused a shift in the shape of her belly, startling us both. My eyes tried their damnedest to exit my skull.

"Nay!"

"I see it, Milo."

Accustomed to our son's daily activities, the movements were nothing new for her. She remained calm, watching as I tilted my head, leaning in closer and projecting my voice.

"Mason. It's Daddy, dude."

Again, there was movement. This time, one side stretched much more than the other. Nature rushed to grab my hand. Her manicured fingers covered mine, pulling them in the opposite direction and forcing them down onto her belly where she wanted them.

"His foot," she announced. "Keep talking to him."

"Daddy needs you to sit tight for a few more weeks and then we're in these streets, son. Strollers, backpacks, car seats, all that shit in the whip, ready to go."

"His head," she told me, moving my hand to the other side where he'd moved. "And he's not going to be in any streets, Milo."

"Shiiiiiid." I laughed. "With the entire Domino gang. Maz waiting on his ass right now. Me and Malachi got matching strollers and shit. You have no earthly idea," I informed her with a shake of my head.

"How over the top the Domino brothers are? I do. I really do."

"I passed your whip, Nay. You have the baby on board sign up already. And I'm over the top?"

"Well, because it's true."

"He isn't here yet."

"So, there's still a baby on board."

"Knock, knock," Marcie called out, entering the room as well. "Dr. Domino. What a pleasant surprise."

"What's good, Marcie?"

"Everything. Everything. Especially with this little boy of yours. He's made this pregnancy a breeze for us both. Heck, Nature could've seen herself for nine months and saved you both some money."

"Nah. She wanted you. Whatever Nature wants, she gets."

It was the truth. Whatever Nature's heart desired, she could have. Prenatal care was covered. She didn't have to spend a dime. Delivery would be covered. Every expense that accompanied our pregnancy was my responsibility. When our son was born, it would be the same.

Because we weren't ready to start thinking of care centers, we'd decided on hiring a nanny, whom we were planning to begin trials for six weeks after the baby's birth. I'd cover the cost for care as well. There wasn't anything within my reach and account range that Nature and my son couldn't have. I'd made that clear the moment the pregnancy test displayed the word *Pregnant.*

"Well, alright then. Let's see what baby is up to today."

Perched beside Nature, I watched as preparation began. Warm, clear gel was poured onto her belly as Marcie pushed the gown aside to reduce restrictions while wanding. When she finally placed the probe on her stomach, the waves began, drowning out the sounds around us.

Shit. Exuberance filled me to the core. Taking Nature's hand into mine, I watched as the skeleton of our son appeared on the screen. Movement was plentiful. He began putting on a show for the camera, bringing a smile to my face.

"And for his tiny heartbeat."

I prepared for the sound of a rapidly beating heart to fill the room. And when it did, mine swelled a thousand times. Breathing became difficult as I tried suppressing the vast emotions surfacing at once. Prickly orbs led to distorted vision as tears cornered my eyes.

Wow. Disbelief silenced me completely. Pride trapped itself right inside of my chest cavity, inflating it just before heartache sucked the air right out of me. Thoughts of our son growing accustomed to two homes, two routines, two cribs, two of everything crushed me.

"Strong. Very strong. I'm going to take a few measurements and get some pictures and let you guys get back to your busy day. He's doing just fine. Not yet in position for delivery, but he still has weeks. I have a feeling we don't have to worry about this one at all. He cooperates."

"We love an easygoing baby," Nature snickered.

"Don't we? Almost makes us want to refund the parents," Marcie joked.

"Almost!"

Zoned in, I continued admiring my son's body on the screen as she measured his frame, his skull, his heart, counted the chambers, and printed images. It amazed me how Nature was able to grow and nourish an entire human inside of her as she went about her life with little to no changes in her daily routine and schedule. She hadn't slowed down a bit. Her bravery and resilience was stunning.

"Alright. They'll schedule your next appointment up front. From here on out, I'll be seeing you every week."

"Yes," Nature confirmed as Marcie made her way toward the door.

"Dr. Domino," she called out to me. "It was nice seeing you."

"Appreciate you, Marcie."

My attention span was limited. Holding the images she'd printed close to my face, I examined every detail of the tiny human stuffed inside of Nature. The fact that I'd impregnated her and one sperm cell was responsible for this moment had me in a daze.

Like a lost puppy without a care in the world other than the images in front of me, I followed Nature with her over-sized bag and book in my hand. It made me feel a bit better, toting anything on her person that added weight to the load she was already hauling. By the time we made it outside, she'd grown sick of my new obsession, snatching the ultra-sound from my hand forcing me to rejoin society.

"What?"

"You're going to walk into a pole if you don't pay attention, Milo."

I retrieved the ultrasound images, lowering them by my side as I gave her my undivided attention. Leaning against her door, I gave a complete once over. The simple leggings and oversized shirt that stopped right under her belly were simple, but the colors complemented her beauty.

With a face free of makeup, the discolored circles under her eyes were visible. I loved them. However, the lack of effort that her attire displayed revealed what she wasn't willing to confess. She was at the point of pregnancy that left her too drained to do the things she loved most.

"Come on," I commanded, grabbing her hand and pulling her in the opposite direction.

"Wait. Woah. Come on? Where? And no."

"Wherever we're going. Come on."

"No. I have—"

"You don't have shit, Nature. We're scheduled for a check-in at 12:00. Your schedule is clear and so is mine. Come ride with a nigga."

"No," she stated, standing her ground."

"Cool."

I folded the images neatly and stuffed them in Nature's bag, which was still dangling from my hand. I added the book to the mix and pulled it up on my shoulder.

"Milo, what are y—MILO!"

Effortlessly, I pulled her into my arms, carrying her bridal-style toward my car. I lowered her down until her ass touched the seat after I'd gotten the door open and in the air. Before closing the door, I leaned in, waiting for her to say anything. Pouty lips and folded arms let me know that her brain was working overtime trying to conjure something, anything.

"Voluntarily or involuntarily, Nay, you coming with me." I settled at once.

"Milo. You can't just–"

"I can and I will so shut that shit up, sit back, put your seat belt on, look pretty, and sing along to these girly ass tracks I'm about to play for your spoiled ass."

Rolling her eyes, she turned her back toward me, dismissing me. With a shrug, I sealed the door and headed around to the driver side.

FOUR

Nature

"CHEER UP. FIX YOUR FACE."

"Being that I've kind of been kidnapped, I don't think I can cheer up, Milo. You have me here at some... place to be serviced when I have patients that need me," I reminded him.

"My son needs you and so do I. I can see it all over your face, Nature. You're exhausted. I'm not here because I just wanted to come. I'm here because you needed to. So, they can wait. This can't."

Blowing out in frustration, I tried to remove the leggings from my thighs but struggled to push them down my legs.

Out of my peripheral, I watched him secure the towel around his waist, rounding the bed and approaching me with stretched arms. He lifted me onto the bed that I'd be occupying in the midst of my resentful grunts.

It was pathetic, how I unknotted under his spell. The twists and tangles I was wrapped up in, the walls I'd put up, they dissolved. Still, I was baffled, wondering if it was because the care he took, his patience, his uncompromising smile, his scent, his heart, or his dick that was the culprit. Maybe it was a combination of them. Maybe it was all of them, together, working against my sanity.

One leg at a time, he removed my bottoms. Then, there was my shirt and bra. Carefully, he pulled the shirt over my head. Next, he unclamped the bra from the back, putting it on the chair where he'd laid my purse.

Hurry back, my body begged. His absence reminded me of the torture I'd suffered through my entire pregnancy. *Cold. Lonely. Uncertain.*

My panties were the last to go. Hesitantly, I lifted so that he could slide them from my waist and underneath me. Shame filled me to capacity. My cheeks flushed as Milo's handsome face contorted. My secret didn't belong to me anymore. He was privy to the information I wished to keep to myself. I was a mess down there. In an attempt to explain, words failed me.

"Sorry. I, uh... I..."

"Damn, Nay," he whispered, thumbing my pearl.

I remained silent, stuffing my moans at the root of my mouth as he massaged me near my peak. Pent-up emotions and sexual frustration had me ready to blow a gasket. I placed my hands at the edge of his shoulders and leaned forward, increasing the pressure down below.

As if he knew my body's language, Milo lifted my legs onto the bed, spreading them wide and exposing my center in its eternity. Though my belly was in the way, I could feel the moisture it produced. I caved at the sight of him sticking his hand into his mouth and releasing the gold teeth that lined the bottom teeth.

Flared nostrils and an increased heart rate were indicators that I was well aware of what was to come. One second, he was in my line of vision, and the next, he wasn't. His tongue replaced his fingers.

"Miloooooo."

With haste, he clamped down on my flesh, flickering his tongue back and forward, not stopping until I felt the tingling sensation in the pit of my stomach.

"Milo. Pleeease."

I lifted a hand placing it on the back of his head, warning him not to stop because my peak was near. To my dismay, he shoved it away, never missing his mark as he continued to hammer my clit with his tongue. And within seconds, I untied, releasing everything my little box had to offer. I gifted Milo with a creamy thickness that oozed into his mouth and onto his beard.

"Please. Please," I begged, pushing his head away.

Overstimulated and sensitive, I needed him to unhand me. With pleasure, he released me, standing in all his glory. The towel around his waist fell by his side. I watched his massiveness spring from underneath the fabric. The small space that had gotten between us, he removed in one breath.

His facial hairs brushed against my chin as his lips lie against mine. I tasted myself as he buried his tongue in the warmth of my mouth. Simultaneously, his dick parted me like the Red Sea, stuffing me. Oblivion summoned me, leaving me breathless, clueless, and spineless. I collapsed into Milo's arms as we both stilled, unmoving, while acknowledging the ground that was just broken.

Knock. Knock. The knocking at the door startled me. I raised, eyes darting, as I began panicking. This was a massage parlor. It wasn't a hotel room, but we'd used it for privacy reasons beyond belief.

Our eyes met as he slid out of me. We both understood things far beyond what our words could express at the moment. Silently, he wrapped the towel around his body, covering his hard dick.

Pure ecstasy lingered in his eyes, mirroring mine, as I struggled to close my mouth and close my legs. He watched as my creaminess trickled down my pussy, leaving us both in worse shape than we were three seconds ago when he was deep inside of my pussy. Deep in *his* pussy.

"Ready?" the women asked, making their way into the room as I tried gathering myself.

My sweet aroma filled the room and I was certain it was still on Milo's lips and face. The towel beneath me was soiled. Nevertheless, I turned around and positioned my belly in the large hole before lowering my face into the smaller one.

"Yes," Milo responded, knowing I didn't have the words to share.

I felt him pull the towel over my bottom half. My

personal scent tickled my nostrils as I felt his hand touch my back. I lifted my head to address him. The conviction in his eyes spoke before he opened his mouth.

"I really don't give a fuck what's going on right now. When this shit is all said and done, Nay, we're locked in," he whispered, needing to get that off his chest. He was unable to hold it in a second longer.

"You're different. I'm different. We can't go back to the people we were. *What* we were. Let's not spin in circles, chasing the unobtainable."

"I'ma spin and spin and spin again until you get it through that thick ass skull of yours."

He lifted, revealing his thick print through the towel, forcing me to clench below and pray that I was given the strength to save myself the heartache I knew he would cause me in the future.

Milo · Nature

SOUNDLESSLY, we rode. Not even music played in the background. Both deep in our thoughts and completely relaxed, we indulged in the silence. The short distance traveled reduced the awkwardness. When we finally pulled into the parking lot of Giselle's, Milo was out and by my side within seconds.

He assisted me out of the car and onto my feet. Behind him, I made my way up to the restaurant where they sold breakfast all day and night. The idea of an omelet stuffed with American cheese, chicken, bell peppers, and onions left my mouth watery.

We entered the establishment and found ourselves a seat in a booth closest to the back of the restaurant. My bladder protested against my comfort. The second I was situated, the restroom began beckoning for me. Blowing out in frustration, I slid toward the other end of the booth and stood to my feet.

"What's the matter?" Milo asked, standing to his feet as well.

"Restroom," I sighed with a shake of my head.

"Poor baby," he cooed, extending his hand so that I could lead the way.

"It's fine. I can go al–"

"Shhh."

He placed a finger to his lips and shook his head from one side to the other, letting me know that I was wasting my breath. Taking heed to his warning, I strutted toward the restroom, feeling his glare burn holes in my backside. I'd shed the coat and so had he. I was exposed completely from behind.

Upon making it inside, I quickly emptied my bladder. Relief left me breathless as I squatted over the toilet, hoping and praying I didn't wet my leggings by accident. After cleaning myself up, I stepped out of the stall I'd occupied and took a look in the mirror.

Thank God.

The door of the restroom opened, startling me. In some sick, shameful way, I expected Milo's head to peek around the corner. Instead, I was blessed with a tall, shapely figure that commanded my attention and I was sure she'd commanded the attention of everyone she'd passed to get to the restroom.

"Okay. Aren't you just the freaking cutest," she exclaimed, wiggling her fingers.

"Uh... *Thanks?*"

Her acknowledgment led me to believe she knew me. Unfortunately, I had no clue who she was and how she'd know me. I'd remember a beauty of this magnitude and she was nowhere in my mental rolodex.

"Do I know you?" I probed, pumping soap into my palm.

"Nope," she stated as a matter of fact. "But you will soon. I'm Kleu, Lawe's fiancée."

My eyes bulged, unsure if I'd heard her correctly.

"Lawe? Engaged?"

"No." She chuckled. "We're not. But we're testing the waters. Seeing how it sounds. Neither of us are really interested in marriage, but we figured, what the hell, right? Besides, fiancée has a little ring to it. Literally. We can stop at that point. We don't have to be dramatic and sign papers."

Her humor made my cheeks rise.

"I'm Nature," I introduced myself.

"Nice to meet you, babe."

"The feeling is mutual."

"So, a son, huh?"

"Yes."

"Decided on a name?"

"Mason. We chose that name some time ago in college. We were kids but we wanted to honor the pledge."

"I get it. How far along are you?"

"I'm thirty-five, almost thirty-six weeks."

"Almost at the finish line."

"Yes. Almost."

"Well, you two have been togeth—around each other long enough for me not to have to tell you this, but you have a good one, girl. I haven't met a Domino that's made me turn my nose up yet. They're all..." She paused, struggling to find the perfect word to describe them.

"Men."

"Yes. Exactly. It's that simple. They're all men."

"You're right."

I dried my hands, still stuck on her hiccup.

Together.

We weren't. And just like her, I thought that fiancée had a ring to it. Wife had an even bigger ring, and somehow, my heart still yearned for that title. Milo, it was him I wanted to give it to me but he was dangerous territory.

Loving Milo was equivalent to living life in a minefield. Any movement in the wrong direction could lead to destruction. Heart and body exploding, leaving me unrecognizable and unidentifiable. The risk outweighed the reward, and if I was smart, I'd keep my heart in check.

"Congratulations on the baby."

"Thank you so much. Congratulations on the future nuptials." I chuckled. "Pretend or not."

"Thank you."

I exited the restroom, bumping right into Lawe.

"Damn, move that motherfucker over or something!" he fussed.

"My belly? Seriously? How do you suppose I do that?" I asked, hand on my hip as I tilted my head and waited for an answer.

"Shit, I don't know. Y'all the fucking doctors."

"Hello to you, too, Lawe. Milo, I'm going to sit down."

I started for the booth we'd chosen. Immediately, I felt a hand on my arm, pulling me back in the direction I was fleeing from.

"Nah," Lawe protested. "I know you fucking lying. You trying to wobble your ass over to the table and give me that dry ass greeting like you don't know me or something."

"I do know you. That's why I'm trying to wobble away," I assured him, settling into his embrace.

"You been good?"

"Yes. Just wobbling around."

"I see. Shit. I'm still trying to get over the fact you let this nigga knock you up. Was there a shortage of dick or something?"

"Lawe!" Milo barked.

"What?" He raised his hands.

"Chill."

"No. There wasn't, actually. I saw him as the best candidate. And wherever he's involved, Lawe, there's never a shortage of dick."

His jaw fell as his eyes grew bigger. While he took time to readjust to the wrench I'd just thrown his way, I made my escape. This time, I was successful.

Milo returned as the waitress appeared, taking our orders and bringing out the orange juices we ordered just a few minutes later. When the food arrived, I dug in, immediately. It wasn't until my mouth was stuffed that Milo discovered the words to fill the space between us.

"The birth plan. We're sticking to it?"

"Yes."

"Good. Good. I'll take another look at it when I get home this evening. Is there anything in particular you want during your hospital stay that might not be in the plan? Meal prep? Delivery from a specific restaurant? Photographer? Videographer? Anything?"

"No. There's nothing I can really think of. If you'd like a photographer, then I don't mind that. My mother will have her camera and will take photos and record, I'm sure."

"Cool. The less people, the better."

"Yeah."

"I want to ask you something that I don't want you to answer right now. But I want you to think about. Whatever you decide, I'm cool with but I want to toss it out there, though."

"What is it, Milo?"

"Coming to my home after the birth so that we share the responsibility for at least the first few weeks."

"Milo, I don't know if that's a good idea."

"Give it some thought. That's all I'm saying. I'm not tripping, whatever you decide. I know you feel comfortable at your crib and that's where you've planned to be since the beginning of this thing. I'm not trying to get in the way of that. I'm just making an eirenicon that you come home to me so that this is much easier for us both."

"I understand and I'll consider it."

"That's all I'm asking."

"Have you decided on a middle name, yet?"

He'd been tasked with determining our son's middle name. By the look on his face, I wasn't convinced he had.

Shaking his head, he responded, "Nah. I haven't."

"I could make this much simpler for you."

"How?"

"Maurice."

His features tried their hardest to gather in the center of his face as he dropped his fork onto his plate. Questioning my choice without saying a single word, his crinkled brows and deflated chest exposed him. He tilted his head to one side and then to the other side. I watched as he cracked his knuckles, one by one. The habit still a part of his unnerving.

"Wh-Why'd you... Why Maurice?"

"Why not?" I shrugged.

His long fingers pulled his bushy brows as he shook his head, trying to make sense of my suggestion. Scoffing, he sniggered sarcastically, a failed attempt to gain control of his movement and his emotions. I watched as he continued to unveil the pain that rested deep within.

"Nah," he expressed. "N-Nah." Choking, he continued to shake his head from side to side.

"Mason Maurice Domino."

"Nay," he pled.

"It's perfect, Milo."

"It... Nay, nah. I'll think of something. I promise."

"Mason Maurice Domino," I repeated.

Though a million other names had flowed through my head and matched well with my son's name, there was something special about Maurice and it wouldn't allow me to fall in love with any other combination.

"You serious?"

I nodded.

He grew quiet, tracing the pendant on his necklace, one that the four of them shared. Malachi. Makai. Mercer. Milo.

It was a diamond-studded prayer hand with the letter M hanging on rosary beads.

"You'd do that?"

"Yes. I would. Why not?"

"Thank you," he sighed. "Thank you."

"Of course."

A smile parted his lips as pride sparked in his eyes. "Thank you, Nay."

"Please. Don't. I just thought I'd help ease your worries and give you something to remember your father by. Our son will be honored to carry his name. I'm certain."

"I didn't even consider it."

"I know."

He was forever running from the pain that accompanied thoughts of his parents and their demise.

"Mason Maurice Domino."

"Yes," I confirmed.

"Not the first choice, but—"

"The best choice."

Of course I would've chosen something fun and mysterious for Mason's middle name but nothing suited better than the name we'd just decided on. It was perfect. I loved it for Mason and I loved it for Milo.

"Nay... what are we doing, my love?"

"Milo," I groaned.

"Tell me because I don't fucking know. I feel all of this shit for you and trying to keep it under wraps has got me ready to lose my fucking mind."

"I thought I wanted something between us, wanted more, you know. And I almost made the mistake of gaining it. But over the last week, I realized it's not really what I need. It doesn't matter that my heart is telling me to go for it. My head knows it's the dumbest fucking decision I could make, especially right now."

"Dumbest?" he grimaced.

"Seeing someone at your home was a blessing in itself, Milo. As much as you'd like to believe we can pick back up where we left off, that's untrue. We can't."

"I'm not trying to."

"What are you trying to do?"

"Give my son a two-parent home, stability, and twice the love."

"Without us being together, he'll have that. If I thought otherwise, I would've continued with the plans of using a sperm donor. I don't think for a second he will lack in any category."

"That's true, but what does it hurt to try?"

"My heart."

"Nay, come on. Cut a nigga some fucking slack, baby."

His referral nearly strangled me. I rubbed a hand against my chest, recovering from the blow.

"I don't think you understand Milo."

"Then, help me."

"Without a doubt, there will never be another person in this world that I'll ever love the way I loved you. The way that I love you."

"Love me?" He scoffed, taken aback.

"Please don't act as if that's a surprise."

"I just—"

"The other night, when I poured my heart out, ready to risk it all, throwing all caution to the wind, seeing your company descend stairs that I'd imagined myself coming down countless times in my dreams – day or night – crushed me. I don't think you're comprehending, Milo. The one time I was ready, the universe said, NO. And I'm going to listen. I'd be a fool not to."

Resting his back against the booth, he nodded, accepting my response.

"I won't stop."

Shaking my head, I avoided eye contact by lowering my eyes to my plate.

Please don't.

"A slight delay isn't equivalent to denial."

"There are thousands of girls, Milo."

"I want the one in front of me. The one that I deserve."

"I doubt very much that you deserve me, with all due respect."

Leaning forward, he looked in both directions before speaking. And when his mouth opened, my eyes and ears opened. He had my undivided attention.

"Nay, ain't no nigga out here going to dick you down like me. Ain't nobody going to stuff that pussy in their mouth like me. Nobody knocking that pussy down like me, he chuckled, presumptuously.

"I'm sure of it. And that's just the small shit. My account is expansive. You can have it all if you want. Ain't no limits when it comes to you. I don't give a fuck about you having your own. You've got mine, too. Ain't a nigga in this city going to step 'bout you like I am. Lay my shit on the line if it means saving yours. Plus, that little nigga in your womb, I put him there.

"So, yes, I deserve your fine ass. Niggas haven't and aren't willing to put in the work I am to secure my spot. And furthermore, I'm not concerned with what the fuck they're willing to do unless it's lay down behind it because I'm willing to end a motherfucker 'bout you. I'm down bad and I ain't afraid to admit it."

His face. I wanted to ride his face as he repeated himself.

"Milo," I sniggered. "Scan your roster. I'm certain someone is available. Maybe you can impregnate her and put in the same work. I don't know."

"Don't fucking play with me, Nature." He laughed.

"I have to get back to the office. I have two patients to see before I end my day."

"I'll take you."

"I can manage."

"You look exhausted."

"I am."

"Then let me take you and get you home. I'll have your car lifted to your house."

"Milo, I appreciate it, but really, I can manage. I'm fine. The appointments won't take long at all. I'll be home in the next hour and a half."

"Alright." He laid off, but didn't break eye contact.

"What?" I blushed, hating my cheeks for showing their truest colors.

"You're about to be a mother, Nay. That's big shit."

"Don't try to downplay it. You're about to be a father."

"I know. A nigga nervous a little. I won't front. Malachi makes the shit look so easy. I'm trying to keep my cool and not call him every five minutes with another question that has arisen."

"He'll understand and be happy to help."

"I know. But I'm not trying to wear him out with shit that I can Google or ask Pops."

"Parents," I breathed out, watching Milo peel off a few twenties and lay them on the table.

"Parents," he repeated. "Fucking parents. And a son on the first try."

"Admittedly," I cringed. "I kind of wanted a daughter."

"My dick still work, Nay. You ain't said nothing but a fucking word."

"No," I tittered. "I'm not trying to raise a bunch of babies with a co-parent. Maybe God will send me a husband and he'll give me a daughter when I turn forty."

"He's trying to give you one once you drop this one. What we waiting until forty for? Thirty-eight, maybe? That's what, less than two years apart. Two under two sounds doable."

"I said my husband."

"I know what the hell you said," he assured me. "And I know what our future holds, too."

"Oh, my God. Let it go. Please, sir!"

"Can't."

He stood on his feet, looking like a tall glass of vitamin D. The sudden deficiency left me fiending for his supply.

"Help me up."

Together, we exited the restaurant, making our way to his car. I was considering canceling the two appointments that I had, but decided against it. When I did make it home, I didn't want the cancelations on my conscience. A bubble bath and the bed were the only things I wanted to lend my thoughts to when I walked through the door.

With Milo at the wheel, we headed back to Marcie's

office where my truck was parked. My vibrating phone stole my attention. Assuming it was my mother texting for an appointment update, I unlocked it without hesitation. However, the name on the screen proved me wrong.

Zane. Seeing his name immediately reminded me of the second round of drinks we'd shared at the same bar, a total coincidence. This time, however, I didn't mind accepting the food he offered. With the same chair between us, we dined, laughed, and ended our nights with full bellies.

What's good?

Hi.

The gray bubbles appeared, disappeared, and then appeared again as he considered a follow up.

You crossed my mind. I feel like I miss your company. I could be tripping but I doubt it.

I gnawed on the flesh of my bottom lip, wondering how to respond. I could feel my cheek sharpen at the peaks as a smile split my face. It wasn't until the music stopped and I heard Milo's voice that I snapped out of it and back into reality.

"Who we texting?" he asked, peeking over at my screen.

I snatched it out of eye range, pressing the phone against my chest, eventually.

"We?"

"Yeah."

"Milo, you don't pay the bill on my phone so you have no business worrying about who I am texting," I told him, finding his inquiry comical.

"What's so fucking funny?" he wondered.

"You. Turn the music up."

"Aight. Get you and some nigga fucked up."

"Please drive!" I laughed, pointing toward the green light.

He hiked the volume on the stereo again. I locked my phone, deciding against texting Zane in his presence. He could wait until I was alone and in the comfort of my home.

FIVE

"WHERE'S THE BABY?" Aussie whispered in my ear as if she was sharing news with me that others weren't privy to.

"You know that everyone knows I have a baby on the way, right, Aussie?"

"I don't really care, Uncle Milo," she sassed.

"Oh. Well, alright, then. The baby is still in Nature's tummy."

"He's taking so long," she fussed, folding her arms in front of her.

"I agree."

"Maz took a long time."

"Yes. Babies take nearly ten months to make it out."

"That's almost twelve months, like a full calendar year."

"What don't you know, Aussie?"

"Mandarin, but Mommy says she's going to hire a tutor."

"I believe it." Nodding, I shifted in my seat, facing the woman in question.

Aeir's brown skin with hints of orange reminded me of the woman I'd watched my brother fall in love with when we were just kids. Though I didn't think it could get any better than Anna, somehow, he'd proven me wrong. Aeir was the updated, upgraded version of a woman that was already perfect. That spoke volumes about her and her position in Malachi's life. His happiness allowed me to rest easily each night.

For two years straight, I tossed and turned, praying for his heart's contentment. Aeir's presence quickly became the paracme of his life. He was in his prime. After battling with the discovery of who'd murdered Anna and having to dead that situation, he struggled for a few months, but once Aeir was back in the picture, all was right in his world.

Since, they'd grown closer, and surprisingly, he hadn't grown colder. He was the warm, intriguing fella I knew before the tragedy that shook us all to the core. His smile lit up the entire room and everyone inside would do almost anything to see it because we all knew the pain that still resided in him. It was pain that didn't go away, it lingered and it hurt each and every day.

It was in his eyes, in his words, in his movements, and in that smile that we held our breaths for each time we saw his face. For so long, he was misunderstood. Everyone on the outside looking in, deeming him as uncouth and incapable of being loved. Those were unrealistic, seemingly unscathed people who didn't understand grief and the power of pain.

It was just as potent as love. It had a way of ripping out the best parts of people. *He's changed.* I heard a million times over. But every time, the follow up revolved around the question I'd asked twenty times over.

"If your wife was snatched right from up under you, murdered in cold blood in front of your daughter by someone you loved like the brothers your mother birthed, wouldn't you change to?"

Malachi was dealt a fucked-up hand. And every day, I thanked God that he was still here. It was a blessing that I didn't overlook, even on my best days. With our mother's history of mental health and how their story ended, I prayed daily for the strength of my brother.

Every time my phone rang, I died a little inside, hoping it wasn't a call that Malachi had ended his life. That's how deep his roots with Anna ran. Until Aeir came into his life, I was certain he wasn't a willing participant in it. He wanted out. It was Aussie that kept him grounded. Forever, I was indebted to her.

Extending my arms, I reached for Maz, who was drooling as he stared at me, curiously. His hands went up, immediately. Standing to my feet, I leaned over and scooped him up. His joy was infectious. He bobbed his head and wiggled his body, excitedly.

"Alright, little dude. Alright. My bad. I took too long to get you."

He rested his head on my chest as I tuned back into the

conversation being had among the men surrounding me. But just as quickly, I zoned out completely, taking a good look at everyone around me.

Mercer's humbled nature was a far cry from the man he'd been before his stint, but I loved this version of him even more. Makai, the wicked and wildest of us all, managed the perfect disguise. From first glance, and to any stranger, he was a perfect, sane dude. But everyone at the table understood the complexities of his brain.

Being a man who studied the brain and its functions, I understood those complexities best. There was a tiny switch inside and when it was flipped, he transformed into something unfathomable by the average human. His mental capacity was the one that worried me most. It was most reflective of our mother's. At the snap of a finger, he became a completely different human.

Malachi, the heart of the family, was slowly progressing and it was a joy to see it. Aussie, the Princess, surrounded by soldiers, was thriving. She was the smartest thing I'd ever seen. The family would argue that she was following in my footsteps, but I felt that she was beyond me at her age. College by twelve was my prediction and she was well on her way.

Pops, even in old age, was still as sharp as a steak knife. It was his idea, this night and the gathering at his home. Mercer spent the majority of the evening in the kitchen with Pops at his side. The culinary enthusiast of the family, he could truly burn. The mixed greens, pan-seared chicken breast, stuffed salmon, green beans, mashed potatoes, and mac and cheese spread that was waiting under the heat lamps were his latest creations. He'd popped the cornbread in the oven seconds before sitting at the table to join us.

First Fridays. It was our new ritual and this was the beginning of many first Fridays of each month that we sat down to feast as a family. Though I was surrounded with love, there was still a missing piece to the puzzle that robbed me of the feeling of completion. Wholeness evaded me. The empty chair next to me was a reminder that I was still alone and the person who belonged there, rubbing her growing belly with my son inside, was alone, too.

I shifted Maz in my arm, retrieving my phone from the pocket of my jeans. With one hand, I entered the code and opened the message thread from Nature and I. Chuckling, I admired her dedication.

Just like me, she was burning with desire inside, but remaining cautious, she fed me bread crumbs, just enough to satisfy me for a few before I was back for more. What she didn't understand was that I had every intention of sticking around until I was gifted the entire loaf. It was mine, any-fucking-way.

Have you eaten? I texted her.

Surprisingly, her response was almost immediate. It could only mean her phone was in her hands, already in use, when she received the message. It was read within the same minute I'd sent it.

No, she responded.

Come to Pop's house. We're having dinner.

Milo. *I don't feel like driving. Thanks for the invitation.*

I'll send a car.

No.

I'll come get you.

I don't think dinner is a good idea.

I responded with a sad face emoji before closing the chat. Sliding my phone back into my pocket, I joined the conversation with the guys.

"Pour me some more."

I lifted my glass, waiting for Makai to pour in the Hennessy White. It was the drink of choice for the night. Three bottles sat on the makeshift bar with juices that Aeir was kind enough to supply, however, we were drinking our shit straight. No chaser.

"And then, this nigga Chem and his two cents. Always trying to stick that shit somewhere. I told the nigga to pull up. Stop all that talking and pull up."

"Why are you so damn adamant about tussling with this grown ass man?" Pops asked Makai.

"'Cause I owe that nigga."

"He misses him," I interjected. "And this is his way of expressing it because he can't process his feelings like a normal, sane human."

"Fuck you!"

"Hey," Malachi warned, pointing at Aussie.

"My bad," he apologized, tossing his middle finger in the air.

"Aussie." Aeir chuckled.

"Yes?"

"Headphones, baby."

"Okay, Mommy."

Immediately, she pulled the headphones that were around her neck onto her ears. She canceled the noise around her, watching the iPad in front of her. I expected to see a silly cartoon on the screen, but there wasn't a character in sight. A new word on a large flashcard appeared each time she swiped.

Of course.

"I love you and I miss you. Is there a way I can see you? I'd love to spend time with you, brother. It's simple, Makai. Repeat after me," I suggested. "Chem, I miss you."

With flared nostrils, he cut his eyes in my direction. I leaned back in my chair, finding his discomfort enjoyable.

"Leave him alone, Milo. He'll practice in the shower tonight."

Everyone around the table doubled over in laughter.

"Nigga, go check on the cornbread. Big, sweet ass."

"Ain't shit 'bout me sweet, nigga," Mercer replied, still chortling.

"Now, why would you call that man sweet?"

"'Cause ain't no way that nigga did eight strong without no pussy."

"Niggas do it all the time," Malachi told him.

"So, you think your brother was busting niggas down in there?" I questioned with a smirk, knowing damn well he wasn't serious.

"Or getting took down."

"You hear yourself right now?" Mercer asked, standing to his feet.

He was utterly unfazed by Makai's antics. We all were.

"Y'all really entertaining this dude right now?" Malachi wanted to know.

"Nah. I'm taking my sweet ass in here to get this cornbread out the oven."

"Makai, shut up," Pops finalized.

Mercer disappeared into the kitchen. When he reappeared, he was rubbing his hands together and clapping his hands.

"Time to eat, y'all."

"Not before bowing those nappy heads of yours."

Stretched arms transformed the gaps into passageways to the next set of fingers as we all bowed our heads.

"Aeir," Pops called out.

"Dear God," she began immediately, her voice like soft wool against the skin. "Thank You for this day. Thank You for your grace and mercy. Thank You for Your protection. Thank You for keeping us all safe. Thank You for giving us all another day. Thank You for the food and the hands that prepared it. Your blessings are far beyond our imagination and we can't tell You how much we love You for deeming us worthy of them. We need you. Stay close. Amen."

"Amen."

"Amen."

"Amen."

"Amen."

Maz bounced in my arms, ready to nibble on whatever was passed his way. As I stood to my feet, ready to go grab a plate, the doorbell sounded.

"I got it!" Makai yelled.

Because he was the closest and we all knew that he'd most likely invited one of the many from his lineup, we let him handle it. I grabbed a plate and followed the line into the area where the food was laid out, ready for consumption. I watched as Aeir and Malachi avoided the meaty goods and settled for extra helpings of the side dishes. They were strict vegetarians and refused meat of any kind.

Mercer respected their choices, making their greens separate from everyone else's, which had turkey parts inside.

"What are you having?" Aeir asked. "Or how about I put my plate down and grab him?"

"Nah. It's fine. Load me up. Put everything on my shit. I got him."

I held my plate in her direction as she filled it with a little of everything on the table. The extra-large paper plates were almost too small for the spread but Aeir worked her magic and managed to fit it all on top somehow.

"Appreciate it."

"Of course. If he gets on your nerves, I'll get him."

"I got him. Getting my practice in."

"Yeah?" She smiled. "Admittedly, you look nice with a baby in your arms."

"I can't wait to hold Mason in mine."

"Me either."

My intensity of the waves the voice behind me caused left my heart in shambles. I stiffened, momentarily, hoping my balance wasn't thrown off and Maz didn't fall from my arms as a result. My body's equilibrium was fucked. I knew that for a fact. With a shake of the head, I turned to find Nature standing behind me, wiggling her fingers.

"Can I hold him?" she asked. "So you can fix me a plate?"

Her hair was pushed back off her face into a messy bun. Her face was free of makeup, again. She wore a white button-down that stopped right at her knees. On her feet, she wore platformed Gucci slides that were brown and beige. Gold hoops dangled from her ears.

The Rolex watch I'd purchased her glistened on her

wrist. Though she aimed for simplicity, she was glowing. My heart was heavy, but not with sadness or grief. Instantly, it was filled to capacity with joy and love and happiness and all the other things that Nature brought me.

"Hi," I greeted her.

"Hi."

"You lied to me."

"I had a change of mind."

Inside and out, I smiled. This woman would be the death of me and I'd die happily.

"You're determined to drive me crazy, Dr. Dupree."

"It'll be nice to have you finally join me, I guess. I've been here for years."

"And I'm to blame?"

"Yes. In fact, you are. Give me the baby, Milo."

"Here."

I handed over Maz, who had no issue jumping in Nature's arms. His wet lips landed on her cheek as he grabbed her face, trying his hardest to take a chunk out of it.

"Somebody get this baby some food before he eats my baby's face off!" I yelled. "Malachi, get ya mans."

"He knows a beautiful woman when he sees one," Aeir said, admiring Nature from afar. "I'm Aeir."

"Nature."

"He's a fucking eater," Makai blurted, making us all turn toward him.

"He's a Domino," Malachi confirmed with a shrug.

"This is a baby we're referring to," I reminded them. "You niggas are sick."

"And I'm sweet, huh?" Mercer scoffed. "Sick fuck."

"Whatever."

Makai paid us no mind, bobbing his head to a beat that no one heard but him, apparently. I grabbed the plate that Nature grabbed and handed to me. Aeir loaded hers up, too. After everyone was satisfied with their helping, we gathered at the table again. This time, with an added bonus.

"Hit me one more time. And don't lil boy me this time," I advised Mercer.

He poured a healthy glass of Hen before moving on to Malachi, Mercer, and Pops.

"Y'all heard from Portland?" I tossed out to no one in particular.

"Yeah. He came by yesterday."

"Saw he was in the city. Guess I'll hit the nigga up tomorrow. Lawe putting something in motion for the weekend."

"Where y'all going?"

"As if you're joining us," I responded to Makai.

"I might shut the shop down early and step out."

"I don't know a luxury tire shop that stays open until two in the morning," Pops interjected.

"They're moving tires, Pops. I'm moving bricks. We different."

Nature spat the water she'd just consumed from her mouth.

"Sorry," she apologized quickly. "Sorry."

"It's all good."

I wiped the portion of the table that it had spilled onto.

"Just ignorant," Pops grunted.

"I'm just being honest. Unless somebody at our table working for the people," he paused, looking in Mercer's direction. "Then what's the issue?"

"Don't start your shit," Mercer warned.

I couldn't contain myself and neither could Malachi. The two people that Makai missed most, because they spent so much time away, he picked on. It was his way of telling them how much he loved, cared for, and missed them. For us, it was pure comedy.

"Ion know. You sure you ain't nev—"

"Shut up," Mercer belted. "Just shut the f—"

Taking a deep breath, he restrained by stuffing his face with food and shaking his head.

"A hit dog gon—"

"Shut up, Makai. I'm with your brother on that one."

Pops was fed up with his shit just as much as Mercer. Unfortunately, Makai didn't care.

"I shoot old niggas, too."

"He'll be the last old nigga you shoot," Malachi assured him.

"Makai just loves to hear himself talk," Pops huffed. "Nature, how's my great-grandson doing in there?"

"He's fine, Pops. Almost time to make his debut."

"Yeah? Mason. That's a nice name there. Falls right in line with the rest of these knuckleheads."

There were verbal protests in the form of grunts, grumbling, and blatant disagreements.

"Mason Maurice Domino."

Silence swept across the oak wood table. A pin could drop and it would be heard by everyone in attendance, even Maz, whom quieted as well.

"Maurice?"

Pops recuperated first, swallowing back whatever was lodged in his throat. He loosened the collar on his shirt, pulling it away from his neck to stretch it slightly. I watched his chest rise before releasing a heavy breath.

I straightened my back before allowing my body to slump again. Pride and grief were fighting for residency in my head and my heart, both needing the moment for themselves. I struggled to hand it over, but eventually, pride prevailed.

"Yeah. We decided on Maurice for a middle name."

"That's what's up." Mercer nodded.

"Aw, nigga, he done one upped you. Now you've got to have a daughter and name her Catherine," Makai tittered, staring straight at Malachi.

"Nigga," he barked, ending it there.

"Alright. Maurice," Pops said, nodding in approval. "God, it's been so long since I've said his name."

"Same," I admitted.

"It feels good."

I agreed by lifting my head up and down.

"Hand me that bottle, Mercer," I requested, beckoning with my hand.

"Pour me something when you've poured your helping."

I filled the glass halfway and then tilted it over Pop's glass. He lifted his left hand to let me know when I'd poured enough.

"When are you due?" Aeir's attempt to lighten the load was successful.

"June tenth."

"An end-of-Spring birth."

"I'm just hoping he doesn't decide to stick around until

Summer begins. I'm hot and I'm growing tired," Nature explained.

"I understand."

I forked my greens, watching as Nature handled Maz in one hand and managed to stuff her face with the other. She was a natural. Mason's presence would only enhance her motherly instincts. Admittedly, it was eye opening, seeing her with a boy in her arms that would most likely resemble ours.

It was as if I was seeing our future right before my eyes. The empty ring finger was my only hiccup. It deserved the fattest rock that kept her finger chilled and her heart ice cold when it came to any nigga besides me.

Plates were cleaned and bottles were emptied over the next two hours. No one was in a rush to leave, everyone joking about a sleepover that would more than likely happen in the future. Tonight, however, my bed was calling my name. I leaned over, scooting Nature's chair closer to me.

"You feel so far away," I whispered in her ear.

"You're intoxicated, Milo," she responded, whispering as well.

"Every time you come around."

"No," she hissed. "Like, actually drunk."

"You haven't put Maz down once."

"I'm attached," she admitted.

"You're going to look good with our son on your hip."

"Am I?" She smiled, her cheeks flushing a soft pink.

"I'm ready to go home."

"What's stopping you?"

"Come over."

"No. You asked me to join you for dinner and I have. I'm going home after I leave."

"Then I'm coming with you," I told her, standing to my feet and nearly busting my ass.

"Wooooah." Nature extended a hand to help me keep my balance. I was a bit worse off than I'd assumed.

"Nature," Pops called out.

"Yes?"

"Take him home," Mercer demanded.

"He's in no shape to drive."

I tilted my head, smirking as I waited for her to deny either of them. She couldn't, especially not Pops. Mercer, it was possible.

"Of course," she replied, staring up at me.

"I'll take him," Aeir said, reaching for Maz, who was sound asleep in Nature's arms, looking like it was where he belonged.

Carefully, Nature stood to her feet, taking me by the hand and pulling me closer to her.

"Thanks for dinner. I thoroughly enjoyed it. Mercer, you haven't lost it a bit. Malachi, it was good seeing you. Makai, may God be with you. Pops, talk soon."

She went around the table, sharing her thoughts with each individual.

"Aeir. It was nice meeting you. You have a beautiful family."

"So do you," Aeir responded, smiling up at us both.

"I'm trying to tell her, Aeir."

"Milo, quiet," she barked. "Thank you."

"Appreciate that." Malachi laid a hand on his chest.

"I'm going to get this boy home. I'll come back for my car in the morning. I'll stop by Milo's to grab him first."

"I'll take care of it," Malachi offered.

"I got it," Mercer offered as well.

"I'm the only one at the table with a towing truck," Makai reminded us all.

"What we need a towing truck for when it's more than enough of us here to get the job done?" Mercer asked.

"Exactly," Malachi added.

"Well, it would be great, whoever could get it to my address."

"Don't worry. Just leave your keys inside," Makai instructed.

We made our way toward the door, but not before I stole a few kisses from Aussie, who was still occupied with digital flashcards. Though under the influence, chivalry, for me, still existed.

"Milo, I've got it. I promise," Nature told me as I rounded my car on my way to her rescue.

"You'd better not touch that fucking door, Nay. I'm serious."

With her hands in the air, she stood off to the side, waiting for me to open the door. Once I had, she lowered her body into the driver's seat, reminding me that I needed to look into a new set of wheels, one that would accommodate a family that would need a car seat over the next six to seven years.

Slowly, I made my way to the passenger side, holding onto the car for support. Almost immediately after I was in my seat, Nature punched the gas. With my back pressed against the seat, I couldn't refrain from staring at her bare face.

She's a fucking doll.

Nature's beauty was alluring and the thought that it wasn't a permanent part of my daily routine was agonizing. Waking up to that face every morning would be my personal slice of heaven on earth.

Taking her eyes off the road for a split second, she peered in my direction. Shaking her head, she turned around. The smirk on her face left me with a silly smile on mine. It didn't matter what the circumstances were, I loved this woman down. She could have anything she wanted from me, but most of all, I wanted her to have my heart. That's what we both needed most.

"What?" Nature shrieked.

"Let's get married," I slurred, resting my hand on her belly and inching as close to her as I could as she drove.

"Be serious, Milo."

"I am serious, Nay. You don't think we'd survive marriage?"

"Me, yes. You, no, I don't and I'm not going to set myself up for that big fat failure either."

I lifted my head and turned to her with as much serious-ness as I could muster.

"Damn, you have no hope in your boy."

"Milo, it's not that I don't have hope in you. I do. I want to, at least. But let's be for real. Right now, if I agreed to marry you, tomorrow. Can you honestly, truly say that you're ready and you can be exactly who I need and what I need in a husband?"

Pausing, I thought long and hard about her question.

Realizing there was a lot of work to do on my part, I shook my head.

"Nah. Not immediately, but eventually."

"Eventually?" she scoffed. "Who the hell wants to rush forever just to have a husband eventually?"

"I'm saying there's some shit I know I need to work on but they wouldn't hinder me from being a good husband. But to be the best husband and man for you, it would take time."

"And I know this. That's why I'm saying that I don't think you'd survive marriage right now and no time soon. You're stuck in your ways, Milo. They're not going to change overnight and I'm not willing to take that chance.

"Because, in the end, it's my feelings that'll be hurt. You're obsessed with the idea of having me, but not the idea of the work it requires to get and keep me. That's a problem. But it's not my problem. It's your problem. Besides, I'm enjoying the safety of being alone, even though it's lonely."

"I'm not a bad dude, Nay," I clarified, needing to get it off my chest.

"I know you aren't. I've never considered you as one either."

"I'm human and I made a mistake so many fucking years ago. Why you still holding that over my head?"

"Because it's still held over my heart. Time heals, but it doesn't make you forget. That immense pain I felt didn't go away in a week. It chained me to my bed for months and when I finally saw light again, I didn't recognize it.

"I was in such a dark place for so long, Milo. Life continued for you. It stopped for me, completely. My mental, emotional, and physical health declined. I was a fucking mess, so forgive me for not wanting to go back there."

"You won't. I'm different."

"You're different?"

"I was a kid, Nature. We were the youngest on the campus. I was tutoring all the older, more mature students."

"Making them a priority and putting me on the back burner."

"Okay. You're right about that."

"You did to me exactly what my father had my entire childhood."

"I know and I regret that shit."

"And then—"

"I got the big head and gave your shit to someone it didn't belong to."

"Yes. And a mentee, nonetheless."

"I was on some young nigga shit, Nay. Older broad constantly trying to jump on my shit. Temptation just... Man, I fucked up. But I'm trying to get past that. We're grown now with a son on the way."

"That you agreed to co-parent. Being together wasn't part of the plan, Milo."

"Because I expected us to be by now!" I confessed.

Shaking her head, she asked, "Is that why you agreed to father my child?"

"Part of it, yes."

"Wow. Okay."

"Come on. Don't act like that shit wasn't on your mind."

"It wasn't. Having a piece of you forever, yes, but as a means to keep you in my life to secure a position as what, your baby mother? No, Milo. That wasn't on my mind.

Have you forgotten, I was on my way to have a stranger's sperm injected in my womb so I wouldn't have to deal with any of that."

"But you didn't."

"Because you agreed and now, you're being all... I don't know."

She tossed a hand in the air, unable to explain herself any further.

"Fuck it."

"Fuck it?"

"Yeah. You've made it clear that you're not fucking with me on that level, then okay."

"It's not that simple, Milo," she breathed out.

"Yeah. It is, actually."

Stubbornness plagued us both as silence crept in the spaces that we weren't willing to fill with words. I cracked my knuckles one by one as I rested my head against the reclined seat, staring at the ceiling. It wasn't until the car came to a complete stop that I sat up and tucked my feelings deep into my chest. I exited the vehicle, taking note that Nature hadn't given me a chance to make it around to her side before rushing out of the car.

"Sit back down," I sneered, approaching her.

"Milo, it's fine. I just need to use the bathroom. My blad—"

"Nah, Nay. Sit back down. You're going to make it to the bathroom, but what you're not going to do is be petty because you can't make up your fucking mind about a nigga."

"I don't know what you're talking about," she sighed, lowering her body back into the car and closing the door.

I counted down from three, hoping it was enough time for her to begin getting her shit together. When I lifted the door, I discovered a very flustered, pregnant Nature, moving her head from one side to the other. I offered my hand for assistance but she declined, stepping out of the vehicle by her lonesome.

Before she was able to get around me, I pushed forward, pinning her body against the car. With my index finger, I lifted her chin so that her eyes were on me. She stared straight ahead, right past me, and off into the distance.

"I express myself and you hide. Then, finally, you emerge, confessing your love for me and your desires to be something more. Shit doesn't go your way and you pitch a fit. Cool. I'll give you that much. I push forward, you pull back. I push forward, you pull back. And when I finally decide to agree with you, you got your fucking lips poked out and you pouting.

"Your confusion has nothing to do with me, Nay. I've made it clear what I want, why I want it, how I want it, and when I want it. I'm a fucking man, not some boy, Nature. Especially not the boy I once was. I don't have time for uncertainty. Make your fucking mind up."

Grabbing her hand, I took off for the house with her on my heels. I refused to let her ass piss all over herself because she was being stubborn or because she'd rather make a mess than spend another waking moment with me. I didn't give a fuck that she was in her feelings.

I wasted little time getting upstairs and into the shower, leaving Nature to figure shit out on her own. With the car keys in my possession, I knew that she wouldn't be going anywhere anytime soon. If she couldn't figure our shit out, I'd figure it out for her.

I understood her hesitancy to jump into something with me after what I'd put her through. I wasn't claiming to be a saint at all. I'd done baby girl bad. My focus was my education back then. My obsession with the brain, the way it worked, and what had caused my mother's malfunction was my driving force back then. It helped me conceal the pain I truly felt, allowing me more time to heal and come to terms with her death.

The same complaints Nature had cried to me about pertaining to her father and his obsession with his career, she'd experienced in the years that she dedicated herself to me while I dedicated myself to the books. And on top of the neglect, I cheated. Though I'd known it before, by the time she was walking out of my door, I truly understood the depths of my love for Nature.

My actions might've proven otherwise, just once, but the truth was, I loved her more than I did myself. The love I harbored for her was the same love I'd witnessed in my father's eyes for my mother. It was the same love he showered her with on a daily basis. And putting it lightly, that shit scared me.

To know I was capable of loving so severely with the possibility of inheriting my mother's mental disability was disheartening, forcing me further into my studies to prove that I could love Nature that much and never bring harm to her. My fear consumed me and so did my studies, leading to my infidelity and eventually our departure.

"Milo!"

Her voice lured me from my thoughts. The droplets of

water and steam from the shower restricted my view. Though I could hear her, I could only see bits and piece of her figure through the glass.

"Yeah?"

"I can't find the keys. I'm trying to get home, but the car won't start without them inside. Do you have them?"

I stepped out of the shower, wiping the water from my face with a swipe of the hand. Nature turned slightly to give me the privacy I hadn't requested and shield her eyes from the rigidness between my legs.

"Sounds like a personal problem to me, Nay."

Covering her eyes, she turned around to me and blew out a stream of air.

"Seriously? You have them, don't you?"

"You covering your eyes like you ain't never seen this motherfucker, like it wasn't all up in your guts just eight months ago. Not once, not twice, but three rounds to make sure we made that handsome boy in your womb."

"Milo. The keys!" she yelled.

"If you find them, then you can go home," I informed her with a shrug. "If not, then I suggest you pick a fucking shirt out of the closet and a pair of boxers to sleep in."

"You can't be serious right now."

"I'm dead serious."

"You and I both know that if you've hidden the keys, I'll never find them."

"That's the point."

"Can you put on some fucking clothes?" She grimaced, finally removing her hand from her eyes. "This is considered kidnapping. I just want you to know that."

"You ain't a fucking kid, Nay, and neither am I."

Frustrated with my ability to break down those walls she loved building, Nature snatched my towel, shirt, and boxers.

"*You* pick out a shirt and pair of boxers to sleep in," she fussed, taking off.

My lips curved upward, revealing a smile that reached my eyes and forehead. Nature was such a great performer, but when the act was over, I knew her true desires. They aligned with mine. She was as desperate to be in my world as I was to be in hers. She just had some shit to work through. And after I finished working that sweet pussy of hers well into the wee hours of the morning, I was hoping she'd put her pride and fear aside to give us a chance.

With a simple nod, I clasped my hands together, quietly celebrating the small victory. Nature sleeping over wasn't exactly what I'd awakened with on my mind, but the improvement on my night was appreciated. Her presence had me ready to skip around my crib without a care in the entire world.

Within twenty minutes, my body and skin were hydrated. I'd tossed back two bottles of water and slathered the shea butter all over my body in preparation for my night's rest, assuming that I'd get any. Boxers and a white tee covered my body as I strolled down the hallway, opening the door to each room in my home in search of Nature.

Not here.

Not there.

Not here?

Not in here?

No—

The sound of the running water stopped me in my

tracks. I'd found her in the room furthest from mine. Her level of dramatics was comical. I pushed through the bedroom, into the bathroom where I found her emerging from the shower. She looked up, recognizing me as I slid onto the counter.

"Go!" She pointed toward the door.

"No," I stated, getting comfortable.

"Milo, what is it?"

"Nothing. I'm just here to assist, in case you need any help."

"I think I can manage on my own. I've only being doing so for my entire life now," she sassed.

"Well, now, I'm here to help."

She disregarded my statement, pulling the towel around her body. Casually, I leaned forward and unknotted the thick cloth. Her breast made my dick swell in my boxers but they weren't exactly what I was looking for. It was the round, protruding belly that I loved most for now. When it disappeared, I'd miss it tremendously.

I palmed each side, utterly obsessed with the feeling of her skin beneath mine and our son's underneath hers. It was surreal, even under the circumstances, it was everything to me. So many times, I'd imagined moments like this one, where nothing else mattered but us.

"Thank you."

"Thank you," she responded.

Neither of us had to explain why we were giving thanks. For the life we were creating, it was only right that I showed my appreciation to the woman that was making it possible. Without her, I'd never experience fatherhood and I'd never have the son I'd dreamed of many nights. Watching her belly grow was a pleasure of mine.

"I know shit is not what either of us wished and hoped for right now, but regardless of our situation, I need you to understand that our son is and will forever be alright. He'll forever be my priority. The rest, we can figure out when the time comes. But Mason, you won't ever have to question where I stand with him. He'll always top every list in my life."

"I know, Milo."

Slowly, I re-wrapped her towel and slid down from the counter. I opened the door and exited the bathroom, leaving her alone to handle whatever necessary for her to feel comfortable at my place. Her comfort was a requirement for the night and any other time she visited my residence. As far as I was concerned, it was hers, too, regardless of what she'd witnessed the other night.

While waiting for her to emerge from the steamy room, I removed the decorative pillows from the bed, tossing them over to the other side of the room. I pulled the covers back and rested my ass on the fitted sheet. I scrolled my phone, checking the emails I'd received throughout the evening with intentions to respond during office hours on Monday.

"You're still here?" She groaned, leaving the bathroom moments later.

"Come lay your ass down, Nature. All this fucking protesting. You're wasting your breath!"

Shaking her head from one side to the other, she made her way through the room. I observed with pure adoration as she strutted in my briefs, which hugged her curves and stretched to accommodate portions of the body that they weren't catered to or designed for. The white shirt barely covered her belly.

"You cute." I chuckled, making myself comfortable in bed as she got in beside me.

"Shut up," she demanded, pulling the comforter up and over us both.

"Especially when you're mad."

"I'm not mad, Milo."

"Then bring your ass here, then," I requested, pulling her back into my chest.

When her ass brushed against my rigidness, her body stiffened.

"See, no. Go back to your ro—"

"Shut the fuck up, Nature," I gritted.

Sliding my hand up her body, I wrapped my fingers around her neck and squeezed.

"And take these off."

I pulled at the waistband of my briefs with the other hand. Relaxing against my frame, she began to release the tension that she'd used to border her sanity and her heart.

SIX

Nature

"WHERE YOU WANT THIS MOTHERFUCKER?" he questioned, tapping his massiveness against my pussy.

My body jerked every time it crashed against my sensitivity. I was slippery wet from the tongue down he'd just administered, forcing me to climb the mountain and crash into the body of waves that my ocean created. Now, I wanted nothing more than to feel him inside of me, making us one, again, even if only for a moment.

"Inside of me," I murmured.

"Speak up, Nay. Stop fucking with me," he breathed, desperation stitched into each word that fell from his big, wet lips. My secretions shined the hair on his face. I couldn't bear the thought of the distance between us. I reached forward and pulled Milo into me until his lips rested against mine.

"Inside of me," I repeated, "Inside of me."

After the words left my mouth, I cleaned my remnants from his face with my tongue and ended my task with our lips locking and us exploring each other's mouths.

"Ummmmmmmmm," I shrieked as Milo split me in half, parting my sea to make room for his hard, increasingly addictive shaft.

My hold on him tightened. For once, I didn't want to ever let go. Not now. Not ever.

This is my person. The tears blurred my vision as I began weeping into his mouth. Pulling away, he continued to stroke my pussy like the perfectionist he was. He swiped the tears from my face as he stared down at me, exposing his vulnerability to let me know that I wasn't alone. Realizing his efforts were in vain and the tears wouldn't stop falling, he used his hands in other places. His thump caressed my clit as he continued to slide in and out of me, gliding with ease.

"Mi—ummmm... Milo... uhhhhh."

"Just say the fucking word, Nature, and I'm yours to have. Always have been. That'll never change. Just say the word. Just say—fuck, this shit makes no fucking sense. Shit, girl."

"I'm going to cum. I'm going to cum!" I screamed. "Oh my God."

Before the fireworks erupted below, the pleasure of the moment disappeared. Unplugging himself, Milo swiftly flipped me over, pushing my legs up until my ass was in the air and he had unrestricted access to my entire pussy. And without hesitation, he began to feast.

His tongue slid from my asshole, ending at my pearl. Situating himself right on my most sensitive spot, he sucked my clit like a fresh mango that had fallen from a sun-soaked tree. His breath tickled my flesh, intensifying my climb. Adding another level of gratification to his pleasurable assault, he circled my asshole with his thumb, lubricating it before sliding it inside. I clenched my muscles before releasing everything that was left inside of me.

"Oh God! I'm cumming!"

Milo maintained his position, continuing to ravish my backside as creamy, white fluid shot from my well and into his mouth. Once emptied, I began quivering at every swipe of his tongue. I tried falling forward to reduce the amount of pleasure my body was experiencing, but I wasn't allowed.

Milo held me in place, simultaneously freeing my flesh from his hold. The breath that I was holding, I pushed out and tried my hardest to settle the tingling in my lower abdomen area. It was pointless. Before the mission was complete or the sensation subsided, Milo slid back into me. I leaned forward, desperate to escape his expertise. He was way too good at this. He knew my body way too good. His dick was way too good.

WHAM!

His palm slammed against my ass.

"Don't run from this dick, Nay. Be a big girl. Take this motherfucker."

"Milo," I cried out, lifting my body.

"Hands on the bed," he reminded me, still stroking me

slowly. "Hands on the fucking bed, Nay. Throw this little motherfucker back."

Mustering the strength, I placed both hands on the sheets, clenching them as Milo wrote a beautiful love song on my walls. Once I adjusted to his girth, I matched his intensity. I pushed backward, into Milo, accepting every inch he was offering. The sound of our bodies colliding was music to my ears.

His hand gripped the back of my neck as he tried to fit his soul into my canal. I continued to cream on his dick, producing more lubrication for ease of access. Together, our moans and groans served as ad-libs to our track. And when I assumed that there was no greater feeling than the one I was experiencing, Milo lifted my body, rounding my neck with his hands. His lips tickled my ear.

"I love you," he confessed. "Like, really fucking love you, Nay."

Tears welled in my eyes from the mounting pleasure and the words that he spoke with such sincerity.

I love you more. The words were at the tip of my tongue.

"I'm cummmmmmmmmmm—uhhhhh," I belted, instead.

Together, we climaxed. Everything around me blackened. I fell forward, but somehow, I ended up on my side, curled in a ball as my son flipped and turned in my stomach. With my lids sealed, I began to doze as I heard running water. Seconds later, the warmth of a wash rag jarred me awake. I allowed Milo to clean every part of me his tongue and dick had been.

When his chest finally rested against my back, an indescribable degree of peace swept over me, putting me right to sleep.

Milo · Nature

SEVEN DAYS and six nights had passed since I'd crashed at Milo's place, but every day, like clockwork, he called me around lunch hour. Twice, he'd made the trip to bring me lunch. Though I only saw him for a few minutes because neither of our schedules permitted much downtime, they were an eventful few minutes that once resulted in the steamy office session that the movies didn't quite get right.

The fresh air hit my face as I stepped outside of the doctor's office. The weekly appointments were going to be challenging because I had so many mothers at the end of their pregnancies as well, but I'd be sure to make time for each one I scheduled. For my son, everything stopped.

The calendar alert on my phone reminded me that I'd be seeing Milo outside of the office today. Our meet ups were changing along with my doctor's appointments. As the notification bar disappeared, a message immediately followed. **Mason's Father** appeared on the screen with a text following it.

Scratch the meetup. I'm coming over tonight. You can tell me all about the appointment then.

I prefer the meetup, I responded, knowing exactly what Milo had on my mind. However, waiting that long wasn't in my plans. I wanted dick now, not later.

So. I'll see you tonight.

I'll see you in a few minutes, I almost responded, but shut the phone down and climbed into my truck. Within minutes, I was being handed two white bags full of my favorites from Jet's Chicken. An order of buffalo wings, seasoned fries, and Kool-Aid to drink would satisfy my unhealthy cravings for the day.

For Milo, on the other hand, I'd settled for BBQ wings, seasoned fries, and water. It wasn't that I cared much about his preference, but because I wanted BBQ wings as well without ordering my own portion and looking bigger than I already was. But I had every intention of eating his, too.

Nervousness kept me planted to my seat as I recalled the last time I'd gone out on a limb and showed up unannounced. I quickly shook those thoughts, determined to push forward and lean into the space that Milo and I were in. It was a good one and much better than any space we'd shared in such a long time.

He's come up to my office twice this week, I reasoned, stepping out and locking up behind me. With both bags in my hand, I entered through the automatic doors and made my way to the elevator. As the doors shut, it felt like my throat followed suit. I inhaled deeply and exhaled seconds later in an attempt to regulate my breathing. By the time the doors opened on Milo's floor, I'd regained control.

Stepping into the well-lit space with my head high, chest in the air, stomach growling, and my center throbbing, I scanned it for any signs of the man that my cravings included. There were none. Even the receptionist area was empty. The small bell on the counter, I tapped, waiting for assistance. After two minutes of waiting, shifting my weight, and unraveling internally, I realized no one would be coming.

I, then, resulted to scrambling through my purse to

retrieve my phone, which required setting our food down. However, there was nowhere for it to go other than on the desk in front of me. Reluctantly, I set it all down and retrieved my phone. I dialed Milo's cell number. As it began to ring, voices surfaced, capturing my attention.

"Hmmm," an unfamiliar, feminine voice hummed. "I don't think I could've asked for a better, bigger boss."

"You're out of control, Christina. Make that the las—"

"You said that the last time."

"I mean it this time. Make that the last time yo—"

They rounded the corner one after the other. Christina, who looked awfully familiar, cleaned the corners of her mouth and straightened her face as I came into clear view.

"Oh, sor—Hello," she stammered. "How can I help you?"

Words completely failed me, leaving me soundless as I realized why Christina looked so familiar. She was the same woman I'd encountered at Milo's home.

"Natur—"

"Don't. Don't do that," I interjected. "I jus... I just wanted to return the favor and uh, and bring you lunch."

And hug you and kiss you and fuck you, but someone else has already handled that.

I cringed at the sound of the voice in my head. The fact that I kept making a fool of myself, and in front of the same woman, made my stomach turn. And the fact that Milo, once again, was having relations with someone this close to him, whom he worked with, left me baffled. Pulling myself up from the floor by my imaginary boot straps, I turned, leaving my food and his, and headed out toward the elevator.

As if it heard the shattering of my heart again, it arrived almost immediately after I pressed the button. Milo's lack of assertion confirmed everything I needed to know. I made it out of the building and into my truck before the emotions hit me at once. As fast as my fingers would allow, I found Shayla's name and tapped the call button.

"Hey, babe. What's up?"

"Are you busy?" I cried, exiting the parking lot.

"I can get unbusy for you. What is it?"

"Can you meet me somewhere?"

"I wish I could, Nature, but the most I can do right now is hold this phone."

"I understand. Sorry for calling in the middle of your day."

"What's the matter?"

"He's doing it again. It's like it's happening all over again."

"What?"

"It's his assistant."

"What about his assistant?"

"The person he's sleeping with. The girl I saw at his house. It's his assistant. This feels like college all over again."

"You're lying, friend."

"I'm not. He's been bringing me lunch this week. I just left my appointment and decided to bring him lunch today. Just returning the gesture. I get to the office and no one is at the front desk. I ring the bell, still nothing. I put my things down to call Milo, though I didn't want to ruin the surprise.

"He'd canceled our meetup with plans to come over to my house tonight. I was under the impression that I'd end my night, undressed, and trying to come down from an orgasm. I guess that wasn't the message he intended to send. I'm literally throbbing in the coochie, Shayla.

"I'm trying to cut our wait time down so we could both have a good day, but I see them two coming from the back. She's wiping her mouth and he's telling her that it's the very last time. She's going on about him saying that last time and just... Ugh."

"Did they see you?"

"Yes!"

"And said what?"

My phone vibrated in my hand. I quickly opened the message that was from Milo.

Meet me somewhere. Anywhere. Name the place and I'm pulling up.

Ignoring it, I placed the phone to my ear again.

"Nothing. There was nothing to say. I left both our lunches. I'm hungry!"

Chuckling, Shayla apologized. "I'm so sorry for laughing, but the way you just screamed you're hungry, friend. Do you need me to send you some food? You need to go home."

"I'm not going home. He'll come looking for me. I know he will."

"Then you guys can talk."

"Right now, today even, is not the time. It's not. I will talk to him, eventually, but that day won't be today."

"I understand. My question is, are you venting to me, or are you requesting a response from me?"

"Both."

"Alright," she said, clearing her throat.

The therapist in her was working overtime, collecting thoughts to help shed light on my situation.

"Well, Nature, you're in for a fight. There's no other way to put it. The day that you wanted to make your plans and intentions clear, it turned out to be a disaster. Nevertheless, love, desire, desperation, and forgiveness prevailed. You accepted Milo back into your world. And though you tried to readjust those boundaries, you failed. Miserably. Which led to family dinner and sex, which ultimately uprooted those feelings for him you've been trying to bury.

"The truth is, when it comes to Milo, you're either all in or not in at all. You go from zero to one hundred. There's no in between. Milo, on the other hand, goes from zero to one. Your scales aren't balanced. Do you fault him? No. Because, at the end of the day, you've yet to admit to him that you're expecting more of you guys. Why? Because you're afraid of shit like this happening.

"But I'm here to tell you, as long as you keep running or putting one foot in, it'll keep happening. Milo isn't going to put all his eggs in your basket until he sees that you're ready to empty yours in his. All of them, Nature. Should you be upset right now? Yes. You should. You guys were progressing, or so you believed, but that wasn't exactly clear on either of you guy's ends. No one has declared anything, which leaves room for continued exploration.

"Should he have gotten the memo by now and deaded his ways, I'd say so, but that comes from a place of love for you. It's a biased opinion. But unbiased, he isn't exactly wrong. I know you're triggered and this feels like college again, but you can't run this time, Nature. You have to step into this thing head first.

"Take the time you'll need to get yourself together, but Mason is coming, and for now, you have to put you and Milo's shit aside to bring him into this world a happy, healthy, and joyful boy. You've been focusing on that your entire pregnancy. Get back to that. At this point, and I'm saying this as your friend, fuck Milo, baby girl.

"Get your head in the game in preparation for your son's birth. The last few weeks have been nothing but tears, upsets, and uncertainties. Let it go, even if only for a few months. Revisit it once you're well physically, mentally, and emotionally."

Sighing, I agreed. "Thank you, Shayla."

"Always. I hate to rush you off the phone but I'm headed into my next session. I'll call you this evening. I can stop by if you'd like."

"It's fine. I'm headed to my parents' house. I just need some time to think about this entire situation. I'll call you when I'm feeling better."

"Alright. I'm sending food."

"No. I'm almost certain my mother has made lunch."

"Alright."

Ending the call, I continued the route toward my parents' home. My thoughts consumed me, overwhelming me to the point of no return. With my index finger and thumb, I tapped the steering wheel, chewing on my bottom lip while simultaneously being cautious of the other drivers in my path.

Somehow, the journey seemed to double in length. When I finally arrived, the black Mercedes in the driveway startled me. Though the vehicle was familiar and I knew exactly who was driving it, its presence was still surprising. I mustered as much strength as possible, swiped away the tears that had fallen, and exited my truck. With my tote in hand, I tackled the walkway to reach the stairs. As I entered my door key, the door was pulled open from the other side.

Expecting to see my mother, I sighed, prepared to fall into her warm embrace. However, I was confronted with my father's figure. His long, lean body stepped forward in my direction, forcing me to swallow the lump in my throat and attempt to collect myself. Nevertheless, my emotions prevailed. Not only for Milo, but for the moment. He continued forward until he'd passed me, turning back briefly to acknowledge me.

"Nature," he spoke.

Looking over my shoulder, I tittered, "Dad."

"Good to see you. Headed back to the hospital."

Yet, your daughter is home with a face full of tears and growing belly that you've yet to acknowledge. Can't the hospital wait? The words never surfaced. Instead, I watched as he took the small set of stairs, made his way to the driveway, and slid into his car moments later.

Good evening, baby.

What's the matter?

What's with the tears?

How many more weeks do we have before my grandson is here?

Looks like we're getting ready to welcome Mason soon.

Are you okay?

How can I help?

Is there anything I can do?

How about we go get ice cream, Nature? Will that make it better?

Would you like to talk about it?

The plethora of remarks and questions that could've come from my father played in my head as I removed my key from the door and stepped into the house. I found my mother in the kitchen, plating sandwiches that I'm certain my father was too busy to grab on his way back to work. At the sight of me, her movements halted.

"Nature. Is everything okay?" she questioned with worry lines across her pretty face.

"I will be, Mom. Can I have one of those or two?" I pointed, referring to the sandwiches in her hand.

"Did you see your father?"

"As I always do. The question is does my father see me."

"Oh, Nature, baby. Please cut him som—"

"Slack. I have, Mom. All of my life. At this point, let's just be honest and call it what it is."

"I'm sorry you feel this way."

"Be sorry he treats me this way, not my feelings as the consequences."

"Okay. I'm sorry that he's the way that he is, Nature. But I don't want to focus on him right now. I want to know why there are tears on my daughter's face."

I wiped the fresh ones, trying to clear my face completely. More fell. Slowly, uncontrollably.

"I just... I just need some rest, Mom. I had a shi—bad day."

"Is everything okay with Mason?"

"Yes. Mason is fine. It's Milo."

"Oh, God. What's happened to Milo?"

"He's screwing his assistant. That's what's happened."

"And you found out today?"

"Yes."

"Well, Nature," she sighed heavily. "I wish I had the right words or more comforting words but I don't at this time. I think co-parenting Mason with Milo was a brilliant idea. I couldn't imagine a better co-parent, honestly speaking. However, you have to decide whether you only want to be co-parents or you want to be more.

"From the look of things, you both want something more but you're clueless as to navigating that territory so you're tiptoeing around, stepping on traps in the process. It hurts, every time you step on another one. But if you two sat down and cleared the air completely, you could both clean the grounds so that you can frolic freely without the risk of stepping into another trap, causing more hurt, more pain."

"Every time I think our time has come and we're taking steps forward, something knocks us ten steps backward. As of today, this moment, I'm ready to co-parent with Milo. I want to leave the rest of it alone. I'm the only one hurting in the end, every single time. It's time to let go of the possibilities, time to stop hoping and wishing, and focus on birthing a healthy baby boy."

"I agree. Everything will fall into place just as it should. You have to understand that when the universe is ready for alignment, it will happen. No matter how much you want it, how much you crave it, how much you pray for it, how much your train for it, how much you cry for it, or how much you think about it, if it's not time then it's not time."

Nodding, I silently agreed with my mother.

"Here. Take two of these and get my grandson good and full. It'll help you rest better. A full belly and empty tear ducts is a recipe for great rest."

"Thank you, Mom."

"Always, Nature. Always."

Even in her fifties, my mother was youthful, mentally, physically, and spiritually. Her beauty hadn't fled with age. It evolved. She didn't look a day over thirty-eight. I could only pray that I'd maintain her level of excellence after climbing the hill.

Milo · Nature

BZZZ.

Beep.

Beep.

BZZZ.

Beep.

Beep.

BZZZ.

Beep.

Beep.

I rubbed the exhaustion from my eyes as I tried deciphering if the sound of my pager was part of my dream or a source of reality. The green light that glowed in the darkness the blackout curtains provided confirmed my suspicions. This wasn't a dream and someone needed me.

Leaning over, I removed the cordless phone from the charger and dialed the number that I knew better than I did my own. Immediately, the phone was answered.

"Mona speaking."

"It's Dr. Dupree. What do I have, Mona? And who is it?"

"It's Drea Ignes. She's seven point five centimeters and will be pushing really soon. Will you be able to make it in, Doc, or should I get the doctor OB on duty tonight?"

"No. Tell her to hold that baby until I get there. I'll see her in twenty-five minutes or less."

"See you then, Doctor."

As quickly as my body and bones would allow, I got myself together. Sitting at the edge of the bed, I slid into my sandals and stood to my feet. My phone chimed in the distance, pinging its location without me having to search. Though I was slightly relieved, I dreaded what was waiting for me when I picked it up. Messages from Milo littered the screen. I unlocked the phone and tapped the message box to access the damage.

Nay.

Nature.

Where you at?

I'm pulling up to your crib, open the door.

Nay, real shit, where are you?

Answer the phone.

I'll be here when you get here.

An image of my bedroom followed the last text. Questioning how Milo had gotten into my home or why he felt it was anything more than chaotic for him to invade my space the way he had was pointless, so I didn't bother. I shut the phone off and wobbled across the room, headed to the place that brought me unspeakable peace and content-ment. I loved every aspect of my career and it was possibly the reason I was devastated to take a leave of absence and reluctant to stop working even in the late stage of my pregnancy.

"Hey, baby," my mother greeted me when I reached the living room.

"What time is it?"

I realized I had no earthly idea what was happening around me, what time of day it was, or how long I'd slept.

"It's a little after six. You're headed out?"

"Yes. One of my patients is in labor."

"Nature, baby, when will you go on leave?"

"When the baby comes. Until then, Mom, I have to keep doing what I love because when he gets here, everything will stop to make sure that I'm present."

With a simple nod, she continued to gaze in my direction.

"Fair enough."

There was so much more than words intertwined in that statement and we both knew it. Instead of either of us dwelling, I exited the house and walked the short distance to my vehicle. Before pulling off into the evening, I adjusted my stereo volume, ready to hear the instrumentals of the jazz record because I had no desire to hear words from a track.

When the music halted, my eyes scanned the screen of my dash, expecting to see Milo's contact. My body stiffened as I pinched my lips together, deciding that I wasn't yet ready to hear his voice or ease his frustrations because I had some of my own. However, the realization that it wasn't him calling replenished my fluidness.

"Hello," I answered after tapping the necessary button.

"What's good?" Zane responded. I could hear the smile in his voice and the cheerfulness in his tone.

"Nothing. As much as I'd love to chat, I'm racing against the clock to get to my patient. I'd love to call you back another time."

"Sounds like a plan. Hit me whenever your schedule is free."

"Okay."

That was easier said than done. I would be working until Mason's head sprouted from my vagina and immediately after, I'd be in full-blown, new mommy mode. Communication through messages was still the best form of contact for me until further notice. There was far too much going on in my world, and the fact that Zane appeared almost every time the reality of my situation slapped me across the face made me wonder if he had telepathic abilities.

"Talk to you soon."

"Goodbye."

I ended the call, keeping my eyes forward and on the road, determined not to allow the chaos in my world to cloud my judgment and hinder my progress. A woman needed me and even more than she could imagine, I needed her as well.

SEVEN

Milo

MY DESTINATION WAS SET, but I'd be damned if I didn't contemplate stopping by the liquor store and turning a bottle up. Warm. No ice. No cup. Turn that bitch right up because this shit with Nature had me out of my body, out of my head. Two days of no communication left me feeling as empty inside as that day she left my dorm room.

Then, I felt like a fucking fool and now I felt like an even bigger fool. Not once, but twice, Christina and Nature had crossed paths. I understood her position. That shit would send me up in flames, too, if the roles were reversed. There was little I could do to fix the damage that had been done. My only option was moving forward. The first step in that direction was keeping my word and keeping my dick out of Christina's mouth.

As the five o'clock hour approached, the palms of my hand began to perspire. My nervous system wasn't in overdrive because I was afraid to face Nature. I wanted to. I had to. I owed her a thousand apologies.

It was the hurt on her beautiful face that I was afraid to see. It was the pain in her silky voice that I was afraid to hear. It was the disappointment in her beautiful brown eyes that I was afraid to witness. It was the defeat in her posture that I was afraid to encounter.

With a shake of the head, I rubbed my hands down my pants to dry them. The fabric of my jeans soaked the moisture up immediately.

Leaning against Nature's ride, I scrolled my phone. As if queued, I landed on Malachi's number. My finger hovered over the contact listing, contemplating the call. If there was anyone that could give me sound advice when it came to a woman, one that you loved wholeheartedly, it was him. I brushed a finger over the contact, deciding to put the call through regardless of my hesitation.

"Yeah?"

"When I call, greet me better than that, nigga."

"Or, I could hang this bitch up, Milo."

"Don't do that. I'd hate to have to pull up and show my ass in front of Aussie."

"You won't make it up the driveway for her to see you."

"Is that a threat?"

"It's a promise. I stand on that."

"Nigga swear he a fucking gangster."

"I've never stated that."

"It's insinuated."

"It's understood, nigga, now what's up?"

Blowing out a stream of air, I prepared to tell him the details of the last forty-eight hours of my life. I scratched the back of my head, trying to figure out where to start.

"She won't keep waiting for you to get it right, Milo."

"I haven't ev—"

"You don't have to, Lil Bro. I can hear it in the sound of your voice. The deflection at the beginning of the call was a dead giveaway, too."

"I might've fucked up, again," I explained.

"How?"

"Christina, man."

"Who is Christina? You know what? It doesn't matter."

"It does, though. It does."

"Why?"

"Because she was the same chick Nature saw at my crib. I didn't let her know the business then, but I should've. Nature brought lunch to the office Friday. Christina is my assistant and the receptionist. She was unable to greet Nature when she came in because she was burying my seeds down her throat. It was the last time, though. Without a doubt, that was going to be the last fucking time, bro. We walked to the front, bumping right into Nature as I told her so."

The dramatic whistling from the other end of the line made my stomach knot.

"Chill, nigga, it's not that bad."

His silence was followed by, "If you didn't think it was bad, then you wouldn't be on my line."

He was right.

"My head is all over the place, man. I'm just trying to center myself."

"How bad do you want this thing with Nature, Milo?"

"Man, for real, for real. As much as I do the next breath of air."

"You're my brother, I love you, and I'll always keep shit one hundred with you."

"I know."

"You don't want it bad enough."

"What you mean?"

"Your heart does but you're so programmed to disconnect mentally from a situation to avoid some shit that you don't understand or can't change, due to a past that is not at all your fault, that you don't recognize your self-sabotaging actions.

"Just like you were all those years ago when you called me from campus, face full of tears, admitting that you'd reached a point of no return with Nature and couldn't fathom loving her beyond that point because it would be the death of you both, you're terrified.

"That fear led you to sabotage a relationship and lose a woman that birthed a love so fucking profound in you that you'd never be able to recover from it. Never, bro. She planted something within you that can only survive by constant watering. Not from just anyone, but from her. That hasn't changed.

"She's your solution to a fruitful life but you're so fucking scared, bro. You're so scared that one day you'll become the person you've been studying since a teenager. You're not her, Milo. You'll never be her. And if you ever fell sick like her, your fate doesn't have to be hers. You can let go of that.

"Listen to me, bro. Let that shit go. I'm giving you permission. I'm begging you. Let it go. If you don't, you'll wake up in old age with your mind intact, wishing you'd lost your shit because it would make your loneliness make sense. Make it feel a little less pointless. I've felt that fear. It stiffens you. It paralyzes you. I thought the greatest part of my existence left me, giving me no reason to continue life.

"But then, Aeir picked my shit up and turned it all the way around. That's the power of love. That's the power of a woman. A woman is the strongest creature ever produced. Nothing tops that creation. God did His big shit, bro. Aeir came in, rummaged through the debris and helped me locate parts of me I'd long ago forgotten. She lifted me. She lit me, refusing to leave me in the darkness. She healed me.

"There isn't a person on this planet I think is capable of what my wife is capable of. She carries the weight, graciously. The magnitude of her influence in my world is just... unimaginable, Milo. I run to her. I cling to her. She is my altar. There's nothing she can't handle when it comes to me. Her strength is intangible.

"I'll never be able to duplicate it. The thing is, she's not the only woman with those strengths. Nature, I wholeheartedly believe is capable of loving your stupid ass right through that fear if you'd just give it to her, holding nothing back. She's your altar, Milo.

"Stop running from the inevitable, nigga. Lock it in and make me your best man. I look better in suits than them other niggas." He chuckled to lighten the load he'd just laid on me.

"Uh hmm."

Preoccupied, I hadn't noticed Nature approaching. She was as pretty as the last time I'd seen her. The dress she wore had her belly on full display. Without a doubt, I knew that our son wouldn't last another two weeks inside the womb. He was ready, and by the look on Nature's face, she was ready as well.

"Malachi, I'll hit you back in a few."

"Tell Nature I said hello."

"How'd you ev—"

"Tell her I said hello."

"Malachi says hello."

"Hello, Malachi."

"Alright, big bro. Love."

"One."

I ended the call, still leaning against the hood of Nature's ride.

"Hi."

The gloom in her eyes never wavered.

"Hello, Milo."

"I feel like I owe you some explanation."

"As to why you're on the parking lot of my office and why you sent me images from my bedroom, though you don't have a key to my home?"

Shaking my head, I responded, "Nah. Not that. I got the door fixed. Don't sweat it."

"The door?"

"Yeah. But that's not why I'm here, Nay."

"Then why are you here?"

"To explain myself."

"Though I'm listening, I don't think it's necessary.

Admittedly, I've been unclear with my intentions and expectations of you. But today, I'm clarifying things and letting you know that I expect nothing from you from this point moving forward. If it doesn't involve our son, it doesn't concern me. We're adults and the games that are being played right now, it's time to dead them."

"No games are being played."

"It sure as hell feels like it."

"I know. But misunderstandings and lack of proper communication feels the same too. I'm a grown ass man and you're a grown ass woman with a thriving career. Neither of us even have time for games. We're just... not aligned at the moment. Our balance is off."

"I've attempted to communicate."

"And shit didn't go as planned."

"And then I tried again."

"And shit didn't go as planned."

"It didn't, which translates as stop trying. Stop trying to give life to a situation that is dead. It doesn't matter how much history, how much love, or how much I'm yearning for something more. It just isn't working."

Almost naturally, I nodded, agreeing with everything she was saying. As much as I wanted to counter her statement, I had nothing to support my claims.

"I'm tired, Milo. Every time I stick my neck out there, it gets my heart in trouble. I can't pretend like I'm okay with any of this. I'm not. I wanted this. I wanted you. But I want me more. A healthy me. A better me. I don't think that's possible right now."

"I'm sorry."

"Changed behavior, Milo, that would've been an apology. This isn't."

"Regardless, I'm sorry this shit is happening, Nay."

"And with your receptionist," she grimaced. "It's déjà vu."

Crushed at the comparison, I stumbled with a rebuttal.

"I— It—"

I hadn't considered how similar the situations were. Speechless, I simply stared at her beautiful face, knowing deep down inside, I'd reached the point of doom with Nature. I tugged at the back of my neck, lowering my head as I tried to find the right words. Nothing suited the moment.

"Let's agree to just focus on what's most important here and it's neither you nor me. It's our son."

Nodding, I agreed.

"Thanks."

"Have you eaten?"

"I haven't."

"Can we discuss your last appointment over a bite to eat?"

"As much as I'd love to, Milo, I just want to go home and lay down in my own bed. I've been at my mother's place, being ignored by my father for three too many days."

"Damn," I fussed. "Why didn't I think to ch—"

"Milo."

"I'm just thinking out loud."

"Maybe tomorrow."

"Tomorrow will come and we'll be having the same exchange. You're still processing shit and sitting down with me, pretending that we're not feuding isn't on your list of things to do this week an—"

"Or next."

"Or next, and I understand. A text after your appointments will suffice."

"Thanks for understanding."

"That won't stop me from taking care of you in the final weeks of our pregnancy. Go home and relax. I'll make sure you have food this evening. By noon tomorrow, expect to hear from the person that will be taking care of your meals from now until you feel better after the baby. Aight?"

"Alright."

Her willingness to compromise her independence to allow me to be present for her validated a lot of things for me. She was at the end of her road and our son was about to take his first breath earth side. The thought of his entrance and how much my world would be changing had my heart tap dancing in my chest.

"Friends?" I asked, extending my hand.

Smirking, Nature took my hand into hers. "Almost friends."

"Damn. Real shit?"

"Milo, in no shape, form, or fashion am I okay right now. But I'd rather not fuss and fight."

I'd rather fuck than fight, I thought.

"Understood. Future friends."

"Future friends."

I eased off her truck, moving out of her way, but not before palming her round belly.

"See you in a few. Open the door for a nigga. I don't mind getting that motherfucker fixed again if I have to."

"You're insufferable. Truly."

Shrugging, I jogged toward my car. As I slid in, I instantly remembered the appointment I had at the dealership Thursday. If I found anything on the lot suitable, I wouldn't be the only one in a new whip by the time I left.

Milo · Nature

I PILED the groceries onto the porch, right in front of the door. As I lifted my knuckles to knock, it crept open. I retrieved the bags and stepped inside, finally getting a glimpse of the woman of the hour. I offered her the bag from my right hand. Without a word, she closed her eyes and expanded her nostrils to inhale the smell of the wings I'd provided to replace those that she'd left at my office.

"Ummmmm."

Upturned lips and prominent cheeks stretched my face beyond recognition. Deflecting in an attempt not to get so lost on the woman before me, I headed for the kitchen where I began putting away the items I'd bought to stock Nature's fridge.

Pineapples. Strawberries. Sliced honey-roasted turkey. Orange juice. Apple juice. And a plethora of things that would make her mornings a bit smoother as she made her way out of the door. Upon finishing, I tossed the empty bags in the trash and carried the last one into the living room with me, where I found Nature engrossed in television while cleaning the meat from the bones of her chicken wings.

Her legs stretched across the empty space, resting on the table. The swelling I'd suspected was now in plain view, making the items in my bag feel a bit more useful that I'd initially imagined. Sneakers concealed the condition of her feet, but from a quick glance at her ankles as we stood outside of her office, I had an idea of what was inside of them.

In an instant, her feet were in my hands and the moisturizer I'd pulled from the bag coated them both.

"What are you doing?"

Her mouth was stuffed with something other than my dick, drawing jealousy from my frame that I casually concealed.

"Eat, Nay."

"The fact that you have my feet between your fingers makes that a bit challenging."

"Figure it out. You're a smart girl."

Shrugging, she dropped the conversation altogether and continued brutalizing the box that she had all to herself. The combination of flavors was beneficial. From the looks of it, she didn't have a favorite. She'd had at least one BBQ wing, one buffalo wing, one lemon pepper wing, and one sweet chili wing.

"How long have they been swollen?" I questioned, growing concerned with her condition. I applied pressure as I worked my way up and down them.

"Yesterday," she moaned.

"Maybe we should hit up Marcie."

"I've ran the tests, Milo. It's not preeclampsia. It's nothing more than the load I'm carrying, causing my frame to try its best to adjust. I'm fine. I promise."

"You sure, Nay?"

I pulled each of her toes until I heard them pop.

"Yes. I promise."

"Do they hurt?"

"No, but my back does," she admitted, setting the box on the table beside her.

She cleaned her fingers with one of the wet wipes provided.

"Lay on your side. A massage will help alleviate some of that pain."

I tried rising from the couch but was stopped in the process.

"Un, un. Stay right where you are. We don't want any confusion. Back massages lead to internal massages."

"What's wrong with that?" I chuckled, tilting my head.

"They lead to brain fog and a lot of confusion. Stay right there and keep going. That feels good."

"You petty for that shit, but aight."

Sniggering, she shrugged. "You can't blame anyone but yourself, Milo."

Nodding, I agreed. I was the reason I was in the doghouse where I'd remain until Nature decided to free me. Unfortunately, I'd done time in that motherfucker before and knew she was never in a rush to open those gates.

"I bought compression garments that will cover your feet and ankles."

"Thank you. I planned to stop by the store to grab some tomorrow."

"Now you don't have to."

"Now, I don't have to." She yawned. "I truly appreciate you."

She meant it. From the depths of me, I understood the

fact that her statement was much deeper than she was letting on.

Tired eyes batted the tearful display of exhaustion away.

"My God," she sighed, coming to terms with just how much she needed the rest that was waiting for her.

I removed her feet from my lap, this time managing to stand to my feet completely. The last thing I wanted was Nay to try to keep my company by staying awake longer than her body could tolerate. My departure was inevitable. Though I'd rather stay, we weren't in that space, not yet. We were back at square one. The thought stung momentarily, but subsided once I heard her call out to me.

"Milo."

"Yes, Nature?"

"Can you grab me a blanket?"

"I need you to lock up, Nay. I can grab you a blanket but you have to get up to lock the door."

"I can't," she whined with her eyes closed.

As the words left her mouth, she turned on her side, getting more comfortable on the couch. Seeing as though she had little interest in getting her ass up, I made my way to the basket where blankets were piled to the very top. I draped the blanket over her body before making my way out of the door.

As I stood on the porch, I began typing a message that simply didn't feel substantial enough. I quickly decided to make a call instead. Mercer picked up after the third ring. Silence coated the line. I could feel the heaviness of the load he bore, readjusting to life after his freedom was stripped away for so long. I saw the struggle in his eyes. I heard the struggle in his voice. And I understood the struggle even in his silence.

"I won't make it to dinner tonight, Merc," I explained, lowering my eyes to the ground as I brushed over my waves with my hand.

"Aight." His lack of emotion was directly rooted to his disconnection from the world.

Already, I regretted the decision to cancel. As much as Nature needed me tonight, so did my oldest brother. His mental health was in question. I'd never forgive myself if it overturned his ability to think properly and positively, resulting in something catastrophic.

"I'll be there," I rushed out.

"No you won't," he responded, seemingly unfazed. "Stay with her."

"How do you niggas know what the fuck I'm doing, who I'm with, and my plans without me even telling y'all?"

"Because, nigga. Nature is the only possible reason you'd flake on your family, so I know she's involved. I'm not sweating it. Get it right with her."

"I'm trying, man, but shit isn't looking too good right now."

"It always gets better, *eventually*," he emphasized.

"Eventually, huh?"

"Yeah."

"I love you, Merc. And I'm sorry, bro."

"You sound like a bitch, Milo."

Because he ended the call so swiftly, I was unable to respond.

Chucking up the abrupt end to our call, I headed inside Nature's place. She hadn't invited me to spend the night, but she hadn't exactly forbid it. Not that I gave a damn either way. My concerns were valid, and so was my presence. The swelling of her feet was still heavy on my mind and I wanted to keep an eye on her in case of an emergency.

Suddenly, she wasn't the only one that needed some shuteye. A yawn split my face in two, almost, and the thought of hitting the sack before the clock struck nine for once sounded like the move. Stepping inside, I found her sound asleep with her back toward the television she'd been watching.

Because it was impossible for us both to lie on the couch, and her comfort was my priority, I revisited the basket I'd retrieved her blanket from and grabbed a few of my own. I rearranged the living room slightly by pushing the table and accent chairs across the room to give me unrestricted access to the large rug underneath them. I spread the largest blanket out on the floor before placing the smaller of the two on top. Up the stairs, I ran to grab pillows from one of the guest rooms.

When I finally rested my back against the floor, with Nature in sight, relief consumed me. I'd switched off every light around us, leaving it dark and moody. The low lights from the late setting of the sun cast an orange hue over the sky that peeked through the blinds. The ambiance was a scene straight from a movie.

Gazing over the top of my phone as I opened the emails that had been sent to me in the last few hours, the revelation hit hard. There wasn't a place on earth where I'd rather be than with my son and his mother. Until we figured our shit out, I'd be sure to remind her every chance I got.

EIGHT

Nature

THE GUT-WRENCHING pain that soared through me, landing right at my center was to be mistaken for nothing other than contractions. I leaned over, feeling around in the darkness to locate the lamp switch. After finally producing light, I surveyed my surroundings, quickly analyzing the situation.

The wetness that puddled beneath me was evidence that my amniotic sac had ruptured, and my predictions were correct. Though I wasn't actively laboring the previous day, the random pains I felt every other hour, as well as the tenderness in my vagina were signs that my body was preparing itself for birth. I'd witnessed the process far too many times during my career as an OB.

I reached for my phone but found it extremely difficult to stretch the distance required. Another pain soared through me, causing my entire body to stiffen. I took long, deep breaths, clenching my butt cheeks until it finally subsided. There was no doubt in my mind that my son was coming and it wouldn't be long before he arrived. How I'd seemingly slept through the first half of my labor process was baffling but it also revealed the true strength of a woman in the hours of birth. Our bodies were incredible.

Managing to retrieve my phone, I dialed Milo's number. As the phone began to ring, I tossed the covers back and slid out of bed. I pressed it against my shoulder and began pulling the covers back. The leak-proof mattress pad I'd added proved to be beneficial. Upon snatching it off, I noticed there wasn't a drop of fluid in sight.

It wasn't until I heard Milo's voicemail that I realized I was still holding the phone up to my ear. I ended the call without leaving a message and redialed it. As I piled my linen in the corner of my bedroom, the phone continued to ring, eventually rolling over to voicemail again.

Frustration grew from the pit of my stomach. Another contraction claimed my mind and body as I leaned forward, fully expecting the wall to alleviate the weight that accompanied the contractions. If not physical, it was definitely a mental gain that I couldn't quite pinpoint. The heaviness was unfamiliar and it was anchoring.

My contractions were powerful and they were not very far apart. With my phone in my hand, I wobbled toward the room where I'd been preparing for Mason's birth.

Throughout the course of my pregnancy, I'd been seeing Marcie, but the chances of her delivering my child were always slim. My birth plan had been made early in my pregnancy and was tailored to a home birth, a method I'd admired since I was a teen. Witnessing my first home birth was the deciding factor for my career choice.

As motion was detected, the light of the bedroom glowed, lighting the entire space. The oversized tub in the bathroom was the reason I'd chosen this room in particular. On my way inside, I called Milo a third time. To my dismay, I was greeted by the voicemail again.

Are you fucking serious, Milo? I pondered.

Instead of continuing to dial his number in vain, I made a call to the next best person on my contact list. Shayla answered on the second ring, voice riddled with sleep.

"Hello. Nature. Are you okay?"

"Yes. The baby is coming and I can't get ahold of Milo."

"I'm on my way."

She ended the call, immediately. The key to my home that Shayla hadn't had the chance to use since I'd moved in would finally be put to use. By the time she arrived, I doubted I'd be able to manage the lengthy distance required to open the door.

Another contraction forced me down onto the edge of the bathtub where I gripped my knees, praying this one didn't last as long as the one before it. However, I understood that was simply asking too much. It didn't release me for almost a full forty-five seconds.

"Shiiiiiiiiiit."

Once I was finally able to move again, I started the water that I'd spend the next thirty minutes to an hour in.

With the intensity and closeness of my contractions, that was all the time I'd have to bring my son earth side. Warm water speckled my skin as it hit the bottom of the tub.

I opened the tab that displayed Shayla's location and discovered she was only five miles from my home. She'd be pulling up within the next ten minutes. Though it wasn't her support that I was banking on, it would suffice for the moment. Dwelling on Milo's absence would only make matters worse and possibly affect the trajectory of my son's birth. Our health wasn't worth the risk.

Contractions hit one after the other, giving me little time to regain my composure between them. The satisfaction of the water level prompted me to twist the nob until it halted the flow. I stripped out of my soiled gown and slid into the warm water, hoping for comfort. With the hair tie on my wrist, I pulled my curls into a ponytail and rested my head against the back of the tub.

Just as I closed my eyes, bracing for the build of the contraction that began, I heard Shayla's voice, calling out to me.

"I-I'm... in here." Weakly, I yelled.

However, I was aware that my efforts might've gone unnoticed. The low, wimpy voice I'd exercised probably hadn't made it past the guest bathroom where I was suffering through another vaginal-splitting contraction.

"Here you are."

Despite my assumptions, Shayla found me, immediately removing her slides and pinning her hair up. She wasted little time sanitizing her feet and legs before climbing into the tub and resting her bottom on the edge. Even through the pain, I couldn't hold back the laughter that was a result of her seriousness. One would think that she was the OB and I was the therapist.

"What?"

"Ouch," I groaned, unable to stop laughing.

"What? What's so funny, Nature?"

"I just... You look so serious. Please, lighten up."

"What do you mean, lighten up? A baby is coming!"

"A baby is coming, but the baby's mother is a birth specialist. You can relax."

"I can't."

Shaking my head, I braced for impact. The pressure that budded in my vagina coupled with the contractions, pushing was inevitable. The time was near. I felt the need to bear down and begin the process.

"I need to start pushing, Shayla. Please, come around this way and observe what's happening below. I can't see over my belly. I can only feel."

My phone vibrated in the distance. Preoccupied with the task at hand, neither Shayla nor I budged. I bored down, sinking my teeth into my lip as I pushed.

"One. Two. Three. Four. Five." I counted out loud.

The phone began vibrating again, breaking my concentration.

"It's Milo," I shrieked. The potency of the pain I felt was incomparable to anything I'd ever experienced.

"Should I ge—"

"No. I need you right here."

With each contraction that followed, I continued to push. On the sixth push, there was progress. From the look of terror on Shayla's face, I knew exactly what was happening down below. Crowning was taking place.

"Nature! Nature. Wait. Hold up. Wait."

Jumping back, nearly out of the water completely, she pointed.

"What the fuck, Nature? It's a baby. He's right there."

"Yes," I belted, finding it hard to keep a straight face as I watched Shayla's eyes swell on her face. "That's the point of all of this, Shayla."

"Friend, it's a whole baby right there. You can't possibly get that out of you. It's huge."

I was beginning to think that calling Shayla was a mistake. She was unable to focus and she was making me laugh uncontrollably when I needed to push to avoid vaginal tearing and the need for repair.

"Sh—Ughhhhh! Shayla. Get it toget—Oh my God!"

I was unable to fully articulate my thoughts or feelings. The next contraction wouldn't allow it. I counted down from ten, determined to end my suffering at once.

"Ten. Nine. Eight."

"Oh shit, Nature. A whole hea—a head. Nature," Shayla choked.

"Seven. Six."

"Five."

My heart stopped at the sound of his voice, forcing my eyes open. I watched as he politely moved Shayla aside as he pulled a pair of gloves over his hands.

"Keep going, Nay. You got this. He's right there. I can see his big ass head."

His encouragement gave me a boost of strength in the nick of time. I closed my eyes, accepting his hand as he stepped inside the tub.

"Four. Three. He's almost here. Keep pushing, Mommas. Keep pushing. Two. On—"

At that moment, Milo's hand fell as he rushed to catch our son. Into his arms and out of the water, Mason began wailing immediately, uprooting a new level of emotions from me. A sunken chest and teary eyes welcomed my son into my hands. His wailing filled the entire bathroom, echoing in the distance, confirming his cleared airways and lung capacity.

"Hi." I cried. "Hiiiii. Welcome home."

His brown skin and thick, bushy brows made it obvious who'd taken the lead on this group project. Though his features had yet to settle, I quickly determined that Mason was every bit of his father. My genes were recessive, leaving Milo to paint the blank canvas that we'd go on to name Mason Maurice Domino.

"Damn. This little nigga all me."

"And to think, you almost missed the big reveal."

"I feel like all I've been doing is apologizing, but I'm sorry. I fell asleep watching TV last night. My phone was on the table."

"I'd rather see results than hear explanations, Milo."

"Heard."

"We have to deliver the sac," I reminded him.

"Quiet him before he gives himself a headache. I'll work on releasing the sac."

Though painful, the passing of my son's nutritious home that helped him grow over the last nine months was rather swift. Milo had helped me study for enough tests and snuck into enough labs to know the process and how to perform necessary tasks for a successful birth although it wasn't his area of expertise.

I sandwiched my nipple between my thumb and the rest of my fingers to assist Mason with his latch. Immediately, he gripped my breast with his gums. His little jaws moved in unison as he began sucking, settling himself at once.

Milo · Nature

WITH A FULL WEEK as new parents behind us and my son growing to look more and more like his father, I wondered if I'd even show up in his DNA if a test was conducted. As Milo rocked him back and forward, pacing the floor, with his phone glued to his hand, I watched anxiously. Since Mason's birth, he'd absentmindedly shown up each and every day.

Four nights straight, he'd crashed right beside us as we both adapted to Mason's schedule. Wholeheartedly, I felt as though it was the only time Mason truly had his undivided attention. Feeling my eyes on him, he turned in my direction, staring back at me as I prepared to speak. Before words exited, he responded to the person on the other end.

"No, that's not the file, Christin—uh..." He stumbled over his words after allowing the name to slip.

My breath hiked in my chest as I shuffled around my jumbled thoughts for understanding. Tilting his head, he pled with his eyes for forgiveness. He placed his hand over the phone, pulling it away from his ear slightly as he began to explain.

"I have some shit to handle at the office. I'm just trying not to step foot in there if I don't have to."

"Hand me Mason. I can get him to sleep. Continuing to hear your voice on the phone won't help and I'd rather you take that call in another room."

"Alright. It'll only take a few minutes. I'll get him back when I finish up."

Nodding, I accepted Mason into my arms. I snuggled his body against mine and removed my right breast from the nursing bra that I practically lived in. He settled right in, finding comfort in his mother's bosom. I, on the other hand, was trying to smolder the fire inside of me.

Knowing that Milo worked so closely with a woman who knew exactly how his dick felt and his semen tasted was triggering. The lines they'd blurred to appease their personal fantasies left me muddled with confusion and finding it fairly hard to trust the fact that their relationship would ever be less than sexual.

He's not yours to have, I reminded myself, sealing my lids and sighing in disappointment. Our wires were tangled, too, complicating our situation and leaving me with unraveling feelings that intensified each time I saw him with Mason in his arms. Picking my phone up, I texted the one person I knew would understand my dilemma without judgment.

I want this thing between us to work but I don't know where to begin repairing it.

This is best friend talking, not Dr. Farmer.

More bubbles appeared, and then another message.

You don't know where to begin because it isn't your job. You've done absolutely nothing to

sabotage you and Milo's future. You've only enhanced it. Him, on the other hand, is the one that needs to figure this out. For now, focus. Mason needs you.

I tapped the camera button and took a quick picture of him enjoying another serving of milk. By the time the message was delivered, Milo was walking back into the room.

"My bad. Had some things to take care of at the office."

"Umm hm." I nodded, shutting off my phone and tunning into the episode of *The Blacklist* that I'd shied away from for a moment.

"Umm hm?" he asked, taking a seat on the bed next to me.

"Yes. Umm hm."

He waited, silently, beside me, staring holes into the side of my face.

"What?"

"Something is on your mind, Nay. I know you, and the prettier you get, the madder you are. Talk to me. Tell me what's wrong. What did I do this time?"

Sighing, I prepared to voice my concerns and my feelings toward the situation at hand. Before beginning, I was sure to maintain focus, keeping things centered around Mason because that's what truly mattered.

"You've seemingly been preoccupied with work whenever you're here. I understand that you decided against paternity leave, but when you're here, Milo, be here," I begged.

Nodding, he refused to combat my statement.

"You're right. It feels like I'm trying to be in two places

at once," he admitted. "Maybe that leave of absence should've been on my list of things to do. I just figured I could balance the two, but it's proving to be difficult."

"It's hard and I'm not at the office anymore. I'm home. So, I can't imagine the pressure you must be under. If it's not too late, take the leave, Milo. It'll save us both the headache."

"I'm at the end of this trial, Nature. Taking a leave now would honestly kill all the work I've put into this project. They're willing to shove anything down my patient's throats and I can't allow it. For most of them, it's life or death. For my mother, it was life or death. I don't want to keep shoving drugs in their systems that make them walking zombies. They need solutions, not sedation. They want to live. Most of them, anyway. Not be confined to a facility or a bed because they can't get past the fog the medicine creates. I have to thug it out, and once this ends, I'll take leave."

Remaining silent, I nodded. He sounded so much like my father. There was never the need to confront or argue with anyone who had their mind made up, already. Those people were only listening to respond, not listening to understand. Milo's promises to prioritize Mason hadn't been directly affected yet, so for now, I'd let him continue the work he'd began without the lengthy interruption.

"Don't you have anything to say?" he asked, still gazing in my direction.

"I don't," I confessed.

"I wholeheartedly believe that's bullshit, Nay."

"Well." I cleared my throat. "There is one thing."

"What's up?"

"Calls between you and your assistant, please take them

elsewhere. Not in my bedroom, bathroom, house, or porch. You can get in the car and drive down the street to take them for all I care. Just not here."

"Understood," he responded, both hands in the air as he shook his head up and down.

"Now, do me a big, big favor and put Mason in his bassinet. I think it's time I showered for the day. Are you staying, or should I bring the monitor in with me?"

"Nah," he started. "I'm not going nowhere. I'm staying put."

As the words left his mouth, he removed one of his cells and powered it down. When he laid it on the nightstand beside me, I realized it wasn't the phone I saw him with on a daily basis, which could only mean it was for business purposes only.

"Am I supposed to clap, now?" I tittered with a smile, slightly moved by the gesture, though I didn't want to reveal it.

Just as he rescued Mason from my arms, my phone chimed on the bed. My soul almost left my body completely as my eyes zeroed in on Zane's name. Just as the first message came through, a second notification piled on top of it.

With crinkled brows and lines across his forehead, Milo stretched his neck and lowered his head, staring at the screen as if he was seeing the unimaginable. In an instant, I snatched the phone from the bed, taking off for the bathroom, ready to put the desolate look on Milo's face in my rearview. I managed a few centimeters before I felt his hand on my arm, pulling me in his direction, and back onto the bed.

"Milo!" I chuckled, trying to deescalate the situation in advance.

"Who the fuck is that?"

His nostrils flared, widening his nose on his face.

"I'm not exactly sure yet and neither am I sure why you're screening my texts."

"Get fucked up, Nay," he fussed.

"Your level of delusion is what you should be studying to find a cure for."

"You heard what I said."

I stood from the bed, phone still in hand, finally making my way to the bathroom. My success led me to check the messages from Zane the second my back brushed against the locked door. I didn't trust Milo to mind his own business or stay out of the bathroom, ready to make a fuss of nothing.

What's up?

You crossed my mind. Tell me a time and place. I'm ready to see your pretty face.

He was relentless. His efforts weren't in vain, though, and were slowly easing me in his corner where connections were few and disappointment was nearly impossible. The weight of the world Milo and I created left me with a wet pillow and ass on occasion. The smiles that Zane managed to pull from me and the airiness his presence, though virtually, offered me was refreshing.

Hi. I sent before starting the second message to send over next.

I welcomed my child recently. I'm unavailable for many weeks to come.

Congratulations. Can I get a P.O. Box, a registry, or something to send you something?

I have much more than I need. Thanks for your generosity, nonetheless.

The last thing I wanted was to steer the conversation in Mason's direction but I felt the need to explain my reason for rejecting him once again.

*Be*t.

If this is too much for you, I understand.

If a nigga ain't got nothing else, I have patience. Take your time.

Thanks. Can I text you later? I'm in the middle of things right now.

Yeah. I look forward to it.

Later.

Later.

"Nature!" Milo's pounding on the door startled me.

My heart rate increased tremendously as I held a hand to my chest and exhaled deeply.

"Yeah?"

"Open the door. I need to take a piss."

Turning around, I unlocked the door to allow his entry. He wasted no time probing. Shaking my head, I folded my arms across my aching chest, waiting for him to perform the task he'd entered for.

"You ain't ran a drop of water in the five minutes you've been in this motherfucker."

"I'm still waiting for the point you're trying to make."

"What you been in here doing?"

"Returning Christina's call," I responded sarcastically.

As he tried picking his mouth up from the floor, I started the shower. While he attempted to recover, I removed my clothes and stepped into the shower, leaving my phone in clear view because I was certain Zane wouldn't be texting again until I texted him.

Thirty minutes later, I emerged from the shower feeling like a brand new woman. Mason was sound asleep in his bassinet. His father had buried himself underneath the covers, falling fast asleep as well.

The sound of the doorbell was startling, propelling my body forward to dismiss the person laying on it so that they wouldn't interrupt Mason's nap or wake Milo from his temporary slumber. They'd both be up soon enough. The possibility of anyone waking them before their rising occurred naturally left me gutted.

My feet patted the wood flooring at a rapid pace, putting as much distance between my body and the bedroom as quickly as possible. When I finally arrived, the doorbell began to ring, again. I snatched the door open, ready to plead with whoever was on my porch.

"Malachi?"

His presence was unexpected, but welcomed. I stepped back aside, offering the cool breeze my home was willing to gift him the moment he was close enough to the entrance.

"I'm not here to intrude," he told me, opening his outstretched hand and revealing a key fob in his palm. "That motherfucker nice."

Furrowed brows displayed my confusion.

"I don't understand."

Pointing toward the driveway, he smiled. "Cut him some slack, Nature. The nigga trying. Even if it doesn't feel like it."

As swiftly as Malachi had come, he'd gone, leaving me on the porch with my eyes fixated on the beautiful white

BMW sitting in my driveway with a red bow on the hood. The body on the XM was sickening, leaving me speechless as I stepped back into my home and closed the door behind me. I headed straight for the man responsible, running full force until I reached the bedroom, where he rested his head on my pillow. I leaped on top of him, centering his face as he stirred in his sleep.

"Naaaay," he groaned.

"Thank you. Thank you. Thank you. Thank you. I love it."

He rubbed his eyes, gathering his thoughts and taking a good look at me. He forced my body off his, sliding me down on the bed beside him, showcasing his depleted energy. Milo was exhausted. Juggling Mason and his daily activities was wearing him down. I was instantly reminded of Malachi's words and decided to give Milo the grace I knew he needed. As long as he continued to show up, that was enough for me. The rest would work itself out.

"Good, now tell that nigga to quit texting your phone before I put him in the trunk of that bitch," he grunted, pulling me down onto his chest where I rested my head. "Go to sleep."

NINE

"CBT IS NOT EFFECTIVE FOR EVERYONE," Jim added.

"Neither is the drug you're suggesting. Because once the brain fog clears, the issues still exist. Instead of taking away their ability to think, why not focus on improving their thoughts – about themselves, others, the world, and whatever else matters to them? Couple it with a medication that levels them out and not one that makes them hit rock bottom, and the results are far more promising than what I'm seeing here."

This meeting was dragging and we weren't getting any

closer to the solution. All they were seeing were dollar signs. I, on the other hand, wanted improvements. Not only for the company's reputation, but for my patients as well.

"Justin, the twenty-four-year-old I visited this morning, he can't tell me his name right now. He's only been out of bed twice this week. He'd been throwing up off and on since he arrived. This trial is doing to him exactly what I've been afraid it will do to at least 70 percent of the people who will consume it.

"People want to feel better, not to feel comatose. They want to see the sun, hear the birds chirping in the morning, have a sip of coffee at the kitchen table, watch their children grow, and work among the rest of Americans to earn a living for their families. I think we're forgetting that absolutely none of them chose this for themselves.

"They were chosen. And while your boots aren't on the ground, mine are. While you're seeing their disabilities as problems that need to go away, and quickly, I see them as people, just like you and I. It doesn't matter that our brains don't work the same. Our hearts, all of them, beat the same. That's enough for me. They're human just like you and me, Jim."

The alarm on my phone sounded as the device vibrated in my pocket. Instantly, I remembered the single marker on Nature and I's shared calendar. Mason was now four weeks old and due to see the doctor for his first visit. He'd been able to see Marcie the day after his birth and was given a clean bill of health. This appointment, however, was with his new pediatrician that I was anxious to meet. It was an associate of Nature's, one she referred a handful of her clients to.

"I'm running behind for my son's appointment. I'm signing off. Have a blessed day, fellas."

I slammed the computer screen down without another word aimed in their direction.

"Fucking pigs. Fuck all you fat fuckers. Trying to medicate these people until the day they die. Not on my fucking watch," I fussed, gathering my belongings as I rushed out of the door.

"Dr. Dom—"

"Not right now, Christina. I'm running late. Cancel the rest of my day."

Without a doubt, ass kissing was in my near future. I could see the look on Nature's pretty face as she chewed me out for the second time this week, proving that my promises to make Mason the priority of my life were falling short. My phone buzzed again in my pocket. Upon retrieving it, I watched her name on the screen, debating on answering the call that I knew the nature of. Swallowing back the fear of hearing the disappointment in her beautiful voice, I picked up.

"Yeah?"

"Where are you? His appointment," she whispered just as the phone began to cut out.

I pulled it away from my ear, peeking at the bars in the top right corner. The phone never made it back to my ear. The call dropped.

Fuck.

Dialing her back was pointless. Apologizing, at this point, was pointless. The quicker I got to them, the less brutal the blow would be for us all.

I sprinted toward my whip as if my life depended on it.

Inside, I revved the engine of the brand new XM I'd purchased in addition to Nature's. Instead of the white paint that she loved, mine was wrapped in matte black. The Forgiato rims lifted the body slightly higher and elevated the look altogether. Together, as a family, we'd taken a total of two trips to the store inside of it and it was proven I'd chosen the right ride each time.

I mashed the gas, determined to cut the twenty-minute trip down by at least six minutes. Though I hadn't been to this particular office yet, the GPS wasn't necessary. I could pinpoint exactly where it was and how long it would take me to get there without assistance or the reminder that I had fallen behind.

I took the ramp to the expressway, ready for the freedom it offered so that I was able to open my engine right up so that my destination was reached sooner. The numbers on my dash climbed, reaching the hundreds. And just when I thought the coast was clear, red taillights in every lane put an end to my short victory.

"FUCK."

My tires screeched as I brought my whip to nearly a complete stop.

"What the hell is going on?" I wondered out loud, frustration quickly replacing every other emotion of mine.

Congestion of the road was puzzling. It was a decent hour, ten minutes past eleven to be exact. Traffic at this time of the day was unusual and downright upsetting.

Shit. Shit. Shit. I checked the time on my dash, mentally calculating how far behind the traffic would put me. It wasn't looking too good on my end, but I'd be damn if I gave up.

Inch by inch, I moved forward while considering the words to express my remorse for my tardiness as my finger hovered over the call button. It didn't matter that my intentions were good when it came to Nature and our son. Life kept finding a way to fuck me over. Admittedly, I was exhausted with the constant disappointment, so I couldn't imagine how Nature felt.

She was my heart and so was the son I was growing to love more and more every day. However, I was beginning to learn that the simplicity of our childhood hadn't followed us into adulthood. In college, it was so much easier to keep a smile on Nature's face. A trip to the café, a night of studying together, coffee in the morning, walks to and from class... that's what made those cheeks rosy pink and her lips curve into a smile.

Shit was different now, and the fact that I hadn't yet found the recipe for happiness according to the new Nature, that shit was running me hot. I made no excuses. As a man, I fully understood my role and was determined to improve it.

This is it, I promised. *I've got to get my shit in order.*

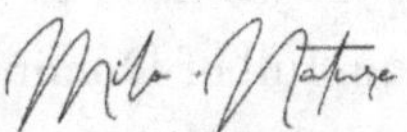

FORTY-FIVE MINUTES LATER, I pulled the door of the doctor's office open, hopeful that there was a lengthy wait and Mason was still being seen by the doctor. To my dismay, Nature was wheeling Mason's stroller out simultaneously. I stepped aside, allowing her to pass through as I grabbed hold of the stroller.

On her angelic face, I could see that she wanted to

protest, but decided against it. Instead, she remained silent, strutting toward the truck that I thought she looked stunning in and beside. No words were exchanged as we got Mason situated in the truck. Nature was strapped in and ready to reverse before I could close the door good.

Because her actions were justified, I allowed her to have her way. Guilt consumed me as I watched them exit the parking lot. I jumped into my ride with my destination set. I felt like shit for missing my son's first appointment, but I still wanted to know how it had gone and what the doctor had said.

When I pulled up to Nature's home, she'd already gotten Mason out of the truck and was headed inside the house. I jogged up the steps to assist her inside. From the weight of his car seat, I could tell my boy was growing and gaining weight. He stayed glued to his mother's breasts all day long, so that wasn't surprising at all.

As quickly as we'd made it inside, Nature had disappeared. I set Mason's car seat near the door and kneeled before him. His dark skin and coily hair reminded me of the baby pictures of us all that my grandfather collected over the years. From the tip of his head to his long feet, he was every bit of us. In a room full of Dominoes, you wouldn't be able to determine which of us he belonged to.

"Hey, little dude. You went to the doctor and they gave that baby some big shots?" I asked, paying close attention to the Band-Aids on his legs, sure not to apply any pressure or mistakenly touch them.

A smile revealed his dark pink gums as he began swarming in my arms. I couldn't remember an instance in the last four weeks of his life that he didn't show me, in some way, that he was happy to see me. Even in the first week of his life, his eyes grew larger at the sight of me. If there was nothing else I was certain of, it was the way my son felt about me.

"You took it like a champ? Or, did you cry to Mommy?"

Finally, I had him unbuckled and in my hands. Leaning forward, I tickled his nose with mine, bringing more of those gums out to play. Even at his young age, he displayed emotional maturity, a level you typically witnessed in infants two to four months.

"Yeah. You cried to Mommy?" I laughed. "It's cool. Daddy about to go do the same thing, little dude. Mommy is not happy with Daddy right now. But Daddy loves Mommy very much and is going to get it together... for you, me, and for Mommy especially."

My explanation made his eyes twinkle as if he understood what I was saying, but I knew that was bullshit. He didn't give a damn what I was saying, as long as I was in his face.

"Let's go see how we can fix this, Mason. Daddy fucked up. You have to be on my side when we get up here, though, or I'm leaving your little ass right down here. Tell me what it's going to be?"

With raised brows, I waited for his response. The smile he widened was good enough for me, pushing me toward the stairs that we climbed in unison.

We entered Nature's bedroom to find that she'd already taken off the clothes she'd worn and replaced them with a silk gown that rose as she slid into bed. Silent tears slipped down her blotchy cheeks. The pained look on her face pushed my heart down my chest, abdomen, legs, and into the soles of my Jordan Ones.

Nudging her over a bit, I sat next to her on the bed. With the back of my hand, I wiped the tears from her eyes. Into the pillow where her head rested, she released more, turning into the fabric completely as her sniffles grew louder. I felt like a million different versions of a fool as I watched her unravel.

"Talk to me, Nay," I requested.

She remained silent. Other than the sound of her cries, she was soundless.

"Nature. The meeting I was in ran much longer than expected. I lost track of time. Five minutes after my alarm went off, I was out of the door and in my car. I bumped into traffic. An eighteen-wheeler was flipped over on the expressway, causing standstill traffic."

Silence.

"I know it feels like we're just in this never-ending loop, but—"

Raising slightly and turning to face me, she released a steady breath.

"You asked for this, Milo. You asked to co-parent. You brought this upon yourself and so did I. You begged to become a piece of this puzzle of mine and now you're acting as if you don't know where you belong, where you're supposed to go. I don't need this shit, Milo. I could've done this on my own. I could've had a son on my own, raised him on my own. I didn't want to deal with the drama of having a child with someone but I thought, it's Milo. This will be fine. And up until the eighth month of pregnancy, it was fine.

"But right now, I'm letting you know that I'm not for your bullshit. I don't have the luxury of excuses, so fuck your excuses. If I can be there, so can you. I didn't ask for this, Milo. You did. You wanted your son, you have him. Do right by him! I'm not a woman that is going to beg for your participation. I watched my mother do it for far too long. Either you're in or you're out. There's no in between!"

"Okay."

"Okay?" she yelled.

"Ain't shit else for me to say that I haven't already said. You're right. I know it and so do you. I'm not apologizing no more. You've made it clear that you want improvement. Shit, me too. So instead of wasting my breath, telling you how sorry I am that this shit keeps happening the way it does, I'm going to show you. But make no mistake, Nature. I know exactly where I belong in this puzzle.

"Don't let the last two months cloud your memory and make you forget that I've been here... right here... waiting, watching, preparing, and being any and everything you need even with the limitations you put in place. That's not to discredit anything you just said, but damn, Nay. You act like I'm a fucking menace. You and I both know that's the furthest from the truth. I just... shit just been fucked up for the last two months but it's going to get better. I put that shit on my Pops."

Silently, she rested her head on the pillow again.

"How was the appointment? Did he cry when he got his vaccinations? What did the doctor say?"

Silence.

"Nay, what the doctor say?"

Silence.

"Nay. Don't be stubborn. What did the doctor say?"

"He's deaf!" she shrieked. "He can't hear, Milo. That's what the doctor said and had you been there, you would've heard it yourself and maybe we could've supported one another instead of me having my heart ripped out of my chest while all alone and trying to remain calm."

The tears she's cried and the defeat on her face made more sense now. The blow to my chest almost made me regret the question I'd just asked. I stood to my feet, tilting my head as the words she'd just spat looped in my head. I stumbled, slightly, remembering his final months inside when my voice seemed to rattle him, causing him to flip and turn in Nature's belly.

How? I asked, but quickly answered my own question. *Cardiac rhythm.* Studies had shown time and time again that it could be determined and acknowledged by babies in utero.

"I'm sor... I'm sorry. He's what, Nature?"

Her words had crushed my heart once, but I begged for the pain again. I needed to verify the information was accurate and I'd heard her correctly, even if it meant physical, mental, and emotional paralyzation momentarily.

"Deaf. His hearing is compromised in both ears. More extensive test will need to be done to determine the degree of his disability but without a doubt, Mason is deaf," she cried.

Managing my emotions was impossible. My nose widened and tightened numerous times. I gazed at my son, still in my arms, trying to comprehend it all. A tear fell from my eyes, onto his shirt, notifying me that I'd failed at maintaining my composure.

"Deaf?"

I swiped my eyes, lifting my head to confirm one last time.

Nature was unable to respond. Her face and head were stuffed into the pillow. Her loud sobs mired my thoughts. I walked over, near the corner of her bedroom where the rocking chair was, and sat down to relieve my legs before my brain stop signaling to them and both me and Mason fell to the floor.

Rocking my son back and forward, I glared in his mother's direction, silently apologizing for my tardiness though I'd promised her I wouldn't. I wasn't above my own chastisement. Internally, I gave myself a good tongue lashing before settling on my next move.

With haste, I removed one of my cells from my pocket and dialed the office's number. Christina picked up on the second ring. Though Nature had made it clear that she didn't want calls made to or received from Christina happening in her home, I wasn't in the space to make the call elsewhere.

"Dr. Domi—"

"Clear my schedule for the next two weeks."

"Mr. Domino?"

"Clear my schedule."

I didn't wait for a response. Instead, I ended the call and peered in Nature's direction. Her right hand and face indented the pillow as she drifted into a deep, difficult sleep. The emotional turmoil she was experiencing forced her to rest.

Her beauty wasn't only skin deep. Inside out, Nature was stunning. Seeing her so broken and battered left me feeling some kind of way. This pain, which was pain I suffered from as well, was the kind that made your gears grind because it wasn't pain that you could snap your fingers and make go away. It was pain that lingered because the circumstances wouldn't change, most likely. Mason's disability wouldn't hinder his success in life, I'd make sure of it, but it would make life a bit more complicated for us all.

Big, curious eyes stared up at me. I quickly pushed the pain aside to reside in the moment with my glossy-eyed son. He didn't have to hear me to feel me, see me, and understand me. That was enough for me.

"We got this shit, little dude. Pops got you. No matter what. We're ten toes down in this shit, Mason. Most kids hard-of-hearing any-damn-way, right? This is lightweight."

Just as the words left my mouth, my phone buzzed in my pocket. I retrieved it, immediately recognizing the email that repeated itself across the screen. The timing couldn't have been more perfect.

"Aussie," I answered.

Ruffling in the background eventually led to her pretty face in the screen.

"Uncle Milo. Name an animal that lays eggs but isn't a bird."

"A snake."

"Good job."

"Name an animal that—"

Before she could continue her quiz, I interrupted. There were more pressing matters at hand.

"Aussie, look who I have in my arms."

Angling the camera, I showed Mason's face. He

followed the light of the screen, eyes glued on Aussie's face as it always was whenever we talked while he was near.

"Ahhhh. Hey, Mase," she cooed, already having gave him a nickname. "Hi! It's Aussie."

Flipping the phone again, I gnawed on my bottom lip before delivering the news.

"He can't hear you, baby," I admitted.

"Babies can hear. In fact, they develop the ability while in u—"

"Not this baby, Aussie."

"I don't understand."

"He's deaf. We found out today. He can't hear us. None of us."

Her furrowed brows straightened and began to lift right along with the rest of her features. Naturally, she began using her hands as she spoke.

"Hey, Mason. It's Aussie. Your biggest cousin. I love you." She re-introduced herself, but this time through signs and words, carefully articulating her words so that he could see the movement of her mouth.

"I'm going to need you, baby girl. Your uncle knows little ASL."

"I'm fluent," she said, still signing.

"I'm not deaf, Aussie. You don't have to sign, baby girl."

"But you are. At least, you have to be or act as if you are to truly adapt to Mason's world. If I were you or Mason's Mommy, I would forbid verbal communication in private settings from this day forward." She emphasized each word with her fingers and body.

Being schooled by a young girl who wasn't even old enough to be in kindergarten might've been offensive for some, but I loved every bit of it. She reminded me so much of myself and my mother. Her brain was simply impeccable.

"You're right."

"You're..." She paused to show me the signs. "Right."

"You're right." I repeated the same movements.

"Good."

"I'll be coming by often. At least three times a week, sometimes with Mason and Nature."

"Uncle Milo, I love you. I really do. But please don't come over without Mason. Okay?"

I bellowed, stirring Nature in her sleep as laughter roared from my chest. I wasn't exactly sure what I'd do with the little girl on the phone, but I needed to find out soon.

"What's good?"

Malachi's neck stretched, exposing his face on screen.

"Your mother is at the table waiting for you. Lunch is ready," he said, removing the iPad from her hand. "I'll take this. Go have lunch so that you can finish your lesson for the day."

"You know, Dad, if you wanted to talk to Uncle Milo, you could've just called him on your phone."

"Aussie, get your little smart a—self out of here and join Mommy at the table."

I listened for a remark because I wouldn't be surprised if there was one. Silence trailed for a few seconds before I heard Malachi sigh in distress.

"I don't know what the fuck I'm going to do with her. She went from my sweet little baby girl to wanting to be the boss of this entire shit."

"At least we both know she'd run that shit well."

"Crazily, I have no doubt about that. Sometimes, her

knowledge scares me. I don't know what in the Milo Domino she be on."

"Did you forget your mother was the originator of this shit?" I chuckled.

His hand rubbed the back of his neck as he shook his head, ready to change the subject already. I was as well.

"Mason had his first visit at the doctor's today," I explained.

"Oh yeah. How'd he do? They shot his ass up?"

"Yeah. Yeah. Almost everything else checked out it seems. There's only one concern."

"His head too fucking big?" Malachi tittered.

"Fuck you."

"Real shit. You don't think your son has a fucking rock on his shoulders?"

"Have you seen Maz's head?"

"That motherfucker big, too. I can admit that, though."

"Alright, nigga, don't mean I'm admitting shit about Mason."

"Denial is a hell of a drug."

"Again, fuck you."

"What's up, though? What's concerning? I don't like the way you sound. The melancholy is all in your voice. Talk to me."

"They ran test that would normally be performed during a hospital birth. We had a homebirth. He went to see Marcie the first week and checked out fine, according to her checklist. Breathing, eating, all of that shit. Well, today, he went to see the pediatrician and failed his hearing test."

"Have them run that shit again."

"He's deaf, Malachi."

"Still, get a second opinion."

"When Nature wakes up, we're going to discuss next steps. She's fucked up about it."

"The last thing she needs to do is worry about Mason. He's going to thrive regardless. With you two as parents, there's literally no way he'll fail another test in life or of life. Winning is inevitable. This diagnosis isn't a sentencing, it's simply a new lesson. Don't let it distract you guys from the beauty of his birth. Enjoy this time. It won't come around twice."

"I know. Shit, four weeks has felt like four days."

"Blink. I dare you, nigga, and it'll be four years."

"Right. Right. Feels that way with Aussie."

"Exactly."

"We're going to need her help. We might slide through a few days a week over the next few weeks. I've paused my schedule to figure this shit out."

"Pull up on us whenever you need to. I'm pleased to hear you've taken the time off to see this through. You'll realize you needed the time off even more than Mason. Your career is a soft cushion for you. It's your comfort zone. It helps you zone out, forget the problems outside of your office. Nigga, you got plenty. One is making sure shit is solid with the mother of your child."

"That's at the tippy top of my list."

"As it should be. I need to get off this line. My wife is calling for me. Hit me up tomorrow with whatever information you learn once Nature wakes up. If we need to relieve her a bit and team up at his appointments, I'm down. I'm sure the rest of them knuckleheads with it, too."

"Four niggas in a doctor's office with a baby?"

"Two babies. I need to bring Maz, too. Sometimes, I think it's air between them ears of his."

"Leave my young nigga alone."

"And five."

"Five?"

"You think Pops going to let us slide alone?"

I thought briefly before responding, "Naaaaaah," shaking my head.

"Exactly. But let me get to the fam. If you haven't hit me by noon tomorrow, I'll call you."

"Bet. Love you, nigga."

"One."

"One."

Mason was fast asleep in my arms, unable to keep his eyes open any longer than the conversation with Malachi lasted. As if he'd miss something, he didn't bow out until the call ended. Patiently, I waited until he was resting well before standing up and taking him to the bassinet where I laid him on his back. I kissed his full cheeks and forehead, watching as he shifted, finding comfort underneath the blanket I'd placed over him.

I stripped down from head to toe, leaving only my briefs. Feeling a few pounds lighter, I lowered my body onto the bed where Nature was sound asleep. Her brown cheeks were flushed a light red, evidence of her emotional state prior to her slumber. I stretched my legs underneath the covers, following up with my arms, pulling Nature into my chest.

The stiffness of her frame voiced her protests, but I continued to slide her across the bed until she surrendered and the silk her robe was created with was pressed against my skin. I wrapped my left arm around her and laid my head against the right one.

Like magnets, our bodies synced, heartbeat and breathing all on one accord. My fingers, with minds of their own, combed her frame, searching until they brushed against her wrist, eventually taking her hand into mine. I kissed her soft, straight hair, pushing forward until I felt the back of her cranium.

"I love you, Nay," I admitted, closing my eyes as shards of pain soared through my heart.

The quietness of the room was our safe space. Nothing more needed to be said. With our bodies intertwined, peace lulled me to a place that only Nature could guide me.

TEN

Nature

"NO. I'm actually bagging the last of my child's milk," I corrected Zane, who assumed I was unbagging groceries.

Over the last three weeks, he'd become the exclamation point at the end of my day. After Mason was down for the night, I took the opportunity to respond to messages he'd sent throughout the day or return any calls I'd missed. In the short time span, my interest had piqued. Not only was his patience commendable, but so was his persistence. Fortunately for him, the perfect opportunity for us to finally sit down and have that meal he'd been proposing for months had come.

"I promise not to keep you out too late, aight? I know you have to get back to the little one."

Though we'd gotten to know each other more, Zane still knew very little about my son, other than the fact that he'd been born almost two months ago and he was breastfed. He wasn't informed of Mason's gender, parental dynamic, or anything else. I was very hesitant to offer any amount of information pertaining to my son to anyone. My protective nature had kicked in and it was severe.

Discovering his disability made it a bit more potent. The urge to protect him from any and all things possible left me with little to say about him when talking to those that weren't in my immediate circle. Concealing his condition wasn't the plan, but until I felt comfortable with sharing, it would be our little secret.

His diagnosis changed little to nothing in our lives. Mason was still growing and thriving as any newborn. He was hitting his milestones with ease, and the way he was bursting at the brim with smiles and giggles made us question the truth in his diagnosis. However, after two visits with audiologist, there was no doubt in our minds.

Because Milo was returning to work on Monday after spending three weeks resting, resetting, and watching our son grow a little more each and every day, he planned he and Mason's first weekend together. This would give me the break from mothering that I desperately needed and allow me to get a fresh breath of air. Each time I closed my eyes since he'd announced his plans, I could feel my hair blowing in the wind and see the endless smile that spread across my face until I began to drool.

Our communication was improving. His willingness to

put his world on hold for Mason was commendable. I appreciated his presence over the last three weeks, but the slight resentment I felt toward him still remained. The strain was felt on both ends, however, Milo still knew no boundaries and crossed mine each chance he got.

"Thank you, for the consideration, but time is not a factor for the night, Zane."

"Oh, yeah?"

"Not this weekend, it's not."

"Shit, don't tell me that, Nature. I might not want to bring you home," he responded.

"Well, I do plan on coming home." I laughed. "Being that we agreed to dinner, I'm assuming I should be home by eleven, correct? Dinner doesn't last too many hours."

"I thought time wasn't a factor?" he reminded me.

"It's not."

"Then let's not time stamp it and just see where the night takes us."

My phone buzzed. My heart leaped in my chest as I realized who was trying to get through to me. An incoming FaceTime call from Milo meant that I needed to end the call with Zane. Reluctantly, I shared the news.

"Someone is on my other end. I have to go now, but I'll see you soon."

"In about an hour and a half," he replied.

"I'm looking forward to it."

Since Wednesday, after agreeing to finally having dinner with Zane, I'd been in knots. Nervousness and anxiousness were attacking my nervous system, leaving me with bubbling bowels and an unsettled stomach. Waiting to see his brown skin and perfect teeth happened to be much more difficult than I'd anticipated. The rawness of our union might've contributed to my vexation, or maybe it was the man on the other end, trying to get through to me. It was still undetermined.

Without waiting for a response, I tapped the green circle on the screen. Milo's face appeared, replacing Zane's.

God, this man is fine, but he is trouble for my heart and my head. I cringed.

His presence was possibly the reason for the strength of my pelvic floor. Whenever he was on my other line, so was my sanity. With his gold teeth gleaming, especially in the dark, and dark eyes glistening, he was the recipe for disaster.

"What is it, Milo?" I sighed with a roll of my eyes, concealing my true thoughts.

His smile widened. He was no fool and knew me well enough to pinpoint my charade. As if he found joy in annoying me, he chuckled.

"You sure you don't want to spend the weekend with us? We can make room."

"No. In fact, I don't."

"Pleeeeeeaaase."

From his position, I sensed he was leaning over onto his armrest with his phone in front of him as he sat in his driveway.

"No."

"Why not? You don't miss a nigga?"

"Milo, I see you almost every day. Why would I miss you? You haven't given me a chance to."

Besides, I don't want or need to miss you. You're no good for me.

"You see me every day, Nature, but you don't see a

nigga, for real. You got ya guard up and shit. Not letting a nigga get at you like I want to. So, when I ask if you miss me, I mean, bend your ass over the console miss me. Arch your back, miss me. Get on all fours, miss me. Suck my dick, miss me. Spread them fucking legs and let me eat that shit, miss me. Sit on my face, miss me. Ride this dick, miss me."

Clenching my jaw, I closed my eyes to rid myself of the visions that aligned with his sentiments.

"That's what type of time I'm on this weekend, Nay. You trying to get dicked down or what?

"Milo," I groaned. "Just stop it."

"Ya six weeks was up last week, Nature, and I ain't hit that pussy yet. What we waiting on?"

"I'm going to hang up on you."

"That's cool, because I'm right outside. I'm going to break the fucking door down again if you do."

"You need serious help. You didn't mention being on your way. I assumed I was bringing him."

"Yeah, well, I saved you the trip. Open the door, I'm coming in."

"He's not exactly ready."

"I'm not in a rush. I can wait."

"I just need to double check his bag."

"Open the fucking door, girl. We can discuss that when I get in the house."

He ended the call, not letting me get out another word. I stood right where I was, closing my eyes and praying to the Lord that I had enough energy to fight off Milo's advances. I was really looking forward to spending time with Zane and the last thing I wanted was to allow Milo to screw that up for me.

He'd contributed to the end of pregnancy blues and I wasn't quite done punishing him for his contributions. It was time to get out of the house, from under his skin, and in some fresh air. A few drinks and conversation that didn't involve Mason, doctor's appointments, next steps, possible delays, breastmilk, or naptime was something I was looking forward to.

Boom.

Boom.

Boom.

Boom.

The thunderous knocking hiked my breathing as I opened my eyes and faced the kitchen exit. Though I wasn't a fan of his beating, I was happy he hadn't touched the doorbell and awakened Mason. Slowly, I walked through the kitchen, into the dining area, through the living room, and into the hallway that led to the front door.

I watched Milo, standing with his legs locked as far back as they'd stretched, hands in his pockets with a smile on his face. His attractiveness should've been labeled a crime. He was the sexiest creature I'd ever seen in my life. The resentment I harbored for him over the last three months was easily forgotten at the sight of him, but I had to stand my ground.

I unlocked the door, hurrying to turn around and head upstairs to get Mason. The more distance between Milo and I, the better I felt. However, he refused to let me get far. His arms were around me, surrounding me and pulling me backward, into his body that smelled like precious wood and sprinkles of black pepper.

"Milo, what are you doing?"

"I'm hugging the mother of my child, showing her that I miss her."

As the final sentence fell from his lips, he brushed his bottom half across my butt, revealing the underlying meaning of it all. It had been two days since I'd seen him. And two days ago, he hadn't been as physical as he was at the moment.

"Seriously?" I asked, sliding from his grasp. "What's gotten into you?"

"You," he stated. "Or the lack thereof, rather."

"Let's not start this tonight," I suggested, waving my right hand in the air.

"Start what?" he asked as if he was clueless.

"This. Any of it."

"Yeah. Aight."

"What's so funny?" I asked, peeved by the sniggering he was doing.

"You."

"Me?"

"Yeah, you. Trying to convince us both that your pussy not wet and your heart not pounding against your chest right now. Yeah, you, Nay. You and these fucking games you like to play."

"I'm not playing any games, Milo."

"Then prove it."

"Prove it?"

Stepping forward, Milo lifted his hand until it reached the seat of my shorts, which were scorching hot and soaked in my secretion. My nostrils flared as frustration mounted in my belly. I gazed into his full, round eyes, waiting for him to say something, anything. When the pressure became too much, I stepped backward, catching my breath as I did so.

"Ugh," I scoffed.

"Exactly what the fuck I thought. Now, you trying to spend the weekend with your nigga or what?"

"You're not my nigga, Milo. And no. The answer still stands. Your son is upstairs. Feel free to grab him while I check his bag again."

I started for the kitchen, only to be stopped, again. This time, Milo wrapped his arm around my neck, placing his lips at my ear as he spoke.

"You can save us both the heartache and anticipation. Your pussy wet, my dick hard, we can handle this like adults before I go up and get *our* son. Or, we can build and wait for the climax. I'm cool either way. Your choice. But making me wait will force me to make you pay."

Swallowing the lump in my throat, I froze in place momentarily. My chest rose and fell, rose and fell. Blood spilled in my mouth as I bit into my bottom lip, needing to release the pressure that was building from my vagina. My womb was tingling, ready to grow the seeds I knew Milo would plant, giving me two children under the age of two.

"Mason is upstairs," I breathed, finally pulling away.

Nodding, with a sinister smile on his face, he set me free and moved in the direction in which I'd advised. The energy required to dodge the fiery bullet left me depleted. I scurried into the kitchen, double-checked Mason's bag, and secured the milk he'd need to get through the weekend. There wasn't much at my home that Milo didn't already have at his, so his bag was fairly empty, mostly filled with ice packs and frozen breastmilk. I pulled it up on my shoulder and transferred it to the console table near the entryway.

"He was awake. Just sitting there, staring into the dark," Milo said to me, descending the stairs.

"Geez, you scared me."

I watched as they both made their way down.

"I'm going to put him in the seat that's already in my truck."

He was headed for the door, already, a little too fast for my liking. It was the very first time that Mason would be away from me for more than an hour or two. Milo had taken him on rides to calm him down during a tantrum and taken him to visit Aussie a few times, but never for an extensive period.

"Wait. I need to kiss his cheeks. And maybe I should let him nurse before you guys take off."

"Nature, don't start. I know that look. The wheels are already turning in your head but them motherfuckers might as well stop. He's coming with his pops and you're going to enjoy your weekend, aight?"

"Okay," I whined.

"Now, don't bring your ass out here in them little ass shorts. I'd hate to have to pop a neighbor for—"

"I'm not coming out and hush. Always talking about violence as if you're not a board certified physician and head of the phy—"

"I don't give a damn. I'm a nigga from The Valley first and foremost and the tool I pack has nothing to do with improving the neurological system but it will rearrange a nigga's thoughts."

Rolling my eyes, I waved him out of the house with

Mason in his arms. But not before stealing a kiss. With the bag on his shoulder and Mason snug against his chest, Milo nearly made me reconsider my plans for the night. Fatherhood looked pretty good on him.

Milo · Nature

NERVOUSLY, I drew circles on my legs as I waited for Zayne's arrival. My punctual nature led to me arriving fifteen minutes early. As a result, I was given far too much time alone with my thoughts.

What am I doing?

What is Mason doing?

Is Milo alright with him? Alone?

Maybe I should call.

Does he miss me? ...Mason. I mean Mason.

Is he being a good baby?

What if he's looking for me and can't see—ugh.

I shook my head, ridding myself of the worries that would surely stress me and ruin my night. Determined to stay busy, I reached into my clutch and removed the lightly scented and pink tinted stick of gloss. I brushed the end of the wand across my lips, evenly distributing my third layer of the night across them.

Staring down at the Rolex on my wrist, I took note of the time. Zane was due at the table in five minutes or less. I continued my quest to keep myself busy. This time, I rearranged the contents on the linen of the table, aligning them all to better suit the eye.

"Straight enough?"

My body froze as a tingle ran down my spine, ending

with my partially numbed toes in the Tom Ford sandals I wore. Batting lashes and curious eyes followed the trail that led straight to his broadness. And there he stood. Draped in a natural-colored shirt with denim jeans, I was led to the conclusion that my date was a man of good taste.

"Hi," I greeted Zane, shuffling my feet underneath the table in preparation to stand.

"No need," he told me, extending a hand to stop me.

Smiling, I sighed in relief, watching as he took the seat across from me. As he did so, he removed the hat from his head, displaying a set of thick curls that weren't there when we'd met but I'd grown fond of since we'd started communicating via FaceTime.

"I Ii," he repeated after settling in. "It's been a long time coming."

Agreeing, I nodded. "I know. Months."

"Months." He chuckled. "I must admit that this moment made it all worth it."

"Yeah?" I leaned in, placing a hand under my chin.

"I can finally buy you a drink and feed you."

"I see. I see."

"You look stunning, Nature. It feels damn good to be in your presence."

"I can admit that I'm feeling the same. I'm wondering if the heat is up or if it's my nerves." I chuckled, fanning my face.

"Nerves? Nah. Can't be."

Mellow was the temperament of my lifetime, but tonight made it rather complicated to remain in control of my thoughts, fears, and feelings. A few months ago, before Mason stretched my body and forced my confidence into hiding, I would've sat at the table across from such a radiant individual with my head held high and my shoulders squared. Postpartum blues was kicking me in the shins, though I had little idea it existed in my world before now.

"Possibly."

"Hello, I'm Monica, your server for the evening. Can I get you started with anything to drink?"

Zane nodded in my direction, instructing her to take my order first. I didn't need a menu to know what drink I craved, sliding down my throat with a slight bitterness that was chased with a sweetness that made your lips lickable. *Joseph's*, the restaurant I'd chosen, was famous for the zesty beverage.

"A lemon drop, please."

"And you, sir?" Monica asked Zane.

"Martell. Neat."

His choice in Brandy was flattering. Brandy of any choice would have you questioning your logic and speaking your truths, but Martell was a bit special. The brother of Hennessy, it was sure to knock you on your behind if you weren't careful.

"Will we be having appetizers?"

"Lumped crab cakes, four. By the time you return, we'll be ready to place our orders."

I admired Zane's aura. There were qualities of his that immediately attracted me, soothing my femininity and softening my soul. By nature, he was a leader. That much was obvious.

But his leadership wasn't accompanied by haughtiness or arrogance. It was quiet, like the eye of a storm, yet dominant like a lion's roar. It reserved your attention in pure, baffling silence. It demanded your submission in the slick-est, mildest manner.

"What is it?" he asked, placing his back against the chair behind him.

"Nothing." Blushing, I shook my head free of the thoughts circling.

"Champagne. I love that color on you."

The slip dress I'd decided on was beautiful, simple, and elegant. It felt so good against my skin, creating a legion of small, fine bumps against my skin almost every time I moved. The fabric was breathable and cool to the touch.

"Thank you."

Two thick pieces hung in my face while the rest of my hair was pulled behind my ears, flowing down my back. Body shimmer made my arms, neck, and chest glisten. I studied the menu, trying to keep my eyes from Zane's hand-some face, though he didn't seem to mind the ogling.

"Admittedly, I'm enjoying the view. It's been hell getting you in a chair across the table, but well worth the wait."

"Here we are," Monica said, setting our drinks in front of us. "Your appetizer is ready. Before I run back, do we know what we're having for entrées?"

"Yes."

"Yeah."

Zane hadn't picked up the menu, but he knew exactly what he wanted, it seemed. After I called off my selections, he did the same. Monica disappeared again, but not for long. Within minutes, she was back with the crab cakes in hand. Soon after her departure, our forks clung to the glass dish in pursuit of decent proportions of the massive cakes that lined it.

"Ummm," I moaned as the texture and taste both paraded in my mouth.

There was the perfect amount of everything balled inside a thin, crunchy crust. I chastised myself inwardly for never trying the dish, though I'd been to the restaurant a handful of times.

"I assume we should start with the basics." Zane chuckled, finishing off the first bite as well.

"Basics." I laughed, "Haven't we covered those over the last few weeks?"

"Nah. There's one thing in particular that has me lost."

"Yeah? What's that?" I took another bite of the crab cake I was working on.

"What nigga was dumb enough to let you get away?" he asked with furrowed brows of confusion.

He hasn't. The words were at the tip of my tongue, but I decided against them. The truth was, Milo hadn't let me get away, not in his mind. However, I was committed to living my life freely from this point beyond. The chances he'd been given, he'd blown, directly and indirectly. Joining in on the fun didn't feel like such a bad idea.

The difference between us was that I was dating for marriage. While Milo was willing to knock down every woman who crossed his path, I was selective with who I lent my time and attention to because ultimately, I desired marriage. Any man in my presence for more than a few minutes must exude the qualities I wanted in my husband or he couldn't share the same space as me.

"I'd rather not," I tittered, letting him know that a change in the subject would be appreciated.

"Me, either, but tell that nigga thanks."

Nodding, I smiled. "I see what you did there."

Conversation rolled freely from our tongues as if we weren't on the first date. Lemon drops and Martell were plentiful, nonstop until dessert was served and shared among us two. An apple crumble cake that was soft and moist, paired with two scoops of ice cream and glasses of water to wash it all down.

Zane was a good time. He listened when I spoke and was engaged in the conversation, no matter the subject. From women's healthcare to the pesky hairs that always found their way on my bathroom floor, it didn't matter. He heard every word that came from my lips.

I listened, too. His exhaustion was apparent, but he wore it well. I craved sleep for him. I craved settlement for him. I craved a good night's rest and sleep well into the midday.

"I'm not ready to leave," I sighed, feeling every particle of the lemon drops I'd washed back.

"The restaurant is closing," Zane shared, waving a hand around.

"I know. Being out of the house just feels... it feels so good."

"No one said you had to go home, Nature. You just can't stay here."

Standing to his feet, he stretched his arm. I stood, taking his hand into mine.

I miss him. I miss my son. I miss Mason. The revelation hit me, dramatically, causing the caving of my chest as a hollowness formed. Tears lined my bottom eyelids, daring me to blink. Behind Zane, I tried swiping them away as quickly as they'd come. The overcast of emotions that soared through me, turning my heart inside out, was unexpected, but left me feeling empty. The happiness I'd discovered over the last two and a half hours was dismantled at the thought of him.

He must miss me too.

Guilt crept in as we continued through the restaurant and out of the door. Valet had garnered a line, patrons pouring out of the establishment at once, all in a hurry to get to their destination. I still had no idea where mine was.

"My home is always an option," softly, Zane whispered to me as he turned in my direction.

He'd read my thoughts. The gap between us closed. His hands brushed up and down my bare arms, rubbing his scent into my skin and making the bumps rise again. His eyes, they were the dreamiest. I quickly became lost within them, forgetting everything and anything on my mind prior.

His hands moved upward, caressing the curves of my shoulder. And then, up again. My neck, my chin, and finally, he held my cheeks between his palms. Still staring into his eyes, I watched as his face moved closer to mine. And when his lips touched mine, I rejoiced internally, accepting him.

Gracefully, our heads moved in sync as my mouth widened and my tongue got acquainted with his liquor-stained, ice cream-hoarding one. I could still taste the sweetness of the chilled treat, complimenting the Martell.

Completely engulfed in one another, we'd lost ourselves. It wasn't until the attendant whistled, reluctant to interrupt, letting us both know that our vehicles had arrived. Flushed, I pulled away, clearing the smeared gloss on my lips while trying to compose myself.

"Sorry," I apologized to the valet team.

Zane cared nothing about our lapse in judgment and lack of movement.

"You don't have to go home, Nature," he reminded me.

But Mason, my thoughts screamed, yearning for him just as much as I did the adventure of the night that was awaiting me if I agreed to follow Zane to his home. Because my son's face was the only one that could fill the void that I felt, knowing my night would end without him, I chose wisely.

"I know. But I... I..."

"Understood."

He didn't require an explanation. I wanted to express the newness of motherhood that chipped away at my sanity. I wanted to share with Zane that though I was happy to have a break from Mason, I missed him more than ever. But I didn't have to. He just... *understood.*

"Goodnight, Zane."

"Goodnight, Nature. I'll call you tomorrow. If you're not busy, you can roll with me."

"I'd love to." Nodding my head, I agreed without knowing any more details. I didn't need any.

"Bet. Be ready by ten. Take a nap because we're out until the sun's up. Celebrating my partner's birthday."

"Okay."

"Later."

"Later."

The wind brushed my cheeks as they hiked in the air,

watching as he made his way to his car and I made my way to mine. In the comfort of my space, I sighed in relief, knowing I'd made the right decision. I didn't need the GPS to guide me out of the lot and toward my destination. My son's heart led me from one light to the other, around every corner, down each street, and right up to his father's door where I stood, dialing Milo's number.

"Nay?" he answered, sleep on the tip of his tongue. I felt utterly awful for waking him from his sleep, but I was in desperate need of my son's touch. His skin against mine was the only way that I could sleep tonight.

"Open up."

"Open up?"

"Yes. I'm outside."

"Nay. You should be home, baby, enjoying your night."

"I know, but I can't sleep without him, Milo. Open the door."

As the final word left my mouth, I heard the locks turn. Behind the door, Milo appeared shirtless, bottom half covered in thin, linen pants that did little to conceal the print of his—

"Nature," he called out to me. "Come in."

It wasn't until then that I realized I was standing still, staring. I stepped inside, removing my shoes and setting them next to the door. Down the hallway, I traveled, feeling Milo's gaze burn holes in my back. Though half asleep, he was inquisitive. I could hear the questions as they circled around his head, begging to be freed.

I found Mason in his nursery with white noises playing as blue waves crashed against the ceiling from the night light that Milo had installed. I was a bit jealous of the serenity the room presented, leaving me wondering if the nursery I'd designed for him at my home compared. Mason was swaddled in the center of his bed, sound asleep. Still, I pulled his body close to the railing and scooped him right into my arms.

I marveled at his dark skin and perfect nose. He was Milo's twin. Malachi's twin. Makai's twin. Mercer's twin. He was undoubtedly a Domino. I leaned forward to kiss his cheek, but the hand around the back of my neck interfered with my display of affection.

"Milo, what are you doing?"

"Don't put ya fucking lips on him, Nature. Not until you brush your teeth."

"Seriously?" I slurred, realizing just how intoxicated I was. Through my entire drive, soberness carried me. Now, the drinks I'd enjoyed were beginning to add up.

Instead of responding, Milo took Mason from my hands.

"Go gargle or something. And yes, I'm serious. Unless you want me to drive your drunk ass home, then, let's go. Head straight to the bathroom."

"You're being so dramatic right now, Milo." Chuckling, I sucked my teeth, trying to figure out what his issue was.

I still managed to get out of the nursery and down the hall in the room I'd grown to love. Secretly, I'd claimed it as my own. I rounded the corner and entered the bathroom, knowing Milo was right on my heels. The counter lights glowed, illuminating the space enough for me to leave the main light untouched. I grabbed the small paper cup from the dispenser and held it beneath the tiny faucet that released the minty blue liquid often used after a good brushing.

I tossed it back, swirling it around my mouth until I couldn't stand the burning. My entire mouth was on fire. I followed up by gargling water and cleaning my lips with a damp cloth. My full bladder urged me to empty it.

And after I managed, I removed my dress completely, stripping down to the half bra and thong that I wore beneath. My breast pads were full. I dumped them both in the trash and grabbed new ones from my purse, ready to release the milk that would carry traces of alcohol that I wasn't willing to give Mason.

I walked into the bedroom, fully expecting for it to be empty. But to my surprise, Milo was pulling the covers back as Mason rested in the bassinet beside the bed. Sighing, I pushed forward, deciding against protesting because it would be useless.

"He's not sleeping next to you. He'll want to nurse and your breasts aren't in the condition for him to do so. Instead of agitating him and making our night miserable, leave him in the bassinet."

Milo laid down the law the second he caught wind of my presence. A response wasn't necessary. He was right. Instead of a rebuttal, I used the little energy I had to drag my body to bed and underneath the cover where Milo met me. He pulled my body into his, hand wrapped around my insecurity, caring nothing about the small pouch that was taking it's time retracting after stretching for Mason's accommodation.

The stiffness of his body made it impossible to melt against his chest. The sound of his widened nostrils inhaling my hair before lowering his head to smell my neck, then shoulder, and my chest left me dumbfounded. And when he flung his body from the sheets, my confusion steepened.

"Where you been, Nay?" He breathed heavily, rounding the bed where I'd scooted and sat up, trying to figure out what was happening.

"What?"

A headache began knocking on the left side of my head.

"Where. Have. You. Been?"

"Out. Why?"

"Out where?"

"Milo, I don't ask you all of these questions when you're out, doing whatever it is you like to do when you're out. Please, show me the same respect."

"Nay, I'm really trying not to blow a fucking gasket. All that other stuff is irrelevant. Where you been and who you been with?"

"A friend."

"You don't have a friend. I'm your friend. Mason is your friend. Shayla, that's your friend. And you talking about disrespect? You climbing in my bed, smelling like some department store cologne and telling me to respect you?"

"Can we talk about this in the morning, Milo? Please? My head is throbbing and I just want to get some sleep."

Not another word was exchanged. I watched as Milo wheeled our son out of the bedroom, shutting the door quietly behind them. I could still feel his energy once they'd left. Thankful for the dark, I was relieved that I hadn't seen the pain the reside in his features. Unfortunately, the strain in his voice was enough to leave me questioning if coming over instead of going home was a good idea.

Maybe I should go, I thought, unsure of what was best at this point.

Before I could move an inch, the door crept open.

"Lay your ass down and don't even think about hitting that door, either."

"I'm not."

They were the only words I could muster before he bolted again, leaving me alone with my thoughts. Instead of laying down, as I'd been advised, I headed for the bathroom again. This time to cleanse my body from head to toe, erasing the memories of my night with Zane until I left Milo's home.

ELEVEN

MY HEART ACHED as I stood over her, watching her sleep soundly, wondering if another nigga had contributed to her exhaustion and peace of mind. The last few months of our lives replayed in my head. Although there were some good times, there was plenty of pain. Nature was on the receiving end of all of it. That shit stung.

Even through my vexation, I knew her actions was justified. Did I give a fuck? I didn't. Because there wasn't a woman on my roster that could replace Nature. She wasn't a fool, though. She was a calculated woman. Anyone she allowed in her space had potential.

Could the nigga replace me? Nah. But for Nature, a runner-up was just as good because she'd tried three times too many with the starting player and he'd let her down.

"Wake up!" I yelled, slapping her ankle.

The abrupt, rude method jolted her from her sleep. Satisfied with myself, I stood on side of the bed, watching Nature pull herself together. One of my white shirts covered her body. The front was soaked in breastmilk, a result of sleeping without a bra.

"Breakfast is ready. Your pump is right there."

"My pum—" She breathed, rubbing her head in confusion. "You went to my house an— what time is it?"

"Noon. Get up and drain your milk before you clog a duct or be in pain. Make sure you dump that shit, too. We can test the next batch."

"Thank you." She sighed, grabbing the portable pump and strapping it to her body, along with the nursery bra I'd gotten as well.

After my run, Mason and I took Nature's keys and her truck. I ran it through the car wash, filled her tank, picked up a few of her favorite groceries from the store, and grabbed her breast pump and a bra. We'd been home for two hours and she was still resting—until now.

Who the fuck is he, Nay? The words were at the tip of my tongue. Instead of asking, I turned to leave. The conversation would be had, but I needed her to get herself together before we began.

When I reached the kitchen, Mason lie quietly in his bassinet, eyes big and bright, waiting to be held. He loved being in your arms, right in your face. His silence and calmness was easily a result of his hearing deficiency but I'd concluded he was simply a chill ass dude, just like his mother.

"Hey, dude. You ready for some milk? You ready to fill that tummy, buddy?"

I squeezed my hand together, balling my four fingers into my palm and creating a pulse for milk in ASL.

"Hungry? Hmm? That baby hungry?"

Mason giggled as I rounded my hand, leaving space in the middle, and rubbed it from my belly to my throat, right down the center.

"Hungry, buddy?"

With him laying on my arm, I made my way into the kitchen and scooped up the bottle of breastmilk that was cooling down. I tested it on the backside of my hand, satisfied with the temperature. I plopped it right into his mouth.

Greedily, he began chugging. The custom design of the nipple on the bottle was a duplicate of Nature's, making the transition simple and heavenly for me. Most breastfed babies despised being bottle fed. With the new technology and companies catering to breast babies specifically, things were much easier.

As he finished up his second bottle of the morning, I moved about the kitchen, making a plate for both Nature and I. The first plate went down on the table just as he completed the four ounces he'd been given. I removed the bottle from his mouth to prevent air from entering his system and causing gas. Just when I positioned him on my shoulder to pat his back, a large burp exited his tiny body.

"Goddamn, boy."

I held him up in the air, trying to make sure that had come from him. His lazy smile and low lids revealed his near future. Mason was ready to hit the sack, again. It was time for his midday nap and I refused to get in the way of that. Quick on my feet, I pulled the bassinet into the living room and removed the blanket that he loved most.

I wrapped it around his body after double checking his diaper. It was still dry. Swaddled, he went back down without a fuss. I didn't have to wait it out or rock him. Mason would, undoubtedly, fall asleep on his own, so I let him be and continued my work in the kitchen.

"Morning." Nature yawned as I set the last plate on the table.

Taking a look in her direction, I paused briefly.

"Okaaaaay," she responded to my silence.

I noticed she wasn't wearing the clothes I'd set out for her to lounge in if that was what her plans were. Just as I fixed my mouth to ask, she explained.

"I'm not sure who left their clothes over here, but I'm not into hand-me-downs, Milo."

"Those are your clothes, Nature, so are the ones in the closet of that room if you'd care to check. I pulled the tag off them this morning."

"My clothes?" she questioned.

"Yes. They've been there since you had Mason. I expected you guys here much sooner than this weekend."

Feeling foolish, she caved, slumping in the chair she'd sat in.

"I know you like to make yourself believe I'm some type of villain in this situation, but I'm not."

"I never said that, Milo."

"Then why would you even fix your mouth to say some shit like that, Nay? Why would that even cross your mind?

Seriously, you think I'd lay another woman's clothes out for you? I'm not you."

"OK." She sighed. "We're getting to the underlying message of this now. I'd appreciate it if you simply said whatever it is on your mind instead of poking around it."

"I'm not poking around. You didn't give me time. I had every intention of saying exactly what's on my mind. I've never had an issue with that."

"OK. Then, go ahead, Milo."

"You fucking him?"

That wasn't the question I wanted to ask, but it came right out because I truly wanted to—needed to know.

"You're asking questions that has absolutely nothing to do with you and that you really don't want to know the answer to, Milo."

Chuckling, I sat back in my seat, uninterested in the food in front of me. My appetite no longer existed. Staring across the table at Nature's undeniable beauty, even in the early morning, I wanted nothing more than to bend her smart mouth ass over the table and fuck her until she forgave me for old and new, put her ass to bed, and then go find the nigga that was gunning for my spot.

"Just answer the question."

"Are you having sex with Chr—"

"Fuck Christina."

Tilting her head, she shrugged her shoulders. Her nonchalant attitude had always been something rather attractive about her, but right now, it was the power source to my displeasure.

"Milo, there's absolutely nothing I have to say about my

private life. If you're looking for answers from me, then you're not going to get them."

"Three stipulations, Nay. I had three fucking stipulations when we agreed to have Mason. Natural conception. Co-parenting. And in the event you decided to date again, I was first in line, giving our son a chance at a two-parent household. How quickly have you forgotten?"

"Me? Forgot? Milo, please be serious right now. *I forgot?* Or did you forget that I initiated things, twice, and both times, I was slapped in the face with your lifestyle and the fact that I didn't fit in it.

"Have you forgotten I came to your home and found your assistant descending the very stairs that my son will climb the rest of his life? Have you forgotten that I tried returning the favor, bringing you lunch at the office, only to discover you and your assistant had already indulged in the very act that I was craving at that very moment?

"Or what about the fact that you nearly missed your son's birth? If that's not enough, you missed his very first pediatric visit, leaving me alone to deal with his diagnosis? Since, have you improved? Yes. But *I* have not forgotten. I'm not a revengeful person. It benefits me none. But I've had my share of heartache over the last few months.

"Excuse me for wanting to feel something else. If that means seeing other people, then that's exactly what I'll do." Calmly, she explained.

"All you had to do was say the word, Nay. Shit, all you have to do is say the word and I'll drop all that. None of that matters. That was just something to do until I got shit right with you."

Snickering, Nature shook her head.

"Say the word? Milo, I've said the word. And I shouldn't have had to. If you truly wanted to get things on track for us, you would've dropped them all because you wanted to, not because I wanted you to.

"Pursuing me doesn't mean falling into a routine because we're used to each other or because we have history. You messed up, yet I feel like I've been doing all the repairing. Pursuing me means actively going for me, showing me, without a doubt, that I'm the one person you want, need, and yearn for. Not once, Milo, can you actually say that you have.

"I carried your son for nine months. Nine months and the most I got from you, aside from harmless flirting, was a text message that said, I miss y'all. And what did I do with that inkling that you truly wanted this? I ran. I ran to you. I ran so fast and so hard that I fell flat on my face when I reached you.

"You've had chances, Milo. Don't act like you didn't know that I wanted this, wanted you. I've always wanted you, wanted us. But I've been waiting and waiting and waiting for you to really apply some freaking pressure instead of thinking things would be a breeze for you and me as they always had been.

"No. It was only always a bunch of talk. There was no action. And last year on my birthday, I thought that maybe it was the start of something different. I thought you'd stop at nothing to secure a spot in my life, no matter what imaginary boundaries I set.

"Those were just tactics. Those were just reasons for me to feel better, knowing that if you'd just pushed on those barriers a little bit, they would've fallen and I would've caved. But you didn't. And when I couldn't take it anymore, I came running to you.

"Even that failed. So, what's the issue now? Why is dating suddenly an issue for you after you've actively shown me that it's not me you truly desire? We just sound good together to you, Milo."

She shrugged, forking her food around her plate.

"That's untrue, Nature."

Her words crushed my spirit. She hadn't lied. Not once. Not until the last few words.

"Honestly, I don't know what's true anymore. My intentions weren't to come and ruin you and Mason's time together," she grimaced, standing to her feet. "I just missed him."

My heart swelled as I watched her eyes gloss over.

"Since we're being honest, Nay, was it really Mason that you came for?"

"After all of that, Milo, after all I just said, your only response is to ask if I missed you or Mason?"

"That's not what I asked."

I'd heard her loud and clear. She'd answered my question without answering it.

"I'm done responding with words. You've made it clear that I must actively pursue you. What the fuck do we have to talk about, Nay? I'm just trying to get myself together. Finding out the woman of my dreams is fucking another nigga got me stuck right here in this seat, trying my hardest not to crumble. Forgive me for needing a minute to pick my pieced heart up out of my glass dish."

"I'm not having sex with him," she blurted, closing her eyes immediately after realizing what she'd said.

Her need to soothe my ache was heartening, beginning the healing process much faster than I'd imagined it would start.

"He's a nice guy, Milo."

"Do it look like I give a fuck? Seriously, Nature. Do it look like I care?"

"I'm going to leave, now. I didn't come last night expecting the morning to transpire as it has."

"Enjoy the rest of your weekend. Please understand that I'm not standing down. I'm shooting my shot and I'm making buckets. You want to be pursued? Prepare to be pursued."

"May the best man win."

She sucked the skin of her teeth with a final shrug. Slightly offended by her remark, I waited impatiently at the table until she'd made it back to the guest bedroom. I found her near the entry, pulling another one of my white shirts over her head. She'd changed out of the stained one before coming to the kitchen for breakfast.

Hemming her against the door, with a hand around her neck, I stuck my tongue so far down her throat that I could feel her tonsils. I used my free hand to slide up her thigh until I reached her pantiless pussy. She had no fucking business walking around my home like this, not expecting to get her back blown out.

"Uhhhhhh."

Biting down on my tongue, she moaned from the entrance of my middle and index fingers. Just as I recalled, her pussy was snug, fitting around my fingers like gloves. My dick jumped in my shorts, protesting my finger's privilege.

Not right now.

In and out, around and around, I worked her pussy while tonguing her down. Completely invested in the moment, Nature devoured me. Her juices coated my hand down to my wrist. She was creaming uncontrollably, making me rethink my sinister plan. It was backfiring, leaving my dick throbbing and my head spinning. The control I'd assumed I'd maintain was a losing battle.

"I'm going to cum," she whispered into my mouth. "Oh, God. I'm going to cum. Put it inside of me. Put it in—"

Abruptly, I pulled away, disengaging completely. Against the door, Nature leaned breathlessly, confusion furrowing her brows and contorting her features.

"Milo."

"May the best man win, Nay."

I didn't give her the satisfaction of sticking around. I made my way down the hallway and into my bedroom, I shut the door behind me before shoving my pants down toward my knees. I fisted my dick, using her creaminess as lubrication as I began to massage my rigidness. Eyes closed, I was immediately back in the room with Nature as she begged me to lodge my dick inside of her.

My nut rose without hesitation. The lump in my shaft and the sound of Nature's voice looping in my head were the end of me. Within seconds, I was releasing my seeds into my hand.

"Fuck."

THE CAMERA in the backseat allowed me to keep an eye on Mason as I drove and at stop lights. It made the ride so much smoother and I worried much less during transit. The truck was massive, making him feel so far away. His condition didn't have me feeling as guilty for the loud, thunderous roaring of my stereo as we cruised.

"And you get flewed out. Leave it in ha raw while she on top and let it ooze out. Her head was so stupid would've thought she had two mouths."

EST Gee spat through my speakers and I matched him word for word, thinking about one person in particular. Nature was the naughtiest of them all, though she was the most educated and reserved. Her head was stupid. Brain was ridiculous. And I'd be damned if I let another nigga lock that shit down.

May the best man win. Her words still sat with me, stirring movement in my chest as I pulled into Pop's yard. I hopped out, made my way to the back, and began unbuckling my boy. He had fallen asleep on the ride, but the kiss I planted on his forehead nudged him awake.

"Alright, dude. We're here."

It didn't matter that Mason couldn't hear me. I still spoke to him as if he could. Understanding was one thing. You didn't need ears for that. A skull with a brain was enough. He had both.

Sleepiness plagued his stretched lips, and pointy cheeks as he smiled at me. It was almost all he ever did. Mason was an amazing baby. We didn't have any issues out of him. He hardly cried. And when he did, it was minimal. His audiologist said that it might have a lot to do with his lack of hearing, but Nature and I believed it was simply because he was a good boy.

"Let's go see our old man. You ready? You ready to chill with the boys? Your uncles over here. Your girl Aussie here. So is Maz. You're in for a treat, dude. You missed Friday dinner, but we're about to make up for it, today."

By the time I got him out of his seat and in my hands, Aussie was rounding the truck.

"Can I help with anything?"

"I got it, baby."

"OK. What is Mason doing?"

"You'll see in a minute, Aussie," I chuckled, watching as she stood on the tips of her toes trying to get a better view.

I strapped him into the carrier that I'd slid up both of my arms. He fit snug into it, laying his head against my chest and closing his eyes to shield them from the bright sun. I tossed a thin blanket over his head to assist and shut the door of the truck behind me. With his bag in tow, we trekked up the driveway and into the yard. Aussie led the way, looking back every few seconds to make sure that Mason was alright.

"This nigga looking like he play on Hangover or some sh–"

"Hello to you as well, Makai. Instead of bullshitting, greet your nephew. Say hello."

"You being serious right now? That little nigga can't hear shit."

WHACK!

WHACK!

Right across the back of his head and neck, Makai received open-hand licks from Mercer and I.

"Ignorant," Mercer growled, lowly.

"That's why I'm not even over on that side of the room. His energy is always off," Malachi shook his head.

"You better be glad you got my little nigga or—"

"Or what?" I asked, beginning to remove Mason from his carrier.

"And you, you just a big, bored ass nigga that pumped weights the whole eight and think I'm about to fight you. Nigga, I'm shooting."

"Make sure you aim high, nigga," Mercer suggested.

"That's the plan. Big ass."

"And big where? This man is a good, what, twenty more than you and me. Twenty that's hardly even noticeable." I sided with Mercer.

"Twenty you gone feel if his—"

"Makai, shut up. All you do is start shit," Pops demanded, strolling into the living room like the cool cat he was.

"Alright, na," I whistled, admiring him in the Nike shorts and tee to match. The hat on his head was Nike as well.

"Boy, be quiet. This ain't nothing. Give me my grandson."

"Technically, I'm your grandson. You want me?"

"Me too," Mercer said.

"Me too," Malachi added.

"Me—"

"Shut up!" He didn't let Makai finish, making us all double over in laughter.

No one wanted to claim Makai sometimes. He was a possible.

"Why y'all always inviting me places if—"

"Shut up!" we all said in unison.

"Bet," he scoffed, leaning back and placing his hands behind his head.

I handed over Mason and watched Pops' grimace turn into a full-blown grin.

"Hey there, Daddy. Hey, man."

It was his third time seeing Mason, and each time, he got a bit more attached. According to him, I didn't bring Mason around nearly as much as I should. Truthfully, I was still getting acquainted with the little guy. It made me selfish with our time together. He knew it just like I did.

We all settled around the living room. Aussie followed the baby, ending up at Pops' side, watching and observing as if Mason was precious glass and would break if mishandled. Without a doubt, I knew they'd be the best of friends, just like she and Maz, who was sound asleep on the blanket next to Malachi.

"I'm trying to get this nigga out of the house for his birthday," Makai announced. "I got a section at Lust tonight."

"Merc, you rolling or what?" I asked, turning toward Mercer.

"Not really feeling it. But this nigga won't let it die."

"And ain't. Get out the house. Rub on some ass and titties. Make me a believer, nigga. 'Cause I ain't saw a piece of pu—I ain't saw nothing come out that crib since you been home."

"Make you a believer?" I scoffed. "You still on that?"

Malachi laughed, still shaking his head. "I don't understand why y'all entertain this man."

"I'm on baby duty," I sighed. "Maybe next weekend."

"His birthday is Tuesday. We hitting the club this weekend."

"I've got Mason. And your babies if you need me to keep them, Malachi."

Silently, Malachi shook his head. It was written in stone that he wouldn't be joining us. No one tried to convince him otherwise. There was so much pain and heartache behind his decline. He deserved to reject the invitation in peace. Watching the glimmer in his eyes transform into gloom made my chest burn. I rubbed from one side to the other, diverting my attention while praying it subsided.

"I'm down," I told Makai.

"Lawe is down," he shared.

"Which leaves you no choice," I said to Mercer.

"Portland in town. Even that nigga sliding."

"Oh yeah. Mercer, you coming out. That's it. That's settled. Even if we have to cuff you to the car."

"Go enjoy yourself, Mercer," Malachi suggested. "It's all on me, bro."

"It's all on me, bro," Makai mimicked Malachi. "Like we broke or something."

He pointed between him and I.

"If you're expecting me to turn down free liquor and a good time, then look a little further, homie. I'm not the one." I held my hands up. "Malachi got it."

My phone vibrated in my pocket. I quickly tuned everyone out, worried that it was Nature trying to contact me. I realized, almost immediately, that Mason was in my care, which settled me slightly. *Lacey.* The name was familiar, one that came across my screen every so often, just like the others.

Before reading the message, I deleted the entire thread. Taking things a step further, I deleted the threads that followed until I was down to approximately seven of them. Of the seven, it included threads from my brothers, Portland, a buddy I kept in contact with from med school, and Nature.

I exited the messaging app and opened my contacts. One by one, I began erasing them, along with the faint memories that each of them held. Before I knew it, thirty minutes had passed and my eyes were still trained on my phone.

"Don't you hear Pops talking to you?" Makai fussed, snatching my phone from my hand. "This nigga zoned out."

"Give me my phone."

"Reesh? You erasing big booty Reesh out ya phone? Man, where my line at? She can get added to my roster."

"Makai, hand me my shit."

"Who else you getting rid of? I've got a few slots."

"Everybody."

"Everybody? Damn, what the hell kind of voodoo Wilderness done put on you?"

Standing to my feet, I cocked back, ready to send a blow straight to Makai's abdomen. However, Mercer's grip on my fist stopped me.

"Call her by her name, Makai. All them games you playing, chill, my nigga. The joke is over."

"Damn, who pissed in your Cheerios? I've been messing around with Nature since I met her. It's never been an issue. Why your panties in a bunch?"

Realizing my level of sensitivity had increased tremendously after the night and morning I'd had, I settled a bit, taking a seat on the couch next to Makai. I rubbed my hand up and down my face, trying to make sense of everything happening between Nature and I.

"Lay off on the jokes, Makai. From this day forward," Malachi told our brother. "Milo, is there anything you need to share with us?"

"Besides the fact that I'm getting my shit together so I can live my happily ever after with Nature and our son, nah."

There was no need to explain everything going on in my head or my heart. It was understood.

"Then, let's make tonight a night to remember because it sounds like it's the last night we'll see you in the streets. Forward them contacts before you delete them all."

"You hitting behind your brother?" Mercer asked, face knotted.

"Have you not seen Reesh? I'd hit that shit behind my pops if it came down to it."

The humor offered at that moment was much needed.

"Just awful," Pops grunted.

He'd rocked Mason right to sleep. My son laid peacefully in his arms without a care in the world, soaking in the love that surrounded him. I rested my back against the couch with every intention of making myself comfortable. I had nothing to do and nowhere to be anytime soon. With my phone in my possession again, I continued clearing my contact list without sending Makai a single digit.

TWELVE

THE WIND TICKLED the tip of my nose. With my eyes closed, I enjoyed the breeze that the retracted panoramic roof allowed inside. It felt amazing outside. The sun had gone into hiding leaving the Berkeley City lights in charge. The tiny dollop of a moon that we were given for the night hardly made a difference.

Zane handled the wheel, effortlessly, traveling seventy-five miles per hour on the expressway, heading for our destination. It was near midnight. While I should've been deep underneath my covers, I was just getting out of bed and out of the house. Our plans to visit a bar prior to our final stop failed because I simply couldn't pull myself out of bed any sooner than the eleven o'clock hour.

As we neared our exit, Zane's car slowed to a creep. Red lights for what seemed like a half of a mile lined the exit, everyone headed in the same direction. Suddenly, I was happy I hadn't driven. Meeting Zane at my parents' house was the best decision I could've made. By the end of the night, I would be sound asleep in my bedroom, waking up to breakfast that my mother prepared.

I wasn't sure what was playing on the stereo but it had a nice tune to it. I bobbed my head, unable to repeat a single word but refusing to look so out of the loop. The engine of the Corvette revved as Zane tapped the gas, stirring up a bunch of commotion from the people that had already parked and were walking toward the club.

Lust. The large sign that could be read from afar said. From the silhouette next to the bright, neon sign, I concluded we would be entering a strip club. I wasn't a night crawler, so I didn't frequent clubs, but I'd been to a handful. Strip clubs, however, I'd only heard about them and never visited one personally. Tonight would be my very first time and I wasn't sure if it was excitement or nervousness bubbling in my belly.

The black miniskirt and black top I wore, along with thigh-high silver boots seemed fitting for the occasion. According to Zane, his friend and old business partner was celebrating his fortieth birthday and he needed to be in attendance, even if it meant stopping by for a few minutes. I'd learned over the last few weeks that Zane was an entrepreneur with investments in the transportation business.

Finally, through the line of cars waiting to enter the parking lot, we pulled up to the front of Lust where I was instructed to exit. Hand in hand, Zane led me up the walkway and toward the long line of people waiting. I'd quickly gathered that this was a spot that people loved to visit for a good time. There was one line after another, making me wonder if we'd ever get inside.

To my surprise, we brushed past the line to another line, one that was much shorter and moving much faster. Within seconds, we were being wanded for weapons and gaining access to the loud, dark space filled with fully clothed guests and the naked bodies of women who worked at the club.

Stunning. Each and every one of them were incredibly beautiful with bodies that would make an insecure woman cower. With my head held high, I strutted as if I belonged, hanging onto Zane as he led us to the booth where a few of his friends welcomed him. The universal awkwardness ensued as I stood beside Zane, who dabbed up everyone in the booth before introducing me as his friend and offering me a seat next to him.

"You good?" he asked once the introductions were out of the way and I settled in.

He, on the other hand, never took the seat beside me. He chose to stand near his friends instead.

Nodding, I assured him I was fine.

"What do you want to drink?"

Over the loudspeaker, he yelled into my ear, but it sounded like a whisper.

"Wine. I'll take wine."

"Baby, they don't have wine here."

"Lemon drop?" I asked.

"Nah. I doubt that either. It's hard liquor. Real hard liquor with maybe a splash of juice."

"Uhhh. Any frozen drinks, perhaps?"

"Don't worry. Sit tight. I'll figure something out."

"OK."

Though I shouldn't have been indulging again after the previous night, I figured one wouldn't hurt. Zane returned within two minutes, though it felt like ten. In his hand, he held a yellowish drink that he handed me and I accepted without hesitation, putting it up to my lips and taking a tiny sip to make sure I was willing to commit.

"Ummm. This is good. What is it?"

I stood, moving closer to Zane.

"Not sure. I told the bartender to hook me up with something girly."

"Oh, wow. Did you really tell them that?"

"Yeah, and I'm glad you like it. Just in case you didn't, I bought this one, too."

He handed me another drink. This one was a reddish tint. I decided to try it as well. It was equally as good.

"I'll take both." I chuckled, holding one in each hand, desperate to loosen up and enjoy my night out. "Thank you."

"My pleasure." Zane laughed with a shake of his head.

He was definitely a good time. Nothing felt forced. He allowed me to have my way while simultaneously remaining dominant and endearing. He was as sweet as he was tart. There was the perfect amount of everything within him.

Instead of sitting back down, I stood in front of him, swaying my hips from side to side while sipping from the first cup he'd handed me. Usher's "Superstar" played over the speakers, encouraging the slow wind against Zane's rigidness. With a hand on my hip, he held me in place, making sure I didn't go too far or fall forward into the table that held bottles of alcohol and pitchers of juice.

The straw from the drink never left my mouth, bringing my sipping to an end as the song did. I set the cup on the table, wasting little time starting the second drink in my hand as Trina's song, "Phone Sex" began to play. I remembered being a young girl, sneaking and listening to songs just like the one playing while my parents were downstairs. The volume would be as low as possible so that I could hear them coming up the stairs and change the selection if necessary. Music like so wasn't allowed in our home or cars.

Right after Trina was Future. The music shut on and off as the crowd sang the lyrics along with him. Every time the DJ cut the music, it was as if a choir was singing.

"You telling me you falling out of love with me?" everyone sang. I'd only heard the song a handful of times, but I joined in, anyway.

In the midst of my performance, my nostrils grew sensitive to the smells around me. Not because I was in a new environment or because of my random allergy flares, but because I recognized a familiar scent among the others. It was loud, boisterous, and dominating, just like the man who wore it religiously. It was his signature, and I knew it well.

I ditched the straw and tossed back the rest of the drink in my hand, unsure of what was going on around me. The darkness offered little assistance. Suddenly, I felt like I was front and center, holes being stared into the sides of my face, neck, and back. My eyes wandered, dreading the moment they came in contact with my son's father. Without a doubt, I knew he was near. I could feel his presence. I sensed him. I smelled him. And I *saw him*.

Headed straight in my direction was Milo. As if in sync, when he moved, so did the three men who were in the booth next to us. I didn't remember seeing a soul there the last time I'd peeped over. To my surprise, it was now filled with Domino men, all dressed in black, blending with the darkness of the atmosphere. It was their gleaming jewels that helped me keep track of their rapid movement.

Shit, I panicked.

Run, a voice screamed in my head.

Shaking my head from side to side, I began to plead with Milo through shifting eyes. Looking straight at me, he continued in my direction, not giving a damn about the look on my face or the panic in my eyes. When he finally reached me, I froze.

Stepping up and into the section that we were in without caring about the people around us, he leaned over until his lips touched my ear.

"You know you got me fucked up, right?"

"Milo, please. I just want to enjoy my ni—"

"You can leave voluntarily or involuntarily. The choice is yours, but either way, you leaving this motherfucking section, Nay."

"Bro, what's up with you?" Zane interfered, placing a hand on Milo's chest.

My bowels began to move and I swore I'd ruin my panties at any second.

"Zane. Please. It's just a misunder—"

"Nigga, if you don't get your dick beaters off my chest

and your hand from around my woman, I'm going to lay you out in this bitch."

"Milo."

"Nature, you know this nigga?"

"I'm the nigga dicking her down. Now, stay up out our business. Come on, Nay."

"She ain't got to go if—"

"Watch out, Nay," Milo warned as he began to scoot backward, partially out of the booth.

"Milo, please." I sighed, watching as he cocked back, his body demanding space beyond what was necessary. And before I could get another word out, he'd let off.

WHAM.

Zane's body tumbled to the floor. Everything happened in slow motion. The drink in his hand fell along with him, spilling on my shoes and legs.

"My God!" I shrieked.

Gasps from everyone surrounding us could be heard above the music. Chaos was sure to follow the mess Milo had made. I looked up, examining the damage, fully expecting those around us to lunge forward, ready to brawl, but to my surprise, no one made a move.

Mercer, Makai, and Lawe stood shoulder to shoulder, arms folded in front of them with their fingers gripping pieces that would shut any party down and silence anyone from the section that got rowdy. Sadly, I knew that it wasn't a front. Each and every one of them fully intended to use their weapons so that Milo wouldn't have to.

They protected his career and livelihood as if he was the president of the United States. It had always been that way. He was their precious gem. He'd worked his butt off to gain his status and they refused to have it revoked, no matter the circumstances.

"Nay. Let's roll."

"I'm so sorry," I apologized to everyone.

Carefully, I stepped over Zane's body, nearly busting my knees as I fell face first. Quick on his toes, Milo managed to catch me mid-air. At that moment, I realized the drinks I'd consumed were kicking in.

"I got it," I fussed. "I don't need your help."

"Cool, then, fall on your fucking face. Just make sure you do that shit over there," he stated calmly, pointing to the section they had just left from.

Trying my hardest to conceal my true state and level of intoxication, I made my way over to their section. By now, there were bottles on their table, too. I plopped down in the first available space, which wasn't too far from the edge. Milo sat down beside me.

"Fix your face," he commanded. "Give me your foot. Let me make sure you ain't break your fucking ankle."

"I am an adult, Milo. I have every right to have fun and enjoy whoever I want to," I slurred. "You had no right. That was egregious. Why would you hit him like that?"

"I'm going to go hit his ass again if you keep taking up for that lame ass nigga."

"Ridiculous!"

He lifted my leg on his own after realizing I wouldn't.

"I'll be that. I told you, Nay. I'm done talking. You want action, then I'm going to give you just that. You want to be pursued, then don't complain about my pursuit. If you want to have fun, you can have fun right here with me and my people. Here," he said, pouring two small cups of liquor before handing me one. "Relax a little."

Hesitantly, I turned the clear liquid up. It burned my chest, making me gag, almost.

"Ugh."

Milo tossed his back without an issue before slamming his cup on the table and pouring himself another one.

"Understand that I'll knock a hundred niggas out if they're standing in my path to you. So, if you want to save me my good hand, stick to what you know best, Nay. *Me*."

With pouty lips, my gaze lingered. Even in the dark, Milo was truly a sight to see. Before standing to his feet, he pecked my lips and pulled me up with him.

"Don't sit down, now. Get ya dancing ass up."

He posted me right in front of him, wrapping his arms around me as he sang in my ear.

"We ain't spoke in so long, probably put me in the past. I can still get you wet and I can still make you laugh. You should call into work if that ain't too much to ask. I could pour you up a drink and we could burn something."

Relaxing against the firmness of his chest, I rocked from side to side along with him, feeling as if Drake was talking directly to us. The song was fitting.

"Come through. Come through. Come through. Come through. Girl you know we got thangs to do."

He was laying it on thick, straining my vagina of its juice.

"Know ya got that thang that I like."

Leaning me forward, he grinded behind me, pushing his hardness against my backside. When he raised me back up, he buried his face in my hair, wrapped his arm around my neck before moving my hair out of the way with his chin and biting down on it.

"Why has it been so long? Why has it been so long?" he asked, following along with the altered version of the song the DJ spun. "Why has it been so long?"

I closed my eyes, allowing him to roam my body with his fingers, forgetting that we were surrounded by a club full of people. The liquor left me careless, free to soak up every ounce of attention Milo was giving me. Like a puzzle, we just fit together.

The song changed and so did the atmosphere. As if something foreign had awakened within Milo, he began chanting the words to the song that I wasn't familiar with. After listening closely, I wanted to crawl under the bench in the booth and hide. Nevertheless, I stood by his side as the lyrics belted from his body.

"If that's yo hoe, that's my hoe too. If that's your hoe, that's my hoe, too."

Rather swiftly, our section filled with dancers who had no problem exposing every inch of their bodies to us. I thoroughly enjoyed the view, watching as the men around me tossed ones in their direction, in no particular order or fashion. Money rained down, seemingly becoming a signal for more women to join us. Milo handed me money from the stack he was pulling from. It was massive, tall like the hookahs on the tables of those around us.

I placed one dollar at a time on the woman who was bend over in front of me, one leg on the couch and the other on the floor while making her ass do things I didn't know were possible.

"Like this, baby," he instructed me, using one hand to push money out of the other.

I followed instructions, finding it much easier to distribute the money.

"I'm doing it, Milo."

"That's right. Throw that shit, Nay," he hyped me.

Shot after shot. Dollar after dollar. We cleared the table of the drinks and the money. By the time Mercer was rounding us all up, my feet felt like nubs and my head was spinning.

"I don't think I can walk," I admitted.

"What's the matter?" Milo and Makai asked in unison.

"My feet hurt," I whined.

"Here." Milo used the back of his feet to remove each of his shoes. "Sit down."

I took a seat on the cushion and watched as he slid my feet into his long shoes. They didn't fit at all, but they felt much more comfortable than mine, which he'd taken off beforehand. He grabbed my heels and purse from my hand before pulling me up.

"We ready," he announced as we proceeded.

He stayed behind me as Makai led the pack with Lawe and Mercer behind us. The club was still in full swing, but we were all toast. Everyone stalked the floor like zombies, finally making it out to fresh air after what felt like forever. I headed for valet, but was quickly redirected. Milo pulled me back into his chest. His dick resting against my ass left a heartbeat between my legs. I tried putting distance between us, but he wouldn't allow it.

"When you start running from this motherfucker?" he

whispered in my ear, dipping his hand into the front of my skirt.

"Milooo," I moaned, feeling his fingers on my swollen bulb. "Everyone can see us."

"So."

"I need to take a piss," Lawe told us all.

"Shit, me too," Mercer agreed.

"And I got some business I need to handle right quick," Milo announced, making everyone turn their head.

"This nigga." Makai chuckled.

"Handle your shit, nigga," Lawe advised with a shrug.

"No he doesn't. Please don't listen to him."

"Yes the fuck I do," he disagreed as we approached his truck.

He pushed me toward the driver side, opening the back door and then the front.

"Milo, seriously?" I groaned, fully intending to go through with his plan, whatever that plan was. I was leaking like a faucet and the quicker he filled me, the better off I'd be.

"Shut up, Nay," he whispered. "My dick hard as a fucking missile right now. Can you suck it? Please."

The sound of a stereo playing nearby made the decision much easier for me. With as much liquor as I'd consumed, remaining silent would be impossible. The last thing I wanted was everyone around us knowing how I truly got down.

"Please," Milo begged, lowering his pants and exposing his long, veiny tool.

I watered instantly, my mouth and my pussy, both releasing fluid. Without words being exchanged, I lowered my body until I was eye-level with the only tool that had the chance to rest in my box. Milo was the only man who could say he knew how my insides felt, how much pleasure it was to be inside of me, and how well I worked my walls.

Puh! I spat directly on his tip before taking him into my mouth completely, consuming as many inches as I could.

"Shit, Nay."

With my right hand on his balls, massaging them, I used my left to grip his thickness, sliding it up and down his length along with my mouth. Each time he touched the back of my throat, I gagged, ready to spit up everything I'd eaten and drank for the night. I knew from experience that Milo didn't mind a bit. He would, undoubtedly, release everything inside of his nutsack if I puked. He was filthy, but I couldn't deny the fact that I loved him that way.

"Suck that dick, baby. Shit."

I did as I was told, silently thanking whoever was playing the music.

"Stand up," he whimpered. "Stand up, Nature."

Obliging, I stood. Milo turned my body around, placing my upper half on the driver's seat. He pushed my skirt up over my waist and ripped my thong to shreds. Shortly after, I felt his tongue against my slit, sucking nearly my entire vagina into his mouth. He flicked his tongue back and forth rapidly, making my legs shake as my body weakened.

"Miloooooo."

Back and forth. Back and forth. He refused to let up, even when I began clenching my legs together in an effort to relieve myself.

"Milooooooooo. I'm cumming."

The levees broke and down came the flood. I creamed

into his mouth, closing my eyes as the tingliness ripped through me, threatening to end me. When he finally freed me, I rested my weight on the seat, gasping for air that I desperately needed.

His thickness tapped against my sensitivity. I yelped in sheer pleasure. Though exhausted, still waiting for what I knew was to come.

"Uhhhhhhhh."

Slowly, Milo entered me. Simultaneously, we released satisfying groans.

"This shit so fucking good."

Slowly, he stroked me from behind, gliding in and out of me with ease. With a hand around my neck, he dug into me, stretching me as he filled me to capacity. He was everywhere. All over me. His hand crawling all over my body and his dick climbing my vagina as if it was an obstacle he desperately needed to conquer.

Time wasn't on our sides. We both knew that our ending was near, but that didn't stop us from enjoying the folds of one another. Milo's thumb crept into my second hole, sending me to a new dimension. Closing my eyes, I altered my position in order to receive the perfect amount of friction and in the right spot. As he massaged my asshole with his thumb and milked my pussy with his dick, I felt the rumbling in my lower half, rising until it reached my vaginal area and began to sprout.

"Please. Please don't stop."

"I'm not," Milo assured me, driving himself deeper. With each stroke, his balls tapped the back of my thighs, sending me into another galaxy. And when I'd made it safely, I began to erupt from the inside out.

"Uhhhhh. I'm cumming. Milo, I'm cumming," I grunted, piercing my bottom lip with my teeth.

"Me too," he confessed, stiffening behind me. "Shit, girl."

His body fell forward as my vagina contracted around him, emptying him of everything he had to offer.

"Oh God."

The tingling sensation still hadn't subsided. My body was ringing, quite literally.

"Hurry up, my nigga. We ready to roll," Makai yelled out.

Chuckling, we both quieted, halting all movement.

"Shut yo' hating ass up," Lawe interjected.

"'Preciate that."

"We have to go."

Tickled, I pled with Milo to end our impromptu session. The liquor was still heavy in my system, distorting my logic, yet I knew that we needed to clear the parking lot, get home, and wash our bodies.

Sliding out of me slowly, Milo agreed. "I know."

He pulled my skirt back over my butt and tapped my backside.

"Climb up and get in."

I obliged, reclining the seat and curling up in a ball. Milo stood outside of the car, mingling with his family as I began to doze. It wasn't until he got inside, slamming the door behind him, that I opened my eyes.

"Nay?"

"Yes?"

"Where's your car?"

"At my parents'."

"Cool."

"Where's my son?"

"Safe."

"Where is he, Milo?"

"At Pops and we're not going to get his little ass, either."

"I don't want to. I want sleep."

"We ain't doing that, either."

"Then take me home."

"Erase that nigga number out of your phone and block his ass. Busy yourself with that and let me worry about the rest."

"Milo, I thought we were past that."

"I'm glad we can both agree on that."

"You're so annoying."

I maneuvered in the seat until I was comfortable. No matter how I twisted or turned, I was unable to settle. Milo's long arm stretched across the truck, landing on my thigh. It was at that moment that I sighed, closing my eyes and settled in. Within seconds, I was counting sheep.

THIRTEEN

Milo

THE BRIGHT LIGHTS and cool setting reminded me of every medical office I'd stepped into since pursuing a career in medicine. It wasn't until then that I realized they were all alike with an array of furniture that made them look different. However, they all felt the same. Brick.

"Hi. Can I help you?" the receptionist asked, wasting her breath.

The one-person suite made it rather easy to locate my target.

"Excuse me, sir. Sir."

I could hear the receptionist as she stumbled behind me,

trying to keep up with my legs, which looked about twice the length of hers. They were the longest things on my six foot six frame. She didn't stand a chance. Within seconds, I was pushing open the door with Newk + Company Trucking sprawled across.

Behind the desk sat the nigga that was responsible for the soreness of my knuckles this morning. By the discoloration of his skin, I wasn't the only one in pain. The eventful night had left us both with unpleasant memories. Wasting no time, I got straight down to business. I had shit to do and it didn't involve prancing around this nigga's office.

"Listen, my nigga, it's best you stay away from that one 'cause I'm pulling up every time 'bout it. That pussy there, it belongs to me and I'ma suck and fuck that motherfucker until the death of me. You feel me? Unless you ready to lay down 'bout it, then I suggest you keep it pushing, partner. These are problems you and any nigga you run with want to run from. Understand?"

"At my place of business, though, homie?"

"At ya crib. At ya momma's house. At Granny's spot. At the gas station. The grocery store. It makes me no difference. The message remains the same. Come up off that one or it's up. I don't give a fuck where we at."

Nodding, he remained silent, gnawing on his bottom lip.

"And go get ya fucking eye checked out. That shit looks painful. Send me the bill. It's on me."

I reached forward, tipped over the cup of toothpicks and shook until one slid out. I popped it into my mouth and made my way out of the door. I shut it back, but not before hearing the receptionist begin her line of questioning.

"Do you want me to call the police?" she asked frantically.

"Nah. I respect the nigga's gangster. I ain't even hit the pussy yet, but I have a feeling it would have me acting like that, too. Get back to work."

With a tilt of the head, I continued on my way, headed to Nature's so that I could officially get my day started. I figured another week away from the desk wouldn't hurt. I had a task list longer than my frame and every task on that motherfucker involved Nature. Until I got shit right with her, the office wouldn't see me.

My priorities were set in stone. There was no second-guessing and no sugarcoating it anymore. Burying myself in work was only a temporary solution. Nature and Mason were the solutions of a lifetime. I needed to make sure they were covered before stepping foot behind my desk.

I hopped into my ride and peeled off. The engine was still running and my music was still pumping. The second Makai forwarded the information to me, I made my way across town to holler at the nigga Zane. I wouldn't be able to focus on the tasks at hand until I handled that. Makai suggested I waited for him, but that was impossible. If I needed him, I knew he was in route, which was good enough.

Handled, I shot over to him through text.

Hardheaded ass nigga. Do I need to slide by, anyway? Reinforcement never hurt.

Nah. He got the point.

I knew that my last message was pointless and Makai

would slide regardless. Yet, I sent it anyway, hoping he'd listen for once.

Within twenty minutes, I was pulling up to Nature's home. She didn't give me a chance to park before she was at the door, standing out on the porch with a mug on her face. From the looks of things, she was privy to information that she shouldn't have been.

"Milo! Really?"

She tossed the bags of milk she'd pumped at me. I caught them mid-air, waiting for more to come from that sick ass mouth of hers. The thought of her on her knees in the parking lot last night had my shit rocking up.

"Really, what?"

"You tracked Zane down? What is the matter with you?"

She folded her hands across her chest, looking better every time she twisted her face a different way. Nature didn't know it, but she looked the prettiest when she was upset.

"If you'd blocked him like I told you to last night, then you wouldn't know shit because he wouldn't be able to contact you."

"That's beside the point."

"That is the point."

"You're insane. Why would you go to that man's place of business?"

"Bet. I'm on my way back up there. I told that bitch to let that shit go, but I see that motherfucker hard-of-hearing."

"Do not! Makai's sick ass is there. That is who made him call."

A smile curved my lips upward. *My nigga.*

"You think this is funny? You guys are ridiculous. It's not that serious."

"You ain't never felt that thang between your legs so I wouldn't expect you to understand. Now, that's the end of that. We're not even discussing that nigga no more. Erase the number and block him."

"I will."

"Right now."

"Milo."

"Right now. While I'm here."

I pointed at her phone, instructing her to do so in front of me.

"Go ahead so we won't even have these problems anymore."

Even through mumbled protests, she opened her phone, unlocked it, and erased the contact. She held the phone up to my face and showed me the screen.

"See. Happy?"

I wrapped my arms around her, pushing her against the door.

"Move."

As much as she hated to admit it, this was the pressure she'd been waiting for me to apply. Though Nature was a well-rounded, well-educated, well-reserved woman, it was my rough edges that got her juices flowing and her heart pumping. My knowledge and extensive education was just icing on the cake.

"Move, Milo. You dropped me off to go be foolish. Move."

"That's what you pissed about. Would you have been happier if I'd dicked you down before I dropped you off?"

The root of her issue was clear now.

"No. And I need some emergency contraceptive. You weren't exactly careful last night."

"That wasn't the plan."

"I just had a baby, Milo. What do you mean, it wasn't the plan?"

"Might as well get them out of the way."

"No. Stop by the store or I'll do it myself."

"Don't play with me, Nay. I better be down there, catching my daughter in nine months."

"I'm telling you now that it won't happen. Worry about going to get our son right now and leave me that hell alone. I'm serious."

"I got him. And we've got shit to do. I'm not bringing him home right away."

"Whatever. Can you let me go?"

"Nope. I'm taking you on a date this week since you want to be courted so fucking bad. I'm going to court you."

"Are you asking me? Because that's something you ask a woman."

"Nah. I'm done asking. I'm telling you. Have your shit together and be ready when I say be ready."

"Demanding much?"

I leaned forward and rested my lips against Nature's. She opened for me, placing a hand on each of my cheeks and pulling me deeper. I pulled back, chuckling.

"You doing all that yapping but wide open for a nigga every time he opens his mouth. Body hot and shit all of a sudden."

Her cheeks flushed with embarrassment. Her skin was fire red as she tried escaping my hold.

"Move, Milo."

"Stop. I'm just fucking with you. I don't mind taking you in the house and bending you over on the couch right quick before I go get our boy."

"Nope. You're on punishment."

"Nature, don't play with me. I ain't even did shit."

"So, you didn't just go to that man's office?"

"What man?"

"Oh, now you have jokes."

Shrugging, I kissed her lips again.

"I'm mad at you, Milo, I'm serious."

"Why?"

"Because you went into that office blindly, risking your life and career, for what?"

I rubbed the seat of her shorts with my hand sure to caress her clit in the process.

"This."

I, then, touched her belly.

"This."

I made my way up to her chest, where her heart beat against it.

"This."

I touched her lips next.

"These."

I tapped the side of her head with my index finger.

"And this."

Silently, she shook her head.

"I just don't get you most days. Everything is so different."

"One thing remains the same, though, Nay, and that's all that matters."

I grabbed her hand and placed it on my chest.

"This motherfucker *still* beats for one girl."

"Go get Mason. I miss him."

"You want to ride with me?"

"No. I'm sleepy and I'm pissed. I need some time alone."

This time, I let her free herself from my grasp. From the lines in her forehead, I knew that she was upset with me. It wasn't about me popping up on ole boy. My safety, freedom, and career being risk factors led her riot. In a way, I understood. But in another way, fuck all that.

I was back in my whip, and on the way to Pop's house to retrieve Mason. We had somewhere to be in the next hour and I didn't want to miss the very important appointment with a very important girl. Dr. Aussie, she'd began calling herself over the last twenty-four hours, and I was feeling it.

Milo · Nature

I WASN'T EXACTLY sure if the television was watching me, or I was watching it. The eventful night I'd embarked on contributed to my sleepiness, making me doze every few minutes. Stretched out on Malachi's couch, my comfort level was questionable. I felt like I was right at home. Mason's presence, though in the other room with his aunt, was the only thing stopping me from passing out completely.

With sad eyes, Aussie rounded the corner where Malachi and I lounged, watching the highlights on the big screen. Out of sheer habit, I checked my phone for notifications, ready to forward any emails I'd received to Christina to handle, being that I was out of the office for another four days.

"What's up, baby girl?" I asked my niece.

From the look on her face, I could tell she was in a slump.

"He's not a very good student," Aussie complained.

"What's the matter?"

"He just keeps falling asleep."

"Baby, he's only seven weeks. He can't help himself. His body tires easily."

"It's not his fault, Aussie. He needs rest and lots of it to grow big and healthy, just like you," Malachi explained.

"But how will he learn to communicate with us?"

"He'll learn. I promise he will. Just keep working with him when he's up and alert. He'll be back each week. We have plenty of time, baby," I assured her.

"I don't know, Uncle Milo. I want him to learn now."

Chuckling, I nodded. "Me too."

"It's been hours. He's been to sleep two times already. And he likes when Mommy holds him."

"Because Mommy has milk in her breast, Aussie. He's a baby and smells her milk."

"But Mommy isn't his Mommy. She can't feed him. Her milk is for Maz."

"Her milk is for Maz, but she can feed Mason, actually. If necessary, she could feed them both. However, Nature packed him enough milk."

"She can feed two babies?"

"Yes. It happens all the time. It's called wet nursing. It's more common than people think. Family members who have babies around the same time do it. Friends who both have babies do it. Even grandmothers, because, believe it or not, they can still produce milk. It takes lots of patience but it happens."

"Really?"

"Yes. Really."

"That's fascinating," Aussie gasped.

"It is. And that's such a big word. When did you learn that?"

"That's a simple word," she sassed. "I know'd it a long time ago."

"Know'd it?" Malachi asked.

"I've known it for a very long time."

"Much better," he complimented.

"Is Mason asleep now?"

"Yes. Him and Maz. Mommy is rocking them both."

"Is that why you're sad? You want one to yourself?"

"A little."

"Well, how about you hang out with your uncle? I can rock you if you want me to?"

Reaching forward, I tickled her tummy.

"Uncle Milo!" She giggled.

"Come on. Hop up here."

As Aussie settled right on side of me, my phone vibrated in my pocket. The unknown number didn't fill me with any urgency to answer. I almost slid the phone back into my pocket before it dawned on me who could actually be calling from an unknown number with a different country code than mine.

"Yeah?" I picked up.

"Congratulations, nigga."

Chem's voice came through, slightly muffled.

"Appreciate that, bro. Good hearing from you."

Knowing that every call made on his end was a risk that he gladly took every time he needed to contact one of us made every call that more special.

"I would've called earlier, but shit," he explained.

"No need to explain. I know your heart. What you been up to?"

"Man, staying out of the way. Same shit, different day. Another damn Domino, huh?"

"Another damn Domino."

"You need to quit playing and lock Nature ass down. That's a good look for you, bro. I only met her once, but I like her energy. She done fucked around and gave you a son. Don't let her slip out of your grasp."

"I don't plan to. I've wasted enough time and so has she. I'm getting that lined up right now. First chance I get, I'm walking her down the aisle."

"That's what I'm talking about, homie."

"I don't give a damn what you got to do to get here. Get here. I need you there. Front and center. Shit, even if I have to come to you."

"Nah. Too much of a hassle. I'll be there, Milo. You know I will. I wouldn't miss that for the world."

"How's the fam?"

"Man, good. Really fucking good. I'm about to have a son myself. Just found out about three weeks ago."

"Yeah? That's what's up. I hope the nigga ain't grown by the time I meet him."

"He won't be."

"Good."

"I can't hold this phone too long, but I wanted to check

in with ya. Tell them niggas I love them, make sure you tell Makai I mentioned him separately. You know how jealous that nigga gets."

"A fucking headache. Love you, too, Ch—"

Before I could finish my statement, the line went dead. I tucked my phone back in my pocket, getting comfortable with Aussie right up under me.

"Chem?" Malachi asked.

"Yeah."

Nodding slowly, he confirmed he was feeling everything I was. It didn't matter how much time passed, we all missed Chem the same and wished circumstances were different. We'd loss our mother and father to death, Mercer to the streets, and Chem to his profession.

We understood there was no coming back for our mother and father, but I'd be damned if we didn't want Chem's return just as much as we wanted Mercer's. The calls that only lasted minutes, sometimes seconds, simply weren't enough.

"Aeir is starting dinner. She wants to know if you're staying so she knows how much food to make."

"Nah. Me and Mason will be out of here by the time dinner is done. I can barely hold my damn neck up. I'm tired. I think we're about to go to the house. Pops robbed me of my last night with him. I'm about to make up for it since I don't have work in the morning."

As the words left my mouth, my phone vibrated again. This time, it was Nature. I held my hand up to halt the conversation between Malachi and I.

"What's up, Nay?"

"Hey. What time are you bringing Mason home?"

"I'm not," I informed her, yawning in the process. "He's coming home with me tonight."

Silence coated the line. I could see her face miles and miles away.

"You pouting?" I sniggered.

"You're so aggravating, Milo." Her voice cracked.

"How? What the hell did I do?"

"Nothing."

"Then why are you upset?"

"Because I've been looking forward to Mason coming home tonight and you're telling me he's staying away another night."

"Quite frankly, you haven't had any time to yourself, Nay. Why don't you enjoy tonight and we come first thing in the morning?"

"Goodbye," she groaned, ending the call instantly.

The slight joy that it brought me to upset her exposed my low level of toxicity but I'd never tell anyone. She was just so damn adorable when she was pissed. And it made her pussy wetter, mouth warmer, and heart grow bigger. In my opinion, it was more beneficial than not because Nature didn't truly care about shit. It was all a front.

Anything that required too much energy, she stayed far away from, including me. So, the minute she felt as if I was becoming too much, she'd put up those walls that I hated. Until then, I didn't mind stepping on her toes just a little. As long as our progress wasn't affected, everything was alright.

"What were you about to say?"

"You need to stop fucking with her," Malachi warned, changing the subject.

"Or what?"

"You'll be at a new nigga's office every month, that's what."

"That's the first and last nigga. If I need to put his eye on a billboard to warn niggas what time it is, then I will."

"Or you could just do better."

"I am. The ball is in motion. It only took one time for me to see her outside like that. One time and I'm a fucking believer."

"Better be."

"I guess I'm not going home then. Looks like me and Mason got other plans that include his mother and a good night's rest."

"Yeah. Take your ass home and I ain't talking about your residence."

"I wasn't thinking of a residence, either," I confirmed that we were on the same page.

I checked to find Aussie sound asleep next to me. Because I didn't want her too uncomfortable, I replaced my body with large pillows that she was able to lean against. I searched through the house to find Aeir, checking on both of the boys, who she'd laid side by side in Maz's crib.

"I'm going to steal him. His mom is ready for him to come home."

"Awww. I was enjoying him."

"He'll be back at the end of the week. His mother and I have a date."

"Okay. Do you need us to come get him? We can."

"I'll let y'all know what the plan is Thursday."

"Okay. Do you have my number?"

"I do."

"Well, you sure never use it," Aeir taunted.

"I haven't had a reason to, yet. When I do, trust me, I will. Malachi keeps us updated on all things Aeir and the kids. Trust me."

"I believe it. Give me a call Thursday. Aussie and I will be happy to scoop him up."

"He'll most likely be with his mom. Can I shoot her your digits?"

"Of course. Yes. Please."

"Bet."

Aeir helped me gather Mason's belongings and get them to the front door where Malachi took over. He walked us out to the car and stood outside until we made it out of the driveway. Mason hadn't budged. He was still sound asleep, unsure of what was happening around him. His disability had its advantages. I'd admit that. Naps were a breeze for us all.

DVSN played lowly as we cruised through the neighborhood, taking the scenic route to Nature's place. I couldn't wait for the day that we all shared the same home and separation wasn't a factor. Mason wouldn't have to split his time with the two of us. Each and every night, we'd both come home to him, lay down with him, and wake up to him before the sun rose. Knowing he was waiting for me on weekdays would get me out of the office and to my residence much faster.

Soon. Very fucking soon, homie.

I managed to get Mason out of the car without waking him. I turned the key that Nature was clueless of, gaining access to her home without disturbing her. The morning I came through to grab her belongings so she could empty her breasts gave me the perfect opportunity to copy the keys on her keyring. In my possession was a key to her front door, back door, and a garage fob. Because it was at the back of the house and used as a storage, she didn't bother parking her vehicle in it. Nevertheless, I had access.

I tiptoed up the stairs after discovering she wasn't downstairs. Mason's room was my first stop. I got him squared away in his crib, swaddling him tightly to keep him comfortable throughout his nap.

"Nigga act like he worked a twelve-hour shift in the ER."

I lowered the light in his room and headed toward Nature's room. Underneath the covers, she lie like a sleeping beauty. She was still trying to recover from the weekend she'd had. It would be a few days before she was back to normal. As someone who was a homebody, she'd had a pretty busy weekend. It would take a lot of water, electrolytes, and rest to whip her back into shape.

Light snores erupted from her body. She was balled in a knot, oblivious to what was going on around her. She made the bed look so damn cozy, I couldn't wait to climb in. The blackout curtains blocked the sun's rays from interfering with her slumber. It was setting, but we still had an hour or two before it was completely dark out.

I twisted the nob on the baby monitor so that we'd be able to hear Mason if he began to fuss. My clothes came off as easily as they'd slid on and within seconds, I was under the covers, pulling Nature toward me. Her body hardened before relaxing at the sound of my voice.

"It's me."

"How'd you get in?" She yawned.

"My key," I confessed.

"Should I even ask?"

"Nah. You shouldn't. Take ya ass back to sleep, Nay. I'm tired."

With both arms wrapped around her, I closed my eyes and waited for the moment I transitioned to a faraway place. Nature's presence made it as simple as releasing the air in my lungs once, twice, and then a final time.

FOURTEEN

"I FEEL like a teenage girl going on her first date as if I haven't spent the last week with this man and we don't have a child together. I need to get over myself, already," I sighed, turning to make sure that Mason was alright.

While the realtor showed my home, Shayla agreed to accompany me to the stores to find a dress for the night. The mention of selling my home got Milo on his toes. Though he had a motive behind selling my home so fast, I was thankful that he was handling it so that I wouldn't have to. In his little head, the quicker he got it on the market and off my hands, the faster Mason and I could claim his home as our own.

I wasn't opposed to the idea and was actually looking forward to it. He hadn't left my home in a week's time, giving me a glimpse of what it would be like to share the same space with our son. Putting it lightly, I was onboard. He managed diaper changes, cooking, laundry, and naps while I focused on feeds, cleaning, rest, and my newest addiction, cycling.

"Are you complaining?" Shayla asked. "Because I'm jealous over here."

"Stop it."

"I'm serious. But more than anything, I'm just happy you two are figuring this thing out and are both on one accord. Shit, if I'd known it would only take another nigga's cologne on your skin to get him all the way together, then I would've been at the department store grabbing some and spraying you down a long time ago."

"Shut up!" I sniggered. "But didn't it get him right together? Men, they're complex creatures. Women push us away. Men push them forward."

"They hate another nigga pissing on their territory. Once they mark it, that's that."

"But did he mark it, though? I wouldn't say he did."

"You see that baby in that backseat?" She pointed. "He definitely marked his territory, friend. If you're thinking otherwise, you're a fool. Milo knew exactly what he was doing, getting you pregnant."

"He's seemingly on a mission to double up. I've been taking more emergency contraceptive in the last week than I think is legal. I'm considering birth control."

"Not you. Not the woman who wants to be fruitful and wants a family before she's too old."

"Well, I did. But with Mason being special needs. I think we should—"

"Special what? Girl, don't play. My boy is not special needs. He's just special. That's it. The lack of hearing won't hinder him from doing a damn thing he wants to do. Don't let that stop you. As a matter of fact, let's call it what it is. Don't let that scare you."

"It's not. I just don't want to... I don't know."

"I know you don't. I'm not saying go get pregnant tonight, but I am saying that you shouldn't let Mason's condition be the deciding factor for you when you are ready. You're the same woman that was willing to go to the fertility clinic to make her dream of motherhood come true. Come on, now, babes."

"I knoooooooow. And Milo's dick is just so good, Shayla. I don't know. This man is always on me and I'm always all over him. We're like two horny ass college kids all over again."

She found that so funny. Tears fell down her eyes as she cackled loudly.

"What? I'm serious. Like, I know we'll do our thing after dinner, but I'm literally counting down the minutes until I see him this evening because I want some before we even leave out of the door. It's bad, friend. I'm obsessed. Truly. Honestly. I don't understand how I went this long without him in my world."

"And he's the only real piece of meat you've had. Baby, you're down bad for that one."

"And I don't see myself coming up off him anytime

soon. Never, honestly. Like, when they bury me, I want him and his dick in the casket with me. You think that's too much to ask?"

"Y'all will be dead, Nature. What the hell y'all going to do down there?"

"I don't know. Rot together." I laughed, realizing how silly I sounded.

"Ma'am, sometimes I forget that I'm talking to a reserved freak."

"I'm not."

"Please spare me."

"Well, after over a decade drought, wouldn't you be famished as well?"

"Nobody told you to become a carpet muncher," she sniggered.

"I wasn't, actually. Tried it, wasn't my cup of tea. Companionship beats loneliness and that's exactly what that relationship was, nothing more. Did I have more orgasms than I can count? Yes. However, I can't tell you how long we went without intimacy before we finally called things off."

"So, basically, dick wins again."

"In my world, it will always win. Milo's at least. I couldn't see myself sliding down anyone else's pole and still can't."

"Not even Zane?"

"Zane came really close. That man is fine."

"I'd love to be the judge of that but I never saw the damn man."

"Well, you won't be seeing him. Milo messed that up for me."

"The way we've been hunting for a dinner dress over the last three hours, I don't think you mind one bit."

"And I'm still on the way home empty-handed."

"Yeah. You're on your own now. You passed up way too many good choices. I'm not sure what the hell you're looking for."

"Something that screams, *Work for it. Work for me*."

"Work? Nature, weren't you just telling me that you want to be buried with this man in your casket?"

"So, Shayla? That means nothing. Milo showed his little behind these last couple of months. He has some catering to do."

"I find it hard to believe he doesn't already plan to cater to your needs, babe, whether he's in the doghouse or not. And giving a man pussy on a daily does not suit the narrative that he's actually in the doghouse."

"What does his penis have to do with it? It didn't piss me off, Milo did."

"Oh, yeah, friend, you're down bad."

We both burst into a fit of laughter as Shayla turned into my driveway. Luckily, the potential buyers and the realtor had already concluded their walkthrough. The large box waiting on my porch struck my attention, making me a bit more anxious to get out of Shayla's car and up the steps.

"And catering he is doing, because I have a feeling you didn't order that. Whatever *that* is... or did you."

"I didn't," I stated as a matter of fact.

"It must be nice, honey, coming home to surprise gifts. Going to dinner. Knowing you're going to end the night with your man. Waking up to your man."

"He's not my man, yet. Slow down, Shayla."

"Girl, are you trying to convince yourself or me? Because you're wasting your breath either way."

"He needs to ask first. I made it clear that we're not falling into a routine. He has to actively pursue me and not assume that anything is other than what's been made clear by us both. So, until there's a ring on my finger or Milo officially asks me to be his, then I'm very much so a single woman."

"Who can't date other men?"

"Who can't date other men," I confirmed with a smile ripping through my face.

"You're so full of shit," Shayla taunted, nudging me.

"His rules, not mine." I sighed with a shrug.

"Girl, get out of my car."

I climbed out of the passenger seat and into the backseat where Mason was staring at the fish that dangled from the handle of his seat, keeping him entertained. Once I unfastened the seatbelt, we were both able to slide across the backseat and out of the car completely.

"Call me and let me know what you decide on."

After hours of shopping without any luck, I decided to wear one of the many items in my closet that still had tags on it.

"I will. Answer my FaceTime tonight."

"Sure thing, babe. Do you need me to unlock the door and let you guys inside?"

"No. I'll be fine. I'm getting the hang of this thing, finally."

"Wait, where will he be while you guys are at dinner?"

"Milo has everything handled. Aeir, Mason's aunt,

agreed to take him for the night. She'll be over to get him at three."

"Alright. Let me know if that doesn't work out because I'll come get the little nugget."

"Okay. I'll call you."

I tried kicking the box inside of the house after unlocking the door and pushing it open. It was resistant, moving only an inch. I got Mason situated in the living room and ran back out to grab it. However, Shayla was already out of her car, carrying it inside for me.

"Here. Whatever the hell is in here is heavy. Now, I'm curious. Open it."

She handed me her keys with the sharp one separated from the rest. I bent over and ran the key along the line of the tape that held the box together. When I finally popped it open, I was pleasantly surprised to see three large boxes, all from different designers, in addition to two smaller ones that matched the logos on two of the larger ones. A note was the final piece to the puzzle that I was desperately trying to solve before my anxiety stole my joy.

Nature,

Don't worry your pretty little head too much about your attire. Focus on the details. Here are a few options. See you at eight, baby.

HINT HINT *The ivory one looks much easier to take off.*

I LOVE YOU LOTS, *Nay.*
— *the nigga dicking you down tonight*

. . .

I LAID the note against my chest as my cheeks peaked and all thirty-two of my professionally cleaned teeth showed.

"I can't imagine what the note says. I doubt that I even want to know. But I do want to know what's in these boxes. Especially the Bottega one."

"Options for dinner," I informed her.

"For the dinner we just spent three hours searching for something f—"

"Yes. That one."

"Girl, what factory did he come from? I need to run by there really quick."

"Be quiet, silly!"

"I'm just saying. This man heard you loud and clearly this time and he is not letting up."

"He better not."

"Let me go. I have some praying to do. God can send me my man at like any point. I'm like really ready, God. I hope You hear that. I'm ready!" She looked upward while shouting, causing me to double over in laughter.

"I'll call you and show you the final fit."

"Please do."

I let Shayla out, happy to dig through the boxes and discover what was inside. There was no doubt about it, though. I was definitely wearing the ivory one. I had no clue what it was, but if Milo wanted me in it so that he could easily take it off, then I'd happily slip right into it.

Milo . Nature

"WHAT YOU BLUSHING FOR, NAY?" Milo asked with that sinister smirk on his face.

"Because what is this?" I asked, holding up the small, square box that Milo brought inside of the house with him, demanding I wait until we reached Saint.

"Something light, nothing too wild. You'll open it soon enough."

I admired his clear skin as he handled the wheel of the Aston Martin, weaving through traffic. His right hand rested on my thigh, which was playing peek-a-boo through the high split in the dress that Milo had chosen out of the two he'd purchased. The other, he swore, would be worn Sunday for our second date.

Admittedly, he was keeping me on my toes. We'd reached a point where I didn't know what to expect from him or when. He was full of surprises. Waking up was a new adventure, each morning, never knowing what I'd embark on next. My jaws hurt from smiling so much, my stomach muscles were sore from laughing so hard, and my heart beat erratically from being loved so intentionally and so loudly.

"Then why'd you give it to me? Why not wait until we reach our destination?"

"Because I love the way your brows crinkle and your thoughts linger when waiting. Anxiousness is written all over your face. You can hardly sit still," he snickered.

"Basically, you live to torture me."

"Only in the best way, Nature. I mean no harm, baby."

"Baby?"

I creamed at the sound of it. Each time it fell from his lips, I wanted to part my lower ones.

"Don't play with me," he demanded, slapping my thigh before caressing the spot he'd made sting.

"Ooch."

"Want me to pull over and kiss it?"

"We'd never make it to the restaurant."

"So."

"Then I'd never know what's inside of this box."

"Something to remind niggas what time it is since motherfuckers been acting clueless."

"So, a leash?"

"You full of jokes tonight, huh?"

"I'm just asking. You're speaking as if I'm some sort of property. I'm just trying to figure this thing out."

"You're not a piece of property, Nature. I've never thought of you as such, either. Never will. But without a doubt, I wholeheartedly believe you belong to me. I want everyone to know that."

"Milo, I've explained that we're not falling in line or falling into a routine."

"I heard you. The second you feel like that message is being lost, tell me. But I doubt you'll need to. I can comprehend."

"Alright."

"Now, can you just sit your fine ass back and listen to the music instead of worrying about that damn box? You'll see what's inside soon enough."

Though difficult, I managed to enjoy the duration of our journey without mentioning the box again. We arrived at Saint, walking into the dimly lit establishment hand in hand. Milo was dapper in the silk, short-sleeve button-down that matched my dress. His pants were a deep, dark brown that made his dark, buttery skin glow.

The gold teeth and jewelry that he accessorized with were the ultimate straw. Making it home to the bedroom would be a challenge that I'd easily fail proudly, knowing that the prize at the end would be well worth my failure.

We reached the lobby where a young woman and man stood with tablets that displayed last names and reservation times. Milo and I changed our trajectory, meeting the woman with his first initial and last name on her screen. Our eight-thirty reservation time was just underneath it, confirming we were indeed the targets.

"Domino party?"

"Yeah," Milo asserted.

"I'm Bridgette. I'll be your host for the night. I'll be serving you all in your suite tonight as well. If there's anything I can do for you, just let me know. There's a button on each side of the table that you'll find helpful in the event that you need me and I'm not within reach."

"Nice to meet you, Bridgette."

"And you are?" Her gaze lingered as she offered me a hand.

"Nature." I shook her hand.

"Nice to meet you, Nature. Such a beautiful name."

"We'll be right back here. We're aware that your privacy is your top priority tonight, so we've made it ours as well. Menus are on the display board inside. However, your meal is being prepared as we speak. Drinks and dessert will be delivered shortly."

"Prepared already?"

"Yes. Mr. Domino took the liberty of choosing the do

not disturb option, which requires selections at the time of reservations. It cuts down my time with you all and gives you more time to enjoy one another's company."

"Appreciate it."

Milo took my hand and led me into the dim room with a table set for two. Champagne was chilling on ice, making me wonder why we needed more drinks. Either way, I wouldn't complain. Mason was stocked on milk and would be for the next twenty-four hours if necessary.

"Can I get you guys anything else before I cut out?"

"Uh, I don't think so," I stammered, noticing the enormous bouquet of flowers that were next to the table in a large container that stood at least four feet from the ground.

"Enjoy your time at Saint."

Alone, Milo and I stood, both taking in the ambiance. The space was gorgeous. Without a doubt, I knew the ticket was well over four digits. Admittedly, it fit the bill.

Milo moved closer to my side of the table, pulling my chair for me to sit. I lowered my bottom until it touched the soft velvet and then waited patiently for him to round the table and do the same. Upon resting, his lips parted as if there was something he needed to say. My sight was set on his perfectly lined facial hairs and the shiny teeth that lie just beneath those succulent lips that I loved pressed against mine.

"What?" I blushed, feeling my cheeks tingle.

"You're so pretty."

His smile reached his eyes, eyes that I could fall in love with over and over again.

"Stop staring," I whined, covering my face.

"Move your hands, Nay."

"So you can stare at me all night?"

"That's the perfect plan, isn't it?"

"No. It's awful."

"Not when you plan to do the same."

Uncovering my face, I admired the features of Milo that I loved most. His distinctive nose, piercing eyes, and kissable lips.

"Maybe you're right."

"I know I am, baby. Now, go ahead. Open that box you've been impatiently waiting to open."

Momentarily, I'd forgotten about the box that was in the YSL bag that dangled from my shoulder. I unbuttoned it quickly, placing it on the table so that I could remove the tiny black box. In a haste, I popped it open, finding it completely free of jewelry and stuffed with a note instead. My heart paraded in my chest as I cut my eyes toward a sniggering Milo. He found my confusion amusing.

"Seriously?"

"Are you going to read it, or are you going to sit over there looking pissed?"

"Both, because where is the ring that belongs in here, and why is it a ring?"

There were questions that needed answers and Milo wasn't giving them to me fast enough.

"Just read it. The front first."

"It has front and back?"

"Read the damn note, girl."

I removed the folded piece of paper. The frown I wore was quickly swiped from my face as I began to read.

Be mine? Yes or No.

If, yes, flip over.

When I flipped the piece of paper over, there was more writing with a checklist to match.

"Aw, shit, Nay. You willing to rock with a nigga?" Milo asked, taking note that I'd flipped the piece of paper, meaning my answer was yes.

Since you've promised to be mine, here are the things I'm promising:

Love and cherish you, through the good and bad days.

Respect your wishes.

Create space for every version of you.

Be a better man, partner, and father.

Listen.

Make you and Mason my top priorities.

Graffiti your walls with my semen.

Eat that pussy sun up and sun down.

Tearfully, I looked up to find that Milo had obliterated the space between us at the table. In his hand was an incredibly gorgeous diamond ring that glistened under the low lights of the room.

"I promise."

"Yeah?" I nodded.

"This is just a token of my love for you, Nay. Something to remind you daily of the promises I'm making and keeping. If ever I should fall short, and I'm too bullheaded to realize it, lay this at my bedside. I promise I'll get back right and make sure you're alright in the process. Nothing, I mean nothing, Nay, means more to me at this point in my life than your happiness and Mason's well-being.

"Everything I ever wanted to accomplish in life, I've accomplished, except walking you down that aisle. I'm going to work my fingers to the bone until that accolade is on my back. Becoming your husband, that's my aim. This is only temporary. Exercise for your finger in preparation for the real rock, so don't get too comfortable. It will be replaced any day now."

He slid the ring onto my finger. It fit perfectly, offering him even more points in my book. I marveled at the ring's beauty, moving my finger in a circular motion to see it glisten from every angle.

"And this is just the promise ring?" I coughed, tears streaming down my face, blurring my vision and smearing my makeup.

"A hell of a promise, Nature. The lifetime commitment ring shitting on that one."

"It feels impossible. This one is... it's everything."

"I did good, huh?"

"You did so well, baby."

"I love you, Nature. Know that. Today. Tomorrow. Next week. Next lifetime."

"I know, Milo. I've never doubted your love for me. I just wanted you to love wholly, without fear and without reservation."

"I'm working on that. Every day, actively working on silencing all that shit and listening to your heart, your voice, your requests. They tell me everything I need to know without having to overthink shit or lean on what I know best —work."

"Nothing's going to happen to us. We're not your parents."

"I know that. I know we're not. It's just so much easier said."

"I understand. I won't push you to see past such a

defining moment in your world. Just like you promised me, I promise to hold space for you and my understanding that your head and heart are warring."

"Like a motherfucker. But I'm rocking with my heart this time. My head, it made me act foolishly and cost me the best thing that had ever happened to me. I still can't tell you I'm sorry enough. There will never be enough time on earth to make up for what I've done."

"You don't need any more time. Let's wipe our hands with everything that has happened up until this moment. Let's start anew. Let's start over."

"Let's."

The door opened, grabbing both of our attention. Our server appeared with two large boxes stacked, obscuring her vision. However, she managed to make it to the table unscathed. I turned to Milo, clearing my face of tears.

"Such a fucking crybaby," Milo teased. "Clean your face, Nay. No more tears."

I whipped my head from the man across the table to our server over and over, unsure of what was inside the boxes or what I'd done to deserve whatever it was.

"Milo, what is this?"

"More boxes."

His smile was heartening. He was proud of himself and the work he'd put in to make this night special for us. Without a doubt, my gratitude would be felt before the sun rose and our son came home.

"Choose one."

"Bottom."

He stood and removed the top box, handing me the one at the bottom. I slid back in my chair to accommodate the massive block of cardboard. The bow that held it together was orange, resembling the box with one of my favorite designers sprawled across the top.

I unboxed a classic black Birkin with gold detailing that made me sick to my stomach. It was stunning. The leather was quality, easily distinguished by its thickness and sturdiness. Our server made her way out of the door just as my eyes landed on the second, identical box.

"Milo. Baby, you didn't have to... have to do this."

"I did."

"Then what's in the other one?"

"A Kelly. In white."

"Seriously? Were you just giving Hermès all your money?"

"Baby, if that was all my money, you shouldn't be fucking with me." He chuckled, finding my question hilarious. "That's less than a hundred bands. You into broke niggas?"

"I'm not into anyone, Milo."

"Better not be," he stated, nodding his head. "Nevertheless, if it makes you feel any better, that didn't even dent my account. I promise I won't miss a dime of what was spent on any of this. I won't even notice it's gone. And don't act like your account isn't massive, Nature. You're in a realm that will never see a day of downtime."

"Tell me about it. I'm not sure what my account looks like. I don't check it, honestly. My accountant handles all finances."

"See. The luxury of never having to check your account and needing an accountant tells me you're swimming in bread."

"Mason's tuition has to get paid one way or another," I tittered.

"By his father."

"If you insist, but I hope you understand that I can handle some of the finances."

"I know you can, but that doesn't mean you will. I got it. I got you. Stack your bread, baby. Leave it to the kids for when we get on up out of here."

"Hopefully, that won't be for another one hundred years."

"Hopefully," he agreed. "Just want to make sure they're straight. Their children are straight. Their children. And their children."

"They, huh?" I blushed, visions of several mini Milos swarming me at once.

"Don't play with me, Nature Dupree."

"I'm not, Dr. Domino."

"She likes you," he blurted.

"Hm?"

"Our server. She likes you."

"Milo, she's just doing her job, which she happens to do well."

I hadn't noticed the lemon drop in front of me, neither had I noticed the drink in Milo's hand. Completely lost in those dark eyes and that alluring smile, I didn't see her re-enter or exit.

"Hey, maybe I'm wrong, but I highly doubt it."

Milo consumed the contents of his glass and removed the chilled champagne from the ice bath. He stood, casually, without haste, and removed the wire from the top of the bottle. Under the pressure of his thumb, the cork slid out.

Pop!

The champagne rose to the top of the glass bottle, happy to be freed, spilling down Milo's fingers. He tilted the glass in front of me to the side and filled it halfway.

"Pump and dump?" he asked, referring to the milk that would be produced after consuming alcohol.

"Yes. I emptied them before leaving home."

"Good."

"But that doesn't mean get me drunk and try to get into my panties tonight."

"Nay, I don't need you drunk to get in your panties. Them motherfuckers damn near slip off from the well that is immediately activated at the mere thought of me."

"Feeling yourself much?"

The bubbles in my drink danced around the glass, sizzling and crackling.

"I'm just saying, baby, you getting dick regardless. You don't need liquid courage."

He shrugged, filling his glass to the top.

"Hmmm. Maybe you're right."

"To starting anew," he announced, holding his glass in the air.

"To starting anew."

Clink.

Our glasses touched each other before touching our lips. Almost immediately after our toast, toasted mozzarella bites, spinach dip, and lumped crab meat was served as three different appetizers that we both enjoyed until dinner was served. Over fresh, authentic seafood, we laughed until our bellies hurt and smiled until the muscles in our faces stiffened.

My heart filled, overflowed, and spilled into the space between us until reaching Milo's side of the table. My hand rested underneath his, neither of us wanting to disconnect, although we were in the same room and mere feet apart. Comfort clung to me. Milo made it so easy to fall deeper in love with him with every word that came from his lips.

I could sit and talk to him for the rest of our lives and still wouldn't be tired of that deep, addictive baritone and low snicker at the realization of the hold he had on me. Though prideful, he was humbled by the reconnection we were establishing, assuring me of how much of an honor it was to finally be in my good grace.

Admittedly, I was just as honored to be part of his world, again, and as more than the mother of his son. Finally, I was his again.

His woman.

His comfort zone.

His safe haven.

His heaven on earth.

His therapist.

His medicine.

His heart.

Melting under his gaze, I pushed a piece of hair behind my ear. Filled to the brim, there was hardly any room left, but somehow, I still wanted to be stuffed by Milo. My mouth. My vagina. And my stomach.

"I know that look," he said, putting the glass of water up to his lips.

"Do you?"

"Yeah." Nodding, he cleaned his mouth with the dinner napkin that had been in his lap. After tossing it on the table, he slid his chair backward, eyes never leaving mine. "I know that fucking look."

"I almost thought you'd lost your telepathy abilities. You couldn't read me."

"For a few months, there, the signal was interrupted. The wires were crossed. I couldn't quite get the messages you were sending. Never again, though. Now that the connection has been restored, I'll be damned if I lost it again."

"Yeah?"

"Yeah," he assured me, loosening his belt.

Taking a peek around the empty room, my anxiety rose along with my temperature.

"Milo."

I watched from afar as his dick sprung from his pants.

"Baby."

"Baby, shit," he fussed.

"We can't."

"Yes we can and yes we will."

The low groan that left his mouth as he wrapped his hand around his pole left me breathless.

"If Nature wants her nigga's dick, then Nature gets her nigga's dick. No matter the place... no matter the time... no matter the situation... it's yours to have."

I swallowed back the mound of saliva that piled in my mouth. Afraid I'd miss something, I refused to blink. His erection was as beautiful as he was.

"Come 'er, Nay," he groaned, still fisting his dick.

"Milo, please."

"Come 'er, Nature. You're going to regret it if I have to

get up, baby. Not even the Lord Himself will be able to pull me up off you."

Taking heed, I stood straight, smoothing the wrinkles out of my dress.

"Take that off," he instructed.

Taking a look around the empty room, my thoughts moved a mile a minute.

"Nobody's here. It's just you and me."

His reminder made the decision easier. Slowly, I lifted the dress with my fingertips until it was over my head completely. My nipples tingled as they began to release milk. The pads I'd strapped to them filled quickly.

"Take them off."

He nodded toward my panties. My focus was altered as I tried splitting it between Milo's hard dick and not falling flat on my face trying to get out of my thong. Somehow, someway, I managed, never taking my eyes off him.

"Those, too," he said, nodding toward my breasts.

"They'll leak."

"Those, too," he repeated.

Following orders, I removed the nursing pads one by one. To my surprise, milk didn't spill from them.

"Now, come 'er."

I approached him, standing in front of him, waiting for instruction.

"Put 'em in your mouth," he insisted.

Falling to my knees, I opened wide and welcomed Milo into my mouth. His hand caressed my head as he guided it up and down his girth. His grip tightened as he pulled upward and tilted my head so that he could gaze into my orbs. With flared nostrils, he watched as I left a trail of saliva, spitting on his dick as I freed it from my mouth. Immediately, it was in my mouth again as I tried to suck it bone dry of the lubrication I'd just provided.

"Shit, Nay, stand up and sit on this motherfucker."

"Milo," I protested, wanting to devour him completely.

"I just wanted you to get him wet, baby."

Tucking in my lip, I stretched my legs, preparing to mount him. With his assistance, I settled in his lap, reaching behind me, feeling for his dick simultaneously. His entry was blissful. I placed a hand on his shoulders to balance myself. His hands around my waist sent chills up and down my spine.

"You feel so good," I admitted, lowering my head so that my lips could meet his.

"I love you," he confessed. "I fucking love you, girl."

"I love you."

Releasing those words made me delirious. It was true. I'd hung onto them for so long. Finally letting them go felt like a sacred act. Holy. Righteous. *Perfect.*

"Ride this motherfucker," he encouraged.

My nipple went into his mouth. Gently, sure not to extract milk, he licked in circular motions, upping my sensitivity a few notches.

"Yessssss."

I felt his thumb as it snaked around my body, ending right at my clit where it stayed. Applying the perfect amount of pressure, he worked it up and then down repeatedly. My knees buckled, complicating my ride.

"Un, un. On them feet, Nature."

Leaning forward, in an attempt to relieve myself of the

pleasure that was being administered, I took his lips into my mouth, moaning inside of it.

"Ummmmmm. Yesssssss."

Gratification threatened to end me.

"Milo." I jerked as the initial wave smacked me right in my pussy.

"That's it."

My legs shook uncontrollably, making it hard to continue my ride.

"Don't stop, baby. Get yours."

He added more pressure below, stuffing his mouth with my nipple again. With each stroke of his thumb and tongue, he untied the bow that held my box together. But once the knot was loosened, I split wide open for him.

"Uhhhh. Uhhhh. Mi—Oh God. Please."

"That's it. That's it. Cum all on that dick."

I laid my forehead against his as my stomach flipped and twisted, knotting and unknotting. Gasping for air, I rode the final wave until it subsided. The vibration beneath me startled us both. Milo hurriedly pulled out his phone, frantically waiting to see who was calling him. From the look on his face, I sensed he believed it was Malachi or Aeir with concerns for Mason.

The unsaved number was an instant stress reliever. However, he still slid the bar over to answer, placing it on speaker phone immediately. He placed the phone near my mouth, waiting for me to greet the caller.

"Helloooo?" I moaned as he began sliding in and out of me.

"Hello?" a feminine voice yelled through the line.

"Tell her ya nigga busy digging into your guts and can't talk. Not today, tomorrow, or any day moving forward."

"Milllllllo."

He wasn't playing fair, making it hard for me to focus as he placed his hands on my waist, stuffing me over and over. The sound of our wetness made the most beautiful tune.

"Tell her what the fuck I said, Nay."

Without warning, he lifted us both from the chair and stretched my body out on the table, making the dishes fall onto the floor, shattering the dinnerware.

"Hello?" the female voice called out again.

"Tell her, baby."

He drilled into me.

"Tell her."

"Uhhhh. Fuck. Miloooooo."

"Tell her, Nay."

He wasn't letting up, deepening his stroke, driving me to the point of oblivion.

"Milo?"

"He's... he's... Oh my God, baby. Busy."

"Tell her what the fuck I said. Stop being so fucking nice," he gritted, biting into my shoulder, "Fuck this shit ridiculous."

"I don't know who this is, but where is Milo?"

"Inside of me," I moaned. "Make... Make this your last time ca—lling."

"Tell her who dick this is, Nay."

"Minnnnnnne. Oh my God, Milo. I—Uhhhh."

The line went dead as I began to splinter. Milo was digging for gold that I was certain he'd find.

"I'm 'bout to nut all up in this shit. Here it come, baby. Get up."

Milo pulled out of me abruptly. Sure not to cut my hand on any of the broken glass, I fell to my knees again. Just as I hit the carpet, Milo shoved his dick into my mouth and pulled it out. He massaged the tip of it, making my mouth water. It was so sleek, shiny, and inflated. I watched intently until I felt his fingers in my hair, forcing me to look up at him just as warm semen splattered onto my skin.

"Urgh. Shit."

The door of our private suite opened almost immediately after his seeds erupted from his volcano. My eyes darted in the direction of our waitress who froze, unable to comprehend what she was witnessing, but unable to tear her eyes away as well.

"I'm sorry. I, uh... I..."

She swallowed, still unmoving.

"What I tell you, Nay?" Milo chuckled. "You can have her if you want her."

The idea crossed my mind, but my selfishness quickly dismissed it. I wanted Milo to myself, now and forever.

"Baby girl, you can put that pretty mouth of yours to work and we won't tell a soul."

"Milo!" I hissed.

"No?" He looked down at me.

"No." I chuckled, allowing him to help me up from the floor.

Still, the waitress stood, unable to speak.

"You sure?" Milo asked with lifted brows.

"I'm positive."

"Can we get some wet linen, baby girl? Maybe next time."

"Uh, yes. Sure. Can I get you anything else?"

"Two glasses of water and a check. Add all this shit to my tab."

"Ye-Yes. Sure thing."

She shuffled her feet, tearing her eyes away from me finally.

"She wants a taste, baby. I told you that when we first walked in."

"She made me a believer just then."

"I'm not tripping. If you're with it, then so am I."

"I'm not sharing you tonight, Milo. Get that out of your head if that's what you're thinking."

"It wasn't."

"Liar."

"I was trying to share you. I just want to watch." He chuckled, dodging my fist. "Come 'er, let me wipe your face."

I stood still as he cleaned me with a dry dinner napkin. While waiting for the wet ones, I managed to get back into my dress and a new pair of nursing pads strapped on my chest. By the time the waitress returned, I was back in my seat, watching as Milo buttoned his shirt.

"Appreciate that."

"Of course."

"N—"

I shot Milo a warning, silencing him instantly.

"Don't worry about the dishes. We break them all the time in the back. Here's your ticket."

She handed Milo a small tablet.

"You can check out when you're ready. It's been a pleasure serving you."

"Bet."

She disappeared again, leaving us alone to settle the ticket and prepare to exit. On wobbly legs, I followed Milo out of the establishment, unable to take my eye off the new rock on my finger. If he claimed it was practice for the engagement ring, I couldn't imagine how beautiful it would be.

"Baby, my gifts," I gasped, finally recalling the bags and bouquet.

"They'll be delivered."

Sighing, I pushed forward, ready for whatever the night had to offer as long as Milo was included.

Home sweet home. As the thought crossed my mind, I rested my head against Milo's arm, waiting for the moment his car arrived at the curb's edge so that we could pile inside.

FIFTEEN

A WEEK of pure bliss after so much bullshit had me feeling as if I was overdosing.

Overdosing on pussy.

Overdosing on happiness.

Overdosing on laughter.

Overdosing on pleasure.

Overdosing on comfort.

Overdosing on hugs.

Overdosing on kisses.

Overdosing on quality time.

Overdosing on cuddles.

Overdosing on peace.

Overdosing on Nature.

Every-fucking-thing was OD. But admittedly, I wanted it no other way. Seeing that smile on her face every time I opened my eyes, it was sensational. Skin to skin, body to body, we slept in each other's arms as if one of us would vanish in the night.

And Mason, having him in my line of vision almost every second that I wasn't busting my ass in the office was quite pleasurable. My first week back in the office had me wishing I was back home, smelling his toes and rocking him while we watched Mommy shower.

My level of clinginess had increased to shameful levels, but somehow, I didn't give a fuck. If she didn't have to, I didn't want Nature to even breathe without me and vice versa. As if she'd heard my thoughts, her name crossed my screen, prompting me to answer.

"What's up, baby?"

"Babe, seriously?" she whined on the other end, sounding as cute as I was sure she looked.

Chuckling, I rubbed a hand down my head. Without her revealing her frustrations, I knew where they stemmed from.

"Hello?"

"I'm here, Nay."

"Milo, everything is gone."

"Making it easier on us both. Why you pouting?"

"Because, where is it all?"

"Getting unloaded at the crib as we speak."

"You couldn't wait?"

"Nah. I couldn't. We have shit to do this weekend and I wanted to get it out of the way."

"The house hasn't officially sold yet."

"It's a cash offer and the buyer happens to be Lawe. It's as good as bought."

"Lawe?"

"Yeah. I ran it by him Wednesday at the barbershop, forgetting this nigga buying up everything in Berkeley. The money will be in your account Monday. The transfer takes a few days."

"He bought it already?"

"Wired the money before we left the barbershop."

"Jesus, Milo, and you said nothing."

"Because I told you I'd handle it and I meant it."

"Thanks. I just wish I'd had a heads up and time to prepare for this move instead of coming home to an empty house for the most part. And what do we have to do this weekend? I had every intention of resting while you take father duty way too serious the entire weekend."

"You can watch, but it won't be from either of our homes. We're skipping town and will be back Sunday night."

"Skipping town?"

"Yeah. I booked a cabin stay for us. I think we could both use some quiet and some calm after such a whirlwind."

"Whirlwind?" she questioned.

"Mason's birth. Pregnancy. Doctor appointments. Relationship shit. Diagnosis. Shit hasn't been exactly chill lately, Nay."

Sighing, she agreed. "I know. Hearing you say it out

loud makes me realize just how busy our lives have been over the last few months."

"Exactly. Some time together, away from everything and everyone, just to hear ourselves think and get some much-needed rest will do us both some good."

"Baby?"

"Yeah?"

"I keep waiting on someone to pinch me."

"Pinch you?"

"Because I have to be dreaming. A year ago, if someone would've told me we'd be here, I'd swear they were gassing me up just to let me down."

"Is that what this feels like?"

"Sometimes. I just keep waiting for something to destroy this life and love we're trying to build."

"Nothing is going to happen because neither of us will let it. And even if something out of our control was to happen, all that matters is we both know where we stand with one another. As long as our foundation is solid, we're good."

"Then, we're good?"

"We're impeccable, baby. Solid. So, stop worrying. It hinders your joy in moments that it matters most. It's counterproductive for us both. I'm better, Nay. I won't hurt you. Never. Don't wait for it because it won't happen. Okay?"

"Okay."

"Now, get out of that house and find something to do with yourself until it's time to roll. I'm leaving my car here, so scoop me in two hours."

"Two hours? I have to get packed and Mason nee—"

"I've handled it already. So, when your man says scoop

him in two hours, quiet your thoughts and scoop him in two hours."

"Yes, sir."

"Daddy. I think I like Daddy better."

"Yes, Daddy."

"Yeah. That's the one there. Do you want me to send you some money to keep busy until I'm ready?"

"No. Mason and I are going to visit Mom. She wants to spend some time with us. I guess we'll leave there and come straight to you."

"Bet. See you in a few."

"I love you."

"I love you back, Nay."

Simultaneously, we ended the call. Hearing her voice left a smile on my face and joy in my soul. Better days were always obtainable with her in the mix. She was the reason my latest decision was so simple. Nature didn't have to voice her concerns a thousand times for me to hear her loud and clear.

Her comfort with Christina just feet away from me each day had everything to do with the trust she was gaining for me, but I knew for a fact it was a struggle for her. To alleviate her stress and worry, I knew that it was imperative that I removed Christina from my payroll. Our time together at the office was coming to an end.

Nature's comfortability was my greatest concern and I'd tweak every section of my life until she could love me freely without those little voices in the back of her head promising heartache. Without a doubt, I knew she'd do the same for me. In fact, she had. I wasn't above alterations. Tailoring our lives to better accommodate one another's wishes, desires, boundaries, and worries was the key to the solid foundation we'd just discussed.

I walked through the office, ready to end my day so that I could climb under the sheets and listen to the fire wood crackle as Nature went on about the day she'd had with Mason while I sulked because of my absence. S'mores. Reruns. New action movies. Love stories. New chapters in her latest book. Silly family pictures. I was anxious for it all.

"Dr. Domino, Dr. West is wondering if he can push your observation back for a day next week, preferably after Tuesday. He's adamant that you don't need to visit the hospital today because he won't be there."

"For his patients, but I still have to see patients of my own, or have you forgotten?"

"Right."

"I won't be there long, but there are two new admissions that I'd like to spend some time with and then I'm cutting out for the day."

"Alright. I'll let him know."

"Christina."

"Yeah?"

Her chest swelled as she looked at me with wandering eyes, waiting for me to say something that was beyond business and that she could cling. A little fix. That was what she needed after so much silence since Nature and I decided to work our shit out, but I couldn't give that to her.

"You'll receive an email shortly. It's scheduled for... it'll be in your inbox within the next twenty minutes."

"Okay, is it something that I need to ad—"

"It's in regard to your termination."

"Ter—I'm sorry. I don't understand."

"Things between us... they never should've happened. You're a superior employee but we crossed lines that we can't return from. It is affecting our employee-employer relationship. Unfortunately, your time here has come to an end. I have a few colleagues that could use an employee with your work ethic and knowledge. It's no longer an asset of mine, but more of a liability."

"Dr. Domino, are you really serious right now?"

"Yes. I am." Nodding, I confirmed.

"So, because we had sex, I can no longer work here?"

"Because we had sex, you can't separate business hours from personal hours, and you've made it your business to make contact with me unnecessarily on numerous occasion since I put an end to things, and—I'm sorry, I feel like I'm explaining myself too much right now. We both know why this won't work out here. The work relationship has been tarnished and it's affecting the work you do here in the office. We've both noticed the change in the last few weeks."

"After shutting down your schedule at a moment's notice?"

"That's why I have my own practice, so that I can practice following my own rules and living my life, Christina, answering to you and no one else. From Monday until Wednesday, you walked around with a chip on your shoulder and we know it had absolutely nothing to do with me needing to take an emergency leave. I'm done with this conversation. Check your email in a few. I'm heading to the hospital to do my rounds."

I didn't wait for a response before tapping the button on the elevator and heading downstairs. The walk to the hospital was only eight minutes and I could complete it in six. Seeing the patients' lives I was making a difference in was one of the highlights of my day. Being their personal advocates was my life's path and I felt as though I was doing a damn good job, leaving my footprints in the process.

Milo & Nature

WITH A LITTLE PEP in my step, I pushed forward, into the complex where my office was located. My two-hour deadline was up twenty minutes ago and getting in contact with Nature felt impossible. After her initial text that let me know she was on the way thirty minutes ago, I hadn't gotten a response or answer. My calls were going straight to voicemail.

The parking lot was my first stop. I walked straight out of the door on the opposite end of the building that faced the parking lot. In the spot reserved for expecting and new mothers was her truck. I peeked inside to find it completely empty, no sign of Nature or Mason.

Her location was apparent, now. And within three minutes, I was stepping off the elevator and into my office where the tone of Nature's voice made fine bumps rise along with the hairs on my arms. Crinkled brows and squinted eyes helped me identify her though her voice had confirmed her presence.

Nature. A woman who only spoke when spoken to. A woman who you'd never hear raise her voice unless it was in cheer. A woman who was as kind as she was gentle. A woman who avoided confrontation at all costs. A woman who cherished peace and made sure her life was soiled in it. Stood behind the receptionist desk of my office, grimacing as she demanded something of Christina that I wanted of her, too.

"Honestly, shut the fuck up talking to me before the calm and collected version of me tags the slightly crazy, uncouth version of me. Neither you nor me want that, so do us both a favor and tell me where Milo is."

"He's your man, ma'am. Not mine. I'm not obligated to tell you that information, either. You're not an associate, doc—"

"In fact, I am."

"Nay," I called out.

She was so enthralled in the conversation that she hadn't noticed my entry. As quickly as possible, I made my way by her side, making contact immediately, my skin against hers as a calming mechanism.

"Milo, please make it completely clear to your assistant that I am not her enemy and I come in peace unless she cares to go about things otherwise."

"Nature," I whispered in her ear, wrapping my arms around her waist and pulling her into my chest. "Never let a bitch see you sweat, Mommas. Never."

Silently, she turned to face me with sad eyes and a sunken chest. My heart ached for her. The discomfort that I'd tried to avoid was written all over her face. Her nostrils widened as she tried finding the words to say. Shaking my head, I informed her that none were necessary.

"Christina, fuck what that paper say. Gon' gather your shit and cut out of here. Your account will reflect pay for the next two weeks, but don't bother coming in after today. Your energy isn't welcomed in this office."

Sighing, Nature mouthed, *Thank you.*

Instead of responding, I took her by the hand and dragged her toward the opposite side of the office, away from my personal space and into the common restroom where I locked the door behind us.

"Milo, what are you doing?"

"Getting your lick back," I explained.

"My lick back?"

"Ummm hmmm. By getting the dick you deserve and the dick she desires but can no longer have. She done pissed my baby off. She don't get to experience peace right now—on any level."

"Are you seriously this petty right now?"

"Nah. I really just want some pussy, but sliding on your opp in the process makes it so much better. I told you, you look too fucking good when you're pissed."

I pushed the sundress up over her hips, a bit peeved that niggas had the chance of seeing her ass wobbling in that motherfucker all day.

"Baby, I don't have an opp."

I could smell her arousal. It made my tastebuds tingle as I produced extra saliva.

"Shid, by the time you walk out of the restroom you will. Hands on the sink, Nay."

"Miloooooooo."

I slid right into home base. Nature was always hot and she was always ready, like the donuts when the sign was on in the window. And just like them, she was always glazed with the sweet, white stuff that I loved.

The second my bone was buried, I knew it would be spitting up soon. But not before blowing Nature's back out. I grabbed ahold of her waist, stroking her slowly to reduce the chances of soreness after. Once I was completely lubricated and unwanted friction was not a concern of mine, I increased the speed of my strokes, not stopping until my balls slapped against the bottom of her ass cheeks.

"Milo! Miloooo! Baby."

Her right hand appeared, stopping me from deepening our connection and pissing me off.

"Baby, please."

I slapped it away, digging deeper, giving her every inch of me.

"Un, un, move your fucking hand. Let me in my shit, Nature."

"Ummmmm. Shit. Milo."

"You feel that dick? You feel that dick inside you?"

"Yesssssss. Yeeessss!"

"Who dick this is?"

"Minnnnne. Baby."

"Fuck me back, Nature. Fuck me back."

Her knuckles whitened from the pressure she applied while gripping the sink. Meeting my strokes, she pushed backward as I pushed forward, our bodies meeting time and time again. Using my right hand, I wrapped my hand around her neck and pulled her upward, still hammering into her gently, yet intensely. When her lips were close enough, I stuck my tongue down her throat.

"I'm 'bout to nut in this shit," I warned her, tightening my grip on her neck as I felt my nut rise.

With my left hand, I tickled the little nub between her legs, making them buckle as she fell forward. That thick creaminess that was my mission to extract came seeping from her, coating my dick completely, announcing her arrival. I came shortly after.

"Fuck."

Silently, we both got ourselves together. Before Nature pulled her panties up and her dress down, I cleaned her with the wet wipes from the cabinet. When she had her shit in order, I unlocked the door.

"You ready?"

"I'm starting to think you have a thing, a kink, for public sex in forbidden places where the chances of being heard, seen, or caught are sky high."

"And I am starting to think that you don't have a problem with it because you opening your legs, bending, or getting on top over every single time."

That brain of hers and extensive vocabulary failed her. Instead of responding, she slid past me and out of the restroom.

"I'll be out in the truck."

"What's wrong with your phone?"

"The charger is broken in the car. I planned to charge it on the way but that plan failed."

"Aight. We can get the one from mine until I replace yours. Where's Mason?"

He was sleep when the two-hour mark approached so my mom told me to leave him and circle back after I get you."

"Bet. But I'm ready. You don't have to go down to the car. Wait on me to grab my shit. And here."

I handed her my phone.

"033444. Find the last email to the new prospect and tell her that I need her to start her trial a little bit sooner than the intended start date. Shit changed a lot quicker than I intended."

"You sure?" Nature hesitated, almost afraid to take my phone.

"I'm positive. Take the phone, Nay. If you find something in that motherfucker you don't like, address it, but I promise I'm on the straight and narrow. I have nothing to hide, Mommas."

"Okay. What's her name?"

"Trish Adams."

"Okay."

"That's cool with you?"

"What?"

"Another assistant? Female?"

"Is that too much for you to handle?"

"No. I told you, Nay, I'm good on all that shit."

"Then it's cool with me. I trust you, Milo. I trust that you've learned a few lessons."

"After all these fucking years, you damn right."

Chuckling, she followed me through the common space of the office, past a seething Christina, and into my office.

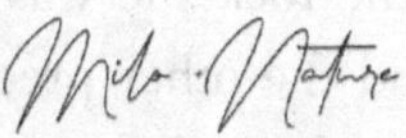

WITH MASON BUNDLED in the blanket and snug in my arms, I descended the stairs of the plane right behind Nature. Flying private made our travel much more pleasurable and tolerable for Mason. He slept the entire hour and a half flight, allowing Nature and I to spend the hour catching up on business before putting our phones on do not disturb and tunning out completely. Our distraction-free getaway was dedicated to centering ourselves and expanding upon our foundation.

The Range Rover waited for us on the tarmac. As requested, there was a brand new car seat in the center of the backseat. I strapped Mason inside and covered his body with the blanket he was once wrapped in before joining Nature in the front as our bags were loaded into the very back.

Her hand joined mine as I settled in. My brows relaxed on my forehead as I admired her long, thin finger and the ring I'd put on it. As much as I wanted to chastise myself for taking so long to ice her out, I fought to remain in the moment. She made it easy, expelling a lengthy breath as she slightly reclined her seat and yawned.

Her delicacy was my kryptonite. It left me fiending for an ounce of power after being stripped ever so gently. Though soft as a feather, she held so much weight and possessed every part of me when in my presence or on my dome.

Lifting her hand, I kissed her ring finger, impatiently waiting for the day that I slid a more permanent solution onto it and replaced the rock she was wearing. One hand gripping the wheel and the other preoccupied, I whipped the truck off the lot and headed toward our destination, excited for the weekend ahead of us.

The forty-five minute drive whooped Mason and his mother's ass. They were both sound asleep when I pulled up to the cabin, let myself inside, and unloaded our bags. Before waking Nature, I got Mason situated in the portable crib that was also a special request of mine by the owners of the cabin.

When I made it back to the truck, I scooped her into my arms, brought her inside, and laid her on the couch underneath a thick, knitted blanket. I stripped down to my briefs, removed the pillows from the sofa and climbed up, pulling Nay into my arms as I got comfortable. And just like that, the first order of business was underway.

Rest.

SIXTEEN

Nature

I WOKE with renewed strength and energy. The enthusiasm in my bones convinced me of a full breakfast spread, which I pranced through the house with on my way to wake my sleeping bear. The home that we now shared was massive, much bigger than the one I'd spent the last decade in. The open-floor concept on the first level worked wonders for my anxiety and mental health.

"Ohhhh, Milooooo," I sang, tiptoeing barefoot into the bedroom.

He stirred awake, rubbing his eyes as he pushed himself up in bed. The skin of his back slid up the headboard, where he distributed his weight. From the yawn that nearly split his face in two, reminded me that we'd had another late night and an early morning probably wasn't the best idea.

"Nay," he tittered. "It's your day, baby. Why are you serving me breakfast in bed?"

"Because, over the last month, you've made every day my day, so I want to celebrate you on this day, too. Besides, I'm sure this is nothing in comparison to what you have in store for me today."

"You have a point there." He nodded, accepting the large tray.

I set it on his lap before kissing his crusty lips and running around to my side of the bed.

Adjusting to life with Milo felt so natural, almost as if it was a requirement for my next stage of life. The way everything aligned for us after being misaligned for so long was mind-blowing. Somehow, everything just fell into place without us trying to piece any parts of our puzzle together.

And since he'd promised, he hadn't stopped applying pressure, keeping me guessing, happy, and on my toes. Our days were blissful, even the ones that I wanted to lock myself in a room and scream for hours. By the time Milo came home to save the day, I was beyond vexed, but quickly soothed by his presence. It was as if he always had a solution, always able to change things around, always able to shift odds in my favor.

My naked bottom rested against the sheets of our new bed, one that was designed to our personal specifications. I loved every feature of it, down to the television that rose from the footboard if we wanted our entertainment closer than the distance between us and the television mounted on the wall. Milo had put a lot of thought into the design and seeing it come to life was incredible.

The large plate held enough food to feed us both. Using the button on the side of the bed, I lifted the television and made myself comfortable. Milo flipped through channels while gnawing on a piece of bacon, in search of football highlights.

"Happy birthday, Nature."

Leaning over, never taking his eyes off the television, he kissed my cheek.

"How many times will you tell me?"

"As many times as it crosses my mind."

"Okay, because we're on like number five since midnight."

"Umm hmmm. Your point?"

"Nothing, baby."

"Alright. Now, do me a favor and reach behind your pillow for me. Grab that box for me."

"And the games begin." I chuckled.

"They have indeed begun."

I peeped behind the pillow to find the box that he was referring to. It was flat, velvety and slightly heavy.

"I'm not waiting to open this one," I explained.

"I don't expect you to."

"Good."

I lifted the lid, opening the box to see what was inside. The sparkling diamonds of the necklace quickly caught my attention. They looped the gorgeous piece, ending where the pendent hung. An M was covered with the same quality diamonds, forcing me to look over at a snickering Milo.

"Is this my gift or yours?"

"You like the necklace or what, Nature?" He stuffed a piece of bread in his mouth, finding his antics comical.

"I love it, almost. Can you have the jeweler take the M off?" I joked.

"Don't play with me, baby. You know what it is."

"You're trying to brand me. Is your name like my new label now?"

"The best thing about it is you're the only one with this label."

"Oh, you're so full of shit."

"Just wait until you see your new license plate, then."

"Milo, what have you done?"

He lifted his hands, shrugging his shoulders. I bolted from bed, running full force toward the closet where I snagged a shirt and pajama pants. It felt like forever before I reached the driveway where there weren't any sign that my truck was ever parked out front. Confusion plagued me. I turned to find Milo scratching his head, giving me that look that crossed his face when his nerves were on the line.

"Baby, what have you done?"

He aimed a fob in his hand immediately starting an engine. Ducked off in the shade, where the concrete carved a secluded space for cars to avoid the excessive heat and the Berkeley summer sun, was a sleek black Bentley truck, complete with black rims and a black bow.

"Baby! Where's my truck?"

"Right there." He laughed, nodding toward the Bentley.

"Milo. I just... You just bought the other truck."

"And I felt like you needed something a little more sophisticated. Something that screamed I'm a boss, my nigga a boss, and my pussy is the biggest boss. That motherfucker got him emptying his wallet ever—" He got carried away, describing his sentiments in detail.

"Milo."

"Okay. Okay."

"But babe, seriously, my truck was brand new."

"So is this one."

"I know, and it's gorgeous. Thank you so much."

Running into his arms, I wrapped my body around his as best I could, climbing him like a tree.

"Happy birthday, love. Now, we have to get dressed. We've fucked off half our morning sleeping in. We have shit to do and money to spend. Whatever your heart desires today, it's on me. I'll get Mason together."

"My mom said she'll take him."

"I already scheduled a play date with Maz."

"Okay. I'll let her know."

"If you want him to cancel, he can."

"No. I'd rather he be around the children than all alone at my parents' home."

"Alright, then we'll drop him off before dinner this evening unless you want him to leave earlier."

"No. I want to spend my birthday with my little baby."

"Good, 'cause I'm not ready for him to leave yet."

"Keys, please! Let me have a look before we jet inside."

Handing me the keys, Milo nodded toward the truck. I sprinted in its direction, opening the door to see the B attempt to show up on the concrete. It failed, but I was sure it would light through the night. Circling the truck, I encountered the tags he'd warned me about moments prior.

Dr. Domino.

Turning around, I glared in his direction. With a tilted

head, he grabbed the back of his neck and shuffled his feet slowly.

"When did you become a liar?" I asked.

"I don't know what you're talking about."

"Is this your truck, Milo?"

"Nah. It's yours."

"Then, why does it say Dr. Domino? I'm not Dr. Domino."

"Not yet."

He was so full of himself. Tossing my thoughts to the back of my head, I rounded the truck, ending up on the driver's side again. I hopped inside, admiring the leathery goods and exquisite interior. They'd taken their precious time designing the vehicle that I'd get to enjoy until my man decided I needed something else. With Milo, I'd never know when that would be.

Milo · Nature

"WHAT DO YOU THINK?"

I twirled in the dress that Milo had chosen for the night.

"I think the same thing I thought when you put that motherfucker on in the store. I can't wait to take that shit off."

"Baby." With my lips stuck out, I dropped my shoulders, wanting to hear something else come from Milo's mouth.

"I think you look stunning, baby."

"Thank you."

Coming closer, wrapping his arms around me, he leaned down and kissed my neck.

"I'm sorry. I wasn't trying to upset you."

"You haven't, baby. I just... I wanted to hear you say it."

"Say it? Say what?" he asked softly, though he already knew the answer.

"That I looked beautiful."

Smiling, he turned me around to face him.

"You look beautiful, Nature."

"Thank you."

"Every single day. Even when ya breath stink and your brows look like bushes."

"Okay, you can stop now."

"Even when your face crusty and your lips are swollen."

"Milo."

"Even when you ain't showered."

"Baby, stop."

I slapped my hand against his chest as I stood on my toes and pursed my lips.

"Even when your mustache needs a lineup."

I couldn't hold back the laughter. The second his lips were close enough, I planted them between my teeth and bit down.

"Ummmm. Ummmm! Aye."

"I said stop."

"Damn, aight. You tried to take a nigga's lip off."

"No I didn't because you're going to need those to eat my pussy tonight."

"Nature, girl, don't talk like that," he warned.

"Hmm. Why not?"

"Because, first off, you don't talk like that. And second, I'll fucking do it and feed you dick for dinner. Please don't play with me."

"Okay. Okay. No. Let's go."

Taking off in my heels, I headed for the door, hoping I didn't bust my behind on the way down the stairs. Milo was right behind me, adding pressure. Thankfully, I made it to the truck safely without incident.

Milo held the door open for me as I climbed inside. Still the ultimate gentleman, he waited until I was inside and settled before closing the door behind me. When he made his way to the driver's side, I watched his lanky frame from the front windshield.

God, did you have to make him so Black and so beautiful?

"Ready to roll?"

"Yes."

The night lights of Berkeley shined against our skin as we traveled south toward the restaurant of Milo's choosing. He'd planned our day down to a science. I was instructed to enjoy the day and worry about nothing. I'd been doing just that.

The diamonds on my finger, wrist, and neck glistened in the dark, matching the pieces on Milo's neck and wrists. Unlike mine, his ring finger was empty, creating a void within me that I couldn't wait to fill. As the thought occurred, so did the urge to spend the next few weeks searching for the perfect piece to represent my love for him and the future we planned to spend together.

"What's on your mind, pretty girl?" he asked, lowering the volume of the music.

"How empty your ring finger is."

"What about it?"

"I don't like it."

"You trying to put a ring on it?" he toyed.

"In fact, I am."

"Nah, for real? You ready to take that leap?"

"Milo, I've been ready since I was sixteen years old. If you'd asked me then, I promise I would've said yes without hesitation."

"Yeah?"

"Yes," I assured him with a nod.

"So, what about tonight?"

"What do you mean, what about tonight?"

"If I asked you to be my wife right here, right now, would your answer be the same?"

"Yes."

As soon as the word left my mouth, the truck swerved.

Scrrrrrrrr!

The smell of burned rubber seeped through the vents. My brows centered on my face as my heart rate increased. I watched as Milo's chest rose and fell as he stared straight ahead, contemplating and scaring me simultaneously.

"Baby, what are you doing?"

"Nay, this is not a birthday dinner that we're on the way to."

"It's not?"

"No. It's an engagement party I set up with the help of your mother. Our friends and family are waiting to hear good news. All day long, all fucking day long, I've been trying to find the words, trying to come up with the perfect combination and the most sentimental way to ask you to be my wife, but I have come up with nothing. Nothing feels good enough, no moment has felt perfect up until now. So, I'm telling you, I don't have anything over the top to say or any clever ass speech. All I have is my heart, baby, and I'm wondering if that's enough to get you to rock with a nigga for the rest of 'em. The rest of our lives. The rest of our good days. The rest of our bad days. All of that shit?"

He dug into his pocket, removing a band that nearly made me orgasm at the sight of it. My heart galloped, pounding against my chest to be freed.

"Milo."

"I'm telling you, Nay, I'm the nigga for you. You'll never have to worry about shit as long as I'm around."

"Milo."

"I got you. I got us. We'll forever be good."

"Milo."

"Say yes tonight, Nay."

Nodding, I allowed my emotions to spill over into my verbiage. "Y-Yes."

"Yes?"

"It was always yes. You just took so fucking long to ask," I choked. "Made me wait all this time. I could just hit you right now. What took you so long?"

Smiling, he slid the ring onto my finger, right on top of the other one. I thought it would collapse from the weight. The combination was massive.

"I'm sorry about that, baby. I promise to never make that mistake again. No more waiting."

"No more waiting," I cried. "Milo, it's beautiful."

"You have to pull it together, baby. We have a photographer and shit. I don't want you trying to beat my ass because your makeup smeared on every picture he snaps."

He knew me so well.

"Okay. Okay. Oh my God, baby. I'm going to be a wife."

Still in shock, I stared at the rings, tears still falling.

"Not just a wife, baby. My wife. That's a big fucking flex."

Nodding, I agreed.

"God, I have to get it together."

"Cry it out, baby. We can wait right here. When you're ready, we're rolling, but not until you say the word."

"I don't want to wait," I blubbered.

"Huh?"

"I don't want to wait. I don't want to wait anymore. I don't want to wait to marry you, Milo."

"Then you won't have to."

"I'm serious, baby."

"You have no fucking idea how serious I am, Nature. It's whatever you want, love."

"Thank you."

Leaning over, I grabbed both sides of his face and pulled him closer so that I could taste his lips and tongue.

"Can I put a ring on it, now?" I sniggered through a tearful smile.

"Whatever you want to do, Nature."

"I don't want to go into the new year as Dr. Dupree."

"I wasn't planning on letting you."

"Is a wedding in two months possible? I return to the office in three."

"Baby, a wedding in two weeks is possible if that's what you want."

"I do."

"No shit?" he belted, turning toward me to make sure I was serious.

"No shit, baby."

"Nature, tell me you're fucking with me."

"I'm not. But I don't want to pressure either of us unnecessarily. I don't mind a November wedding."

"Money talk. You not fucking with a square. I'll pay a motherfucker to reduce our stress and get you down that aisle in two weeks if you want it. It's September third, baby. We have the entire month."

"So, October?"

"If that's what you want."

"Okay. October."

"Then, October it is."

"Oh, baby. I love you so much."

"Yeah?

"Yes."

"Forever?"

"Yes."

"Thank you."

As we pulled into traffic, I cleaned the tears from my eyes, still coming to terms with the fact that I was about to be Milo's wife. My plan was falling together so beautifully. It had taken so many years, but timing was perfect.

Milo · Nature

CHAMPAGNE SPRAYED the room as Makai popped another bottle, sending the room up in cheer. The energy in the room kept my spirits high and my cheeks higher.

"I want to propose a toast to Albert," Makai started, "and his future wife, Hermione. I hate it for Mason 'cause the young nigga will never get away with shit. They know everything. And I mean everything. The only niggas I know graduating from college still in diapers and shit."

"Whatever," I chanted, amused by his narration.

"Nevertheless, I have been waiting on this day for a hot minute. A couple times, I thought this nigga had clipped the final straw, but oh how quickly I forget how us Domino boys slanging that d—"

"Aye. Aye. Aye," Malachi interrupted, standing to his feet. "Forgive him. He's—"

"Makai," Milo shouted. "Don't blame that on the liquor."

"Sadly, I can't. But what my brother is trying to say is, congratulations, Milo and Nature. We've been patiently waiting for this day and we're honored to be included."

Nodding, I clapped, lifting my glass as we all toasted.

"Pops, you got anything to say?" Malachi asked.

Touching his chest, Mr. Domino shook his head as he waved his hand and smiled.

"No, son."

The sadness in his eyes touched parts of me that I didn't know existed.

"You sure, old man?"

"Yeah." Nodding, he lowered his head as grief thickened in his chest.

"Well, I do." Lawe cleared his throat, standing up.

"Baby, let's not do this. Don't get your ass up there embarrassing me," Kleu warned, bringing humor to the room again.

The couple was unintentionally hilarious.

"I got this. Do I look like an embarrassing nigga, Kleu? Fuck I look like, baby? A clown or some shit."

"Depends on the day."

"Oh, really? What's that supposed to mean?"

He tuned us out, lending his attention to the woman standing beside him that I'd grown fond of. They were a perfect match. She matched his energy, though I didn't think that was even possible.

"Man, you gon' talk your sh—your stuff or sit down?" Mercer shrugged.

"I'ma sit down because my girl think I'm a clown ass nigga and I need to hear about this shit. Move on to the next person. Come back 'round to me."

"No one else has anything to say," Makai informed him.

"Well, forget it. I'll say something at the wedding. Kleu, what that supposed to mean?"

He scooted his chair closer to hers as she tried her hardest not to laugh in his face.

"Boy, we can talk about it tomorrow."

"Nah, we talking tonight."

"Well, I would like to share a few words." My mother cleared her throat, standing to her feet.

"Hi, Mom." My cheeks flushed.

The empty seat beside her that Milo had reserved for my father made my stomach turn. However, the fact that my future husband was still holding space for him warmed my heart. My father was alive and well and couldn't show up for me. Milo's was buried many, many years ago and I'd bet my last dollar that he'd be in attendance if he was still living. As disheartening as it was, I didn't let the thoughts linger.

"Hi, baby," she responded, projecting her voice. "On behalf of Nature's father and I, I'd like to officially welcome

Milo to the family, although I feel like he's been a part of us since you two were teens."

Everyone agreed at once.

"Strangely, I've never worried about Nature, how her life would go, or who she would grow old with. The answer was always so clear to me. Every year, like clockwork, I accepted gifts on Nature's birthday, some Christmas Eves, and whenever she accomplished something big, like opening her own practice.

"One thing Milo wouldn't allow was for Nature to forget him. Every chance he got, he tried reminding her how much he was thinking of her and how special her day still was to him. Admittedly, I felt like I was in a love story that was never-ending, just waiting for the day that I turned the page and the couple were kissing and making up. Hearing that Mason was baking and who'd fathered him felt like that moment for me.

"And since, it's been bliss watching this story and the starring characters evolve. Tonight, we celebrate such a beautiful love story and I'm so happy that it is Milo and Nature's. I couldn't wish for a better partner for my daughter. I have no doubt that you two will move mountains together. Congratulations, baby."

I love you, I mouthed.

I love you, too, she mouthed.

The chatter quickly began again. I felt Milo's head against my shoulder. Intoxication might've played a role in his actions, but I doubted it was the case. Milo was mindful of his drinking, knowing that he was the designated driver tonight.

"Hey." Smiling, I looked down at him.

"Hey."

The wetness on my dress startled me, exposing his true state. Immediately concerned, I covered his face with my hand, reserving his emotions for us, shielding everyone else out momentarily.

"Everything okay?"

"Perfect, Nature. Everything is perfect."

Tears fell from his beautiful eyes, forcing me to spring into action. Still shielding his face, I slid my chair backward.

"Come with me."

I stood, pulling him to his feet as well. Without resistance, he followed me into the hallway that led to the restrooms. My feet didn't stop moving until we were alone, in a space where it wasn't likely we'd be interrupted.

"Milo, are you okay?"

"Yes, baby. I'm good. I'm just... I wish my people were here."

My heart broke for him.

"Moms would be proud of me, ya know. Pops, ah, Nature, he'd be having a ball tonight, knowing his boy was becoming a man. A real fucking man. Because that's what you've made me. They'd love you. They'd love Mason. They'd... Fuck, man. She– he should've just let them help her. He should've just left her at the facility. I'd rather have pieces of her than none of them. I was going to make her better. I just needed a couple of years. I was well on my way. I was going to fix it, fix her. She didn't have to just... She just killed him, baby, then killed herself."

"She was sick, Milo."

"I know, baby, but that doesn't make it hurt any less."

"I understand. I understand. I'm so sorry."

"Nah. I'm sorry. I'm not trying to ruin this night for you, for us. Shit just got my chest hurting."

"Milo, you're not ruining my night. My night is perfect, even now. Good days. Bad days. Good moments. Bad moments. I'm here. I'll always be here."

"I know. I know, Nay."

"Are you sure you're okay?"

"I don't know. Seeing everybody so happy is hurting me and healing me at once. It's like I can't have one without the other."

"Then we'll leave."

"You sure?"

"I'm sure, baby. We've been here for two hours. We can leave. I don't mind."

"Alright."

"I'll let everyone know we're taking off. I'll meet you at the truck, okay?"

"Aight."

Before taking off, I kissed his lips and then his forehead, wishing I could take away his pain or at least ease it. The defeat sat on his shoulders like bricks as he took off in the other direction.

Oh baby, I crumbled inside, watching him from afar.

By the time I made it back to the truck, Milo was waiting with the engine running.

"I can drive if you'd like."

"I'm good. You've been drinking. I got you."

"Okay."

I reached over, taking his hand into mine. I reclined my seat slightly and kicked my shoes off my feet, attempting to find comfort for the ride home. Musiq played in the background. One of his most recognized records soothed my heart as he spat about love and how so many people used its name in vain.

Somewhere along the way, my eyes closed, peace overcame me, and I'd dozed off. When I woke up, fresh air was brushing the tip of my nose and Milo was standing beside me. Because there was no way I was sliding back into my shoes, I stretched my arms, praying that my man had the strength to tote me inside. I wanted nothing more than to curl up next to him and sleep the night away.

"I need you to wake up, baby, and listen to me."

The seriousness in his voice was startling, forcing me up in my seat. I wiped the blurriness from my eyes, finally realizing we weren't home and it wasn't our driveway I was waiting to be carried up. We were parked beside a private place with the lights glowing and the engine running.

"Milo. What's going on?"

"That wedding you wanted to happen in two weeks... it's happening next Sunday, baby. Your mother and I have been working overtime for the last month to pull this off for you. On that plane is your mother, Kleu, Shayla, Aeir, and Mason. You'll land in Paris in a few short hours where you'll meet some expensive ass designer your mother had to make you three different dresses. You can choose any one of them you like and if you don't like any of them, you have an appointment at a dress shop at two tomorrow evening. I want you to have the wedding of your dreams, baby girl. And I don't want you to stress doing it. I've handled it all. Just pick the prettiest dress you can find and meet me down that aisle. Aight?"

"Baby. Seriously?"

"Yes, Nature. Now, go. They're waiting on you."

"How'd they even get here? We just left them."

"Baby, they left immediately after us. I've been driving in circles, making sure we didn't beat them. I let you sleep."

"Milo, you're just... I love you so much, baby."

His sadness hadn't subsided, leaving me conflicted.

"Will you be okay without me?"

"I have my brothers, baby. They share my pain. I'll be fine."

"Okay. Call me if you need me."

"I will."

"Promise?"

"I promise."

"You gon' let her roll or you gon' hold her hostage, my nigga?"

An unfamiliar tenor sparked concern within us both. However, my furrowed brows looked nothing like Milo's lifted brows. Confused, I searched through the darkness to find a slim, nearly identical figure headed in our direction.

Caving immediately, Milo gasped in disbelief. I watched his chest deflated as he held his right palm against it. A face I hadn't seen in ages brought my smile to my eyes. From the looks of things, I wasn't the only one who was in for pleasant surprises.

"Chem?" I questioned in disbelief.

"You not expecting me to answer that, are you?" he asked, spreading his arms.

"No. Not really. My God. It's been so long."

"Yeah. Sorry about that. But I'm here, and for good reason. I heard this nigga put a rock on that finger of yours."

Walking into his chest, I allowed him to wrap his hands

around me before pulling back. He lifted my hand to examine the rings on my finger.

"He did well."

"He did well," I agreed.

Milo, still speechless, took a few steps back, trying to gather his thoughts and find words. Hearing his soundless brother and knowing exactly what he needed without words, Chem stepped forward and grabbed Milo. The two embraced, openly displaying their love for one another and the appreciation for the filled void that Chem's absence created. Tears cascaded down Milo's cheeks.

"Bro," he cried.

"I know, nigga. I know."

Knowing that they needed the moment to themselves, I made my way to the plane where I climbed the steps. I took a final look over my shoulder, admiring the pure, unfiltered love that I was witnessing. When I finally made it onboard, everyone was waiting, ready to make their way to Paris.

"Not she don't want to leave her nigga," Kleu scoffed, making everyone onboard laugh.

"She has no other choice. I really need this break."

"We're going to double the fun. Bachelorette party in pear—ee," Kleu taunted.

"Sounds like a plan to me," I agreed. "Tell the pilot we're ready when he is!"

"I know that's right, babe!" Shayla cheered.

I got comfortable in the designated seat, leaning my head against the cushion with one thing on my mind. *God, I love that man.*

SEVENTEEN

"THERE," Pops said, stepping back to marvel at his work. "How does that feel?"

"It feels fine, Pops."

"Good. Good."

The tux that he'd made sure was pressed by his own hands fit perfectly.

"Son, I just want to tell you that I'm proud of ya. Ya know? I never doubted you once, always knew she was the one. I'm just happy you didn't waste another second letting her know. I'd be rolling over in my grave if you let me get out of here without seeing you walk down that aisle."

"Don't talk like that, old man."

"I'm just saying, Milo. I'm not superhuman. I can't live forever."

"I wish you could," I admitted, feeling the strain in my voice from the overflow of emotions.

Since I'd asked Nature to be my wife, I couldn't seem to keep my eyes dry or my heart from aching. Our wedding and the week leading up to it unburied so many unwanted feelings of mine that I'd tucked away so many years ago. This week was such an eye opener, revealing just how deep my pain ran, and just how long I'd been running from it.

"No you don't, Milo. You just think you do. It would kill me to live to see any one of you leave me. I'm supposed to go first."

"I know. I just don't want it to happen. I don't think my heart can take it."

"Baby boy." Rubbing my back, he smiled at me. "You'll be alright."

"Pops, you believe in that wedding luck stuff?"

"Not at all. Whatever is going to happen is going to happen. Why?"

"Because I need to see her. I need to hear her voice."

"Better not be cold feet, Milo."

"I've already married her, Pops. My feet warm. This is just the lightshow. The real magic took place Wednesday, just us two."

"Well, I don't think it would hurt. However, I doubt if those girls will let you get to her because they damn sho believe in that shit."

"I need the room."

"Alright. When you need me, I'll be outside the door.

We only have a few minutes before we're lining up, so don't be too long."

"I won't. I just need a minute."

After another pat on the back, he let me be. I wasted little time searching for my phone; I found it within seconds. Nature's contact was the first on my list. I tapped the screen and listened as her phone rang. The first call eventually rolled over to voicemail.

Come on, Nay.

Pick up, baby.

I tried again, this time getting an answer on the third ring.

"Milo?" she rushed out, panic in her tone.

"Everything is fine, baby," I assured her.

"Are you alright?" Her voice lowered. "Hey, can you guys give me a second?"

There were a few seconds of silence before she asked again.

"Are you okay?"

"I'm trying to be, Nature, but this shit is hard, much harder than I imagined. I want my Pops. I want my Ma. When I look out there today, I won't see either of them and that shit eating me alive."

"Listen to me, Milo. You have every right to be as hurt as you need to be, as scared as you are, as angry as you are. Grief doesn't have a timeframe. It doesn't have a clock. It never stops. It just hurts a little less. I will always hold space for your pain, even on our biggest day. If I have to hold your hand myself to get you down the aisle, then say the word and I'm on my way. I don't care, Milo. Whatever it takes, baby."

"Whatever it takes."

"Yes, baby. And not just today, always."

"I know. That's why I love you."

"So, what's it going to be?"

"I'ma be there already, Nature. Just meet a nigga, you know, whenever you get time."

"Luckily, I've got time now."

"Then I'll be waiting."

I ended the call with a lighter heart and a bigger smile. I two-stepped toward the door, pulling it open to find my brothers all waiting on me, Chemistry included.

"Ya niggas ready?"

"Born ready," Makai responded.

"I love y'all niggas. I appreciate your support on this day."

"One love," they all said in unison.

Milo · Nature

JUST AFTER THE last few petals from Aussie's basket hit the floor, silence coated the room. Nature rounded the corner, leaving everyone speechless. The cream dress she wore hugged every curve on her slim frame. It was perfect, just as she was.

Shit, Nay.

I rocked back and forward, shifting my vision from her to the ground, desperate to find the smallest form of relief. Her beauty was staggering. Watching her make her way down the aisle with her father at her side rocked me to the core, leaving me dismembered. My heart was in pieces and so was my head.

Fuck, baby girl.

Staggering. She looked like a dream, *my dream*. Her cinnamon-colored skin was hardly concealed underneath the sheer veil. Not even the mesh could hide her beauty. The sound of Anthony Hamilton's voice serenading us all as she made her way to me as promised was too much for my heart to handle. Leaning forward, I placed my hands on my knees, trying to steady my breathing.

"You a bitch, nigga," Lawe whispered in my ear. "Handle this shit like a G, nigga. Stand up. Chin up! Bending over like you done dropped your fucking soap."

He forced my hand, not letting up until I made him my best man. But even with the official title being given to him, I truly had four more best men. They all shared equal roles in my big day, however, I was happy that he was the one standing beside me.

Unable to avoid his comical presence, I found humor through the intensity of the moment. I mustered the strength to pull myself up. Standing tall, ten toes down, I joined my hands in front of me, nodding as his words replayed in my head.

Chin up.

Eagerly, I stepped forward and pulled Nature closer to me once she was within reach. The veil she wore was no match for me. I lifted it instantly, drawing her lips into my mouth and tasting her sweetness.

"That part hasn't come yet," Makai bellowed.

The entire congregation, that was filled with colleagues of Nature and mine. Neither of us were members of large families, but we had a plethora of associates that we wanted to enjoy our special day. The email blast I'd sent two weeks prior to the wedding announced our nuptials and the secrecy of it all. Nature's email went out while she was in Paris with the girls.

"Ummmm," she moaned, finally breaking away.

She was even prettier up close.

"Hi."

"Hey, baby," I replied, filled to capacity. Her love surrounded me.

"I told you I'd meet you here."

"And I told you I'd be waiting. You look so... so fucking pretty, baby," I stuttered.

Blinking away her tears, she smiled up at me. "And you, you look so handsome."

"I love you so much, Nature."

"I love you so much."

"Y'all gon' let us in on your secret ceremony or what?" Lawe asked, bringing the crowd to their knees almost.

By the time they went home, they'd need a change of bottoms because he'd surely make them piss them. Between him and Makai, they didn't stand a chance.

"Hush," Kleu demanded.

"Well." Minister Keaton chuckled. "Let's begin with a very warm welcome to everyone, especially the bride and groom who both look incredible. Who gives this bride..."

Completely zoned out, I watched everyone and everything around us disappear, leaving us at the altar alone.

"You look like a doll," I whispered.

"I'm so happy," she responded lowly, so that only I could hear her.

"Today is your day."

"Our day."

We were both lost in one another's eyes, taking the time to clean our faces with the back of our hands as much as we could until we finally settled and were able to control the rivers that flowed down our faces. So much time passed us by, neither of us breaking eye contact nor the physical connection that our hands maintained as words were spoken to and about us. It wasn't until we were instructed to recite our vows that I snapped out of the faraway place Nature and I were visiting and returned to the banquet hall where our guests were waiting.

"You first?" she asked.

Nodding in her direction, I encouraged her to lead the way. She peered at me with sincerity in her eyes and undeniable love in her heart.

"Milo. It's been such a long time coming, but there's nowhere else I'd rather be right now than standing before you, in front of our friends and family, confessing my love for you. I've never felt anything so trivial, yet revolutionary.

"So ugly, yet so beautiful. So recessive, yet so dominant. So old, yet so new. So painful, yet so pleasant. So subtle, yet so overwhelming. So understanding, yet so intolerable. So polluted, yet so pure. So heavy, yet so light. So mysterious, yet so obvious."

Nature blubbered, crying uncontrollably as she continued her vows.

"Never, until I met you. You stirred my soul the very second I saw your face, and it hasn't settled since. It craves you on a daily, sits quietly, in waiting, wondering when it'll be blessed with your presence again. Over the last few months, I've been the happiest, knowing that my soul was getting a good stir every single morning and every single night before bed.

"You are the epitome of love. And your unwavering love for me and our son leaves me wondering if I'm even loving you hard enough, boldly enough, loud enough, unapologetically enough. And then, I quickly remember just how incomplete, just how empty I am when you're not around and know that I must love you as much as you do me. Because there's no other way to explain it.

"I want to live and die beside you, baby. That's my life's wish and today, we're making it come true."

"You trying to have me on the floor, kicking and screaming?"

Chuckling, she shook her head. "I'm just speaking my truth. It's your turn."

Nodding, I exhaled loudly.

"Uh," I stammered, wiping my eyes. "Shoot, I done forgot what I was about to say."

Laughter erupted from the guest.

"Let's see. Nah, Nay. That's unfair. You really came up with all of that, baby? Where the paper? How'd you remember all of that?"

The guests cackled, finding my confusion humorous, but I was serious.

"I didn't need a piece of paper to explain my love for you when it's written on my heart."

"See, you're just too good at this."

"Go ahead, baby."

"Alright," I sighed again. "Nature, the only woman besides my mother that I've had the pleasure of loving, I wish I could relive the day I met you a million times over.

Because that was the day that I was met with my future. That very day, as young and foolish as I was, there were a few things I was certain of. My education. My path. And my person.

"That was you and to this day, it's still you. It'll always be you. I love you from the depths of me that I don't even know exist. Each day, you root yourself deeper in my heart, deeper in my soul, making me aware of places that were undiscovered prior to your presence.

"You're so good at this, Nay. Loving me for who I am and exactly where I am without compromising your beliefs, morals, or sanity. You're so good at this, baby. Forcing me to see that I have potential beyond the books. You're so good at this, my love. Helping me understand that I don't only have a brain but I have a heart, too.

"And when I say that it belongs to you, I'm talking wholly. Every piece of that moth—every piece of it. It's yours. I don't even know why it's still in my chest. It beats for you. It longs for you. It waits for you. And just like me, it's ready to spend the rest of its days loving on you."

"Rings, please," Minister Keaton requested.

The loud clearing of a throat caused everyone in the room to turn around. Just as the culprit was spotted, words came flying out of her mouth.

"Whatever happened to speak now or forever hold your peace? That's the part I came for," Christina yelled across the room, rolling her neck with disdain written all over her face. "Isn't it before the vows, or am I mistaken?"

Silence.

Livid. I planted my feet on the ground, convincing myself that Nature's side was where I needed to remain unless I wanted to end my wedding day in a cell. My heart shattered a thousand times. Too afraid to see the look on my wife's face, I held my gaze, wondering why the hell Christina was among our guests and where her knowledge of the wedding had come from. Our guest list was small and everyone RSVP'd ahead of time. Christina wasn't welcome. Had her name come up on the guest list, I would've noticed it.

The ruffling of Nature's dress grabbed my attention. She was trying her hardest to gather it at her waist. Without a doubt, I knew that she was attempting to make a run for it.

"Nature."

"What the fuck is this?" she said, barely above a whisper. "On my wedding day?"

"Who is this bitch?" Kleu's whisper could be heard loud and clear by anyone near. "Baby," she called out to Lawe.

"Nature, listen—" I tried, but didn't have the words.

"Fuck this. Fuck her and fuck you!" she hissed, finally managing to get her dress up high enough so that she wouldn't fall flat on her face.

"Somebody get that bitch up out of here before I go to jail," I advised.

"You ain't said nothing but a word," Kleu responded. "See, I don't mind a few hours behind bars for a good cause because I'm 'bout to drag this bit—"

"Nature!" I called out, taking off behind her.

As if I was cemented into the ground, I moved like a snail. Though everything was happening in lightning speed, it felt like I was moving at a snail's pace. My long legs weren't a match for her. She was out of the building and headed toward the awaiting car by the time I made it out of the banquet hall we'd reserved for our ceremony.

When I finally reached the pavement, the car she'd hopped into was speeding out of the parking lot. I patted my pockets for keys out of sheer habit, but quickly remembered that I was in a tux, on my fucking wedding day, and my car wasn't anywhere to be found. We'd hired drivers to get us to the venue.

"FUCK."

Malachi, Makai, Mercer, Chem, and Pops all joined me outside.

"Keys. I need somebody's keys, man. I have to... Keys. Anybody got their keys?"

A hand on my shoulder made everything around me come crumbling down.

"Chasing after her and risking you both getting hurt on your special day ain't the answer, Milo," Chem said to me.

"Special day? Somebody jus... She ruined her fucking day, man. I need to get to her."

"What will it change?" he asked me, tilting his head while waiting for an answer. "Exactly. What she needs right now is space and a little time to see that this wasn't your fault and you have no control over other's actions. If you could've prevented that, she knows you would've. She just needs time to realize you're not her enemy right now. Whoever that bitch is, that's the fucking enemy."

"I have to go find her."

"He's right," Pops agreed.

"Real shit," Makai added.

I looked to Malachi and then to Mercer, watching as both of them nodded their heads.

"I'll put somebody on it to make sure she's straight. When you're ready to talk to her, you'll know where she is. I promise," Malachi expounded.

Feeling the weight of her heart on my chest, my body weakened until my ass was flush with the ground. I rested on the concrete, unfastening the button of my tuxedo as I watched the guests file out of the building and make their way to their cars.

"I feel like I'm forever fucking over Nay. She a good girl, man. She doesn't deserve this."

"Don't start beating yourself about this. You made her dream wedding a reality," Mercer reminded me.

"Only to fuck it up."

"You didn't do that. Someone else did," he elaborated.

"The same motherfucker that's been the source of her pain since she was eight months pregnant. You think she trying to forgive a nigga after this?"

"There's nothing to be forgiven, Milo. You're blinded by pain right now and don't see it. Soon, you will. Nature will, too." Calmly, Chem voiced. "And when she does, pay for this shit all again. You got it. Show you ain't afraid to spend it to make up for the next motherfucker's maliciousness."

For the first time in the last few minutes, I agreed.

"I have to get out of here, bro. I'm leaving a line open for you. Call me if you need me. The number is in the pocket of your jacket."

"You had room in that tight motherfucker?"

I didn't have the strength to laugh at Makai's joke. This was no laughing matter. My baby was hurting and I needed to get to her.

EIGHTEEN

THE DIM LIGHTS of the cabin shined against Mason's dark skin. It was black and perfect, just like his father's. The hollowness in my spirit ached. Even the thought of him, the thought of us, hurt. Closing my eyes, I tried blocking out the pain but it was impossible.

The aching of my eyelids reminded me of the tears I'd cried continuously over the last twenty-four hours. The scratchiness of my throat and raspiness of my voice wouldn't allow me to forget it, forget him, or forget her, although I desperately wanted to.

I reopened my eyes, afraid to face the visions behind my lids. I'd seen Christina's face a hundred times over. The sight of her made my stomach turn. She'd managed to ruin the most precious day of my life due to the misery she was drowning in.

Mason's latch on my breast loosened, signaling the beginning of his sleep pattern. I lowered my shirt and snapped the flap of my bra back in place. The darkness that neighbored us was soothing and the reason I'd chosen this flight over the others leaving Berkeley and heading to my destination. It boarded closest to Mason's bedtime.

With any luck, he'd sleep the entire seven-hour flight, but traveling with an infant was always unpredictable. Nevertheless, staying behind in Berkeley to soak my body, heart, and mind in memories of my wedding wasn't an option. This trip, it was necessary. I needed to unplug.

The vibration of my phone prompted me to tear away from my anguish momentarily. Though gloominess coated my spirit, the message that appeared on my screen after unlocking my phone forced a smile on my face. A group between Kleu, Shayla, Aeir, and I had been formed to discuss wedding details over the last week. A new message from Kleu was in the thread.

Nature, I know that your heart is hurting right now but please find comfort in the fact that that motherfucker's eyes, forehead, nose, jaws, mouth, chin, teeth, gums, chest, arms, back, stomach, legs, and feet are hurting right now.

Nature: 20

Hating ass bitch: -8

At the end of the day, you're up, babe. I made sure of it.

It brought me very little comfort, but comfort, nonetheless. Because I had no words, I shut down the screen of my phone and reclined as far as the seat would allow, which wasn't very far at all. Just as I closed my eyes, wincing from the pain their swelling and irritation caused, my phone vibrated again.

"Ouch," I whispered, feeling utterly miserable.

Our doors are open. If you need somewhere to rest without interruption or worry, come to me. I'm here. I don't mind taking Mason off your hands. I know that the next few days will be the toughest of your life, but please understand you're not alone. I'm here. Malachi is here. And it's your heart that we're aiming to protect. You won't have to worry about anything here with us. Just say the word and we'll come running. I know that we've only known each other for a few months now, but you feel so much like a sister I never had. When you hurt, I hurt. I'm praying for the day that our pain subsides. We're all gutted.

Aeir's message reactivated the faucets, however, I was all out of tears. Silently, I cried, but there were no physical evidence of the occurrence.

Call me when you land. I love you, babe. Head up.

Shayla's message was as short as it was sweet. With everyone in the group still awake and active, I felt obligated to respond. Before I could, more messages came through.

Land? Where are you and do I need to board a plane? Kleu wanted to know.

After much consideration and convincing, she's not letting the honeymoon reservations go to waste. I wasn't going to let her, either. She needs this time alone, Shayla explained.

Oh, babe. Good for you, Aeir texted.

Take all the time you need. Don't come back until you feel better – from head to heart to heel, Kleu encouraged.

We can never get it right. Finally, I released the thought that had been haunting me since I fled my wedding.

Life keeps showing me that we shouldn't be together, yet we keep trying to force what simply isn't meant to be aligned.

As the words formed through the movement of my fingers, simultaneously, the confession smacked me against the chest, nearly knocking the wind out of me.

Nature, I'd have to disagree, Shayla added. *That man loves you down. Life just keeps getting in the way of his efforts to show you just that. Yet, he has yet to give up. I've received a hundred calls since yesterday. I haven't told you because I didn't want to pile onto your pain. But he's hurting too and he's trying everything to fix this, to make it right. Though this isn't about him, I can't let you forget how much Milo loves you. When it's all said and done, that's what will matter most here.*

He does, Kleu sent.

I've never seen him so miserable, so broken, Aeir shared.

Locking the phone, I closed my eyes again. Images of Milo, my entire world, appeared. My heart wouldn't allow me to envision a broken, miserable version of that man. It hurt too much.

Another vibration stirred me out of the trance. I unlocked my phone, searching for a new message in the group. To my surprise, there wasn't one. I exited the thread, finally realizing there was a message from Milo sitting atop the others. My heart's gape widened as I expelled a full, lengthy breath. Bracing myself, I tapped the screen to open the message.

Nay.

Another message rolled in as I read the first one.

Talk to me, baby.

A low squeal released the pressure that quickly accumulated in my chest. I closed the message and pressed the side button until my phone shut off completely. Closing my eyes for the final time, I forbid their opening until the cabin lights came on and the plane landed in St. Lucia.

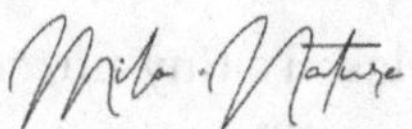

NATURE DOMINO, the sign read as I stepped off the semi-private flight that only sat twenty passengers. After marrying Milo in downtown Berkeley on Wednesday, I was at the government offices, adjusting my identification and going through with my name change.

Nature Dupree, I corrected in my head, chastising myself for being in such a hurry to carry a last name that had caused me so much hell.

"I'm Nature," I announced.

"Right this way. Luggage?" the driver asked, pointing toward the section of the plane where luggage was being unloaded.

"Yes. The Louis Vuitton luggage with the pink tag."

"Okay. Let's get inside and I will get luggage."

I followed him to the Lincoln truck and waited for him to open the door before Mason and I climbed inside. Sighing at the sight of the car seat I'd requested, I was instantly relieved. As quickly as possible, I got my son inside and strapped down. The carrier he was strapped to my body in helped tremendously, but freeing my body of his weight completely felt much better.

The driver rejoined us shortly after with my luggage in tow. He lifted the rear gate and sat it across the carpet. Once he made it back to his seat, our journey began. The beauty of the island was muddled by my broken heart. As we journeyed to the villa that was reserved for the newly married couple, all I saw was darkness and agony.

To my surprise, the drive was relatively short compared to my expectations. Mason's tiny fingers gripped my index finger, pulling them toward his mouth in an effort to extract milk. According to his philosophy, milk would pour from any part of my body if he sucked hard enough. He was mistaken.

"We have arrived."

Unstrapping Mason, I prepared to exit the truck. My door swung open and my luggage was sitting right beside it as the driver waited for me to exit. He led the way up to the private, all-inclusive villa where he produced a key and handed it to me.

"Thank you."

"My pleasure."

"I don't have any cash on me," I explained. "I can g—"

"It's fine. It's taken care of," he told me, turning to leave without another word being spoken.

I tapped the card against the door and waited for the green light to enter. When I heard the lock deactivate, I lowered the handle and pushed the door open. The freshness of the room was convincing enough. The staff had certainly cleaned it for our stay. Red roses sat on the table with a table sign beside the vase that read *Congratulations*. Pushing out the unwanted arm, I groaned as I flipped it over, not ready to be reminded of my disastrous wedding.

Though I'd managed to get a few hours of rest on the plane, my plans were to sleep my pain away over the next four days before returning to Berkeley. The living room of the villa was gorgeous, but it was the bedroom that I would enjoy most. It was where the bulk of my time would be spent.

I pushed through the openness, rounding the corner of the sleeping quarter after only a few seconds. Instantly, I was hit with a whiff of familiarity. Flared nostrils and a bleeding heart controlled my line of vision. The withered frame that sat on the bed before me left me dumbfounded. Woeful eyes peered in my direction as I stood still, unable to move, unable to blink.

"We don't get to run away no more."

"Mi— Wha— what are you doing here?"

"I'm here because there's nowhere else in the world I'd rather be, nowhere in the world I can be right now. I meant every fucking word, Nature. I meant every word. *It beats for you. It longs for you. It waits for you. And just like me, it's ready to spend the rest of its days loving on you.*" He recited his vows.

Silently, I listened, unsure of what was expected of me. My stomach and heart were still in knots, dropping every time I thought about that day.

"You don't get to run away and neither do I," he continued. "My life ain't shit without you. Don't do this to me, Nature. I'm sorry. I'm sorry for all the shit I've put you through, all the pain I've caused, all the shit, everything, anything. Hit me. Yell at me. Ignore me. Fight me. Hurt me back. But whatever you do, don't quit on me. I can't come back from that. Don't quit on me, Nature."

I unfastened the carrier to free Mason because I was unsure how long my legs would manage my weight. Every word Milo spoke tested my strength. Without a doubt, I was weakening.

"Talk to me. Say something. Say anything," he begged.

"I ha-have nothing to say, Milo. I have no words."

"Then what are you feeling?"

"Pain."

"I'm sorry."

"Embarrassment. As I stood in front of the witnesses of our nuptials, there was a sick, fucked-up individual sitting feet away, plotting on destroying them. You don't understand how humiliating that is."

"Fuck standing in front of them people, Nature. I stood in front of you days prior and told you what it was. When I said until death do us apart, I meant that. I'm not a fucking boy anymore, Nay. I'm a grown ass man and I'm not backing down. Neither am I letting you run away this time. I'm ten toes down. If you need a week or two—shit, a month or two to sort your feelings, I'm all for it.

"But one thing about it, two things for certain, when it comes to your block, I'ma spin it. So, let me know what's up. You need space? You need time? What's up? 'Cause ain't no such thing as separation and divorce ain't an option. Ever. Ain't no nigga 'bout to love you like I love you, Nature, and there's not a woman in the world I want to give the chance to love me even a little. We in this shit. For life. What do you need? Tell me what you need and you got it. Just tell me what you need."

"Space."

Milo said nothing more. He took Mason from my arms and left me standing in the bedroom while they migrated to the living room. Closing my eyes, I allowed the tears that stung my orbs to fall down my cheeks.

"Don't think I'm dismissing your feelings, because I'm not. I know it hurts. I know because I feel that same pain. But I'm not your enemy, Nature. I'm your ally, and as your ally, I'm staying right here until we figure this shit out."

Nodding, I silently accepted his response before lowering my body onto the bed, praying to God that I was capable of mustering the strength to push through.

Milo · Nature

DAYLIGHT CAME and went so many times, I'd lost count, yet I still couldn't manage to pull myself out of bed. The door of the villa had opened and closed a million times and Mason's laughter often woke me from my sleep. The father and son duo were finding joy in the midst of misery, yet I was left alone to sulk in solitude.

Darkness covered every corner of the space I occupied. Exhaustion continued to weigh me down to the bed. However, the lack of nutrients and underlying symptoms that accompanied almost every woman's first trimester of pregnancy left me with a dry mouth and rumbling stomach. Unfortunately, I had no appetite. Not even the smell of food appeased me.

Distant footsteps drew closer and closer until I felt Milo's presence in the room. Quietly, he laid our son beside me, searching blindly through the dark to locate my engorged breasts. Upon locating them, he pushed the silk shirt up my skin and assisted Mason in his mission to extract milk.

His fingers traced my skin, trailing my arm until he reached my left hand. Slowly, he pulled it toward his mouth and kissed me gently, soothing my soreness. Even in my state, I still yearned for him, his heart, and his happiness. I missed him dearly, but the pain hadn't subsided and I wasn't ready to push forward. Not because I desired progress, but because I was depleted and unable to press forward.

"I'm sorry, Nature," he whispered.

He was out of the room within the next three seconds, leaving Mason and I alone. Sleep came so easily. It didn't matter how many hours I'd spent resting. My son's heartbeat lulled me into a slumber, following his lead.

Milo · Nature

THE SUN GREETED me right along with soft, strategic kisses on the skin of my vulva. Gasping, I clenched my muscles as my body stiffened underneath Milo.

"Relax," he begged, kissing my clit.

"I don't wanna fight." He sucked it into his mouth.

"I don't wanna hurt." He sucked harder.

"I don't want you hurting." He swiped his tongue across it rapidly, applying the perfect amount of pressure. My legs began shivering just as he slowed to a creep.

"I want to make you feel better, Nature," he explained as he slid two fingers inside of me.

"Miloooooooooooo."

"I love you so fucking much. God knows I love you."

He quieted, continuing his assault on my pussy. I melted in his mouth, unable to withhold my orgasm. Milo knew what buttons to push, how to push them, and how long to apply the pressure to them. Massaging my g-spot with his fingers while sliding his tongue across my clit was a lethal combination that split me right down the center.

"Oh God. I'm cu—Oh God."

Milo lifted until he was on his knees with his veiny tool protruding the air. He stretched my legs, pushing them toward my head until the tips of my toes touched the massive headboard behind me. Slowly, he slid inside of me.

"Ummm, shit," he moaned.

As if the world was ending and this was the very last time we'd make love, Milo stroked me like his life depended on it. Naturally, I received him, opening so that he could fill me to capacity. Our lips met.

His kiss possessed healing powers beyond my comprehension. My broken heart began to mend.

"I love you," he protested. "I love you, Nay."

Over and over, he repeated himself, making me a firm believer. Between the words falling from his lips, my level of sensitivity, and the intensity of his stroke, I could not think clearly.

"I fucking love you, girl."

The wetness of my gown exposed his tears before I saw them running down his cheeks. With my palm, I swiped them away.

"I'm sorry, Nay."

Nodding, I assured him that I'd heard him loud and clearly. I pulled him closer, needing to feel him against my lips as I mounted.

"I'm sorry," he whispered.

With sealed lids, I braced for the volcanic eruption that began within the pit of my stomach.

"Cu–m– Uhhhhhhh."

Maintaining his speed, Milo continued digging into me. Tender to the touch, my body jerked with every stroke. Labored breathing and erratic movements continued until I felt him grip my waist, steadying me. Completely zoned out, he slid in and out of me easily, stirring my creaminess and continuously coating himself with it.

"Fuck."

Never missing a beat, he helped me settle after the explosion he'd caused while meeting his own. The tightening of Milo's muscles announced his arrival. The hairs on my arm stood as his movements intensified, eventually ending with his chest against mine.

"Fuck."

Just as we were, we remained until our bodies grew warm enough to start a fire. It wasn't until then that Milo released me from his grasp.

"It's our last day, Nature."

Sadly, I responded, "I know."

"You slept the week away."

"I know."

"There's too much pain in this room. Let me take you to another place. Somewhere just as beautiful. Somewhere you can smile. I miss your laughter. Just let me help you feel better."

I laid in silence, considering his words. Because I had none to offer, I opted for alternatives. Grabbing Milo's hand, I laid it on top of my stomach. Though flat, the gesture revealed the secret I'd planned to share with him in some elaborate pregnancy announcement after we returned from our honeymoon. However, I felt as though we could both use a bit of sunshine after so much rain.

Immediately, Milo sat up in bed. Staring down at me, he tried gauging my position and where my mind was. The faint smile that tugged at my lips but failed to fully form was enough to address his concerns. His features stretched across his face as he exhaled in relief.

"Real shit?"

Nodding, I confirmed.

"How far along?"

Shrugging, I admitted that I wasn't sure. The lack of periods due to breastfeeding Mason made it complicated in terms of determining when ovulation peaked and our date of conception. However, I was sure that I was still in the very early stages. Five to six weeks, possibly.

"Tell me you're happy, Nature. Tell me you want this as much as I do. Tell me this will all be alright, we'll be alright. Tell me that we're in this shit till death do us part. Tell me."

"We'll be alright, till death do us part, Milo."

EPILOGUE

"WHITEBOY, stop playing with my boy before I hold him up so he can kick your ass."

"I'm just saying, his hair cut takes as long as these grown motherfuckers in here. Boy got a fucking noggin'."

Mason checked himself out in the mirror while paying close attention to the words Whiteboy was spitting. His lack of movement as he stood on top of the vanity let me know what he was up to. Without a doubt, he understood everything we'd said.

At fourteen months, he was a beast with his hands and had a vocabulary that was more complex than most adults.

Both Aeir and Aussie were to be credited for his advanced communication skills. As if he had been signing for years, Mason could manage a full conversation with five to six word sentences.

You ready to go? I asked him.

Yes, he replied. The frown on his face let me know he was unhappy about something.

What's wrong, dude?

I don't like these niggas, Dad.

My eyes widened as I cackled in disbelief.

Yo, who taught you that?

Uncle.

Referring to Malachi, he revealed his source.

Tell Uncle he's going to get your butt whooped.

I don't, he emphasized.

"Nah. Talk. Y'all over there speaking in code and shit. What he say?" Whiteboy asked, dusting the hair from the drape.

"He said he don't like you niggas and I don't blame him."

"He said that?"

"Damn right."

"How do I tell his little ass I don't like him either?"

I doubled over in laughter, lowering Mason from the vanity. On the way down, he grabbed a lollipop from the bowl of treats.

"Nah. Tell his little bad ass to put my shit back."

"He understands and he don't give a damn. This his sucker, nigga, and we dare you to reach for it," I taunted.

"Don't get your ass whooped in front of your boy."

"Try me and I'll bring all the Caucasian out of you to remind you that you're only a quarter of nigga."

"Half."

"Same difference. Regardless, almost doesn't count."

"Find yourself a new barber."

I'd only been sitting in his chair for a year. He was one of the coldest things out of Channing. Lawe had put me on after my barber got booked on with manslaughter for spazzing on a nigga that refused to pay his dues after running up a tab in the shop.

"Working on it."

"Fuck you, my nigga."

With Mason at my side, I headed out of the door. We had shit to do and it didn't include going back and forth with Whiteboy. I strapped him into his seat and unraveled the lollipop that he was struggling with.

Your mom is going to take it when she gets in. Hurry up and eat this.

I can hide, he suggested.

No, Mason. Just hurry up before we both be in trouble.

Okay, Daddy.

I slid into the driver's seat and pulled off the lot, prepared to make the thirty-minute drive.

On my way. I shot Nature a text as I pulled up to the red light that caught us right out of the parking lot.

Gray bubbles appeared and then disappeared. Shortly after, a reply surfaced.

Okay.

Est Gee flowed over the sickening beat, serving as background sounds as I bent the blocks of Berkeley. Bobbing my head, I joined after every few words. The bright sun shined against the front windshield, obscuring my vision from certain angles while serving as a source of vitamin D simultaneously. I tapped my fingers against the steering wheel, determined to cut the thirty-minute trip down by at least two so that I didn't keep Nature waiting too long.

The camera positioned right across from Mason's car seat convinced me of his comfort. He was still going to town on the sucker he'd stolen without a care in the world. Though he couldn't hear a damn word Est was spitting, he bobbed his head to the rhythm, able to feel the vibrations and gauge the tone and pace of the song through his own method.

As I pulled into the space dedicated to Nature, she came wobbling out of her office. Her belly was so much bigger and so much rounder this pregnancy. Mila was a whopping eleven pounds and Nature had every intention of pushing her out in a natural home birth.

Our due date had come and gone, making us all anxious as we waited for her to make her debut. Though Nature was still making her rounds daily, I'd taken paternity leave and would be home for the next three months. Mistakes I'd made in the wake of Mason's arrival prepared me for Mila's birth. Not only did my wife need me, but so did my children, and I'd be damned if I was walking the hospital halls or sitting behind a desk while she struggled at home alone.

The look on my baby's face spilled secrets she refused to. She was tired. With a shake of the head, I jumped out and ran around to the passenger side to open her door. Any day, our daughter would be here, yet she refused to rest. She was fully invested in the health and births of the mothers who'd entrusted her and refused to let any of them suffer through the practices of someone who knew nothing about them or their unborn children if she could help it.

"Any day now, Nature."

"Until that day, I'll be right here, Milo."

"Stubborn," I groaned, leaning over to kiss her lips before shutting the door.

"Umm hmmm. You love me, nonetheless," she said as soon as I was within earshot.

"It's true."

"So then stop complaining. Guess who popped today?"

"Who?" I nearly broke my neck wondering who'd shown up to her establishment. Automatically, my mind began trekking through unstable territory.

"My father." She released a stream of air, still partly surprised, herself.

"Bullshit, baby."

I nearly was stunned speechless. My face mirrored hers, both in sheer disbelief.

"Dead ass? You serious right now?"

"I'm serious. I couldn't believe my eyes when he walked through my office door mid-day —without my mom dragging him. According to my mother, he's been plotting on his retirement since the wedding. Walking me down the aisle made him come to terms with how much of my life he's truly missed. Do you that today is his first time at my practice?"

"No shit?"

"Yeah. He left in tears. I'm not sure what's happening or what has gotten into him, but I can't say that I don't appreciate the change of heart. I just wish it wasn't so late."

"Better late than never, Nay. He has Mason and Mila to pour into now that he has so much time on his hands."

Seeing my baby's world come full circle was heartening. This, all of this, was all she'd ever wanted.

"You're right. Have you guys eaten?" she asked, peeking at the camera to check on Mason. "Is tha—Is that candy?"

I stared straight ahead, pretending not to hear her as I maneuvered the whip out of the parking lot.

"Baby!" Her voice upped a few notches.

"What's up, Nay?" Finally, I looked over at her, sensing the concern in her tone.

"My... my sack has ruptured."

Fluid leaked from her vagina, staining her dress and spilling onto the floor. Remaining calm, I grabbed her hand and brought it to my mouth.

"Any day," I repeated myself, ready for the moment my baby girl took her first breath.

THE END.

HUFFINGTON NEWS

Join over 8,000 honorary Huffington residents for monthly broadcasts delivered right to their preferred devices.

Broadcasts include but aren't limited to:

- A beautiful monthly newsletter detailing everything happening in Huffington
- Extensive snippets of upcoming projects (sneak peeks)
- Release day reminders that include links (to remove the guest work from searching for books on Amazon/Ghuffington.com)
- First to hear about surprise releases
- Exclusive discounts + offers for Huffington residents
- A monthly wrap-up detailing everything that has happened in Huffington since the release of the Huffington Newsletter

Ready to become a resident?
Click here.
[https://huffingtonnews.ck.page/4693a79283]

MORE FROM GREY HUFFINGTON

Find the entire collection of Grey Huffington titles below.
Titles in the catalog are available in eBook (amazon.com, +
ghuffington.com), paperback (ghuffington.com), or
audiobook (audible + ghuffington.com) formats.

Syx + the City
Syx + the City 2
Syx Thirty Seven
Syxth Giving
Syx Whole Weeks

Wile + Reckless
Wilde + Relentless
Wilde + Restless

Mr. Intentional
Unearth Me

The Sweetest Revenge

The Sweetest Redemption

Half + Half
The Emancipation of Emoree

Sleigh
Sleigh Squared

The Gifted
Memo
Give her Love. Give her Flowers.

Unbreak Me
Uncover Me

As we Learn
As we Love

Just Wanna Mean the Most to You
Sensitivity
10,000 Hours
Darke Hearts
muse.

Softly
Peace + Quiet
Press Rewind
Jagged Edges
My Person
The Realm of Riot Thimble
Whose Love Story is it Anyway?

Unhand Me

Home*
Blues*
31st*
Now That We're Here.*

Then Let's Fuck About It*
Giving Thanks

A Month of Sundays Ep 1
A Month of Sundays Ep 2
A Month of Sundays Ep 3
Dinner at Ever + Luca's
Saylah
The Mayor's Ball
Elm

THE EISENBERG EFFECT
Luca
Lyric
Ever*
Laike
Baisleigh*
Liam

THE DOMINO EFFECT
Ledge
Halo*
Lawe
Kleuless*

BERKELEY BRED
Malachi
Anna*
Milo
Makai
Glacier*
Mercer
Vallei*

THE GREY LIST
Chemistry "The Chemist"
Egypt
Rather "The Therapist"

—

* signifies the publication is available EXCLUSIVELY on ghuffington.com.

—

Prefer Audiobooks?

Did you know **there's a library FULL of audiobooks on ghuffington.com** for the lovers who listen?

We're building so you can continue to listen to the books you've been hearing good things about. There are currently over 17 audiobooks waiting for you to indulge.

In addition to our audiobook library, we have an audiobook club for those who care to save 40-50% off their audiobooks. **Heard is not mandatory to shop audiobooks but we do recommend taking a look at the perks.**

Audiobooks Available (**exclusively on GHuffington.com**)

Chemistry
Egypt
Ever
Baisleigh
Halo
Kleuless
Anna
Glacier
Vallei (coming soon)
Muse.
Elm.
Sensitivity
The Realm of Riot Thimble
Whose Love Story is it Anyway?
Unhand Me

www.ingramcontent.com/pod-product-compliance
Lightning Source LLC
Chambersburg PA
CBHW011148310726
48973CB00010B/2816